The Heritage

Jack Michonik

ISBN: 9781977042859

To Celia, with love;
and to our children,
Ghila and Jorge,
custodians of the heritage

Lárida, August 29, 1961

Yitgadal ve-yitkadash shme rabah.

Leon trembled. Whenever he heard those mysterious words, he felt a shiver accompanied by the sensation of something pressing on his chest. Hebrew has such a strange resonance! He felt goose bumps on his skin. *Ve-yamlich malchuteh...* Then he remembered that the Kaddish, the prayer said for the repose of the dead, was not written in Hebrew but in Aramaic. He still remembered the teachings he received in the *cheder,* the humble little school in Golochov, more than forty years earlier. "The Kaddish is not a prayer for the dead, but it is *also* a prayer for the dead," the old *lerer* used to tell them in one of his typical explanations that served more to confuse his young students than to throw light on the subject. Then, gently stroking his white beard, *Rav* Zuntz would begin explaining the difference between the complete Kaddish, the half Kaddish, the Rabanan Kaddish, and the mourners' Kaddish.

Yeheh shme rabah...

"Even though it is said for the dead," Zuntz would explain, stroking his beard the entire time, only stopping to gesticulate with his hands or scratch his nose, "the mourners' Kaddish makes no allusion to the deceased, says nothing to console the relatives, contains not a single word about death; it only says praises to God."

Yitbarach, ve-yishtabach, ve-yitpaar, ve-yitromam, ve-yitnaseh, ve-yitadar, ve-yitaleh, ve yitalal... A thunderclap interrupted the prayer. Some people looked up at the gray sky with its threat of rain. Leon Edri observed the people who were standing around the grave, rendering a last homage to the man who in his lifetime had become

1

one of the region's most outstanding industrialists, businessmen and philanthropists.

A lot of people had attended the funeral; so many that they barely fit into the small Israelite Cemetery of Lárida. Besides relatives and friends of the deceased, high company officials from his diverse corporations, numerous individuals connected with his industrial enterprises and several persons whom he had helped at one time or another were also in attendance. Most of those present were Jewish but, unlike other occasions, a good number of Gentiles were also there. Edri couldn't help but notice how silent and still they remained.

Imitating the Jewish men, they covered their heads with the little black *yarmulkas* they had picked up on entering the cemetery. It was the first time they had ever attended a Jewish ceremony, and the absolute silence was more a matter of curiosity than respect. They all watched Saul Lubinsky in rapt attention, with the lapel of his fine jacket torn, reciting the Kaddish before the grave of his father. Some of them, those standing farther back, discreetly stood on tiptoes to see what was happening. If it weren't such a sad occasion, Leon would have smiled. He had noticed the same expressions of curious interest among Catholics who had been invited to Jewish weddings, or a *Bar Mitzvah* or *Brit Milah* ceremony; especially at the latter, where Christians generally try to get a closer look (but not in the first row where they might call attention to themselves) in the hope of observing the fascinating rite of circumcision.

The presence of distinguished personalities from industry, banking and commerce did not go unnoticed, especially among the members of "the colony," as the Jewish community of Lárida was dubbed. The leaders of the regional economy who were present did not stand out so much because of their manner of dress, subdued and elegant, but for their Spanish physiognomy. Among the most important of them were Joaquín Pabón Pabón, president of the National Union of Industrialists; Gonzalo Villalobos, president of

2

the Securities Exchange Bank; Pablo Pinto Zamora, president of the Farmers Association; Ulpiano Méndez Carrizosa, owner of an endless string of important business enterprises, among them Lanatex, Ríohondo Livestock, and Andean Investments; Elías Jamal, head of Lebanon Textiles; Carlos Concha Camacho, "Triple-C" as his close friends called him, president of the Chamber of Commerce and Director-Owner of the prestigious newspaper *The Progressive Times*; and Fernando Olano Parra, owner of Vita Beverages and ex-minister of the treasury. Never had such a gathering of distinguished personalities been seen at the Israelite Cemetery. These powerful men huddled more or less together, like any other group of persons who share a common bond and feel out of place at a particular event, much the same as Jews behave at a Catholic ceremony.

Moisés Birenbaum approached the group and exclaimed, while extending his soft, pudgy hand to the president of the Securities Exchange Bank: "Don Gonzalo, so nice to see you!" He shook the banker's hand more effusively than the occasion called for and then went about greeting a few others: "Doctor Pinto, how are you? I missed you at the last meeting of the Executives Club." Birenbaum spoke in a boisterous voice, trying to impress on his co-religionists how well connected he was.

Leon also greeted some of the members of the group, from a distance, with a nod of his head. He heard Emilio Gluck behind him saying to someone: "All that money and what good does it do?"

Somebody made a vague remark and Gluck added: "Oh, absolutely! You can't take it with you."

Making his way through the crowd of people, Leon went up to the grave. The prayer was concluding. *Hu yaaseh shalom aleinu ve-al kol Israel, ve-imruh amen.*

A brief silence followed, as if no one knew what to do. Suddenly, a voice was heard shouting: "Chaim! Chaim! Why have you leaved us in such an unexpected way?" Everybody turned their

3

attention to a thin, awkward-looking figure standing next to the grave and shaking his fists at the sky. It was Mendel Fuchs, the community's jack-of-all-trades. He called himself "Rabbi" even though he himself didn't take it seriously. In Lárida he was the one who prepared the boys for their *Bar Mitzvahs*, killed chickens twice a week and slaughtered a cow once a month to sell *kosher* meat, and led the congregation in prayers whenever the rabbi was sick. He attended all the funerals and had a fondness for delivering melodramatic, annoying, and unsolicited eulogies that produced tears in some and a repressed smile on the lips of others. "Chaim, you have left us so sudden like," Mendel Fuchs cried in a clamoring voice, addressing the casket that rested at the bottom of the grave.

An initial surprise for the Gentiles present at the ceremony came when they saw that plain wood box, with unvarnished panels, in accordance with Jewish usage, instead of the luxurious coffin that one would have expected for the funeral of someone like Jaime Lubinsky.

A second surprise came when an old man who seemed to be directing the ceremony approached Saul Lubinsky and cut the edge of his lapel with a knife. Then, grabbing one of the severed ends of the cloth, he ripped the jacket in one big tug, thus fulfilling the ancient custom—the rending of a garment as a symbol of mourning. Young Lubinsky stood there, at the edge of his father's grave, between his mother and sister, with the look of a lost child and the strip of cloth dangling from his chest.

The third surprise was Fuchs's strange monologue. In a voice laden with emotion, insistently addressing the deceased in broken Spanish, he proceeded with his lament: "Chaim, it was only yesterday you was alive with all the living people, now you are with the dead in the cemetery that is the gift you gave us...."

4

An especially fine drizzle, nearly imperceptible, began falling, a kind of delicate mist that didn't get anyone really wet and which, for those who did notice it, seemed to give the air a special glow. *As on that long ago August afternoon in the Golochov cemetery*, Leon thought to himself.

"Chaim, you was always a just man, obeyer of the Law, a generous man who love your people."

Mendel felt that what he had just said was incorrect, or on the contrary, had come out pretty good. He paused a moment to judge the effect of his words on the people, to adjust the jacket of his threadbare suit, and to clear his voice. "You will leave a big hole in all our hearts. Your wife and your children will cry for you always. You were so young, so good person, so really good. Chaim, why did you go away? *Far vos bist du avec gueganguen?*"

And as if not realizing it, Mendel continued speaking in Yiddish. Most of those present didn't understand what the old man was saying, but all the same they maintained a respectful silence. Mendel Fuchs was no longer shouting; he had begun speaking haltingly, and as he proceeded with his lament, his words became laced with tears. Several women began sobbing as well. The old man, of ashen skin and sunken eyes, continued speaking in Yiddish, his arms crossed on top of his striped, coffee-colored suit. The widow wept disconsolately. Leon remembered that on that long ago August afternoon his mother had also asked amidst tears and wailing: "*Chaim, far vos bist du avec gueganguen?*" He shivered once more, as if he had heard the echo of the Kaddish.

"*Shoin, shoin.* Enough, already!" Bernardo Zuckerman shouted, tugging on Mendel Fuchs's arm.

The old man fell silent, the eulogy over. He pulled out a handkerchief from his pocket and noisily blew his nose. His discourse had ended.

The same man who had torn Saul Lubinsky's jacket approached him once more. This time, instead of a knife, he carried a shovel. He handed it to him while uttering a few words in his ear. Saul dug the shovel into the mound of dirt next to him and tossed some of it into the grave. He repeated this a couple of times before sticking the shovel back into the mound. Then, Bernardo Zuckerman approached, took the shovel and did likewise. After him, Leon stepped forward, took the shovel that Bernardo in turn had left buried in the mound of dirt and followed suit in filling the grave. And so, the shovel was passed among the relatives, friends and acquaintances of Jaime Lubinsky: Mordechai Lubinsky, his brother; Hans Guggenheim, his chief physician; Matías Kopel, whom destiny placed twice in his path; Leopoldo Reiss, his long-time friend; Max Russo, his long-time enemy; Erich Halberstam, his financial advisor; Moisés Birenbaum, the moneybags who envied him his fortune; the Liffshitz brothers, whom he had helped get established… One after another they came forward and continued filling the grave, thus rendering their final respects to the departed.

Understanding the symbolism of the ritual, the Gentiles joined those who waited their turn to toss in some dirt. Dr. Joaquín Pabón Pabón was the first to take the shovel. He performed his part vigorously and then passed the shovel to Dr. Pablo Pinto Zamora who, while tossing in some of the earth, reflected on the irony of undertaking the same labor as any of his one thousand four hundred workers carried out day after day. The hands of Dr. Alvaro Escallón, his fingernails painted with a clear enamel nail polish, also grabbed the shovel to do his part. Bankers hands, workers hands, the hands of creditors and debtors, the hands of suppliers and clients, the hands of relatives, of acquaintances who had had social or commercial dealings with him, the hands of Jews and Christians, all seized the shovel and did their part until the grave was filled in. Jaime Lubinsky was laid to rest in a hospitable land, eight thousand miles from the one where he was born.

The community's rabbi intoned a sad chant, a kind of melodious lamentation. Minutes later, the ceremony was over.

The people began departing, without saying goodbye to one another, barely speaking. Leon observed the widow and her children leaving, surrounded by their relatives. *Shouldn't I be among them?* he wondered, indecisive, watching them withdraw. His eyes rested for an instant on the cemetery's oldest grave, Nathan Gottlieb's, maybe because it was the only one that wasn't aligned with the others, jutting out into the path, and, for that reason, was impossible to miss. He picked up a stone and placed it on the gravestone, next to the others that previous visitors had left there. He noticed the dates engraved on the headstone: *1876-1936.* The cemetery was twenty-five years old. And already so many graves!

The very fine drizzle began letting up. Leon walked over to the small fountain on one side of the portal, where several Jews were washing their hands. He remembered that on one occasion, when leaving the cemetery with Jaime Lubinsky, he stopped to wash his hands, in accordance with ancient Hebrew tradition. "Make sure you wash your hands after touching the dead, that way, you'll be spared from the black plague," Jaime had told him with his dark sense of humor. "But remember, they'll accuse you of having started it just because you yourself didn't catch it."

Jaime…He passed away so unexpectedly. How Leon would miss him so! He shook the water from his hands and dried them with his handkerchief.

As soon as he made his way to the street, a band of little kids, ranging in age from five to twelve, rushed up to him. "Hey, mister, some coins!" one of them shouted. "Me, me!" came the voice of another. "I watched the car for you," a third boy said, pleading with him. They were all jabbering away simultaneously and holding out their little hands, eager for a few coins, pushing and shoving each other, competing for Leon's attention. They were barefoot and ragged. Leon walked towards his car with the band of urchins circling him. David was waiting for him in front of the black sedan,

"All right, enough! Stop pestering!" David shouted, but the kids kept up the racket.

He tossed a fistful of coins as far as he could and the kids went scampering after them. He laughed as he opened the door for his father. Leon wasn't in the mood for humor. Quiet and serious, he settled into the back seat, next to his wife. She, like David, had left the cemetery, accompanying the widow, a few minutes ahead of Leon.

"Straight home?" David asked, turning on the ignition.

"The office," his father answered. "Now I'll have to work twice as hard."

He said nothing more until they reached his office downtown. During the entire twenty-minute ride, Leon kept his face turned aside, absorbed in his thoughts, not noticing the city streets he had seen multiply over the years. He had arrived in the Obondó Valley thirty-five years earlier, when Lárida was a "small town" of some one hundred twenty thousand inhabitants. Now it was a thriving city of more than one million.

They drove down a four-lane avenue. Leon leaned his forehead against the window and closed his eyes.

"A lot of people came," his wife said.

"Hm, hm," David murmured.

"And a lot of *goyim.*"

"Hm, hm."

"When I die, I don't want to be buried with so much fuss. I just want my family and closest friends to be there, the people who really care about me."

"Mom, after you're dead, it won't make much difference to you who shows up."

"David!"

The car, a luxury sedan, moved quickly down the avenue, passing through the city's poor neighborhoods in the southern district, between two endless rows of dilapidated houses. At the other end of the avenue, two and three story buildings began to appear. Along the route, the number and size of the buildings increased, as did the volume of traffic and the level of noise.

They stopped in front of a modern, fifteen-story building. On its façade, in thick, stainless steel letters it read: SILEJA BUILDING. Leon got out and said goodbye with a wave of his hand, without uttering a word.

"Good morning, Don León," the doorman said.

Leon walked right past him.

"Good morning, Don León," the elevator operator said.

The elevator door opened on the fifteenth floor, in front of a small but luxurious reception area. On the wall behind it, a sign bearing the company's name stood out in glittering copper letters: SILEJA S.A. A young receptionist, in turn, greeted him.

"Good morning, Don León."

Edri went straight to his office and drew back the organdie curtains that covered the picture window, which offered him such a splendid view of the city, with the Obondó Valley in the distance and the imposing hills of the mountain range on one side. Light flooded the big room, decorated with an excess of luxury, which made it seem more like a waiting room than an office. Leon settled into his leather embossed chair. On top of the huge mahogany desk, his secretary had set out the daily correspondence and a sheet of paper with a list of priority messages. The first thing he did was to read over the list.

"The spare part for the generator was sent this morning by plane. Don Lisandro Martínez wants to know what was decided about his plot of land; he's asking that you call him immediately. The final price quotes for the beer factory equipment arrived."

The beer factory! Jaime was really enthused about it …

Leon pressed the intercom button.

"Melba, get Martínez for me, please."

It was then that he saw among the stack of correspondence, the envelope with familiar handwriting. It had been months since he had heard from Baruch. He noticed the postmark: August 3. It was already the 29th of the month. The intercom buzzed. He automatically pressed the button:

"A *month* for a letter to arrive!"

"Excuse me?"

"Oh, nothing, nothing. What is it, Melba?"

"Don Lisandro Martínez left and won't return before five."

"Okay, leave a message saying I called."

He opened the envelope, prepared to read what surely was going to be a dissertation on Zionism. All of Baruch's letters were the same. Leon enjoyed the correspondence from his old friend, who wrote him so assiduously. Their mutual affection hadn't diminished despite the long years of separation and, in Leon's mind, Baruch was still the romantic dreamer, the eternal idealist, the passionate Zionist. However, on this occasion, his friend's letter barely mentioned the Promised Land. Written in Yiddish (the maternal tongue of the two men and the only one they had in common), the letter touched on a universal subject of special significance for Leon Edri that day. He read it deliberately and with great interest. When he finished, he

10

remained pensive for some time. Baruch's letters always left him feeling that way. This time, more than ever. His friend had written him on the subject of death and—how strange!—on that mysterious luminosity that fell from the sky in the form of a delicate drizzle and which he had just seen an hour before, for the first time since that long ago August afternoon in the Golochov cemetery. Leon dwelled not only on the contents of the letter but on the strange coincidence of having received it precisely upon his return from the cemetery. In truth, it was such a strange coincidence.

Jerusalem

August 2, 1961

Dear Leon,

Please forgive me for taking so long to answer. I confess I have no excuse. Writing letters is one of those things that a person puts off until the next day, and "the next day" never comes. "Baruch," I told myself, "if you don't write him, your friend is going to think you've died." So, here I am, alive and even in good health.

Last week I turned fifty. A good number, right? Nice and round. Five decades. Half a century! This got me to thinking, thinking a lot about death. For the first time in my life, I've had a feeling that I'm going to die.

I'll try to explain, because I don't want you to misunderstand. It isn't that I think I'm going to die soon, or that I've grown morbid. It's something else. I don't see death as something imminent, but I sense its eventual arrival as a reality that I had never felt until now. How can I explain it? We've always known that we'll die one day, but we believe that day to be so remote that we tend to see it as unreal. There's still so much that awaits us, so many projects or problems with their deadlines growing shorter, that death gets lost in a distant and nebulous future. Now, suddenly, the future grows less distant, less nebulous, and death takes on an aspect that becomes more real. I don't know how long it will take in coming—it can be thirty years or thirty days—but I see it clearly and sense for the first time the seriousness of what is in the offing.

I've asked myself the why of that change in perception and it occurs to me that life is like a highway that's always moving uphill until, at a certain point, it begins its descent. Death lies at the end of the road, but while you are moving uphill you don't see it. You don't see it even though you have a clear, straight road ahead. The highway itself hides it. Only when you reach the summit and begin descending does the end become clear.

*You know that I'm not a believer. I wouldn't dare say I'm an atheist because I really don't know if I am one. At times I think that God doesn't exist and at times I think He does. The idea that there can be "a creative force" strikes me as reasonable and there are even times when it seems evident to me. If we want to call that creative force "God," I've got no problem with it. God serves to "explain" all the mysteries of the universe that we can't understand. Without God, we could never understand the "how" much less the "why" of our existence. So, for me, God is the incomprehensible. And the possibility of His existence is no less valid because of it. If I label myself a non-believer, I do it not because I don't believe in God, but because I don't believe in religion, neither in ours nor, of course, in any other. Even if God is ever-present, man still can't communicate with Him, through prayer or anything else; all these rituals are nothing more than ridiculous ceremonies. God doesn't demand anything, any more than He forgives, or rewards, or punishes. Those are all strictly human acts. God simply... **is**.*

Not being a believer places me at a disadvantage in relation to the one who is. The believer can find comfort in his faith and calm his spirit with prayer; what's more, he has a supernatural being he can turn to for help whenever he's in need. I have none of that. The distinction I make between good and evil is more difficult to understand, because these aren't absolutes that religion has given me but notions I must judge for myself. While the believer's concept of the world is resolute, mine founders on the seas of uncertainty. You might say—and please forgive the irony—that it pays to be a believer just for the convenience.

If I've got any advantage at all over the believer it's that I don't have to fear death. After death, there's nothing. Do you remember what you were before you were born? Nothing. That's exactly what you'll be after you die. When the heart stops beating and the

13

thousands of nerves and capillary vessels that make up the brain are destroyed, thinking disappears much the same as a radio transmission when the tubes and cables of the transmitter are destroyed. When the body is used up, so is the spirit. For the person who dies, everything ends, and nothing good or bad can befall him.

As I said, the prospect of dying doesn't scare me, but it does produce in me a profound sadness. One becomes fond of life. The idea of being and then not being seems terrible to me. One is transformed from something concrete into a memory...and sometimes not even that. But the worst thing of all is to be left not knowing how things will turn out. Life is like a novel, like a movie, do you see? One wants to know how the story ends, what the children accomplished, what became of the loved ones, what fate your friends and enemies encountered, your business, your country, the world...But no. Half way through the movie, the lights go out forever.

I don't know why I'm telling you all this. Could it be because of what happened today?

This morning I witnessed a very painful event: the burial of Ilan Gaon, my son's best friend. Ilan was twenty-five. He was tall, handsome, intelligent. Shortly after getting his chemical engineering degree, while on patrol duty as an army reservist, he was the victim of an ambush by Arab gunmen. The funeral took place at the Mount Herzl military burial grounds. It was a heart-wrenching scene: his broken-hearted parents, his sobbing relatives, his friends with their faces etched with pain; a young woman sobbing bitterly. Was it a girlfriend? A sister?

After the funeral, I remained in the cemetery. I walked among the rows of graves, reading the inscriptions on the small, white stone markers, all the same size and shape, perfectly aligned in long columns that line the mountain from one side to the next. At first, I read the entire inscription; afterwards, just the dates of birth and

14

death. While I walked with a heavy heart, I did the math: eighteen years old, twenty-one, nineteen, twenty-two, eighteen… Boys as handsome and intelligent as Ilan, younger than he…and so many of them, so many…

I was absorbed in my thoughts when it happened. It began drizzling. It was a truly singular phenomenon, since it never rains in Israel this time of the year. What's more, from May to October, for five long months, not a drop of rain falls. At least, I don't remember it ever happening since I arrived here, thirty-three years ago. I believe it was because of the rain that I wrote you on the subject of death. It wasn't a typical rain that fell. It was a gentle drizzle, nearly imperceptible, you could barely feel it, or get wet from it; it was a kind of luminous dew descending from heaven… as on that long ago August afternoon in the Golochov cemetery.

Affectionately,

Baruch

1

"Nothing exists. Nothing. Suddenly a violent explosion—inexplicable, in the midst of an absolute void—propels millions of stars across the universe, and one of them, small and inconsequential, is the one that we call the *Sun*. Around it, other smaller celestial bodies revolve, the planets, among which there is a very special one: Earth… All right. It could have happened that way. But what caused that explosion? How do we conceive of absolute nonexistence, that is to say, the total absence of matter and time, and then their appearance, without a Creative Will?"

Rav Zuntz paused to allow his question to really sink into the minds of his students. The class wasn't supposed to be about Creation, since this was only taught at the beginning of the first year of *cheder*. The few years of education that followed were barely enough to prepare the students in the multiple subjects of religion. Nevertheless, from time to time, the old *Rav* liked to return briefly to the subject of Creation and say a few words before starting class, as if to reinforce the foundations of the building that would house the religious heritage of the youth of Golochov.

"Take this planet of ours. A wonder of wonders! If it were a little farther from the sun, we would perish from the cold; a little closer, and we would burn up. Can it be by chance that its position and trajectory in space are precisely the only ones to allow for human life?"

The boys listened in silence to their *lerer* explain once more the arguments they already knew so well and which the old man expounded upon with such enthusiasm.

"But the most extraordinary thing about the Earth is that there is order. Yes, *order!*" he reiterated, with special emphasis. "An absolute, divine order. Everything is held in balance: the rain falls from the clouds, forming the rivers that feed into the lakes and oceans. The water evaporates from the lakes and oceans, rising into the sky to form clouds, to fall again to earth in the form of rain. Thus, a cycle is completed. You see how wonderful that is? But that cycle is part of a more complex mechanism. The rain falls to earth, which needs water to produce vegetation, which in turn produces oxygen needed by man and beast in order to breathe. Do you realize how beautiful that is? Everything harmoniously complements one another. Men get their sustenance from plants and animals, which in turn feed off other plants and animals. The species reproduce and destroy one another, maintaining an equilibrium of existence. That equilibrium, that absolute order, is found in every sphere. It is in our bodies which function like flawless machines. It is in plants and animals. It is in the center of the Earth, at the bottom of the ocean, in space, in the precise movement of our planet, which gives us days and nights and the four seasons of the year. In all of God's creation, hallowed be His name, there is order."

Zuntz cut short the flow of words bursting forth at such a rapid pace and observed the faces of his students, one by one. No one dared look away. That was the interval he needed to bring home his final dramatic point.

"There is no order in an accident... Imagine the house of a painter, filled with canvases, brushes, and jars of different color paints. Suddenly, an explosion rips through the air. You'll agree that there isn't the slightest possibility that the canvases will fall face up across the floor and that the paints will spill over them forming landscapes and portraits, right? Of course, not. In an accident there can be no order."

He had achieved his goal of delivering his idea with a certain impact; at least, so it seemed to him.

He scratched his nose. Then, as if realizing he had been standing too long, he sat down. The boys, seated on benches around two tables, kept their gaze fixed on him. They, with diaphanous looks, and he with his deep-set, tired gray eyes, surrounded by wrinkles, surveyed each other: the baby-faced boys and the old man with the white beard. *What's this generation coming to?* old Zuntz wondered. *Look at them: not one of them with peyot or tzitziot. God help them*!

Rav Zuntz was aware that the Bolshevik Revolution had forever altered the image of the Russian Jew. The doors of assimilation were open and the process that had been initiated in Western Europe a hundred years earlier was beginning to affect Judaism in Eastern Europe. But assimilation did not necessarily mean abandoning the religion, and Zuntz was equally aware of that. He knew that the Jew would more and more take on the *outward* appearance of the Gentile—in his dress, his manner of speech, certain habits—but he wasn't sure to what point the Jew would distance himself from his faith. He considered it a sacred duty to introduce his tender students to the world of the Holy Scriptures, to teach them the traditions and prayers, to infuse in them the Jewish moral values and, above all, to inculcate in them the concern for preserving their religious heritage and to transmit it to the future generations.

It wasn't a big classroom. A single window without shutters or curtains illuminated its white walls. This wasn't a classroom like those in an ordinary school. The students had no desks. There were no posters or children's drawings on the walls, much less a blackboard with chalk and erasers. The four walls of the *cheder* were bare, like the floor and ceiling. A long, narrow wooden table occupied the center of the room. Another smaller one was next to it. The students were seated on benches around the tables, two or three of them sharing the books that were available. At the head of the big table, on the only chair in the room, sat the *lerer*.

19

Rav Zuntz looked into the gentle faces and sighed. Then he opened the old Bible that lay on the table and searched among its yellowed pages.

"All right," he said at last. "Today we'll study the *parashah 'lech lechah.'*"

Berl winked at Leib from the other side of the table.

" *'Lech lechah'* is the third chapter in the weekly readings. It gets its name from the fifth and sixth words of the chapter under study, which begins like this: "God said unto Abram: *'Lech lechah.'* ""

Leib tried saying something to Berl by exaggeratedly mouthing the words, but all Berl could understand was: "When class is over…" He placed his hand behind his ear, indicating to his friend to speak a little louder.

"Go!" Old Zuntz's voice resonated across the room.

Leib, startled, turned his head. Berl felt his heart drop to the floor. Pale with fright, they looked at the old man whose severity all had learned to fear, but the *rav* seemed unaware of anything. The boys breathed a sigh of relief when they realized that the exclamation wasn't directed at them. The teacher continued his explanation.

"*Lech lechah* means 'go.' Literally, it could be translated as 'withdraw yourself,' but literarily, it should be translated as 'Go.' Listen to the special sound the words have in Hebrew, how poetic it sounds: *lech lechah*."

Several boys smiled quietly. A few whispered into the ear of their neighbors. Leib tried again to transmit his message. This time Berl managed to get it: "When class is over, we're going down to the river."

"God told Abram," *Rav* Zuntz said, pointing to the lines of the Holy Scriptures that he was translating, while stroking his beard with

20

the other hand, "get thee out of thy country, and from thy kindred, and from thy father's house unto the land I will show thee. And I will make of thee a great nation and I will bless thee, and make thy name great, and thou shalt be a blessing. I will bless those who bless thee, and curse those who curse thee; and in thee all families of the earth will be blessed."

An hour later, class was over. The boys left the *cheder* running in different directions. Leib, Berl, Itzik, and Zvi ran through the streets of Golochov towards the outskirts of town, not stopping until the last little houses of the *shtetl* were at their backs.

The sun had already begun going down that precious August afternoon, but the sky was clear and it was warm. It was a couple of kilometers to reach the river and the boys hurried along the dusty road. In the distance, approaching in the opposite direction was a horse pulling a cart of hay. As it got closer, one could hear more clearly the creaking of the wheels. The boys stepped aside to let it pass. Two boys, more or less the same age as Leib and his friends, were riding on top of the hay. The four friends watched the two boys pass in front of them, who, in turn, with their eyes fixed on them, watched Leib and his friends standing by the side of the road. They crossed paths without exchanging a word, staring at each other like aliens from another planet, as did their parents, as did their grandparents, generation after generation. Christians and Jews lived on the same land and under the same sky, in two separate worlds.

The boys reached the ravine that bordered the river, panting and sweaty.

"Oh, no!" Zvi exclaimed under his breath. "Look: those guys have taken our spot."

The four of them stared down at some older boys who were splashing around in the water and making a ruckus.

"Who are they?" Leib asked, keeping his voice down.

"I don't know," Berl said.

"Let's go to the small pond," Itzik suggested.

The older boys were horsing around in the water and shouting in Russian.

"Yeah, let's go!" Zvi agreed, lowering his voice. "I don't like the looks of these muzhiks."

Leib and his friends silently withdrew and set off walking to the "small pond," which was less than a kilometer upstream. It was a kind of swimming hole that led out towards the river.

The boys stripped down to their underpants, leaving their clothes folded on top of some rocks, and jumped into the water. None of them knew how to swim, but one didn't have to know how to swim in order to have fun in that shallow fresh-water pond where there was no current and the water barely reached their waists. Typical of boys their age, they began jumping up and down excitedly, submerging themselves completely in the water. Then they began splashing water in each other's face and pushing each other around. They were happy. Limited by poverty, by religious constraints, and by the insecurity of belonging to a weak and persecuted minority, they knew but few of youth's pleasures. The summer, which barely lasted two months, offered them a chance to have the kind of fun they so eagerly awaited most of the year. The boys delighted in the feeling of freedom that came with being outdoors, in the warm air and cool water.

They decided to engage in some horseplay, to joust against each other like knights on horseback, and so they split up into two teams. Leib straddled Berl's shoulders, with his legs under his friend's arms, and Itzik did likewise with Zvi. While gripping the head of his companion with his left arm, the "rider" with his right arm tried to unseat his opponent. The game consisted of knocking the rival into the water. They played until exhausted, then sat down in the field beneath the sun.

"If we stayed in the sun all day, every day, we'd turn into black people," Itzik said.

Zvi looked at him: "That's not true. If we stayed in the sun all the time, our skin would burn and we'd get blisters, but we wouldn't turn black."

"That's only if we stayed in the sun a couple of days, but I said every day, for many years."

"Not that either," Zvi said. "No matter how long we stayed in the sun, we'd always be Jews."

"Don't be stupid," Berl intervened. "What does being a Jew have to do with being a black person?"

"It's because Itzik said we'd turn into black people, and if that happened, then we'd be Negroes and not Jews."

"You don't have the least idea of what you're talking about, and neither does Itzik. In the first place, you can't become what you aren't, no matter how much you stay in the sun," Leib asserted.

"That's what I said. What's more, it's not even sunny every day."

"My God, you're stupid! We're talking about what would happen if it could be sunny every day. *If... it ... could.... be.*"

"I'm just saying that anybody who stays out in the sun for many years turns into a black person," Itzik insisted. "That's how the races were formed."

"So, how come the Negroes who live in the United States don't turn into whites?" Leib shot back.

They all burst out laughing. Itzik hesitated before answering.

"It's not the same thing. Skin is a little bit like clothing: It can be dyed more easily than it can be bleached out."

"And what about the Jews of Palestine, how come they haven't turned into Negroes?" Berl asked. "It's always sunny in Eretz Israel."

"The Zionist has spoken," Leib said in a mocking tone.

"Who said it's always sunny in Eretz Israel?" Itzik protested.

"My mother."

And with that, Berl considered the matter closed.

Leib went to the edge of the river and began relieving himself. Behind him, he heard Zvi's voice: "Can't you pee somewhere else?"

"I'm peeing on those who took our spot.

"Pig!" Itzik shouted.

"That's the world for you," Leib said, trying to sound introspective. "Those on top shit on those below."

"The philosopher has spoken," Berl said, getting even with his friend.

The four boys continued talking until it began to grow dark. They got dressed and started back home, carrying their wet underpants in their hands. They reached their small town just before dark. After chatting for a few more minutes, they said goodbye and each one set off for home.

On turning a corner, Leib saw his house in the half-light, about a hundred yards or so in the distance. He immediately understood that something had happened. The modest dwelling was all lit up and there were a lot of people squeezed into the doorway. Some were outside, standing in front, talking in low voices. With the presentiment that something bad had happened, a pang of anxiety swept over him. He changed his pace to a slow walk, as if trying to delay the moment of recognition. People hastened to let him pass, moving aside without saying a word. He stepped inside and right there, in front of him, he saw it on the floor: a long bundle covered with a blanket. It was a human body and he didn't need anyone to tell him who it was. His mother's sobbing from somewhere in the house was enough to confirm his worst fears. His eyes clouded over. Someone put his arm around his shoulder and affectionately squeezed it, but he never knew who it was. Often, years later, he entertained the idea that no one had seen who it was, because it was none other than his own father giving him a farewell hug.

2

All of Golochov turned out for the watchmaker's funeral. It wasn't that Chaim was an important person—no one was important in Golochov—but in a small town where nothing ever happens, the sudden death of a relatively young man, strong and healthy like Chaim, was an event. People didn't suddenly die in Golochov. Sudden heart attacks weren't in vogue at that time or, to be more precise, other illnesses took their toll on the population before the onset of age and heart problems. In the *shtetl*, people generally died around fifty or older, after some known or unknown illness had them bedridden for some length of time. Children died too from "childhood diseases," according to Leib's mother Sara, who had already lost three children, or else a person just died of "old age" if he managed to reach seventy. Certainly, life was harder and shorter, but no one died at the age of thirty-eight like Chaim the watchmaker.

Leib was numb, there in the midst of sobbing relatives while they waited next to the small building, in the middle of the cemetery, where the members of the *chevrah kaddishah* had finished preparing the body. He pictured the scene of the old men washing the naked and lifeless body of his father. "When a Jew dies, the community is obligated to give him a proper burial in accordance with the Law," *Rav* Zuntz had taught him. "The *Chevre Kadishe* takes care of that for practical reasons, but the responsibility belongs to the entire community." Leib had a dazed look in his eyes. Unlike his mother and the rest of his relatives, his eyes were dry; he wasn't crying, perhaps because what he was feeling more than anything was fear rather than sorrow.

The door of the small building opened and the first one to step forward was *féter* Yankl ("Uncle" Yankl, as he was known in the *shtetl*). His small eyes searched among the mourners for a few men to assist him. With a wave of his hand, he called them over to help carry the casket with the body that had been prepared for its final rest.

The funeral procession moved slowly towards the burial site. It was hot that mid-August afternoon. Suddenly a very fine drizzle began falling, a kind of invisible dew that didn't really get anybody wet but which imbued the air with a strange glow. So soft was the drizzle (if that's what it was) that very few noticed the mysterious light that slowly descended from the sky, like a heavenly blanket that spread itself over the Golochov cemetery. Leib would never forget it.

When they lowered the casket into the grave, Sara cried out: "Chaim, why did you leave us?" Several people tried to calm her, but she pushed them aside and rushed toward the grave. Someone grabbed her when she seemed about to fall—or throw herself?—in. Beside herself with grief, she gazed down at the box that rested at the bottom and let out a shriek of pain before fainting. The women were shouting, the men were giving orders, and Leib stared disconsolately as they led his mother away.

The ceremony had to go on. "Uncle" Yankl approached Leib and told him to tear his shirt. Yankl was the one who led the *chevrah kaddishah* and was in charge of all the details of the funeral. He was the one who, the night before, had asked Sara for her husband's *talit* to wrap the body and bury it in accordance with tradition. Leib grabbed the collar of his shirt and firmly yanked at it, but it didn't tear. The fabric was moist from the extremely fine drizzle and it seemed to Leib that it had become harder. He then grabbed his shirt pocket and ripped it loose with one big tug. But seeing that the shirt itself wasn't torn, he put away the little patch of cloth, thinking that it could be sewn back on. Days later he would recall with shame that fleeting thought. How could he be concerned about his shirt at a tragic moment like that? Or maybe the moment wasn't all that tragic for him. Maybe he was still too much a child to understand death.

28

"Courage, you're the man of the house now! Here," someone said, and handed him an open book.

Leib took it without losing the page. It was a book of prayers and was open to the Kaddish. Sure, he wasn't a child anymore; he had already had his *Bar Mitzvah*. His brothers, Jonathan and Peretz, hadn't yet turned thirteen and so they weren't brought to the cemetery. Holding the book in both hands, looking at it without really seeing the words, he began reciting:

"Yitgadal ve-yitkadash shme rabah..."

It was about four in the afternoon when they returned home, where Sara, Leib, Chaim's brother Shumel, and his sister Lea, were to remain until the end of *shivah*, the seven-day period of strict mourning. For those seven days, no one was to leave the house, no one was to sit in a chair, or cut his hair, or change his clothes; they would remain seated on the floor, without shoes, with their clothing ripped, in the company of their relatives and friends. A lighted candle would burn the entire time. At night, a prayer would be said, and many who normally went to the synagogue would come to the house to pray.

Leib observed his mother's drawn look. She didn't seem to be the same woman who had sent him to the *cheder* just the day before. Her spirited eyes had turned opaque, the color had disappeared from her cheeks, her cheekbones seemed more prominent, and big circles under her eyes marked her anguished face. Thank goodness she can't see herself, Leib thought. All the mirrors in the house had been covered with towels and rags. They were to remain like that for the seven days of mourning and no one could say if it was being done to fulfill a religious precept or because of superstition.

That afternoon saw many visitors come to the house to offer their condolences and they stayed a good while, seated or standing, but without speaking. Sara remained seated on the floor with a lost look. From time to time, someone spoke a few words of consolation to her, which, instead of consoling her, made her break into tears. At sunset, a prayer was said that would be repeated every night for a week.

With the passage of days, the number of visitors diminished and those who stayed to keep the mourners company—generally the closest friends—became a little more talkative. Even those in mourning began to say a few words. The return to a normal life was inevitable.

"*Chaim* means *life*," Shloime the Tailor said one afternoon, "and what poor Chaim had least of all was *chaim*."

No sooner had a laugh escaped the lips of Pinky the Half-Pint than it turned into a grimace when he saw the others fire a harsh look his way. Surely, it was an indiscretion, but it served to slice through the gloomy atmosphere that filled the house. It happened on the fourth day of *shivah*. That was the day when Frimca the Dispenser of Advice came to offer her condolences. Leib was to remember Frimca's arrival the rest of his life, but not because of Frimca herself but because of her daughter Ruchel, who accompanied her.

"First, say hello to Mrs. Sara," Frimca instructed her as soon as they came in.

Leib saw an angel walk through the door. He already knew Ruchel (who in Golochov didn't know everybody else?), but it had been a long time since he had seen her. Now, precisely at that age when a young man begins to notice the allure of the opposite sex, the girl's lovely face appeared before his impressionable eyes. Leib watched her with great interest as she walked over to greet his mother. Her blonde hair, of reddish-golden tones, was an abundant and wavy mane that fell over her shoulders and gracefully cascaded behind her neck and down her back, and seemed to radiate light. She had big, dark, expressive eyes, which in contrast to her shimmering blonde hair, looked even darker than they were. Her long neck, oval face, refined, straight nose, and ruby lips harmoniously complemented each other to give her beauty a touch of elegance and distinction.

"I'm so sorry for your loss, Mrs. Sara," the girl said in a soft voice, and went to sit down on a stool next to Leib.

The young man was so befuddled he didn't even think to ask himself if it was by chance that she chose that spot.

"Leib, I'm truly sorry about what happened."

"Yes." It was a clumsy reply, and immediately it troubled him that he had said "yes" instead of "thank you."

Neither of the two spoke another word; they sat for a long time, listening to the conversation of the adults while mutually ignoring one another. Just the same, Ruchel caught Leib by surprise more than once looking at her.

Sara did not join the conversation. Silent, seated on the floor, she lifted her reddened eyes from time to time to see who was coming and who was leaving. Those who came to pay a visit generally did not address her, just as those who were leaving didn't say goodbye. If someone did greet her, Sara did not answer; she seemed oblivious, as if not hearing a word that was spoken.

"Enach the Giant," Big-Nosed Simcha said, "was strong like an ox until one day he really took sick and died just like that."

"That's because they didn't use leeches," Frimca was quick to answer.

"The reason they didn't use leeches," Simcha said, "was because they didn't find a single one. I should know, since I was there, helping them look, but the pond was completely dry at that time."

"Why leeches if you could have bled him? Bloodletting is much more effective," Shmuel said, scratching his four-day-old beard. "Enach could have been saved if they had bled him."

31

"He would have died just the same," Hersh the Carrot Top said. "The day a person's gonna die is written and when that day comes, that person dies, bloodletting or no bloodletting."

"Still, how come some people are saved when they're given medicine?" Frimca asked in a defiant tone.

"Because they weren't going to die anyway," Hersh replied, faithful to his theory.

Pinky the Half-Pint laughed. Everything he heard struck him funny. Just then, Fishel the Milkman and his wife, Haya the Madcap, showed up to offer their condolences. Afterwards, Ghitl the Matchmaker arrived. Every fifteen minutes or so, someone was either coming or going. When Frimca decided to leave, she stood up and signaled to her daughter.

"See you soon, Leib," Ruchel said in a very gentle voice. "I'll come again to visit with you."

"All right."

All right, he told himself. *I sound like an idiot. Is that all I can think of to say?*

As soon as mother and daughter left, Leib withdrew to the small room that he shared with his two brothers. Neither Jonathan nor Peretz was there. During that seven-day period, friends of the family were watching the boys for Sara.

Leib stretched out on his bed. He was tired of sitting on the floor all day. He stared up at the ceiling and thought about his father. He saw him seated at his workbench, hunched over and looking through his eyeglass at an old timepiece he was holding in his hands. Leib marveled at how his father held the lens in place, with no help from his hand. Whenever he tried it himself, the lens immediately fell from his eye. His father would laugh while explaining to him, in vain, how he had to squint in order to hold the lens between his eyebrow and cheek. He would also explain to him the delicate workings of timepieces, revealing what, to his mind, was the fascinating world of miniature pinions, ratchets, screws, and washers.

Leib pondered the consequences of his father's sudden death. From that moment on, he would either have to become the sole support of his family or, at least, bear part of the responsibility with his mother. In the mere span of four days he felt he had grown up. Seeing no future in Golochov, at least not seeing anything he wanted for himself, he thought that he would do well to go off in search of new horizons. He had already toyed with the idea on several occasions, although more to amuse himself than to really plan for the future. On this occasion, for the first time, he gave it serious consideration. If there are better worlds, why stay in Golochov? But if he were to leave, what would happen to his mother? And he began thinking about her; not about the tormented woman with the drawn face and teary eyes who sat in the next room, but about the happy mother who played with him, pampered him, and prepared the best honey cakes in the world. His mother reminded him of his aunt, who looked so much like her. He remained in bed for a long time, face up, staring at the ceiling and letting his mind wander. A series of images ran through his head. He thought about his Aunt Dora, his Uncle Godl, the dear, old Zimmermans, Zaharia the Seer, *Rav* Zuntz, Berl, Itzik, Etl (Itzik's sister), and almost without realizing how or when, he came to Ruchel. How lovely she was! He had never seen such a beautiful girl.

At fifteen, Leib was experiencing the first pangs of love. In his mind he saw Ruchel's angelic face with those big, dark eyes, and she was looking at him and smiling. His vivid imagination needed nothing more than this image to leap into the candy-coated world of a young boy's fantasy:

"What's that noise?" the girl with the angelic face suddenly asked.

Leib looked out his window and saw a band of Cossacks, so menacing in their demeanor, brandishing their arms as they advanced on horseback, atop steeds that sauntered from side to side.

"It's nothing," the intrepid hero said.

The girl with the alluring face rested her head on his shoulder and closed her eyes. She appeared to have drifted off to sleep. With the greatest of care, Leib picked her up and walked to the door; kicking it open, he fled the house, with her in his arms. Like a bolt of lightning, he ran but without feeling his feet touch the ground. Maybe he wasn't running but gliding over a slippery street or flying barely inches above the ground. Other Jews were also running in all directions, seeking to escape being massacred. Leib looked back and saw a band of Cossacks bearing down on him. The sound of gunfire, the noise of thundering hoofs and shouting could be heard everywhere.

"Oh, Leibele, I'm scared," the maiden said in a tremulous voice, still in the arms of her hero. It was the first time she had called him by that name.

"Ruchel, don't be afraid. I won't let anything happen to you."

As soon as he said this, he spurred the horse with his feet. Yes, because now he was no longer running. He was mounted on a handsome white stallion with a strong neck and an elegant gait. At the signal from his rider, the horse began galloping, leaving a cloud of dust behind. The Cossacks rode after them in pursuit, firing their guns and brandishing their sabers, but little by little they were being left in the distance. Not even the most skillful riders in Russia astride their best horses could have caught up with him. His fiery steed galloped at such a pace that the girl's hair rippled in the wind, fluttering like a golden banner. Once on the outskirts of town, Leib pulled on the reins and the mighty horse stopped hard in his tracks, neighing and rearing up on his hind legs. Twilight had descended and the sky was now a dark gray, but the clouds had a reddish hue that seemed to be the reflection, not of the sun that had just gone down over the horizon, but of the village that lay behind them. Leib and the girl turned their faces to look back and saw the little houses of Golochov in the distance, engulfed in flames.

"Leib." He didn't know if he had been dreaming or what, but the voice of his Uncle Shumel brought him back to reality. "Yes?"

"Everybody is here now. Time to begin the prayer."

"Coming."

Leib sat up and left his room. At the end of the prayer, he had to recite the Kaddish. He would do it not only for the seven days of *shivah*, but for many more days, on specified dates throughout his life, for the eternal rest of his father's soul.

That night, while saying Kaddish (how strange!) the vision of Golochov consumed in flames came again to his thought.

3

Springtime's first balmy days not only warmed the village but also lifted the spirits of the inhabitants. After the harsh winter, the most beautiful of seasons came as a welcome relief. During those days when the sun shone bright, the people hastened outside and onto the streets of the *shtetl* where it was warmer, for their houses still held the cold of the long winter months. The women came out to chat with their neighbors, the boys to play and the men to see to some task. It was the chosen time of year for repairing the roof of a house or mending a fence.

Leib and Berl sat on the grass a short distance from their friends who were playing with a wooden wheelbarrow.

"Today I'm going to tell my mother."

"You'll give her a heart attack," Berl said.

What was on their minds was the journey that Leib was about to embark on. The young boy had gotten it into his head to go to the New World in search of fortune and a better life. The idea came to him shortly after his father's death and grew stronger as the days progressed. At first, he thought that he'd have to wait several years, since before all else, he had to make sure of his family's well-being; but when he saw that his mother was getting along all right with the help she was receiving from relatives and, what's more, that it cost more to keep him at home than what he himself could contribute to his family's budget, he made up his mind to leave as soon as possible.

"When?"

"Right after Passover."

"But *Pesach* is barely a week away."

"True. And two or three weeks after that I'll be gone."

"I'm leaving too one day."

"I know."

"For Eretz Israel.

"Yes, I know."

"Where it's always sunny."

Leib smiled. There were few idealists and romantics like his friend.

"Where the sky is completely blue," Berl continued, "without a cloud, and at night a thousand stars shine above."

"You're an incurable dreamer. What will you do there?"

"Rebuild the homeland."

"You're joking, aren't you?"

"And what about you, what will you do in America?"

"Get rich."

"You'll always be a Jew in a land of strangers."

"No. It's different in America. All the people there are immigrants, and I'll be just another one of them."

"A Jew is always different."

"Not in America."

"You have no idea what it's like in America."

"I have a better idea about that than you do about Eretz Israel."

"I'd like to see you in twenty years; to know what you did with your life."

"You'll know. Wherever we are, we'll stay in touch. I'll write and tell you about my life, and you'll do the same. Okay?"

"It's a deal."

That same afternoon, while his brothers were playing outside, Leib spoke to his mother. Sara was in the kitchen, doing the traditional cleaning—for the third consecutive day—to leave the house spotless for the Jewish Passover.

"Mom, could you stop working for a minute? I have something very important to tell you."

With those words, Leib began his explanation, having prepared and rehearsed it in his mind the previous day. He began by telling his mother how much he loved her and appreciated the sacrifices she had made for him. He went on to praise the merits of his brothers and the valuable help they would provide her when they were older. He praised the generosity of his aunts and uncles and thanked God for protecting his mother and his brothers, Peretz and Jonathan, from hunger and want. He then proceeded to examine the conditions of life in the *shtetl*, the poverty and the struggle for survival. He spoke of the impossibility of changing the conditions of life there and talked about how dark the future looked to him.

With a degree of impatience, Sara listened to her son, knowing that what he was telling her was leading up to something, but no matter how much she pondered his words, she had no idea what it was.

"*Nu?*" she asked when the boy reached a point where he didn't seem to know how to continue. "So, tell me already."

"Mom...I'm leaving Golochov."

The eruption Leib had feared didn't happen. Instead, an absolute silence engulfed the room. Two tears burst from Sara's eyes and began trickling down her cheeks. Leib felt his own eyes tearing up.

"Mom, don't cry, please."

They embraced.

"But you're still a child…"

For a moment he thought of protesting, of explaining that he was no longer a child; but he kept quiet. He had said enough and maybe, after all was said and done, he was really just that, a child. His mother could be right, as always. He hugged her tight and heard her sob.

She said nothing that day—she was too upset to talk—but the following morning they had a long conversation. Contrary to what Leib had guessed, his mother was not opposed to his leaving. She knew—as he did, as all knew—that there was no future in Golochov. Still, she implored him to postpone his trip, to wait until he was older. In vain, Sara explained her reasons. But Leib's mind was made up.

The discussions went on daily, until Sara finally accepted the fact that her son was leaving. On one occasion, she told him:

"I'll never see you again."

"My God, mom! Don't say such a thing," Leib exclaimed, feeling his eyes once more welling up with tears. "With the first money that I put together, I'll send for you; for you and Jonathan and Peretz."

"Son, take good care of yourself…"

"Mom!"

"Never forsake your heritage, your people. Someday, when the time comes for you to get married…"

"Mom, please, stop…"

"Let it be with a Jewish girl."

"Of course! How could you think otherwise!"

The idea of marriage was so far removed from Leib's mind that he found it ludicrous to even speak of it. At sixteen, he would have been hard pressed to find a more absurd subject. The idea that he'd get married one day had never entered his thought. His mother was suddenly coming out with things that were so far in the future and that—so it seemed to him—had nothing to do with his leaving. Still, it was precisely at that moment that the image of Ruchel came to mind. It was a spontaneous association of ideas that the mind makes automatically, independent of one's will. The incursion of the girl into his thinking, at that moment and under those circumstances, struck him as quite bizarre.

"Promise me you'll marry a Jewish girl," his mother insisted.

"I promise."

The news that Leib was going to America spread like a whirlwind among the inhabitants of the *shtetl*. Everybody had an opinion to offer. Leib couldn't walk down the street without someone stopping him, either to encourage him in his resolve, or to dissuade him.

The first *Pesach seder* was held at Uncle Shmuel's. Year after year they all got together at his house because he, being the most prosperous member in the family, was the only one who could afford the luxury of hosting all the relatives at the same time. Shmuel enjoyed having guests and he took great care in attending to them in the best way possible. He had a large table that could be made longer by joining together some extensions he had made with his own hands, just as he had built much of the furniture in the house. The uncle sat at the head of the table with Aunt Dora seated to his right and Sara, his sister-in-law, to his left. Uncle Hoisie and Aunt Lea had their places in the middle. Also invited to the dinner was Gabriel, the bachelor. Shmuel had given Leib the honor of sitting at the head of the table at the other end, where his father would normally have sat. Surrounding Leib were his twelve cousins, and

41

his brothers, Peretz and Jonathan. Jonathan, being the younger, had to read "the four questions."

Leib thought the table looked magnificent. The silverware was the same that was used all year long, but Aunt Dora had a set of special china that she only used during the week of *Pesach*. Everything looked so clean, so shiny. Neatly arranged on the lace tablecloth, which was immaculately white despite a few places that had been mended, were the traditional dishes of the *seder* meal: a plate with a little piece of *beitzah* or toasted egg, *charoset*, green herbs as well as bitter herbs, hard-boiled eggs and salted water, three plates of *matzah*, bottles of wine and wine cups for all the guests, besides an especially pretty cup reserved for the prophet Elijah. The family scene of everybody smiling and dressed in their best attire, seated around the table celebrating *Pesach*—the feast of freedom— filled Leib with happiness. But this time, his feeling of happiness was mixed with apprehension

"Why is this night different from all the other nights?" Jonathan said, beginning to recite the four ritual questions.

Because I'm going away, Leib thought, *and this is the last time I'll be with the whole family*.

"We were Pharaoh's slaves in Egypt…"

Shmuel was reading the Haggadah, the traditional "legend" of Pesach, in a dramatic voice. Every once in a while he would raise his eyes to glance for a few brief moments at one of the guests, but without pausing in his recitation. When he reached the part that deals with the four children and their distinguishing characteristics—the wicked, the wise, the simple, and the one whose mind is too limited to ask—his eyes rested on Leib. The boy swallowed hard.

The week of *Pesach* went by quickly. During the days leading up to his departure, Leib, on several occasions, found his mother in tears.

"One day I'll resign myself to having lost your father," she said with tender sagacity, but Leib knew that the tears were being shed for him.

Sara handed him the pocket watch that had been Chaim's most valuable piece. When she was looking for it among her husband's possessions, she found a little box with spare parts and the name and address of the watchmaker who had sent it from Paris.

"Schwarzbard is his name," she said. "I never met him, but he was a friend of your father. Chaim corresponded with him. When you get to Paris, try to look him up. I'm sure he'll help you."

Aunt Lea gave Leib two gold coins and a faded photograph of her and her two brothers, Chaim and Shmuel, taken at the end of the last century when they were children. The boy found it the most extraordinary photograph he had ever seen. He accepted it as a family heirloom and promised to keep it his entire life.

Uncle Shmuel presented him with a small book of prayers and a little packet of money.

"Take good care of it," he said, counseling him. "It will serve you well on your journey."

Leib never knew if his uncle meant the *sidur* or the money. The day before his departure, one of his friends from the *cheder* came to inform him that *rav* Zuntz wanted to see him.

"Leib Ben Chaim Halevy, come here, my boy," old Zuntz said when he saw him come in. "You're going to America."

A characteristic of the *lerer* was to toss out a sentence like that, without the other person knowing if it was a question or a statement. Leib took it as a question.

"Yes, sir."

"You've decided that Europe isn't for you."

"Yes, sir."

"What will you do in America?"

(*A question, at last!*)

"Work."

"And here a man can't work?"

"Here, if a man doesn't work, he starves to death; but if he works, he barely earns enough to eat. I'm going there to become rich."

"You think so?"

"Yes, sir, very rich."

"From your mouth to God's ears. If you do succeed, I hope you'll know how to be generous with your fellow man."

"Yes, sir."

"But I didn't call you here to talk about the riches you'll acquire there, but about the ones you'll take with you from here. Guard them well, my boy; never lose them."

"I'm not taking anything."

"Nothing?"

"No, sir...I mean, a little money, very little, a watch, two gold coins..."

"That's what's in your suitcase; what about what's in your head? Nothing? What I've instilled in you the last few years, you're going to leave that here?"

"No, sir."

"Well, Leib, that's what I mean. Do you know the value of your religious heritage? Of your cultural tradition? Of your principles?"

"Yes, sir."

"So, don't go and lose them. Hold on to your heritage. It's worth more than any fortune you'll ever acquire; and believe me, it can be lost just like any material asset."

"Yes, sir."

"Always remember, you're a Jew."

"Yes, sir, I will. Always."

"It'll be easy for you," the old man said with one of his rare smiles, "since there'll always be someone to remind you of it from time to time."

Leib understood the irony and nodded.

"To remember that one is a Jew is easy; to be one, isn't," the *rav* continued. "We have obligations that others do not. Ever since we existed as a people, each generation has taken up the task of transmitting its knowledge to the next generation. And just as your parents inculcated in you your Judaism, so you must inculcate it in your children."

"Yes, sir."

"Your offspring must be Jewish; they must maintain the faith, continue the tradition. That is *your* responsibility."

"Yes, sir."

"The heritage is very important. Do you understand?"

"Yes, sir."

Rav Zuntz took a deep breath and concluded:

"Okay... that's all."

"Yes, sir," the boy repeated, taking a deep breath in turn.

The following day, after saying goodbye to his large family and hugging his mother, he climbed into the horse-drawn carriage with four other passengers. Sara was not only able to control her tears, but

45

even managed a smile when she said goodbye to her son. How hard it must have been for her! Leib couldn't respond in kind, knowing as he did that hidden behind the bitter smile was a broken heart.

The coachman gave a couple of shouts, shook the reins, and the two horses set off. Berl and Itzik went running alongside, calling out to their friend. Leib was standing, looking back. While holding onto the railing with one hand, he lifted the other above his head to wave to the relatives and friends who were waving back at him, on the other side of the cloud of dust that was spiraling upward from the road. At that moment, he noticed another person waving to him, not from among the large group of people but behind it. It was Ruchel who had come out to say goodbye to him. An immense joy swept over Leib. For a few brief seconds the only thing he saw was the splendid blonde mane that seemed to glow like a star in the distance. For months, he had been secretly in love with Ruchel, with that pure, platonic love of which only youth is capable. They had never spoken to each other again since that day when her mother brought her to their house to offer their condolences, but on several occasions they had run into each other by accident. When that happened, they pretended not to see each other; but there were times when their eyes did meet. Then they would greet each other with a smile and go their separate ways without exchanging a word. Leib would have given anything to know if she had the same feelings for him that he had for her. Ruchel's presence that sunny morning put his doubts to rest. His heart bursting with joy, he raised his arm higher and waved more vigorously. It seemed to him that Ruchel was doing the same. Suddenly, when the carriage went around a bend in the road, the crowd disappeared from view. Rather than sit down right away, he remained standing, observing the little houses of Golochov growing smaller and smaller each time, until another bend in the road made them disappear. That was the last time in his life that he was to see them.

4

The horses never went at full gallop, as the young traveler would have liked. What's more, to his great disappointment, the horses never galloped at all, but rather sauntered at a casual pace, pulling the open carriage that swayed incessantly from side to side.

"The reason the carriage is swaying like this is because there's a wheel that's off-center," one of the passengers said, not addressing anyone in particular.

The man, small and pallid, and frail in appearance, with a prominent nose and an intellectual air about him, went on talking.

"That is to say, the axle is, of course, positioned through the center of the wheel, but the wheel itself is not set at ninety degrees to the axle, but like this instead," he explained, holding the index finger of his right hand against the palm of his left hand. No one showed any interest in the explanation, and the man, seeing this, fell silent, though not for long.

"The danger of traveling with a wheel off center is that it can break apart at any moment," he remarked after a few minutes. "And then we'd be in a real mess!"

No one said anything. They ignored the little man as if he had never opened his mouth. Leib felt ill at ease. He wanted to engage the man in conversation but couldn't think of anything to say. He lowered his eyes and stared down at his folded hands. He would have preferred gazing out at the landscape, but was too shy to turn his head sideways to look out, not wanting the other passengers to think he was looking at them. In fact, he had gotten the worst of the seats. Each of the other four men occupied a corner of the carriage, while he was stuck in the middle, on the rear bench, squeezed between two of the passengers.

The journey soon became monotonous: the coachman up front, the four adults and the boy behind, all swaying with the motion of the carriage and no one uttering a single word. After some time had passed, the passenger with the intellectual air and the explanation about the carriage wheel made one last attempt to strike up a conversation.

"The reason the driver isn't going faster is so the horses don't tire. If they falter out here, there's no way to relieve them."

One of the passengers glanced at him, expressionless.

"What I mean," the man said, "is that it would be impossible to change horses here without calling attention…that is to say, to ourselves."

No one said anything and the man fell silent, this time definitively. The sun was low on the horizon when the carriage stopped beside a small pasture, in the middle of which stood a rustic stone building with a wood roof. It was a stable of sorts, since from a distance one caught the odor of hay and manure.

"We're here. Just keep your seats," the coachman said.

He got down and walked towards the building. When he drew closer, he stuck two fingers in his mouth and gave a sharp whistle. A corpulent man, dressed in coarse peasant clothes, boots smeared with cow dung, soon appeared from around one side of the structure, walking clumsily. The two men quietly exchanged a few words and Leib saw the coachman hand the other man some money. The driver returned to the carriage and announced: "You can get down."

All rushed to grab their belongings.

"This is Dimov," the coachman said, pointing to the hulking figure, now standing next to him. "From here on, you'll be in his care. Dimov doesn't speak Yiddish." The husky peasant laughed. "But I'm sure you won't have any difficulty getting along with him. Safe journey."

Having said this, the coachman climbed up into his seat, turned the carriage half way around, and headed back on the same road.

"Goodbye," Leib shouted.

He was the only one to say anything. The other passengers remained as silent as they had the entire journey. The giant laughed again.

"Come. This way," he said, motioning to them with his arm.

He spoke in Russian. For the passengers, all Jews, Russian was not their native tongue, but they knew enough of it to understand what the man was saying.

They followed him behind the stable and across an open field, making their way through beet, potato, and cabbage crops. It was difficult to walk, not because of the terrain but because of their luggage. Each one carried a single suitcase; small to be sure, but which became heavier by the minute. Fortunately, the distance they had to cover was not very long, about two kilometers at most. By the time they reached the bank of a wide and placid river they all knew as the Dniester, it was already dusk.

"Hurry, hurry! It'll be dark soon," Dimov said while helping them to board a boat that was waiting for them.

The Russian arranged the suitcases, assigned each one a place, gathered up the rope that anchored the small craft, then sat down in the middle and began rowing. For some fifteen minutes, the passengers could rest while Dimov worked. Despite the husky peasant's efforts, the boat advanced very slowly, propelled down river by the current and moving diagonally across the waterway. The travelers, as before, remained silent. Upon reaching shore, they renewed their journey on foot. This time the terrain was more

49

difficult and the stretch of ground to be covered longer. They passed through a wooded area where there was no trail and very little light until they came to a clear path where they rested for a few minutes. The visibility had improved because the absence of trees allowed the moon to bathe the open terrain in its tenuous light. They followed the path for about two hours. Leib felt himself faltering when Dimov called out: "We're almost there."

In fact, in the distance they could see the silhouettes of houses, all dark inside, maybe because it was already late at night. Few and isolated at first, the little houses became more numerous as the travelers drew closer, until well-defined groups of dwellings, bounded by unpaved streets, came into view. They had entered a town on the other side of the border. Dimov continued guiding them until they came to a house situated in the middle of a vegetable garden. He knocked on the door. From inside someone said something in a language that the others did not understand.

"Dimov," came the burly reply.

A young man opened the door. Next to him was a white-haired man and behind him, a woman with several children.

"May peace be with you!" the old man said in Yiddish.

On hearing the traditional greeting, Leib's heart swelled with joy. He was in a Jewish home! He suddenly felt safe, calm.

"May peace be with you," the others answered.

The Russian peasant looked at them and laughed.

"Come in, come in, please." And as the old man was saying this, he grabbed Leib by the hair and gently shook his head.

Leib was so filled with emotion that he had to make an effort to hold back his tears.

All this happened in the spring of 1926. In that year, as in all the ones that preceded it since the Bolshevik Revolution in 1917,

50

hundreds of thousands of Jews left Russia in the same way that Leib and his companions had left: illegally. They crossed the borders of the immense country in order to join their people in the great migratory tide west.

The border that Leib and his companions from Golochov had chosen to cross was the one facing Rumania, and the town they arrived in was Chotin. Its proximity had allowed the Jews from the area to establish the necessary contacts to maintain a modest flow of clandestine emigration. Leib didn't have time to see much of the town, for he found himself the next morning in another horse-drawn carriage, with another coachman and new traveling companions, advancing along the road that led north to Kamenetz-Podolsk and connected with the main routes that crossed the Ukraine, and towards the south, through what at the time was Rumania, linking the Dniester River with the Prut. It was in this latter direction that they were traveling and, like the first leg of the journey, this one also lasted almost an entire day.

By late afternoon they reached their destination: Cernauti, the political, cultural, and economic center of Bukovina. Cernauti was a cross between a big town and a small city, but compared to Golochov it looked like a metropolis, or at least so it seemed to Leib, who regarded the three and four-story houses with astonishment as the carriage advanced along the cobblestone streets. More than seven years had passed since the city was incorporated into Rumania, after the fall of the Austro-Hungarian Empire, but everybody continued calling it by its German name, Czernowitz.

"Whoa! Whoa!" the coachman shouted, bringing the carriage to a stop.

The passengers got down, said goodbye to one another and went their separate ways, each carrying a small suitcase. Leib set his down on the sidewalk and stood on tiptoes to stretch and extend his arms over his head.

"Tired, eh?" the coachman asked while shaking the dust from his jacket. "Have anywhere to go?"

"Yes, sir," Leib answered, and reading a slip of paper that he pulled from his pocket: "Number twenty-three Harvest Street."

"You're not far, son. See the house on the second corner, the one with the two little windows?" the coachman said, raising his arm and pointing to a house about a hundred yards away. "That's Harvest Street. Number twenty-three should be on the right, up ahead."

When Leib knocked on the door, a heavyset woman answered. She looked thrilled to see him, and holding both his hands in hers, exclaimed in Yiddish:

"You're Leibele!"

"Yes, ma'am."

"Bruno! Bruno! Leibele's here! Come in, my child, come in."

And taking the suitcase in one hand and his arm in the other, she had him come inside. Bruno Schechter was a cousin of Leib's mother, and Chana, his wife, had been a friend of hers since childhood. When they got married, they left Golochov, but stayed in touch with Sara. A few days prior to Leib's arrival, they had received her latest letter, in which she told them of her son's imminent visit and asked them to help him continue his journey.

"Your mother is crazy if she let you leave home at your age," Chana said after she greeted the boy, blessing him and asking about the whole family.

"Let him be, woman! Don't you see he's already a grown man?" Bruno grumbled without really believing what he was saying.

Uncle Bruno, like his wife, was a big, cheerful, good-natured person, and he couldn't do enough in making Leib feel at home. Over the course of the next few days, he introduced his nephew to his friends and took him all around Czernowitz, sometimes by himself and sometimes in the company of his three daughters. There wasn't much to see, but Leib was fascinated. Above all, the fact that the streets were paved amazed him. That, he thought, was something one could only see in the great capitals, but not this close to Golochov where, beyond the main street, all the others were dirt roads.

Bruno Schechter had the necessary connections and money to "arrange" the papers that his nephew required. In less than a week, Leib had "a Rumanian passport," with his name printed in Latin letters and his place and date of birth listed as Bucharest 1908, two years before his real birthday.

"A boy under eighteen shouldn't travel alone," Bruno told him with a smile. "Of course, that's not your situation," he added, giving him a wink.

Leib laughed while he examined the passport.

"Look how nice he looks in the photo!" Chana said. "Such a fine young man."

"And what will they say of a Rumanian who doesn't speak Rumanian?" one of the daughters asked.

They all burst out laughing.

A few days later, on a beautiful April morning, just after dawn, Leib said goodbye to his relatives and began the trip west on a small bus that carried twelve passengers. This was the first time he had ever ridden in a motorized transport and was so excited that he didn't stop smiling, several times voicing his delight. The road followed a course more or less parallel to the Prut River, upstream, to its origin in the Carpathian Mountains. The first stage of the journey went smoothly, but problems arose as soon as they began crossing the mountains. The bus frequently overheated, making it necessary to stop and wait at least half an hour for the engine to cool down. Whenever possible, they attempted to stop next to some stream so they could add water to the radiator which was belching puffs of steam. By starting and stopping so often, the crossing of the Carpathians, which should have taken them some four hours under normal conditions, required an entire day. It took them another whole day to reach the town of Baia-Mare, in Transylvania, the end of line for the railroad that came from the west. But the delay caused by the bus's frequent breakdowns made him miss the train that stopped in Baia-Mare only twice a week. That distressed him. More bewildered than worried, he didn't know where to turn. Straddling his small suitcase, he sat down on the edge of the sidewalk merely to let the time pass, with no idea of what to expect. Maybe something would happen. He didn't have to wait long before something, indeed, did happen. It was the most inconsequential coincidence imaginable: two men walked past him. That was all. But when a Jewish boy finds himself in a foreign country, alone and confused, sitting on the curb, in a town where he doesn't know a soul, and two men walk by, chatting, the event can be transcendental if the language they are speaking is Yiddish. Leib jumped up, grabbed his suitcase, and began trailing after them.

"Excuse me," he said. "Could you, perhaps, tell me where I might get something to eat and spend the night?"

The men turned around to look at the person who had spoken to them. The older of the two asked:

"Where are you from, my boy?"

Leib was more than happy to be able to tell his story, which he did with grace and ease. The men decided to take him to see Moses Aaron Krausz, the rabbi of the small community. When Krausz learned of the situation, he concluded that the opportunity to perform a *mitzvah*, a good deed, was heaven sent. He took Leib home with him and went about seeing to his needs. The young boy remained in the rabbi's house for three days, waiting for the next train out of Baia-Mare. This experience left a profound imprint on Leib, something that was to be reflected throughout his life in acts of generosity and solidarity with his fellow Jews.

At six in the morning, an hour before the train's departure, Leib had already settled into one of the coaches. As soon as it began filling up, he laid his head against the window, closed his eyes, and pretended to be fast asleep. He remained that way for almost the entire trip, fearing that someone might initiate a conversation with him and discover he didn't know a word of Rumanian, which could arouse suspicion. The "Rumanian" who didn't speak Rumanian and which had the Schechter family laughing so much now found himself facing a real danger. That same afternoon, when he would have to change trains to cross the border, they would be checking passports. Leib's wasn't a fake but a genuine document; yet it contained false information and had been expedited for someone who was a citizen of another country. Still, there was no way to detect any irregularity on a routine examination of the passport. It all looked legitimate, even the small photograph, which was really his. The only thing that could do him in was the fact that he didn't know how to speak Rumanian.

Several hours had passed when Leib felt the locomotive slowing down. A prolonged whistle accompanied the screeching sound of the brakes until the train came to a complete stop with its normal jerking motion. He could no longer pretend to be asleep.

They had reached the city of Oradea, the last stop before crossing the border. The train would continue south, towards Arad and Timisoara; the passengers who wanted to cross to the west had to get off and go through the passport checkpoint. A few people picked up their luggage and exited the train. Leib joined them. They walked to a small waiting room furnished with half a dozen long wood benches and sat down to await the arrival of the emigration officers. Minutes later an inspector from the Ministry of the Interior showed up, accompanied by two policemen, and in a loud voice made an announcement whose only intelligible word for Leib was *passport*.

55

For a split second, he thought that if need be he could pass himself off as a mute, but immediately realized that mutes can understand what is said to them, and in his case he wouldn't be able to understand a thing.

The passengers had taken out their identification papers and patiently waited their turn. The inspector began at the opposite end of the room. Leib observed his modus operandi. He went from person to person, examining the documents that were handed to him. He began by saying a few words to the passenger. They were always the same and apparently meant: "Your papers, please," or something like that. The inspector would then take the documents and examine them, spending about a minute for each person. In most cases, he said nothing, but simply returned the papers to the passenger and went on to the next one. In effect, there was no need for the passenger to speak. Consequently, the probability that everything would turn out all right was relatively good. Still, from time to time, the official would ask a few questions of an individual passenger. This happened more or less in one out of every four cases. Leib felt his heart pounding furiously and he was beginning to sweat. A little bit before it was Leib's turn, there was an incident that made him even more nervous. The inspector, without looking up from the passport he was examining, queried the passenger about something. The man answered. The inspector studied the document for a while and asked him another question. Again the man responded. Then came another question, and another and another. Clearly there was something wrong. The interrogation continued mounting in tone until the inspector began shouting. Suddenly, he signaled both guards to come over and arrest the passenger. One of the policemen forcibly removed him from the room while the man put up a big fuss. Accompanied by the other policeman, the inspector continued checking the passports. Leib was afraid his nervousness would give him away. He took a deep breath, lowered his eyes, and tried to appear composed. His turn came. The inspector asked him for his papers and Leib held them out. Then what he feared most happened: the inspector said something to him. Leib felt his face turn red. He looked up and saw a smile on the man's face. He understood that the inspector had said something in jest. Making an extraordinary effort, Leib returned the smile. Was it with a grimace? Had his hand trembled? The inspector examined Leib's documentation and handed it back to him, saying something. Leib nodded and took the papers. The inspector proceeded to the next passenger.

Four hours later, aboard another train, Leib was unable to contain his elation. He had just entered Hungary. The train proceeded slowly through the countryside, and the more distance he put between himself and the east, the happier he felt. Several times he realized he was smiling to himself.

Night had fallen by the time he reached Budapest. All the station's ticket windows were closed and there was no one to give him information. He then decided to spend the night there, and sitting down on a bench, he began thinking about all that had happened on his lengthy journey. It had been a long day, like all the others since he departed Golochov. How many in all? Ten? Twenty? It seemed as if months had gone by. He felt sleep coming over him. He then remembered his Uncle Shmuel's advice and, fearing for his suitcase, he placed it on the bench and lay back, using it as a pillow for his head. *No one can make off with it without waking me up*, he told himself. Before drifting off to sleep, he patted his stomach and felt the cloth purse his mother had sewn inside his shirt. The money he was carrying with him, the small gold coins his Aunt Lea had given him, and his father's watch were all safe.

The following day Leib boarded another train, the cleanest and most modern he had ever known. Through the window Western Europe paraded before his eyes. He spent the trip tasking in the majestic landscape: the green fields of northwestern Hungary; the Danube River, which wasn't blue, as Strauss's waltz had made him imagine it to be; the lakes of Austria which at times were indeed blue; the grandiose Alps with their snow-capped peaks; the forests of Germany; the vineyards of France; dozens, maybe hundreds, of towns and small villages, picturesque little houses and, once in a while, factories and buildings of imposing cities. He felt pleased and at peace with himself. He saw three countries, but was unable to say that he visited any of them. To have traveled so much and to have grasped so little! All he knew of Hungary was the train station in Budapest; of Austria, the station in Vienna; of Germany, the ones in Munich and Stuttgart. He had crossed three borders without any difficulty whatsoever. At the last one, in the city of Strasbourg, the custom's officer who examined his passport, a kindly gendarme with a bushy red moustache and a face nearly the same color, greeted him with a big smile.

"Bienvenu en France, Monsieur Edri."

Golochov

May 6, 1926

Dear Leib,

You don't know how happy it made me to get your letter. It's been five weeks since you left without our having any news of you. When your letter arrived this afternoon, I ran to see your mother to tell her, only to learn that she had also received a letter. Her face was beaming with happiness. Surely you can imagine how worried she was until today.

More than the letter itself, the fact that you wrote me made me happy; I mean, the fact that you kept your promise. Now I know for certain that we'll stay in touch the rest of our lives. Believe me, I've thought about it a lot. You went west and I, as soon as I can, will go east. Who knows if we'll see each other again. I have faith we will. We're young and life is full of surprises.

It seems incredible to me that you're in Paris. I can just picture how you must look in your new suit among so many elegant people. Is Paris really as magnificent as they say? It must be very exciting to walk along wide avenues, to see the plazas and the monuments. I've heard that the Jews in Paris don't speak Yiddish. Is that so? How do you make yourself understood there?

I want you to tell me about everything you see, everything you do. It's a lot easier for you to write, since you have so much more to tell. Nothing ever happens here in Golochov... nothing ever will.

Starting next month and for the whole summer, I'll be working, helping my Uncle Elimelech. He's going to teach me to be a furrier. I'm very fond of him and appreciate the fact that he's teaching me his trade, although I doubt that selling furs will do me much good in Eretz Israel.

I've run into Ruchel several times of late. Occasionally, she's given me the impression that our encounters aren't accidental, but that she's arranged for them to happen. And do you know why? Because she wants to know about you. She always asks me, in the most casual way, if I've received a letter from you. Today, when I told her yes, her eyes grew large. She asked me to let her read it. Of course, I told her no (I don't know if you'd like me showing it to her), but I spoke in general about what you wrote. She showed great interest and asked me to send you her regards in my next letter. As you see, I'm doing as she asked.

It seems everybody was expecting me to get a letter from you, because Ruchel wasn't the only one who asked about you. Half the shtetl did. Zvi and that crazy Itzik don't let a day go by without mentioning their friend Leib. Everyone in the cheder wants to how you're getting on. Even Rav Zuntz asked me if I've heard from you yet.

Speaking of the lerer: A few days ago, in the middle of class, he turned as white as a sheet and collapsed. We thought it was a heart attack; but it wasn't. From where he lay, sprawled on the floor, he asked us what we were all doing standing around him and told us to sit down. Then he sat down in his chair and asked fat-tub Hersh to bring him a glass of water. He took it from him and—can you believe this?—went on with the lesson as if nothing had happened. Poor Rav Zuntz. Who knows what got into him. Itzik says that the old man is off his rocker. Maybe he's got a screw loose, but there's no doubt he's an extraordinary man.

I read with great interest the verses your boss wrote. It seems very admirable to me that someone is both a watchmaker and a poet. Although why not? If there are similar cases in Golochov, all the more reason to have them in Paris. Just think: We've got my Uncle Elimelech who's a furrier and a poet, too; Shloime Rubinstein who's a tailor and a violinist and composer; Marc Shostak who's a carpenter and sculptor; Daniel Marx, a coachman and playwright; not to mention Rav Zuntz, a teacher and philosopher. I showed Mr.

60

Schwarzbard's verses to my Uncle Elimelech and he thought them very good, but not as good as his own, of course.

From what you tell me, I see that Shalom Schwarzbard must be a very interesting person and I think you were lucky to find work there. If you want the advice of a friend, stay in Paris a few years to get experience and save up some money. I don't see why you're so eager to get to America. It can't be any fun there, being broke. Don't count on the good luck you've had in Paris following you around.

I nearly died laughing when I read your name on the return address. Leon! It never occurred to me that you'd change your name. Do you want them to be afraid of you in the New World? "Leon" sounds like a ferocious animal, while "Leib" is totally tame, like everything that's said in Yiddish. Did you ever stop to think that expressions of anger, threats and orders lose their force in our language? Yiddish is definitely a language that only works for laughing and crying. "Leon" instills respect. I like it. I think that's what I'll call you from now on. "Leon."

Affectionately,

Berl

5

The first time he crossed paths with her, he wasn't sure he had seen right, but this time he felt certain. There was no mistaking it; the woman had pursed her lips at him. It was early evening, shortly after he had left work. He was on his way "home," a small room he had rented a few days earlier on the Rue Monge, not very far from Boulevard Saint Germain, when he saw her coming toward him, strolling casually along the sidewalk. He couldn't take his eyes from her; he thought her attractive and felt uncomfortable when she, instead of lowering her eyes, gazed straight into his. Just as they passed each other, she blew him a kiss of sorts. The youngster kept walking, not turning his head to look back at her, as if nothing had caught his attention, but the woman's flirtatious gesture left him flustered. A few days later he saw her again. He felt a shiver. She was coming his way, looking straight at him, and smiled. Leon continued on his way, but this time a sense of excitement took hold of him. When he reached the end of the block, he rounded the corner, then turned on his heels and cautiously poked his head out along the edge of the wall. Captivated by the svelte body, the thin waist, and the sensual walk, he watched the womanly silhouette slowly move away, then began following her, keeping a safe distance. The woman stopped when she reached the corner, but didn't cross the street or disappear around the side of the building; instead, she remained standing on the sidewalk. That was when Leon admitted to himself what he had suspected all along: she was a prostitute. He crossed the street to observe her from the opposite sidewalk. How common that nocturnal figure looked, with her tight-fitting blouse, her short skirt, and high heels! *How common, but how beautiful*! Leon thought, and immediately felt ashamed for thinking like that. He noticed that the people who passed her on the street turned around to have another look. *I'll bet she gives the eye to all the men who walk by and makes indecent gestures to them*, he told himself.

He had never seen a prostitute before in his life, and the woman's presence made a deep impression on him. For sure, there wasn't a single woman like that in Golochov. There was a certain Eniele Grossman, of whom Leib remembered his father saying— above the vehement objections of his mother and his aunts—that she was a whore. But that was crazy! She was a woman like any other in the village. At least, he had never noticed anything out of the ordinary in her behavior. They called her "Feiguele" and the gossips said that she got her vocation from her mother.

Whenever Leib and his friends in the *shtetl* got together, it often happened that they would start out talking about sports or pranks, or something on that order, only to end up on the subject of sex, a topic that adolescents find so alluring.

"There are prostitutes in every city in the world," Zvi had told them on one occasion. "In Warsaw there are even Jewish prostitutes." A violent argument then erupted between Berl and Zvi, since the idealistic young man could accept the first claim but not the second one. *We argued without knowing what we were talking about*, Leib thought. From among his friends, he was the first to see a "lady of the night" and found himself captivated by her presence.

A man approached the woman and chatted with her a bit before moving on. The woman also continued on her way until she came to a brightly lit shop window, where she again stopped. She was almost in front of Leon, on the other side of the street. Balanced on one leg and with an arm resting against her hip, she struck a pose that enhanced the curves of her body. Another man approached her and the two exchanged a few words. Then they went off together. Leon didn't have to follow them for long. About two blocks ahead, he saw them enter a building with a dark, rundown façade. Above the entrance to the sordid establishment was an illuminated sign that read: "Hotel Etoile." The couple disappeared behind the doors of the hotel to engage in who knew what kind of sinful pleasures.

Day after day, upon leaving work, Leon found himself inexorably drawn to the Hotel Etoile, where he roamed the adjacent streets in search of the woman who had captivated him. He came to realize that many women who walked the streets of this particular neighborhood practiced the same profession and was surprised he hadn't noticed them before. But she alone, the woman who passed him that night without lowering her gaze, fascinated him. When he spotted her, he followed from a distance, as if drawn by a magnetic force that would have swept him to her side if it weren't for his fear, which constituted an even greater force. Aided by the shadows of the night, he followed the bewitching figure until, sooner or later, the doors of the Hotel Etoile swallowed her up along with her companion of the moment. On those occasions when he could not find her, he stationed himself at a prudent distance from the hotel, hoping to catch a glimpse of her as she came out. She always came down alone; the client would appear a few minutes before or after.

A week had gone by since Leon started spying on her, which he himself began to consider a morbid obsession. One day he left work and went home with his mind made up not to look for her anymore, this woman of the night whom he found so seductive, but yearning down deep that chance would have him cross paths with her once more. The most direct route home passed through the area where she usually took her evening strolls, which offered him the opportunity "to give chance a little nudge," especially if he took his time. Suddenly, he saw her appear on a corner. The silhouette swayed as it came toward him. The sharp click of high heels on the pavement made him tremble. His face turned red and his heart began beating violently. He saw the smiling mouth and her eyes fixed on him, coming ever closer, seemingly beckoning to him.

"Hi," Leon said just as she approached.

Maybe he didn't intend to say it; it just came out.

"Hey, good-looking. Want to keep me company?"

"Yes," he said just above a whisper, and swallowed hard.

"Come."

Leon hesitated.

"Uhh…"

"What's wrong?"

"I don't know if I have enough money."

"How much you got?"

"Twenty francs."

"It'll do," she said and took him by the arm.

They walked in silence. Leon thought about saying something, but he didn't know what. Without realizing how he got there, he found himself walking through the doors of the Hotel Etoile.

"*Salut, Clau.*"

The voice that greeted the woman from behind the reception desk was that of the night clerk, an old man in shirtsleeves who was shuffling through some papers.

"*Salut, mon chu*," she answered.

The hotel lobby was a fuchsia color and had a small reception desk that, although occupying a corner of the room, took up one fourth of the space. A wooden staircase covered in a dirty, threadbare red runner was located on one side of the counter. A strange odor, like perfumed tobacco, pervaded the air.

"Give him five for the room," she said, looking at Leon.

He pulled out five francs and counted them out on the counter.

"Number eight," the old man said without addressing either of the two in particular.

He took the money and laid a key on the desk.

"Don't I have to sign the register?" Leon asked in broken French.

The old man looked at the woman and made a perplexed gesture with his eyebrows. She laughed. With one hand she took the key and with the other, Leon's arm.

"Come," she said, and pulled him by his sleeve towards the stairs.

She went ahead of him and Leon, frightened and spellbound at the same time, followed behind the delectable rump that swayed from side to side. They went up two flights.

"Ufff!" the prostitute muttered when they reached the hallway. "I'm out of breath. And you, my love?"

Leon shook his head no. *A good thing she didn't call me that in front of anybody*, he thought. She laughed as if she had read his mind, then went to the door marked number 8 and opened it. They went inside and she closed the door.

"You're really good-looking, you know?" she said, draping her arms over his shoulders.

"Yes," he said, feeling completely embarrassed.

What a stupid answer! he told himself. She laughed again and Leon thought that when a man and a woman are this intimate, each knows what the other one's thinking.

"You're funny."

Leon held her in his arms and, with his lips closed, pressed his mouth against hers for a few seconds before pulling them away with the sound of a kiss.

"You're really funny!"

Leon stared at her without sharing her laughter. He scraped his lips with his teeth and tasted the flavor of her red lipstick.

"I don't see anything funny."

"Don't be so serious."

"...It's my first time."

"That's obvious."

Leon came out with what until that moment he hadn't dared to say:

"I want you to teach me everything."

She broke out laughing harder than ever.

"What's so funny?"

"Nothing," she replied, trying to contain herself.

"So?"

"There's nothing to teach. You simply do what you want...How old are you?"

"Sixteen and a half."

" 'And a half.' How cute!"

"Are you making fun of me?"

"No, my love. What gives you that idea! I mean what a nice age... What's your name?"

"Victor."

Better that she not know who I am, he thought. He was pleased that he hadn't hesitated in answering, feeling a little surer of himself.

"And you, what's your name?"

"Claudine."

"You're from Paris?"

"Yes; but you're not. You have a very nice accent. Where are you from?"

"Russia."

"*Ouais!* Russia?

"Yes. I've been here a month."

"Incredible! And you learned French so quickly?"

"I barely speak it."

"You speak it in a very strange way, but I wouldn't say you speak it bad."

"It seems so to you. It's because you've not heard me say much."

"And I don't think I'm going to. You don't think we're going to spend the night chatting, do you?"

She said it with a smile, but not in jest.

"Come on, sweetheart," she continued. "Get comfortable and wait for me. I'm going to the bathroom and I'll be right back."

She took off her jacket, tossed it on the bed and left the room. Her footsteps grew fainter down the hallway. As soon as Leon found himself alone, the idea of fleeing crossed his mind, but he didn't move.

He looked around the room. It was a regular size room, without a closet or a bathroom: a pair of long, dirty, wine-colored curtains covered the window; a clean white ironed sheet folded over a floral bedspread at the head of the double bed; the pillow cases also looked clean. A small lamp with a red lampshade rested on the night table, next to the bed. In one corner of the room, a round wooden table, and on top of it, a pitcher of water, a washbasin, and two small, neatly folded towels. On opposite sides of the table, two wooden chairs. At the head of the bed, a wall painted a rose color with the other three walls painted a cream color. Two pictures adorned the room: one of a woman, blonde and fair-skinned, reclining naked on a couch; the other was a landscape of an idyllic countryside.

From the hallway came the sound of the toilet being flushed. Leon sat down on one of the chairs and waited. A minute later Claudine came in.

"What? Still dressed? Come on, fella."

The woman sat down on the edge of the bed, in front of him, and took off her shoes. Leon began undressing and as he removed each article of clothing he carefully placed it on the chair. She watched him briefly before also undressing. While taking off her clothes, she hummed a tune in a low voice. Leon acted as if he didn't notice anything and pretended to be busy folding his clothes; but every once in a while he glanced up for an instant to see the woman undressing, her naked form gradually baring itself before his eyes. First she tossed her blouse on the bed where it landed next to her jacket. Claudine was still in her little red skirt and black bra. Then the skirt fell to the floor, revealing her mesh stockings and the garter belt that held them up. Sitting on the edge of the bed, the woman crossed one leg over the other, resting her ankle on her knee, and leaned forward to examine something at the tip of her foot. Then she unfastened her garter belt and began removing her stockings. Leon thought he would go mad. His heart beat with such force that he felt his temples throbbing. All that Claudine had on now were her skimpy black bra and black, lace-edged panties. Leon's trousers fell from his hands and when he squatted down to pick them up he knocked over the chair. Embarrassed, he rushed to stand it back up and lay his clothes across it, folding them with trembling hands. Everything was happening so quickly. Claudine had placed her garments on the corner of the headboard and was now lying on the bed, completely naked. Leon stopped what he was doing and stood there, unable to take his eyes from her: so fair of skin, so alluring of face and body. She couldn't have been more than twenty-five. The dark eyebrows reinforced the beauty of her large, brown eyes. Her

70

curly, dark brown hair was cut short and came down a little over her forehead. Her nose, though somewhat long, was straight and pretty. Her full lips and slightly prominent cheekbones gave her a certain air of ordinariness, but she was no less attractive because of it. Her breasts were large, crowned with dark, plump nipples. Of medium height, and despite her wide hips, she had a very well-proportioned body. Her toes and fingernails were painted bright red.

"Ready?" she asked, sitting up in the bed.

Leon was in his underpants and shoes.

"Almost."

"Want me to turn off the light?"

"No. It's okay like this."

He removed his shoes and socks and placed his shoes under the chair and his socks above, on the chair. A chill ran up his body. He took off his underpants and placed them on top of his socks. Immediately, like one who has decided that something else is better, he pulled the socks from beneath his underpants and put them on top of his shoes, under the chair. When he looked up, he saw Claudine staring at his penis.

"Muslim?" she asked.

"Jewish."

For a few seconds, no one moved, no one said anything. It was the woman who broke the silence.

"Well, are you coming?"

"I want you to teach me everything."

"Again?"

She laughed teasingly with a slight air of reproach

"I know that I've got to put it in you…but…"

71

"The way it is now, you won't be able to put it in anywhere."

"Are you making fun of me?"

"No, sweetheart. Don't say that. Come here, darling. Come here and let me hold you," she said with open arms. "Give me a little kiss, and you'll see how everything's going to be all right."

Leon hopped onto the bed and threw himself on top of her. Claudine shrieked and bolted upright.

"Jesus! Your hands are freezing!"

Leon pulled his hands away and held them out to his sides, not knowing what to do with them.

"It's cold," he said.

"It's not cold. Rub your hands together."

Leon rubbed them.

"Rub them some more," she instructed him, apprehensive about him touching her again.

With the expression of a little boy who has been chastised, Leon vigorously rubbed his hands together.

"I think they're not cold now," he said.

She took hold of them, wanting to make sure before she let him touch her again.

"They're okay...more or less. Come on, sweetheart."

And saying this, she placed his hands on her breasts.

"Feel them," she said. "Do you like them?"

Leon swallowed hard. He caressed them. She nudged his hands aside and pulled his body tight against hers. He held her close and put his lips against hers, ready to give her a noisy, childlike kiss. When he felt her open mouth sucking at his lips, he became more flustered than ever. He squeezed her body with such force that the poor thing could barely breathe and exhaled a mighty puff of air.

"Not so hard, please," she whispered, trying to catch her breath.

He relaxed his embrace. They remained wrapped around each other, caressing and kissing. Suddenly, they lay still.

"What's wrong?"

"I don't know… I can't get it up."

"You're too nervous."

"I'm not nervous."

He sat up on the bed. Claudine made another attempt.

"You're tense. Relax."

"I don't know what's wrong."

"These things happen. It's nothing, sweetheart. Do you want to leave?"

"No."

"All right, then. Just take your time and you'll see everything will be fine. Relax, sweetie."

Without saying any more, she grabbed Leon's penis and set to work massaging it. Excited, intrigued, ecstatic, and scared all at once, he let it happen, and watched her the whole time. In a matter of seconds he had an erection and an instantaneous orgasm. His ejaculation took them both by surprise.

"Ahh!" came his short, breathless groan.

Like a fountain, his semen leapt into the air, splattered Claudine's shoulder and began dripping down her arm.

"*Zut!*" she exclaimed, releasing his penis. "Damn it!"

Leon was at a loss, unable to move or utter a word. Claudine hurried over to the table for the pitcher of water and the washbasin. She had almost finished washing her arm when Leon managed to regain his composure.

"I'm sorry... I'm really sorry..."

"I'm sure you are!"

"I didn't mean to—"

"It's all right."

"I never would have—"

"I told you, it's all right. Stop talking."

Leon sighed.

"And now what?"

"Sweetie, I think the party's over. If you weren't able to before, you can forget about it now, that's for sure."

Leon looked at his penis, now shrunken to the size of a kidney bean, and said nothing.

The prostitute began slipping back into her clothes. Leon's eyes were riveted on her, but unlike before, when he saw her undress, this time he looked at her more with curiosity than enthusiasm. The magnetic force had evaporated. She's pretty, he thought, but not as pretty as she seemed before when he saw her on the street. Darkness works wonders. Maybe it's the make-up. Now she no longer looked twenty-five but thirty-five. Apparently, only her face reflected the abuses she had taken, since her body still appeared young and inviting. In Golochov, there wasn't a single woman with a body like that. They were all so robust and hefty...

Claudine, already in her bra and panties, had finished adjusting her garter belt and was beginning to put on her stockings. Leon remembered what Zvi had said once: "A half-naked woman is more enticing than a completely naked one." How right he was! But how could he have known that?

"Big eyes," she said with a smile, and continued dressing.

The stockings had a hole in them where her big toe stuck out. *That's probably what she was examining when she took them off,* Leon thought. He saw a small bruise on Claudine's thigh and it struck him that he hadn't noticed it before. How quickly she got dressed! How little she wore! In Golochov, he had never seen a woman getting dressed or undressed, but he was sure they all wore more clothes than Claudine. Her high heel shoes covered the hole in her stocking and the little red skirt the bruise on her thigh. Then the idea struck him: *prostitutes look prettier when they're dressed.*

Suddenly he felt uncomfortable being naked in front of a fully clothed woman. He started to get dressed while she combed her hair and fixed her face in front of a make-up mirror she had taken from her small handbag.

"I'm ready, sweetie."

Leon took out all the money he had with him and handed it to her.

"You're an angel, darling," she said, and kissed him on the mouth.

He again tasted her lipstick, and wanted to wipe his mouth with the back of his hand, but held off, not wanting to offend her.

"I hope we'll see each other again."

"Sweetheart, you know where you can find me."

"Goodbye."

"*Au revoir,* Victor."

Claudine—or whatever her real name was—left the room. The boy who was left standing there alone, in bare feet, his mouth

75

smeared with red lipstick, would exit the Hotel Etoile a few minutes later, more of a man than when he had entered.

6

Everybody called him Samuel, but his real name was Shalom. Shalom Schwarzbard didn't have a safe, like every other respectable watchmaker, but in his workbench, at the entrance to the small shop, he had a drawer which he kept locked and where he set aside certain spare parts and only the most expensive watches clients brought in for repair. If someone brought him a watch with a gold chain, he would remove it.

"You hold onto this," he would tell the customer. "I don't need it to fix the watch."

Since there was absolute trust between the watchmaker and his assistant, Shalom had shown Leon the place where he hid the key for the drawer.

The two had met some time ago, when Leon came to the shop with a letter that his mother had given him. The watchmaker immediately took the young boy under his wing. He felt so sorry for the confused and defenseless immigrant that he offered him a position as an apprentice, even though he didn't need one. Thus, on the day following his arrival in Paris, Leon Edri found himself already employed. A friendship quickly developed between them, as far as there could be one between a boy of sixteen and a man of forty. They didn't go places together, but were very much at ease working side by side. At the shop they chatted endlessly, and after a month they knew each other as well as if they had been raised in the same house. Leon told him everything about his family, his friends, and his plans to travel to America. Shalom, on the other hand, never spoke about his plans for the future, nor did he talk about his family.

"I lost everybody," he told him one day, "and I'd rather not talk about it."

But he did speak of other things, displaying ease and enthusiasm. Leon, as a boy from Golochov, was captivated listening to the anecdotes about Paris that his employer related to him with such grace and, maybe, a little bit of imagination. Shalom knew the stories of the Jewish immigrants of Le Marais, of the millionaires on Rue du Faubourg Saint-Honoré, of the underworld of Montparnasse, and of the Russian nobility who, having fallen into misfortune after the Bolshevik Revolution, could be seen all over "the City of Light" holding down the most menial jobs before the indifferent gaze of the French people. But the stories that captivated young Leon the most were the ones that Shalom had lived firsthand while serving in the legendary Foreign Legion during the First World War.

"Look," he told his young assistant the first time he spoke to him about his adventures, taking out a small wooden case from the drawer in his workbench.

Leon was perplexed by what he saw. There was a cross inside! What did it mean? Had Shalom renounced his religion? He contemplated the bronze cross, which wasn't like the ones he knew from Russia, used by the prelates of the Orthodox Church. This one was adorned with a striped colored–ribbon and had four flared branches.

"What is it?"

"*La Croix de Guerre*!" the ex-Legionnaire said, his voice filled with pride. "The French Government awarded it to me."

Leon smiled with a sense of satisfaction… and relief. After all, he had been raised in an environment of intolerance in the *shtetl*, and religious prejudice formed part of his cultural baggage.

Whenever Shalom was away from the shop—which began happening with greater frequency—Leon was left in charge, with authority for taking in work and returning the repaired watches. On one particular occasion, needing a minute hand, he tried to open the drawer of Shalom's worktable, but didn't find the key. Unable to complete his work without the part, he went searching for a similar one that he could use as a substitute. That's what he was doing when he found the key in a little box full of watch hands. It wasn't lost on him that his employer had hidden it there and, moreover, that he hadn't told him about it. But the real surprise came when he opened the drawer. In the middle of the watches and spare parts, next to the Croix de Guerre, something jumped out at him. A revolver. Shalom with a firearm? He couldn't believe it. The simple idea that a Jew could have a firearm struck him as odd. Why in the devil did Shalom need a gun? What secret affairs could his employer be involved in? These were the questions he was asking himself when a noise made him turn his head. Shalom Schwarzbard had just returned.

"What are you doing at my bench?" he shouted.

"I was looking for a part... Why do you keep a gun?"

Shalom approached the workbench and slammed the drawer shut.

"It's none of your business! Give me the key!"

He locked the drawer and put the key in his pocket. Leon went back to his work. The incident ended there. Neither of the two mentioned the gun again. *Really, it's none of my business*, Leon told himself. Few things could offend him more than being shouted at. The two worked all afternoon without speaking to each other, but by the following day the tension had lessened. They went back to their work as they had done before up to that point, conversing on different subjects. In the days that followed, things went along like this, but the atmosphere had changed. Now they were three: the watchmaker, the apprentice, and the gun. That lifeless object, lying silent and out of sight, was there the whole time, coming between the two of them, hindering conversation, poisoning the air.

One morning, Leon arrived for work at eight, punctual as usual, and found the shop closed. It was the first time that had happened, for Schwarzbard was in the habit of rising early to open for business. Young Edri waited outside, without giving much importance to his employer's tardiness. For him, it was a pleasure to be outside on that fresh, sunny day. He had always believed that May was the most beautiful month of the year and that delightful day confirmed his judgment. Shalom arrived a little before nine o'clock.

"Good morning, Shulem," Leon said, pronouncing his name in Yiddish.

"Hello."

There was some roughness in his voice.

"What's wrong?"

Shalom didn't answer. He took a handful of keys from his pocket, opened the doors to the shop and went straight to his workbench.

"Why such a bad mood?" Leon asked.

"I'm not in a bad mood."

"We have to finish Monsieur Foulleux's watch today," Leon said, sitting down at his table. "We promised to have it ready for him by the twenty-seventh and today's already the twenty-sixth."

Again Shalom made no reply. It was then that the apprentice realized just how much his employer was disturbed about something. He looked pale and tense, and his hands were shaking, causing the batch of keys to rattle.

"Here," he said, tossing them to Leon.

The boy snatched them out of the air. Shalom buttoned his coat.

"I've got to go out," he added. "If I'm not back later in the day, lock up and... we'll see each other tomorrow."

The young apprentice looked at him in silence. Schwarzbard left the premises with his brow wrinkled and a long, somewhat labored stride. At that instant, Leon had a premonition. He rushed over to Shalom's table and opened the drawer that his employer had left unlocked. The gun was missing. Leon reached the door in a single bound, but Shalom was already half a block away, quickly putting distance between himself and the shop. With trembling hands, Leon closed the door. It took him a few seconds to locate the key and lock up. When he turned around, Shalom had already disappeared from view. Leon ran after him and, on reaching the corner, caught sight of him a block away. He intended to catch up to Shalom and grab him, to keep the man from committing who knew what madness; but he didn't dare. He barely found the courage to follow him. He shadowed him for a long time, always staying back, but could have easily followed a few feet behind, for Shalom didn't turn around even once to look over his shoulder. They came to an area of the city unfamiliar to Leon, but one that gave the impression of being a district for the well-to-do. Schwarzbard stopped in front of a five-story building, similar to all the others in the neighborhood; a stone façade, big double doors, long windows with jalousies, and roofs with small garrets.

From a distance, Leon saw him take out his watch and check the time, raise his head and observe the windows of one of the upper floors, stick his hands in his pockets, pace nervously from side to side and lean against the wall. An hour went by like this, then two, with Shalom always alternating the same repetitive movements and frequently checking his watch; and each time someone came out of the building, he gave a start. Finally, a middle-aged individual appeared, but Leon was unable to clearly distinguish the person's features. His somewhat corpulent body stood erect. He was wearing a dark leather jacket over a crew neck sweater. In his hands, he carried a felt hat and a cylindrical-shaped object, like a rolled up paper. Leon understood immediately that this was the person Shalom had been waiting for, because after his initial start, he remained perfectly still, like an animal lying in wait. For a few seconds, the man looked at the watchmaker, who seemed frozen in place, then put on his hat and began walking. He had barely taken two steps when Shalom once more came to life. He must have said something to him because the man suddenly turned around and began shouting at him. Shalom, in turn, yelled back. Leon didn't hear exactly what they were hollering about, but he heard enough to know that it wasn't in French. The man had raised the cylindrical object and was waving it in the air. On seeing this, Leon began running towards the two men, for he had an inkling of what was about to take place. Schwarzbard pulled the gun from his waist. The man in the leather jacket lowered his arms and stepped back.

"Shulem! Shulem!" Leon shouted in desperation, running wildly toward him.

Schwarzbard was shouting, too, like a madman, and couldn't hear anything but his own voice. Suddenly, the dry crack of a gunshot split the air. The heavy-set figure staggered and fell to the ground. Voices and shouting were heard in the distance. Before Leon's horrified gaze, Shalom approached the stricken body and fired another shot into it, and another and another, and didn't stop until he had emptied his revolver.

"Shulem!" a breathless Leon cried when he reached his side.

Shalom looked up and Leon saw a haggard face, taut lips, and eyes aflame, flashing sparks of hatred.

"Leib! What are you doing here? Get out of here! Run, run!"

It was more than an order; it was a plea, a piece of advice. Leon looked at Shalom for the last time and, without saying a word, began running, dodging the curious onlookers who were making their way towards the spot where the shooting happened. Leon ran and ran, and didn't stop until he felt his body had no more left to give. He propped himself up against a railing to keep himself from collapsing and saw shimmering water in front of him. He had reached the Seine.

He was on the right bank, before the Pont des Invalides, where he remained a good while leaning against the railing, catching his breath and pondering what were for him the absolutely incomprehensible events of the day. He crossed the river and turned left, towards the Esplanade des Invalides. *Paris is such a beautiful city*! It was a fleeting thought that crisscrossed with so many others in his confused mind. He followed the route along the Quai d'Orsay, in front of the National Assembly, and turned down Boulevard Saint Germain on his way home, walking slowly along the great artery that is born and dies on the Seine. He left Saint Germain des Prés behind and followed the route that cuts through the heart of the Latin Quarter, crossing Boulevard Saint Michel and passing in front of the Musée de Cluny, where he stopped a few steps ahead to briefly take in the old buildings of the Sorbonne. He thought that studying at the university was a privilege that destiny did not hold in store for him. The education he had received in the *cheder*, plus what life would teach him, was all the education he was ever going to receive and, with God's help, that would have to suffice. Continuing on his way, he took Rue Monge, a street teeming with elegant men and women, Bohemians, students, workers...Leon quickened his pace. He didn't want to see people; he yearned for the tranquility of his room. He noticed a prostitute walking along the sidewalk in front of him and was surprised how he had developed the ability to recognize them from a distance. Just as well it wasn't Claudine. The last thing he wanted was to run into someone he knew.

It was growing dark by the time he reached his building. He climbed the four flights of the grimy stone stairway and locked himself inside his room. With nothing to eat since morning, he still had no desire for food. Throwing himself on the bed, Leon began thinking. He couldn't understand what had happened. Shulem, so noble, so polite, a poet…Incredible…Who was the person he murdered? And Shalom didn't flee, but just stayed put, as if waiting for the police to come and arrest him. "Run!" Shulem had shouted at him, and now Leon understood more clearly the import of the man's plea: *In this immense city, where no one knows you exist, why should you be implicated?* The thoughts came in rapid succession. Leon had to find out what had become of Shalom. Maybe he could help him somehow. He would also have to find a new job. Or maybe it was no longer worth the trouble; maybe the time had come to leave. For the next several days, he would look into the best way to continue on to America. He imagined the look on his mother's face when she got his first letter from the United States, and what the people of Golochov would say. He then began dreaming about his next journey, about the New World, about the wealth and happiness that awaited him until he, still fully clothed, drifted off to asleep.

The light of a new dawn filtering through the window of his room roused him from a deep sleep. As soon as he was awake, his first thought was of Shalom Schwarzbard; then, a short time later, when he went down to the street, the mystery of what had happened the previous evening became clear. Splashed across the front page of the daily newspaper that he bought was a headline in big, bold letters: *SIMON PETLYURA ASSASSINATED IN PARIS*. The caption below it explained the headline: *In plain daylight, General Petlyura, former head of the Ukrainian army, accused several times of being the author of numerous pogroms in Russia, was murdered in Paris by a Jewish immigrant.*

Dear Leon,

We just received the news of the assassination of Petlyura and everyone in Golochov is deeply shocked because it was none other than your employer who shot him. Is that right? We're not mistaken, are we? It seems incredible to me. Did you see or know something that didn't show up in the newspapers? How did it affect you? Your mother is very upset, although we've all made her see there is nothing for her to be concerned about, since you are not involved in the matter. Write me as soon as you can. Tell me everything you know about what happened; tell me about Schwarzbard too, about his past, what kind of person he was.

As for us here in Golochov, you can probably imagine, there is nothing really to tell. A few days ago I began working for my Uncle Elimelech. I know he can't afford to pay an assistant. Maybe he doesn't need one either, but he took me on because I'm his nephew. You know how things are here. There's no work. It's almost impossible to earn a living and for that reason I think that in time everybody will leave Golochov. Zvi told me that before the year is out his family will be going to the United States. Itzik's family will be leaving too, but a little later. The Finkelsteins are getting ready to leave and the Stolers already left. Frimca the Dispenser of Advice goes around telling the old maids in the shtetl that they should leave, and the sooner the better. She herself, with Ruchel and the whole Portnoy family, intends to go to New York within a few months. The day will come—not so far off—when there won't be a Jew left in Golochov. No doubt, the muzhiks will be delighted. They always considered this land to be theirs and no one else's. The fact that we've lived here for over seven hundred years gives us no rights? It's sad to see the roots we've put down here torn from the soil, as if time had no importance. And there are moments when I ask myself:

Is it possible we didn't really put down roots? Can it be we can't put down roots anywhere? This last question must worry you more than it does me. I'll go to Eretz Israel and be done with that problem. I'll return to the land of my ancestors, who upon their departure left a piece of their soul there. That's why I cherish it even before I've come to know it. I was taught to love it from the time I was born and I carry that love in my blood. But you, you're going to foreign lands. You'll probably put down roots in the United States, but will they be deep? What will become of the Jews in America in seven hundred years, if humanity should last that long? Will they feel at home in their land? Or will they be like us, "the Russians," foreigners in the country where our parents were born, and the parents of our parents, for generations and generations?

The Jews are not only leaving Golochov but all the towns and cities around the region. They say that the same thing is happening all over Russia and in Rumania, Hungary, Czechoslovakia, and Poland. It is a general exodus. On the one hand, I'm glad. I've got the feeling that the Jews who are leaving Europe are saving themselves from an ill-fated future, from some as yet indefinable horror. On the other hand, I'm worried. I don't know what destiny holds for the Jews of the West. I'm worried for you. I'm worried for the children that you'll bring into the world. As Rav Zuntz would say: What will become of your heritage?

Affectionately,

Berl

7

The day grew interminable. They continued traveling. More than an hour had passed with the family peering out the window of the train, hoping to see their destination come into view. It couldn't be much farther to Slavuta. It was after eight at night, but the sun, which had come up east of Trilesy that same day—a thousand hours earlier—had not yet set. Immense and fiery red, it had gone down over the horizon to rest for a few moments before sinking into the insatiable earth.

It was 1926, June 21 to be exact, the longest day of the year. Even before the sun came up, Anna Lubinsky had gotten her children out of bed to begin their journey. In the dark, they climbed into the carriage that Yoskele Mednik had procured the evening before, and carrying two suitcases with their most valuable belongings, they departed the town. *Farewell, Trilesy*, Anna Lubinsky said to herself.

They had traveled a good distance when the first rays of sunlight illuminated the horizon. Chaim was to remember for the rest of his life the feeling of relief he felt when the sun came up, because from the moment they got into the carriage, he was tormented by the idea that the horses might not see where they were going and would end up going over a cliff. Mountains (much less precipices) are nonexistent on those long stretches of flat, black soil, the most fertile land among the extensive plains of the Ukraine; but at the age of fifteen, fear is an irrational feeling, and only the rays of a rising sun could put the young traveler at ease.

The sky had barely cleared, distinguishing itself from the unlit earth and then, little by little, the countryside began emerging from the darkness. Chaim contemplated the fields of wheat that spread out on both sides of the road. They looked different that day, blurred and surreal. Could it be some effect of the light at daybreak? Or the drowsiness caused by the swaying of the carriage? Or was it the impression on seeing those fields for the last time?

The train didn't pass through Trilesy. Nothing passed through Trilesy; time barely passed through. That's the reason they were traveling to Fastov. It was the closest place where they could take the train that came from Kiev. They arrived around midday. There was no one in the small station, at the entrance to the town. Yoskele Mednik asked the stationmaster what time the train was due.

"It should have been here by now."

"I was told that the train always comes through here in the afternoon."

"It should have been here by now," the stationmaster repeated.

"I want four tickets to Slavuta: one adult and three minors."

"Who's traveling?"

"Only the woman and children."

"Any of them older than twelve?"

"None," Yoske lied.

"How old is the oldest?"

"He'll be twelve in August," Yoskele Mednik said, lying again.

The stationmaster regarded the Jew with mistrust. He looked inside his leather pouch, pulled out three tickets and handed them to Yoske, along with another at full fare.

"Twenty-seven rubles and fifty kopeks."

"Twenty-seven rubles!"

"And fifty kopeks."

Yoske paid, then rejoined Anna and her children.

"We have to wait," he said, picking up the largest suitcase and motioning with his head for them to follow him.

Anna took the other suitcase and they all followed Yoske to one of the few benches in the station. Everybody sat down, prepared to wait whatever time was necessary.

Chaim was the oldest of the three children. Bertha came next, two years younger, and then Mordechai, six years younger than his sister. The youngest one rested his head against his mother and fell asleep. Chaim looked at his little brother without understanding how he could fall asleep at such an important moment in his life. Mordechai didn't seem to be breathing. Fast asleep, with his rosy little cheeks and red lips slightly parted, he looked like an angel. His mother had placed her arm on top, more to cover him than to hold him. Great distress showed in Anna's face. *Always worried*, Chaim thought. He wasn't. He felt euphoric. He thought that a person couldn't be sad on the day he and his family were embarking on a fantastic adventure. It was too important, too exciting. He wanted to jump and shout for joy.

"What are you laughing about, stupid?" his sister asked him.

"Am I laughing?"

"Yes. You always have that silly little grin on your face, like a real jerk."

"We're going to get on a train."

"So what?"

"Maybe you've already ridden a train?"

"No. And what about it? A lot of people ride the train. There's nothing special about it."

"You've never even seen a train."

"Stupid."

"Children," Anna interrupted, speaking in a harsh, authoritative tone.

About two hours later the train pulled into the station. Yoske carried the suitcases on board and arranged them in the car. He hugged the children and took Anna's hand between his.

"Good luck."

"May God bless you, Yoskele!"

"Give Mahir a big hug for me. Tell him that God willing, we'll see each other again."

"I hope so."

"Goodbye, Anna."

She felt the warmth of his hands as they gripped hers.

Yoske hopped down onto the platform and stood in front of the window where Anna and the children were looking out. He stood there a long time, waving and making faces at the children, until the train began moving. Chaim pressed his nose against the window to keep Yoske Mednik in view a bit longer, the old family friend who was staying behind, waving his arm until the last minute.

Chaim kept smiling to himself, delighted to be crossing the terrain at such speed and listening to the noise of the locomotive.

"Mom, aren't you glad we're leaving?"

"Of course, I am, sweetheart," Anna replied, forcing a smile on her constantly sad face.

"Will Papa come to get us at the station?"

"No, sweetheart. We'll see him afterwards."

"When?"

"Later."

"Then, who'll come to get us?"

"A man... a gentleman who is always happy and ready to help."

"Like Yoskele?"

"Stop asking so many stupid questions already!" Bertha said.

"I don't know him, my love."

"Then, how will we recognize him?"

"I told you to stop asking so many stupid questions," Bertha repeated.

"No, sweetheart, it's not a stupid question."

"You see? Silly."

"Idiot."

"Children, that's enough!"

Bertha put her head down. Chaim turned around to look out the window, and Anna remained pensive. She reached in her pocket and took out the last letter she received from Mahir. It was two pages long, written on both sides in small, distinctive characters. She unfolded it and scanned the evenly spaced lines she had read so many times before. She immediately found the part she was looking for: *Shraga Kopelovich will come to get you at the station. He's Boris's relative, the one I've mentioned before. Shraga is a complete gentleman, always happy and ready to help. You'll recognize him right away. He's short, but not very, with gray hair and very bright green eyes. But just to be safe, we arranged for him to be wearing a gray overcoat and a red scarf. He'll have his overcoat unbuttoned so you'll be able to see his coffee colored jacket. Finally, he'll be wearing an astrakhan skin hat. If for some unforeseen reason, he can't come to meet you, another person will go in his place dressed exactly the same.*

Anna carefully folded the letter and put it back in her pocket. She closed her eyes and let her chin drop against her chest. The train's movement and the noise lulled her to sleep. She drifted off without worrying about keeping the peace between Bertha and Chaim, who had begun squabbling again. She didn't know how long she slept, but when she woke up, she realized that her arm had gone numb from holding Mordechai, who was asleep in her lap, and from Bertha having fallen asleep on the same arm that rested on top of her little brother. Chaim continued peering out the window.

"Chaim, aren't you tired?"

"No, mom."

"You haven't slept a wink."

"I don't need to."

The train slowed as it approached the station and the wheels of the locomotive screeched, holding back the forward lurch of the cars.

"Are we there?" Chaim asked.

"Not yet, my love, but I think we don't have far to go."

They were pulling into the station at Sepetovka, the largest one they had seen on the trip. A stream of passengers got off to change trains and continue on, either to Belarus in the north or to Podolia in the south, since the railroad west approached the boundaries of the immense territories of the Soviet Union. Sepetovka was the last stop they would make before reaching their final destination, an hour later.

The sunset meant the end of the day as well as the trip. Anna and her children gathered at the window, but they couldn't see very much at dusk. There wasn't much to see in Slavuta either: just a small town with a small railroad station.

Even before the train came to a stop, Anna saw the man in the gray overcoat and red scarf. He had his overcoat open, so that one could see the brown jacket underneath. This last detail, like the astrakhan hat, was more than was needed since, among the few people waiting on the platform he was the only one with a red scarf. In that excess of precautions, Anna saw her husband's hand at work. She already felt his nearness and thought the happy moment that she yearned for was not far off.

Mahir Lubinsky had traveled alone to Slavuta about two months earlier in order to arrange for his family's departure. The fact was that the police, who were always on the lookout for "suspicious individuals," had been arresting entire families that had come into towns along the border, not knowing where to turn or who to speak to. Thousands of people were officially leaving the Soviet Union, aided by North American Jewish organizations, or by their own relatives. But the ones who failed to get such help or couldn't acquire papers, had to devise less orthodox methods for getting out of the country.

Anna Lubinsky got off the train carrying a suitcase in her right hand and holding onto little Mordechai with the other. Bertha trailed behind her and, at her side, was Chaim carrying the other suitcase. They had brought only those two small pieces of luggage to avoid calling attention to themselves. They walked towards the man in the red scarf who was watching the passengers stepping down from another car. The man suddenly turned around and saw them. Anna and her children stopped just a few feet away, held back by the look in his eyes.

"Anna!" the man shouted and ran towards her with open arms.

Anna remained motionless, not knowing how to react, while he embraced her.

"Anna! How nice to see you again!" he said, anxious to disguise the fact that Anna and her children were not from that region, for there were informants everywhere.

Mordechai and Bertha looked perplexed while Chaim laughed without knowing exactly why. He thought he shouldn't have, but the look of stupefaction on his mother's face was more than he could bear.

"Shut up, stupid!" his sister whispered, but the boy couldn't contain himself.

"Shraga?" Anna murmured.

The man stepped back without letting go of Anna's hands, winked, and continued his effusive greeting.

"You look wonderful!" he said while looking her over.

Completely flustered, Anna began laughing. On seeing her mother laughing too, Bertha did likewise.

"Shut up, stupid!" Chaim said, getting back at her.

The man with the red scarf grabbed the two suitcases and, laughing like the others, said: "This way."

Waiting for them in the street was a big horse-drawn cart. A boy of about fifteen was sitting up front on the driver's bench.

"In the back, Haskel!" the man said while arranging the suitcases. "He's my boy. Say hello, son."

The young man gave the travelers a nice smile and hopped in back.

"You too," the man added, lifting Mordechai up and setting him down next to Haskel.

Chaim climbed aboard in a single bound, balancing himself on the hub of the axle.

Anna and Bertha climbed in behind him. The man took his seat up front, grabbed the reins, shouted something at the horse, and they were off without wasting any time.

They took a street that ran parallel to the train station and in a few minutes found themselves on the outskirts of town. No one said anything during the ride, but no words were needed to share the happiness they felt. The children would soon see their father; and Ana, her husband. The fresh air invigorated them, clearing their minds of the drowsiness induced by the long train trip. Chaim laid back, resting his head on his hands, stretched his legs out on top of one of the suitcases and began contemplating the sky. He fixed his attention on the moon, so round and aglow that night. A huge halo surrounded it, and Chaim, who in his short life had never seen such a phenomenon, took it as a favorable omen.

Under the moonlight they could see they were on open terrain. The land looked black and the crops blended into the darkness, but the trees were clearly visible and from time to time one could identify a little house by the edge of the road. Chaim didn't even give it a thought that they could go off a cliff, as he had feared when they started out on their predawn journey, on what seemed to be an epic distance.

Two hours later they came to a farmhouse, whose only feature they could distinguish was its bigness. The door opened and a man came running outside towards them. Clearly, he had been awaiting their arrival. In the half-light, Anna immediately recognized the heavy-set figure.

"Mahir!"

The faces of the children lit up with joy.

"Papa!" Mordechai shouted.

Mahir arrived just in time to get a hug from Chaim, who had jumped down from the cart with open arms. While holding the boy with one arm, he grabbed Bertha around the waist with the other. Mordechai jumped down from the cart and also wanted to hug his father, but with his siblings in the way there here was no place to grab on. He then hugged him around his legs. On feeling this contact, Mordechai had a sense that all was well, that he was safe, something he had been missing for a very long time. Excited by his parents' jubilant exclamations, and that of his siblings, he squeezed his father's legs harder. He then he felt the hand that had been holding Bertha resting on his head. He looked up and saw Mahir's smiling face. At that moment he could no longer contain his emotion and, out of happiness, began sobbing.

"What are you crying for, stupid?" he heard his sister ask.

He felt himself being hoisted up by his father's strong arms, without understanding—without it mattering to him—how Chaim had disappeared, because now he, Mordechai, occupied his place and was king. He hugged the neck of that all-powerful being, a mixture of angel and titan. Held aloft as he was, up high, he had reached the pinnacle of happiness and cried harder than ever. He continued hearing, as if in a dream, the voices of rejoicing of his brother and sister around him. His mother tried to settle him down.

"What's wrong, my love? Are you happy?"

He wanted to answer, but the words didn't come. He felt that he couldn't control his sobbing and chose instead to nod his head yes.

"Stop your sobbing, stupid," Bertha said, squabbling with him again.

Then he began laughing and crying at the same time, the way children do sometimes. Chaim looked at him and smiled. The memory of that happy reunion would come to mind many, many times throughout the young man's life.

They went inside, Anna and Mahir hugging each other, Mordechai on his father's shoulders, and Bertha and Chaim dancing around their parents, competing for their attention.

Shraga and Mathilde Kopelovich had a large but modest dwelling; an atmosphere of warmth and love prevailed there and made the Lubinsky family feel at home. Mathilde had prepared a magnificent dinner in honor of their guests, who arrived as hungry as they were tired. They ate and chatted with great enthusiasm, for they had much to talk about, especially Mahir, who brought Anna up-to-date on what he had been doing ever since he left home. Mordechai fell asleep at the table a few minutes after dinner started; Bertha managed to finish her meal before also giving into sleep; and Chaim, trying very hard to stay awake, before succumbing to fatigue, learned that they would be resuming their journey the following day.

When Mahir and Anna woke late the next morning, the children were still asleep. It had been a night of joy, emotion and, of course, love.

"The later they sleep, the better. Tonight will be hard for them," Mahir said.

"What time do we leave?"

"As soon as it's dark."

Around noon, the children began waking up. They spent the afternoon playing with Haskel and his younger brothers.

"Will you be coming with us?" Bertha asked Haskel.

"I'd like to, but my father won't let me."

"Does he always accompany many people?" Chaim asked.

"No. Only twice I remember him taking a whole family. Generally, it's just him and one or two others."

"Why don't you ask him if you can come along?" Bertha insisted.

"What do you think? That it's a stroll in the park?" Shraga shouted at them from the next room.

He went up to the children who didn't know that he had been listening to them and spoke about the dangers of the journey. His purpose was to make them aware of the situation.

"Be very careful," he warned them. "Don't start talking. Remember to stay together and not make any noise."

They had dinner at eight that evening. An hour later, when it began to grow dark, they again set out on their long journey. Like the previous evening, it was a clear night, with a full moon. Mahir carried a large hunter's sack slung over his shoulder with everything that Anna had brought in the suitcases. Shraga, leading the way, carried a smaller sack, with provisions. They followed him, one behind the other: Anna, the children, and Mahir. They entered the forest, setting a good pace along a narrow trail. The visibility was poor and every once in a while someone bumped into the person in front. Mahir and Anna took turns carrying Mordechai, but when they put him down, the child was able to keep up with the adults. Occasionally, Shraga would suddenly stop and listen for any sounds in the night. At one point, after listening a bit longer, he put his index finger to his lips and, motioning with his arm, signaled for the Lubinskys to follow him. Taking Anna by the hand, he moved off the trail and entered the underbrush. They were all walking very slowly, holding one another's hand. They must have gone some fifty yards when Shraga stopped again and for the second time signaled them to remain silent. There was no need for the warning, since they were all maintaining absolute silence, barely letting out a breath. With outstretched arm, Shraga pointed over to one side. Mahir and his family looked in the direction he had indicated, but couldn't see the three dark shadows some thirty yards away that could be mistaken for black tree trunks. But they heard voices, and although it wasn't possible to make out what was being said, the language being spoken was unmistakable: Russian. No sooner had one of the border guards lit a cigarette than Mahir saw where they were: so close that after the match went out, the red glow of the cigarette was clearly visible. The travelers furtively withdrew until the guards' voices could no longer be heard. They trudged through the forest for half an hour until they reached the same trail they had been following previously, but coming out at a point well past where they had left it. They spent the entire night walking. During the long trek, they had to leave the trail for a second time to circumvent the route. Anna felt herself faltering, but her children's spirit and stamina gave her the courage to keep going. It was dawn by the time they reached open terrain. Having crossed the forest from one end to the other, they experienced a feeling of relief when they realized that their destination was practically within reach. They sat down on the ground to rest, although it could really be said that they collapsed, overcome by fatigue and the thought of not being able to take another step. They were exhausted to the point of being too out of breath to talk, to congratulate one another for having come this far. They simply remained as they were, half dazed, unable to move, just listening to the silence. Shraga alone gathered up the strength to say a few words. Reaching out with his arm, he pointed off in the distance.

"Look...over there...Rovno. In a couple of hours we'll reach Boris's house."

Yes, there it lay. In the distance, beneath the first rays of sunlight, one could see the Polish city of Rovno. One more Jewish family had emigrated from "the Soviet homeland."

8

Boris Kopelovich lived in a small house on the shores of the Ustye River, on the outskirts of the city. A tall, thin man, whose physique provided an absurd contrast to that of his wife's, for Rosa was short and fat, and barely came up to his chest. Boris was a distant relative of Shraga Kopelovich.

"He's a second cousin of my father, or something like that," Shraga told the Lubinskys as they approached the house. "His real name isn't Boris, but he makes everyone call him that because he's comfortable with it. Boris is an ambiguous name: it's Russian, yet Jews, Ukrainians, and Poles also use it."

Anna and Mahir never learned his real name. Maybe not even Shraga knew it, despite knowing him and having worked with him for many years. Shraga devoted his life to bringing Jews across the border and Boris took them in, helping them obtain papers and sending them on to the West. The two men coordinated their efforts and were able to earn their living trafficking in refugees.

Shraga stayed the night in the Kopelovich house and the next day set out on his return journey, taking the same route he had followed, crossing the forest on foot at night. There was nothing for him to do in Rovno, except miss his family.

"Aren't you afraid of making the journey by yourself?" Anna asked.

"If I'm afraid of doing it in the company of others, how am I not going to be afraid of doing it alone?"

Always with a sense of humor, Mahir thought. *God bless him*!

"You ought to give up this sort of work," Anna said.

101

"I will, but first I need to save up a little money. Just one or two more years, and then I'll make my last trip to bring one more family out: mine."

As darkness fell, before departing, Shraga Kopelovich embraced Anna, Mahir, and the children. With nothing more than a piece of honey cake and a bottle of tea for provisions, he set off for the woods. Mahir and his family watched him until—they weren't sure which—either the darkness or the distance swallowed him up.

The house on the shore of the Ustye River had the look of something straight out of a fairy tale. It was a log cabin, with margaritas and tulips growing all around it, and hyacinths in front of the windows. The curtains always looked freshly washed and ironed; the furniture was rudimentary but pleasant; the copper pots sparkled from regular polishing, just like the ornaments on the shelves, which were simple and cheerful. The house's charm could be attributed principally to Rosa, who spent most of her time cleaning and decorating her modest dwelling, watering the plants and trying to beautify everything around her.

Rosa had one son, a likable boy who had celebrated his *Bar Mitzvah* a few months earlier. He was a happy kid, restless and talkative. People thought that his name was Motl, because they called him Motty from the day he was born, but his real name was Menashe. He was seven when his mother, a widow of one year, married Boris Kopelovich. Rosa had lost her first husband during the pogroms inflicted on the Jews of Rovno in 1919. Boris had lost his spouse too during that same horrific period, and the coming of little Motty into his life was a source of comfort for his tortured soul. He bestowed on him his name, his protection, the comfort that his limited resources allowed for, and all the love he could give him. In those nightmarish massacres of Rovno, Boris had lost not only his wife but also the child that the unfortunate woman was carrying in her womb, her parents, his parents, and their sisters and brothers with their respective families. In other words, only Boris had survived. His loved ones fell victim with the other sixty thousand Jews who were murdered in the anti-Semitic violence of the time.

"That was how the Cossacks celebrated their independence," Boris would recount, sounding a note of bitter irony.

He was referring to the brief period in history, between January 1918 and August 1920, when the Ukraine declared its independence. Led by the president of the republic, General Simon Petlyura, bands of Cossacks poured out their savage fury against the Jewish population, pillaging, murdering and burning right and left until the Red Army defeated them, putting an end to the "glorious" days of independence. Petlyrua and his henchmen fled to Poland for refuge, where the majority of them took up residence; some, however, went into exile in Paris a couple of years later.

The outrages committed against the Jews were not a novelty in those regions of Eastern Europe, but the violence and cruelty of those years had not been seen since the massacres of Chmielnicki, around the middle of the seventeenth century.

Because of the assassination of General Petlyura, which occurred a month before the Lubinskys reached Rovno, those tragic events once more became the topic of frequent conversation among the inhabitants of the city. Boris fervently exalted the unknown Jew who, like him, had lost his entire family in those very same pogroms and who then had had the courage—*the privilege*, he corrected himself—to execute the swine. Mahir and Anna were engrossed in what Boris had to say, listening to him talk about the political situation in Poland and the Ukraine, about the loved ones who disappeared, and about the countless sad and vivid stories of horror.

"Do you think that the Jews of Rovno were the only ones to suffer?" Mahir knew that his rhetorical question wouldn't do much good in consoling Boris. "Scarcely fifty miles south of Kiev," he continued, "close to where we're from, you'll find the town of Belaya Tserkov, 'White Church,' in Russian. The Jews have lived

103

there practically since it was founded, in the sixteenth century. Every two years or so there was a pogrom in that area. In 1919, the year they murdered your whole family, Petlyura's and Denikin's gangs entered Belaya Tserkov and massacred nearly a thousand Jews. I also lost family and friends. My Uncle Velvel, my father's brother, was murdered, savagely quartered by the blows of an axe."

"Enough already!" Anna shouted; then, after composing herself, she added: "May those be the last misfortunes we ever have to face."

"Amen," Mahir said, bringing the subject to a close as if concluding a prayer.

Little did Boris and his guests, as well as all the Jews of Europe, imagine that barely fifteen years later the greatest crime in the history of mankind was to be perpetrated against them. The Nazi extermination machinery, with diabolical precision, was going to eliminate from the face of the earth six million men, women, and children…one million children. A third of the Jewish population! In Poland, the Nazis would attain such a degree of efficiency that the Jewish population, more than three and a half million souls, would be reduced to less than sixty thousand. Ninety-eight people out of every one hundred would meet their death! Among them, Boris… the only member of his family to have survived the pogrom.

The Lubinskys lived for an entire month in the little house on the shore of the Ustye, until Boris was able to provide them with the necessary papers to continue their journey. It generally took Boris a few days to get the papers required of the refugees, but this time, owing to the presence of a Committee of Inquiry that had come from Warsaw to look into certain irregularities in the administrative affairs of Rovno, the acquisition of the documents had become difficult. The cost of the papers, just as the stay in Boris's house, was included in the price that Mahir had paid Shraga Kopelovich beforehand, even prior to his family's arrival in Slavuta. The four weeks that the Lubinskys stayed in Rovno were ones of great discomfort, physically as well as psychologically, since not only did they find themselves crammed together, but the unforeseen delay was costing Boris an additional sum of money that the good man did not have the heart to ask them for, nor which the Lubinskys, aware of the situation, could afford. Only the children were happy. They never had a better vacation than this. They played endlessly from morning to night. They made masks and disguises, set traps in the woods to capture rodents, made perfume from flower petals... Chaim and Motty had the most fun, building a tree house and setting up a "telephone" for those who wanted to call them from down below. Generally, it was Motty who organized the games, despite the fact that Chaim was two years older than he. A close friendship developed between the two boys. Motty Kopelovich—like his mother—was full of smiles and good-natured fun. He made Chaim and Bertha and little Mordechai laugh, infecting them with his constant joy. The only time the Lubinskys saw him sad was when it came time to say goodbye. The boy was quiet and pressed his lips together in what seemed to be an effort not to cry. With a warm embrace, Mahir and his family said farewell to Boris, Rosa, and Motty. To good luck wishes and hugs, the boy answered with a single word: Goodbye.

Mahir Lubinsky and his family traveled from Rovno to Kovel by train. Whoever made that trip today, or at any other time after the Second World War, would be traveling inside Russia; but on July 23, 1926, when the Lubinskys made the journey, it was clearly inside Poland.

They also went by train from Kovel to Lublin, and Mahir was surprised when they passed through Chelm, believing, as did many Jews, that the city only existed in Yiddish folklore. But no other place stirred the Lubinskys as much as Warsaw. The Polish capital was the first great city they had seen in their lives. What really impressed Mahir, Anna, and the children were not the buildings, or the avenues, or the cars, but rather the number of Jews. Accustomed to being a minority and living apart in their own communities, it made a deep impression on them to find themselves among so many Jews; it puzzled them to be surrounded by thousands of their own people and not see anyone they knew.

Strangely enough, as Russian Jews, the Lubinskys did not feel at ease among the Polish Jews. It seemed to them that the sense of solidarity that existed among the Jews of Russia was not as strong among their Polish counterparts. They felt uncomfortable in Warsaw, inside as well as outside the ghetto, because everything was different to them: the customs, the food, and even the Yiddish.

They stayed in Warsaw a week, barely enough time to sell two silver chalices at the best price possible, thus acquiring the money they needed to resume their journey west. Gradually, along the way, they would sell one of the few objects of value they carried with them.

The ultimate goal was to reach South America, but exactly where and how, not even they themselves knew.

Mahir had a cousin—Alexander Lubinsky—who had been his lifelong friend. From earliest childhood, they spent their days and, sometimes, their nights together, since Alexander frequently stayed over at Mahir's house, or vice versa. They sat together in the *cheder* on the same bench and read from the same book. They studied and played together, and on more than one occasion they got sick at the same time. More or less around the same period, they got married: Mahir to Anna, and Alexander to a girl from Belaya Tserkov. Then, after that, the two cousins couldn't continue seeing each other because Alexander moved to Belaya Tserkov, where he went to work in his father-in-law's small business. During the riots in 1919, many Jews from the town lost their lives. It was during that period that Velvel Lubinsky, Alexander's father, who was in Belaya Tserkov visiting his family, was brutally murdered with an axe. Alexander, his wife, and their children were spared from the massacre by hiding in the attic of their house. Faced with the horror of the tragedy, Alexander Lubinsky promised himself he'd leave the Ukraine in search of a better world. As soon as the situation calmed down, without telling anyone, he took his wife and children, and disappeared. For four years no one heard from him, until one day Mahir received a letter. It came from Peru and took three months to arrive. Alexander and his family were well. They ended up in a bountiful, virgin land much to their liking, and had settled there. The children were growing up happy and healthy, and he, even though he worked hard, had the satisfaction of seeing that he was earning a good living and comfortably maintaining a home. *Mahir, what are you still doing there?* the letter asked in Yiddish. *How long are you going to continue living among enemies? Do you think that you, or your children, will survive the next pogrom? Only here will you be able to give your family a decent existence, to make a future for yourself. What are you waiting for? Take hold of your own destiny! This is the land of opportunity. The ground is sprinkled with gold, waiting for you. Come and claim it!*

It was because of this letter—the only one that he ever received from his cousin and which he kept among his papers as if it were an important document—that Mahir Lubinsky, his wife and their children were now traveling from city to city, en route to the West. They had joined the migratory tide of Eastern European Jews that was moving to the coasts of America in search of the new Promised Land.

In Poznan they found a buyer for two more silver chalices, and the last two of what was originally a set of six, they sold in Berlin. From the German capital they traveled to Hanover, in order to continue on to Amsterdam and finally to Rotterdam, where they had to get the ship that would take them to South America.

The trip from Rovno to Rotterdam lasted more than three weeks. Still, the journey overland turned out to have fewer complications than the one they would make by sea, for they ran into a problem that no one had foreseen: there were no passenger ships for Latin America and the Dutch authorities did not allow civilians to board merchant vessels.

"There are cargo ships, though, that have a limited number of cabins for passengers," the port official explained. "Some have four, six, and even twelve cabins. Every few days one of them comes into port bound for the Pacific Coast. I'm sure you'll be able to find space easily."

The Lubinskys waited several days, but the ship that could take them to South America did not appear. In anguish, they watched the days pass, their meager funds diminishing and the date of departure postponed indefinitely. They began to grow uneasy, no longer expecting to find passage to Peru. Any destination was fine with them, provided that it was in the magical world of South America, the land of the future, where the ground was sprinkled with gold, waiting for them to come and claim it. Mahir went to the port every day and each time he was told that there would probably be a ship within two or three days. A week went by, two weeks. Anna began to contemplate the possibility of traveling to the United States, since ships bound for North America left almost daily, or of staying in Holland, which also seemed to be a good place to live, but Mahir looked at her as if she had taken leave of her senses. Before leaving Trilesy, Mahir had but one goal in mind and he wasn't going to change it now, not in midstream.

One afternoon Chaim asked:

"Papa, what if we go to the United States first and then to Peru?"

"What an idiot you are!" Bertha said. "Don't you know that the United States is up and Peru is down?"

"You're the idiot! Isn't it true, Papa, that both are on the same side because both are in America?"

108

"Moron!" Bertha said. "That would mean two trips, what about that? And twice the expense, what about that?"

"I'm not talking to you, stupid."

"Children! That's enough!" Anna demanded.

That put an end to the arguing.

Then Mordechai, who generally kept quiet whenever his brother and sister quarreled, asked: "Papa, the boats that go to Peru, do they only leave from here?"

Mahir turned around to his youngest child with a look of amazement.

I'll be! How come I didn't think of that?

9

"We have three ships that leave this week for South America, but none of them is equipped to carry passengers. I'm sorry, *monsieur*," said the old shipping clerk of the *Société Maritime Transatlantique*, in charge of the office at Le Havre. "The next one that can take you will be leaving... Let me see," he added while consulting a handwritten list, "September... September... fifth."

Mahir looked at him, disconcerted.

"September fifth?"

"What do you think, *monsieur*, that ships are like buses that leave every half hour?"

"No...but I thought—"

"If you wish to travel as soon as possible, I advise you to cross the channel to England. Several ships leave here daily for Portsmouth, and from there to South America the departures are more frequent."

"When is the next ship for Portsmouth?"

"Today, at two o'clock. There it is, over there."

Looking through the window, they saw, at the end of the dock, several workers loading boxes onto a merchant vessel.

"Will you take it?" the clerk asked.

Mahir glanced at the clock on the wall. It was eight-thirty. Then he looked at his wife, who opened her eyes wide and smiled nervously at him.

"Yes, I'll take it," Mahir said.

"What papers do you have?"

Mahir presented his Polish passport and a "*laissez-passer*" for his wife and their three children. The clerk examined them.

"If you don't have your papers in order," he said, "they won't let you get off in England... All right, they look okay."

Having said this, he began filling out a form with their names and some particulars from their identification papers. He signed it and affixed several stamps to it.

"Fifty francs, please."

Mahir paid the clerk and took the document he handed him.

"Is this all?"

"*Oui, monsieur*. Present this for boarding. Your crossing will be on deck, so I hope you'll have good weather, and since there's no food on board, I advise you to take something to eat with you."

Mahir and Anna left the office.

"We're leaving this afternoon," Anna told the children, who were waiting for them outside.

The youngsters burst into shouts of joy.

"That's the ship," Mahir said, pointing.

"That's the ship?" Bertha repeated, looking disappointed.

The fact was that there were much larger and better-looking ships.

"I want to go on board to see it," Mordechai said.

"Not now, my love," his mother replied. "We have to go and get our things."

"There's barely enough time," Mahir warned. "Let's go now."

"Let's go!" Chaim shouted, and abruptly turning around, he took off running.

Before he had time to see where he was going, he collided violently with a boy more or less his own age. The impact was so great that both were sent sprawling on the ground. Bertha broke into uncontrollable laughter.

"Oy!" was the first word out of Chaim's mouth.

He wanted to say he was sorry, but since he didn't speak French, all he could do was flap his arms in an awkward fashion.

"Oy!" he sighed again, shaking his head from side to side as if to say: "Excuse me, it's my fault."

The other boy got to his feet, dusted himself off, and gave Chaim a defiant look before going on his way.

At one in the afternoon, the Lubinskys were back at the dock, carrying their meager luggage. They boarded the small ship that would take them from the continent to the British Isles. Anna was carrying a sack filled with rolls, cheeses, fruits, and drinks she had bought at the grocery store, at the entrance to the port.

Chaim strolled around the deck, agog at the thick cables that held the ship in dock, at the smokestack that had begun billowing puffs of smoke, the lifeboats, and the people coming up the ramp. He felt an atmosphere of festivity in the air.

Several men were engaged in lively conversation next to the rail of the deck, conversing in English, a language that Chaim had never heard before, and he drew closer, attracted by its strange sound and by the men who were speaking it. English-speakers always held a kind of fascination for people whose culture was considered less sophisticated. Chaim had been listening to them for only a few seconds when he noticed that the boy he had run into on the dock was also listening to the conversation at a prudent distance from the group. In turn the boy noticed Chaim and they exchanged smiles.

"Exciting to travel by ship, isn't it?"

He was speaking Yiddish! Chaim was dumbfounded. He hesitated an instant before responding.

"How did you know I was Jewish?"

"Only a Jew says 'oy' when he sighs."

The two boys laughed.

"I'm really embarrassed about this morning! I wanted to say 'Excuse me,' but I didn't know how. Why didn't you say something when you realized I was Jewish?"

"It only occurred to me later. I went running off as fast as I could because I felt ridiculous in front of your family."

They laughed again.

"Nice to meet you," the younger of the two said, extending his hand. "I'm Chaim Lubinsky."

"Leib Edri," the older boy answered, shaking his hand.

"Do you understand what those men are talking about?"

"Not very well, but I know they're commenting about this."

And Leib showed him the front page of the newspaper he was carrying.

"I don't read French."

"I do a little, just enough to figure out that yesterday a woman swam the English Channel."

"Swam?"

"Right."

"Incredible."

"Gertrude Ederle, a North American. It caught my attention because I thought her name came from the Hebrew word 'eder,' like mine," Edri said. "It was really an astounding feat."

"And why did she do it?"

Leon shrugged his shoulders.

"Just because. To show she could do it. She's the first woman to do it and she broke the existing record by two hours, set by a man."

"That's amazing!"

"It took her fourteen hours, thirty-one minutes."

The boys got on with each other from the very start.

"Are you traveling alone?"

"Yes."

"To England?"

"Only passing through. I'm on my way to the United States. And what about you, are you going to England?"

"Also passing through. We're on our way to South America."

"You've got a long trip ahead of you."

"So do you. Aren't you afraid of going by yourself?"

"I'm used to it by now. I left home four months ago. And who are you traveling with?"

"With my parents and sister and brother. Come, I want you to meet them."

They found Chaim's family seated on one of the stairs leading to the top bridge.

"Papa, this is Leib."

"Nice to meet you, young man."

"Aren't you the boy Chaim ran into this morning?" Anna asked.

"Yes, ma'am."

Bertha began giggling.

"Don't pay attention to her," Chaim said. "My sister is daffy."

Bertha stuck out her tongue at him.

"Where are you from, young man?" Mahir inquired.

"Russia."

"Yes, but where in Russia?"

"Golochov."

"Who are you traveling with?"

"No one, sir."

"And what about your family?"

"They stayed in Golochov."

"What family do you have?"

"My mother and two younger brothers. My father died a year ago. I also have uncles and aunts, and many cousins."

"And why are you traveling alone?"

"Papa, you sound like the Russian Secret Police."

"That's enough, son," Anna said. "It's interesting to learn about another Jew so far from home."

"I wish I could have had company on my trip, but I'm doing this on my own because my mother couldn't come with two small children and I wasn't about to waste my life away in Russia."

"We're from Russia too," Mordechai added, trying to get in on the conversation.

"Who asked you!" Bertha blurted out, silencing him.

116

"Where are you going, young man?" Mahir inquired.

"The United States of America," Chaim said, answering for his new friend.

"Do you have family there?"

"No, sir."

"What about friends or acquaintances?"

"No friends or acquaintances either."

"It takes a lot of courage to do what you're doing, on your own, alone in the world. How old are you?"

"I'm going on seventeen."

"But you're a child," Anna said.

Leon smiled.

"What do you intend to do in the United States?" Mahir asked.

"Get rich."

"Doing what?"

"I don't know… Working."

"Everybody wants to get rich; not many succeed."

"I'm going to," the young man exclaimed with conviction.

Mahir looked at him approvingly. Energy, confidence, and faith in the future: that's youth.

"Do you think it's so important to be rich?"

"I know it's not."

"So?"

"It's a goal I've set for myself; a kind of personal challenge."

"If you really want to get rich," Chaim ventured, "South America is where you should go."

117

"The United States is the *Goldene Medine*. Everybody's going there," Leon said.

"Chaim's right," Mahir asserted. "South America is the land of the future. It's a rich continent, virgin territory, waiting for people like you, ready to offer you its wealth. Take my word for it, young man: nowhere else in the world will you have the opportunities South America has to offer."

Edri had never contemplated the possibility of settling anywhere else but in the United States. Mahir Lubinsky's words resonated with him.

"Wherever a person goes, things can always work out," Anna said. "A person only needs to work smart and have a little bit of luck."

Just then a strident whistle sounded.

"We're leaving!" Chaim shouted.

They all stood up to go over to the rail of the deck.

"Leib," Anna managed to say to the boy while holding him back by the arm, "I want you to stay with us. I brought good things to eat."

"Thank you, ma'am," he replied and went to stand next to Chaim to watch as they left port.

Little by little the ship began moving away from the dock, pulled by a small tugboat. Chaim raised his arm and waved farewell to the sailors and stevedores who stood unresponsive on the dock, indifferent to the ship's departure and to the passengers gathered at the rail.

The ship was filled with cheerful travelers, laughing and talking in high spirits. But misfortune had also come aboard. Silently, ready as always to deliver a low blow, it waited patiently until the tugboat pulled the ship out of port to initiate its mortal game. The ship's

118

propeller had no sooner started churning, almost as if that was what had been the cause, than Mahir felt the first stabbing pang in his stomach. The pain was so intense it was as if a knife had been driven into him. He remained quiet, but Anna noticed it immediately.

"What's wrong?"

"Nothing. I felt a sharp pain, but it's passing now."

"Come, sit down on the stairs."

"Wait... If I move, it hurts."

Supported by Anna's arm, he struggled towards the stairs leading to the top bridge. Once there, he let go of Anna and took hold of the handrail for support.

"Sit down," Anna instructed him.

"All right."

"I told you that those French cheeses weren't going to agree with you."

A second jabbing pain in his stomach left Mahir drained of color. He bit his lips in an effort not to groan.

"It really hurts," he moaned.

He barely got the words out as he slid down until he was seated on the step.

"I'm going to look for a doctor."

"Wait. You're always an alarmist... It'll soon pass."

Anna looked at him, frightened, and he tried to calm her with a smile. She took his hands and held them a minute.

"Feeling any better?"

"Yes."

But the pain was not letting up. They waited in silence for a while.

"It's getting better," he said, again not being honest with her.

"You're in pain. I'm going to get a doctor."

"Don't be silly. It's passing, I tell you."

"You're pale."

Mahir gave her a look of impatience and Anna kept silent. They stayed where they were a long time, he seated, doubled over, and she by his side, holding his hand. Some fifteen minutes had passed from the time the pains started to when the third jabbing pain came. Mahir writhed in agony on the step.

"Mahir, what is it?"

He didn't answer, but it was enough to see his contorted face to understand. Anna screamed in anguish and went running along the deck.

"A doctor! A doctor, please!"

Her cries for help caused several persons came to her aid, Chaim and Leon among them. When Anna returned to her husband's side a few seconds later, he was lying on the deck, face up and surrounded by people. Someone was bent over him, examining his condition.

"*Où est-ce que ça vous fait mal?*" asked the man while tapping him on the chest.

Mahir didn't answer.

"*Where does it hurt?*" the man asked, trying his best to communicate in English, but with such a strong French accent that Mahir, who spoke neither English nor French, did not notice the difference in languages.

"*Here?*" the man continued, this time tapping him on the left side of his stomach.

Mahir seemed to understand and moved his head from side to side.

"*Here?*" he asked, applying pressure to the lower right side.

Mahir cried out. The man stood up and looked around. He was young, slightly bald, wore round glasses, and had an intellectual air about him. He understood from the look of anguish on Anna's face that she was the person he needed to speak to.

"Acute appendicitis," he said dryly. "He ought to be operated on as soon as possible."

There was nothing to do except to wait. They had been at sea for nearly an hour and seven more hours lay ahead of them before reaching Portsmouth. Mahir Lubinsky was carried to the infirmary where they placed him on a stretcher and covered him with a cotton blanket.

"I'll see to it he's taken to a hospital as soon as we reach port," said Dr. Deparcieux who, along with Anna and the children, did not leave the patient's side for a single minute the remainder of the trip. "God willing, he'll be fine," he added in a reassuring tone.

But that was not God's will. The pains continued increasing until they became unbearable. An injection of morphine eased the pain, but did not solve the problem. His temperature continued to climb. An hour later, it had reached 102 and Mahir's body was not responding to the drugs they were administering to lower the fever. Leon detected for the first time that the doctor appeared less confident than he had been at the beginning.

"How bad is it, doctor?" he asked, expressing the anguish that Anna was unable to communicate to the physician in any language.

"Well, it's like this... the appendix burst and is infecting the blood... If he could be operated on..."

Another hour passed and Mahir's temperature exceeded 104. Deparcieux covered the immigrant's naked body with wet towels, in a desperate effort to lower his temperature.

Mahir Lubinsky never reached England. Two hours later he went into a coma and never regained consciousness; he died a few minutes before the ship pulled into dock.

Crying practically in silence and with a demeanor of insuperable will, the Lubinsky family acknowledged the death of the man who was husband and father.

"Look after your mother and your sister and brothers," the doctor told Leon in a low voice, taking him for the oldest of the siblings.

Night had fallen when Anna and the four young people disembarked, that tragic seventh day of August 1926. It was raining in Portsmouth. The port authorities were very understanding and polite. After finalizing the formalities, Anna and her children remained with the body while Leon went to look for help. His was not an easy mission: how to go about locating a Jew in an unfamiliar city, on a Saturday night, under rainy skies, and not knowing the language? But Leon's ingenuity and insight came to his aid, as they would so often in the future.

Very early the following morning, Leon found himself back at port, accompanied by two elderly men whose dark suits, striped ties and black fedoras conferred on them an air of ill-fated solemnity. They were representatives of the *chevrah kaddishah* of Portsmouth.

10

They had been at sea ten days when the merchant ship *Leicester Maiden* reached the Azores to stock up on fresh fruits and vegetables. It was all the islands had to offer. Since there was no wharf where vessels could dock, supplies had to be carried out to the ships aboard small boats crammed with merchandise, with one or two people on board hawking their produces. There was no contractual arrangement for provisions between the ship owners and a supplier; instead it was something like a floating market where the vendors competed against each other for business with the captain, who decided on the spot what to buy and from which vendor. While watching the boats rocking in the blue water, Leon wondered if behind the picturesque scene, full of light and color, there was not a hidden struggle for survival, the same cruel struggle that he had left behind, in Europe, and which—who knows?—perhaps awaited him on the other side of the Atlantic, to confront him once again.

The trip proved monotonous and every day seemed longer than the one before. Leon hadn't thought to bring along anything to read and all that was available aboard ship were a few books in English that no one could read. What was available, however, was a chess set, which helped to fill the long hours of idleness with some measure of enjoyment. Leon and Chaim played every day and set their minds against each other in a kind of friendly competition that was to reverberate far beyond their chess matches. Bertha and Mordechai also managed to keep occupied, she drawing or embroidering and he "piloting" the ship on the bridge, alongside the captain, a leathery-faced Scot who had taken a liking to the amusing little boy. Meanwhile, Anna Lubinsky knew no end to her suffering:

123

first, the pain caused by her husband's death was still an open wound; secondly, out of fear of the future—more pronounced than ever by the fact that she was now a widow, —she knew the full responsibility for her family had fallen on her; and lastly, as if that weren't enough, she was experiencing seasickness. She suffered constant dizziness and only on rare occasions, when the sea was calm and she ventured out on deck, did she feel some relief from the terrible queasiness. But if she had suspected what awaited her the rest of the way, she surely would have disembarked in the Azores even if it were only to wither away there the rest of her life.

The following day after the ship weighed anchor, Anna really began to feel ill, and it was just the start of the voyage, since two more weeks of sailing lay ahead of them before reaching the continent and then another five days journey to the Peruvian coast. Anna remained inside the small, dirty cabin she shared with her younger children, refusing to go out on deck and barely eating, which did not prevent her from throwing up several times a day. Feeling as ill as she did, she had no desire—perhaps neither the strength—to bathe, dress or, from time to time, to stand up. She spent the days and nights in bed in the dim light of the cabin, praying to God for the voyage to be over as soon as possible. But the days seemed interminable. She asked her children to leave her be and refused to heed Chaim's pleas to come out on deck for some fresh air. When she was by herself in the cabin, she burst into tears, sometimes over the memory of Mahir, but most of the time over the desperation of feeling so ill. The ship's nurse visited her several times and always gave the same verdict: "It's nothing. Just a bad case of seasickness, that's all."

Ten days passed and Anna continued to grow more pallid and haggard. Unable to look after her children, she contented herself with knowing they were well. She heard Bertha and Mordechai coming and going, getting into bed and getting up, but all this in a kind of fogginess. *May God keep watch over my children!* she thought. It was because of them, more than anything else that Mahir had decided to go to South America. During those moments when she felt the uncertainty and fear of facing an unknown world, without her husband, far from friends and relatives, she wondered if so much suffering was worth it.

The journey had cost what little the family had taken out of Russia. Anna no longer had anything of value to sell. She had sold everything in Portsmouth: jewels of great sentimental value, many of them given to her by Mahir to commemorate special occasions. The ones he hadn't given her held even greater sentimental value, for they came from generations back, having inherited them from her mother: three amber necklaces and several broaches, bracelets and silver rings with topaz, agate, lapis lazuli and other semiprecious stones; highly prized jewelry in Russia but considered ordinary in the West. The money from what she sold, plus a good portion of the money Leon had brought with him, barely covered their lodging in England for five days and the ship's fare. The burial had not cost her anything, for the small Jewish community of Portsmouth, possibly the oldest in England after that of London's, had covered all the expenses out of consideration for her tragic situation. The widow had boarded the *Leicester Maiden* with all the money she had left—a few pounds Sterling—and that had to last her until either she or her son could earn their first wages.

Even though she felt like she was dying, Anna kept a mental account of things: three more days for the ship to make its first port of call in America, a thought that helped her to bear up under the torment.

The long voyage would soon be over: two more days to go. But besides feeling generally unwell, Anna also suffered a continuous sensation of unsteadiness, as if she were falling backwards. Still, she did not lose track of time: one more day remained. Lying prostrate on the cot in her dark cabin, physically exhausted, she willed the time to pass.

Hours and hours—years perhaps?— she remained like this until the day Chaim came bursting into the cabin.

"Mom, get up! There's land in sight!"

Anna got up, using all the strength she could muster, and went out on deck leaning on her son's shoulder for support.

"See?" Chaim said, pointing with his finger. A gray line ran across the horizon, where the sky kisses the sea. "The New World!" he added, bursting with excitement.

Two hours later the gray line had dissipated and what one could now see was a wide, green strip, indicative of heavy vegetation. As they drew closer to land, they could see a small village.

"It's Bellavista," Leon said. "We'll spend a day here."

The *Leicester Maiden* dropped anchor about two hundred yards off the coast. As in the Azores, there was no wharf in Bellavista for large ships, and so a half dozen small craft came out to meet it. From a motorboat, several officials from Customs, including police and port authority personnel, came aboard. They were received in the captain's office where they remained for about twenty minutes. As soon as the port authorities left, an announcement in English came over the loudspeakers. Seeing how the other passengers reacted, Anna grasped the meaning: those in transit who wished to disembark could do so by boarding the small craft that were waiting next to the stairs of the bridge below. The same boats would provide continuous service between the dock and the ship until six o'clock that evening. Passengers whose destination was Bellavista had to carry all their luggage down to the lower bridge and wait for the arrival of a few larger boats that would soon be departing from the port.

"Chaim, get our suitcases," Anna said.

"What?"

"Get the suitcases. We're getting off here."

"But, mom! We're not there yet! We're going to Peru."

"No, son, we're staying here."

"Mom! We've only got a little way to go now."

"Son... I can't take another day."

Chaim observed his mother. She was emaciated. The fresh air had given her a boost of energy, but she still looked very sick. The youngster hadn't realized until that moment how thin she had grown in only two weeks.

"Then..."

"Yes, son, this is it and no farther."

Chaim sighed and turned to his friend who had followed the conversation without daring to say anything.

"Leib, come on, let's get our things."

"Ma'am..." Leon began...

He wanted to explain that the hardest part was over, that five more days remained, including intermediary ports of call, before reaching the destination that Mahir had so eagerly set his sights on, and that in Peru they would find family, whereas here in Bellavista they had no one to turn to. Worse yet: they didn't even know exactly where they were. But no words were needed. His face said it all and Anna interrupted him with a movement of her hand.

"I know," she said in a weak voice, "but I can't go on."

And so it was that Leon Edri and the Lubinsky family never reached Peru. Instead, on a sun-drenched September morning, they found themselves disembarking at Bellavista, a picturesque maritime port in a majestic Latin American country. Destiny had brought them to that country—whose very existence had been unknown to them— so that they might make it their new home. Destiny had not played a dirty trick on them, for here, as in Peru, the ground was sprinkled with gold waiting for those who came, determined to pick it up.

When they reached the dock, a port official approached them and said something. They stood there, looking at him, not understanding a single word. Another official came by and tried his luck, speaking very deliberately and exaggerating every syllable The pains he took yielded nothing.

"*Ne comprends*," Leon said, trying to give a Spanish accent to what was sort of French.

Then it was the officials' turn not to understand. They exchanged glances and laughed. The first one who had spoken addressed them again, this time adopting his colleague's approach, which consisted of speaking slowly and exaggerating every word. He got the same result as his companion. Leon raised his hands to his face and moved his arms back and forth with his palms turned outward, giving them to understand that none of what they said had been understood. The agent replied by motioning with his hand for them to follow him. Both had resorted to a language that Leon would be using daily in the days to come: an improvised sign language.

They followed the man down the hall of an old building to an office where there was a third official, apparently of higher rank, seated behind a desk stacked with papers. The agent who ushered them in explained to the senior official that the immigrants did not understand one iota of Spanish. While listening, the supervising officer surveyed the new arrivals. Everything about them was strange: their pale skin, especially Anna's, for she was still ashen from seasickness; their features, which belonged to people of another race; their language, which bore no resemblance to anything they knew; their clothes, which were bulky and old fashioned… Taking an autocratic air, maybe to impress his subordinate, the supervisor addressed Anna and the boys. He spoke in English, a very poor English, but in this case it made no difference, since they did not understand one bit of the Anglo-Saxon language any more than they understood a single word of Spanish. The supervising officer, confidently expecting a certain reaction, became flustered when he saw none forthcoming. Leon and Anna and her children stood there with a perplexed expression that wounded his vanity. But he was one of those men who do not give up easily.

"*Parlez-vous français?*" he said in French, and turning to Anna, added, "*Madame?*"

"*Oui, un peu,*" Leon said, answering for her.

"Ah!" the officer exclaimed triumphantly, satisfied with having achieved some measure of communication.

He cast a glance at his subordinate as if to say, "You see?" —and grinning, he turned towards Leon; but when he looked directly at him, his smile immediately vanished. "Parlez-vous français?" was the only thing he knew how to say in French.

If they weren't going to understand him no matter what, it was better to speak in his own language. Once more he addressed the Lubinskys and Leon in Spanish. They understood but one word, which is more or less the same in all languages: *pasaporte*. Leon pulled out his Rumanian passport and Anna did likewise with Mahir's Polish passport and her and the children's *laissez-passer*. The supervisor examined their documents, but seeing that he couldn't decipher them, he decided to call in another officer to explain the problem to him. The two officers discussed the case and at moments it seemed they were arguing. Leon grasped a word here and there, but the thread of the discussion escaped him. He had the impression that the first officer wanted to make them get back on the ship while the second officer was ready to let them enter the country. Unable to resolve the impasse, they decided to take the case to their superior and left with the documents in hand, leaving the immigrants alone in the room. Ten minutes hadn't passed when a young woman came to accompany them to the office of the port director, who greeted them with a slight nod of the head and then addressed the two officers who stood next to his desk. While he spoke, he looked Leon and the Lubinskys over, one by one, especially fixing his attention on the children's mother. That same night, pondering matters before falling off to sleep, Leon couldn't help but think that the long look that the chief supervisor had given Anna was the one that made him decide. He couldn't say if there was an improper motive in that decision (since Anna, besides being a widow and in need, was relatively young and attractive) or if it was out of compassion that he decided to help her; but whether his motive was noble or immoral, he had made up his mind while looking Anna over. The supervisor's words were brief. When he finished, he again acknowledged them with a nod of his head, as if to say "you're free to go."

As they filed out of the room, the official who seemed to look favorably on their situation gave them a wink. A few minutes later he himself affixed the necessary stamps to their travel documents and accompanied them to Customs to help them with the formalities.

It was probably close to four in the afternoon when Anna and the children walked past the sign that read "Administrative District of the Port of Bellavista" and exited the building, tired but happy. Two porters carried their luggage. The street was crowded with people and there was a faint odor in the air, difficult to define, something like a mixture of fresh fruits and cow dung, and a pleasant tropical breeze. The younger of the two porters, a cheerful mulatto who was humming to himself the whole time, approached Leon and asked:

"And where to now?"

Leon looked at him without understanding a word and smiled. Chaim observed his friend and correctly interpreted his smile. It was the expression of a person who was confused and wanted to know the same thing that had been asked of him: "And where to now?"

11

Standing next to the boat, a muscular mulatto was shifting restlessly from side to side, boisterously greeting all his cronies who walked by and frequently shaking with huge bursts of laughter at his own remarks. He was barefoot and had his pant legs rolled up to his shins His multicolored shirt hung open, outside his waist, leaving his smooth chest exposed.

"Hurry up, fella!" he shouted, waving his arms in the air.

Leon quickly picked up his suitcase and passed it up to Chaim who was on board grabbing hold of the luggage. A canvas canopy propped up by wood poles cast a shadow over the rear section of the vessel, which looked more like a raft than a boat, not only because of its wide platform and shallow hull, but because there were no benches to sit on. After handing up the last piece of luggage, Leon jumped on board and began helping Chaim to arrange the suitcases so they wouldn't be in the way.

"Hurry up, kid, hurry up!" the mulatto shouted at a boy who showed up with a big bundle slung over his shoulders.

He bellowed at everybody who arrived at the dock, harrying each one as if it was that person's fault that they were delayed in getting under way.

A total of twenty passengers settled in, twenty-one counting the big mulatto who was the "captain" of the boat and probably its owner. Leon, the Lubinskys, and one other passenger were the only ones with suitcases. The remaining passengers had also brought baggage on board, but theirs consisted of sacks, and baskets.

"Yes sirree! It's kicked in! It's kicked in!" the mulatto cried out when he finally got the motor started after fifteen minutes of effort.

The boat was pulling away from shore and entering the gray-brown waters that led to the virgin continent. The river was incredibly wide—so wide, in fact, that it was difficult to determine the direction that had to be taken to go upstream and not towards the opposite shore. In addition to its size, the river wound through marshy terrain in such a configuration that one could not see a substantial stretch of land along the way, creating the impression among those who navigated it that they were on a lake the whole time, advancing towards a shore that for some inexplicable reason was impossible to reach.

Leon gazed out at the little houses of Bellavista lined up along the banks of the river, in that murky outlet to the sea. *How pretty they are from a distance*, he thought. But close up, they were miserable huts, mere wood structures with tin roofs and dirt floors. Leon and the Lubinskys had spent three days in a filthy boarding house, not very far from the port. That was two days more than Chaim and Leon needed to see the city and realize that there was nothing there for them to do.

In the entire city, there were but four paved streets, all quite short and located in the "downtown area" next to the port facility. It's only brick and mortar constructions consisted of two-story buildings, which did not all sit adjacent to one another but rather were separated by houses, also two-stories high, with only the façade made of mortar and cement and all the rest of wood. The mayor's office and the various government departments—national and municipal—had their offices in that section of the city. There were also two banks, two canteens, a pharmacy, and a movie theater. The other premises were occupied by retail businesses. Walking at a brisk pace, a person could cover the entire business district in ten minutes, which is not to say that Bellavista was a small town. Next to the four paved streets, a network of dirt roads spread out, providing access to a sea of miserable dwellings. Since there were no sidewalks, the water that collected in puddles during the rainy season turned them into quagmires. Many of the city's neighborhoods lacked drainage, a deficiency that oddly enough resulted in an advantage for them, because when a torrential downpour fell— something that happened several times a year—those neighborhoods that had sewers were worse off, because the drain pipes, instead of absorbing the deluge, spewed out huge rivers of putrid water that completely flooded the streets, dragging away everything that stood in its way, including rats, dogs and cats, and depositing all of it in foul-smelling puddles whose pestilence lasted whole days to the delight of the buzzards. A substantial part of the population was black and lived in appalling misery. There were children everywhere walking or crawling around completely naked, neglected, their bellies swollen because of worms, and their noses running with snot. The adults wore the most rudimentary clothing: the women, in a simple blouse and skirt, the men in shirt and pants. Everybody went about barefoot. Even among the minority of whites and mulattos who wore better clothes and ran the city's businesses, there were many who did not wear shoes. The people who walked the streets barefoot were perhaps what left the deepest impression on Leon and the Lubinsky family.

When he finished checking out the city and sizing up its possibilities, Leon couldn't help but ask himself what in the devil he was doing there. That world of ignorance and misery, where everything was so strange to him, frightened him. He felt like running to the port and boarding the first ship he saw, to sail far away, to North America if possible, or back to Europe if necessary. Yet, at the same time—how strange! —he felt he wanted to stay, having already breathed in the warmth of the tropics, having already walked on the fertile soil and eaten some of its delicious fruits, and having already experienced the magnitude of its spaciousness; he had taken note of the voluptuous bodies of the black women and on two occasions, at least, had come across the tempting gaze of some coquettish dark-skinned girl. He had already caught the subtle smell of that mixture of violence and lethargy, of liquor and gaiety that permanently permeates the air in Latin America, intoxicating the spirit of all those who discover it. He was a marked man. Instead of a ship to take him to the United States or back to Europe, he had boarded a small craft to carry him to the interior of the country.

According to the information that Chaim and Leon obtained, conditions were much better inland. There were urban centers with highly developed industry and commerce, not to mention the capital of the republic that was a thriving metropolis where women wore the latest Paris fashion and men dressed in suits made of the finest English wool.

Transportation to the interior of the country was provided by a fleet of small boats belonging to the Santa María River Transport Company, which went from Bellavista to La Playada and back, trying to put in at each port every two days. In practice, this program didn't work that well, not with the boats frequently breaking down or running aground on the sandbanks when the river was low, indefinitely prolonging a crossing that normally took eight days upriver and five downriver. A large wheel attached to the stern propelled these picturesque riverboats. Sixteen people could travel in first class, on the top deck, and some sixty in second class, on the bottom deck.

Leon and the Lubinskys traveled neither in first nor second class, but in the only class available aboard the mulatto's boat. They had decided not to take the Santa María line for three reasons: In the first place, they wanted to leave Bellavista as soon as possible, and the shipping line was scheduled to leave a day later; in the second place, Anna flatly refused to board anything that remotely resembled a transatlantic ship; and lastly, the mulatto charged half the amount of the Santa María line, which allowed them to stretch the little money they had left.

"Mister, want one?"

Leon turned around to the person who had addressed him. A man of short stature, round face and ruddy complexion, was offering him something in his outstretched hand.

"Muchas gracias," Leon replied, using two of the few words that he had learned since his arrival.

"Pure sugar," the man said.

"No comprende," uttered Leon, trying to express himself in Spanish.

Like so many of his fellow immigrant Jews, he was to learn the language astonishingly fast, but without ever getting to master it.

"Taste it," the man insisted with a smile.

"Muchas gracias," Leon repeated.

He took the offering. It was a bland fruit, brown in color, somewhat larger than an egg. Imitating the man, Leon split the fruit open, pulling it apart until he had both halves on the tips of his fingers. Behind the thin, fuzzy skin, a dark reddish pulp emerged. He pressed the fruit to his open lips and squeezed it with his fingers, forcing the pulp to slide into his mouth and leaving the squashed skin in his hand. A wonderfully sweet, fragrant flesh filled his mouth.

"Delicious, isn't it?" the man said, watching Leon savor the fruit.

"Hmmm." Leon's mouth was full as he voiced his approval, much to the delight of the little man.

"They grow juicy like this all over La Cicuta. My *compadre* has a parcel of land around there, and he gives me loads of it."

"No comprende."

By day's end, the twenty passengers had become friends. Differing in age, color, size and sex, they had evolved into a sort of floating family, with lively conversation. All were eager to teach Spanish to the foreigners.

Anna marveled at the thick vegetation and the reed and mud shanties that appeared every once in a while along the shores, sometimes solitary and sometimes forming picturesque villages. Whenever she saw someone on land watching them pass by, she waved and the greeting was always returned.

She was suddenly baffled by Mordechai's shouts of excitement. The child was standing next to his brother and sister. Anna rushed towards them.

"Look, Mama!" he exclaimed, holding up his arm and pointing.

Anna looked towards shore, but saw nothing in particular.

"There they are, at the foot of that tree," Bertha indicated, also pointing.

Then she saw them: a number of small crocodiles, a few of them inching along while most of the others remained perfectly still, more motionless than the bushes around them.

"*Caimanes*," said one of the passengers in a friendly manner.

"*Caimanes*," Mordechai repeated.

By nightfall they reached Marañón, a small but well-known locality, considered the heart of the banana region. Many passengers got off to have a look around, some in search of a bar and others simply out for a stroll. Leon, Anna, and her children chose to stay put. The little bit of breeze that was blowing when they were sailing up river had stopped and an infernal, sultry heat, laden with smells and humidity, descended upon them. From the nearby swamp came the annoying symphony of the jungle: the endless shrill sounds of a thousand cicadas, augmented here and there by the croaking of a frog, and from time to time enhanced by the chirping of a tropical bird. To these tormenting sounds of the jungle, was added the worst of all: the maddening buzz of the mosquitoes. Those hellish pests mercilessly attacked everybody, buzzing in their ears and biting them all over their bodies, especially on the face, hands, and ankles. Small welts instantly appeared, with a red pinprick visible in the center. Squeezing them forced a clear ooze to the surface— sometimes mixed with blood—that contained part of the infectious secretion injected by the insect. The children were asleep and Anna tried to protect them by flapping her headscarf in front of them, but the persistent mosquitoes returned as soon as she stopped.

As the warm night wore on, the passengers gradually stretched out on the floor of the boat, amidst bundles and packages, to sleep under an open sky. Leon tried to fall asleep, but the buzz of the mosquitoes gave him no respite; they persisted in their buzzing, which might have been tolerable if it had only been a continuous humming sound. Several minutes could go by without hearing anything and suddenly, just when he felt himself dropping off to sleep, the buzzing resounded almost inside his ear like an alarm, startling him and keeping him awake and on edge at the same time. Leon learned to react, slapping his ear as soon as he heard the buzzing, and more than once he had the satisfaction of feeling one of them get squashed against his face. From time to time he heard other passengers slapping their ears. Anna continued huddling over Bertha and Mordechai almost until dawn when, overcome by fatigue, she finally gave in to sleep. Leon had no such luck and couldn't get a wink of rest the whole night. Only when they were under way again, very early in the morning, did he feel any relief from the mosquitoes' lashing assault.

The boat advanced slowly, laboring to overcome the gentle current of muddy waters, and as it went deeper into the green continent, the terrain became less swampy and the banks of the rivers more defined. Twice a day they put in at some village to take on provisions of water and fuel, but those intervals were not long enough for the passengers to take care of their necessities, and it frequently happened that one or more of them had to relieve themselves over the side of the boat. When that happened, everybody nonchalantly looked the other way, seemingly oblivious to the moment. That trait of delicacy among the people of the region was not lost on the newcomers, who were beginning to adapt to a new culture.

Around five in the afternoon, they reached a large village where they would have to spend the night. This time, since it was still early, Anna decided to disembark and have a look around. Leon and Chaim and the two little ones accompanied her, walking along the unpaved streets and taking in every detail with great interest. In turn, they were objects of curiosity to the locals, since it was obvious, even from a distance, that they were foreigners.

Here, just as in Bellavista, the people were poorly dressed and went around barefoot. The little white houses—all neatly aligned—were of whitewashed adobe, with red-roof tiles; some had dirt floors and others were tiled with different colors. All the interiors had a faux baseboard painted on the wall (almost always a faded burgundy color), about fifteen inches wide and bordering the entire floor. From time to time, there would be a house with the front door wide open, and one or more older residents sitting outside on chairs, watching the passersby. There were no cars on the dirt streets, not even horse-drawn carriages, but there were men either on horseback or on mules. The town consisted of a main stretch of road almost a mile long, with two or three streets running parallel to it, and a dozen shorter ones, perpendicular to them. There was a plaza in the center of the town, with palm trees and leafy shade trees, and across from it, standing out from all the other buildings, was a church with two cupolas that was, without question, the town's most noteworthy structure. Also in front of the plaza, were the only two-story buildings in the entire village, and it was there that the municipal government, the State Bank, a canteen, and several businesses had their operations.

Anna and the children were in good spirits. They walked the length of the town several times and returned to the boat before dark.

When night fell, the situation was more tolerable than it had been the night before. It was hot, but the suffocating oven-like heat had dissipated. The same couldn't be said of the mosquitoes, but there weren't as many compared to the previous day's inferno. Leon lay down on one side of the boat and began to meditate. He was exhausted and it wouldn't take him long to fall sound asleep, but first he went over in his mind the things he had seen that afternoon. Without any doubt, it was the poverty of the people that made the profoundest impression on him. Even though to a lesser degree than in Bellavista, misery could be seen everywhere; an endemic wretchedness that seemed to be more a companion of conformity than of desperation. Before drifting off to sleep, the emaciated faces of the farmers, the dirty, half-naked bodies of the children, the hands of beggars reaching out paraded before him… and brought to mind the town's ironic name: *Valle Rico*.

The journey continued without incident and the days began to take on a sort of routine: getting under way at the break of dawn, brewing coffee in a pot over a small kerosene-heated stove and from which anyone could help himself, stopping two or three times a day at some village, chatting with fellow travelers and spending the night in the last town to be reached before nightfall. During the fourth day of the journey a tropical rainstorm soaked all the passengers and much of the luggage, despite the canvas roof that covered the boat.

With every day that went by, the current grew stronger as the width of the river narrowed, consequently, slowing the journey, if not making it more difficult. Frequently, the current dragged tree trunks, and at times whole trees, downstream. From time to time, bodies of dead animals could be seen floating down river. The heat and the mosquitoes persisted, although to a somewhat lesser degree. On the horizon, the first mountains appeared.

On the sixth day of the journey, in late afternoon, they reached the town of Almavivas. The mulatto was tying up to one of the pylons that supported the rickety wood platform, which also served as the dock, when a group of about thirty people rushed forward. Everybody was talking simultaneously, in loud voices, all competing for his attention. They were part of a larger contingent of passengers from the ship that had docked a short distance away from where they stood. With the water level having gone down and the vessel unable to continue its course upstream without running aground on one of the sandbanks, they found themselves stuck in the town for three days. The day before, a few of the passengers had continued their trip aboard two boats that the shipping line kept for such emergencies and which transported people to another of the shipping company's boats that waited beyond the sandbanks. But on this particular occasion, there wasn't room for everybody and those who had to stay behind were desperate to reach their destinations. Some vociferously explained how urgent it was for them to reach their homes and others stretched out their hands with tempting sums of money in front of the mulatto's eyes. He suddenly decided that he had room for six more passengers, and in the ensuing confusion he ended up letting ten additional people come aboard with their luggage, loading the boat far beyond prudent capacity. As it turned out, the ten passengers departing Almavivas paid altogether more than the total passage paid by the twenty who had started out from Bellavista, none of whom got off, not so much because there was nothing to see or do in Almavivas, but out of fear of losing their places on the boat.

The passengers broke off into three groups of revelers, besides the one composed of Leon and the Lubinskys who, because they didn't know the language, stayed to themselves. In one of the groups, the happiest and most boisterous of the three, someone pulled out a bottle of *aguardiente* that was passed around from hand to hand, and from mouth to mouth, amidst much laughter and shouting. A little later one of the happy merrymakers began singing. Others started singing along with him. Loosened up by the alcohol and in high spirits, one of the other groups began singing too until, finally, everybody joined in. Sometimes they sang together and other times one person alone did the singing, with the group joining him in the refrain that was repeated after each stanza. Apparently, the new passengers hadn't the least intention of getting a night's sleep. Aboard the company ship, those in first-class had cabins and those in second-class were free to hang up their hammocks. It wasn't surprising, then, that they weren't at all inclined to lie down on the floor of the mulatto's boat, instead preferring to turn the evening into one, long night of merrymaking. They drank, made jokes, and sang to their heart's content. Lying face up, with his hands behind his head, and contemplating the starry sky, Leon listened to them singing, amazed that they knew so many songs and that they had the strength to drink and sing all night long. He was captivated by the tropical atmosphere, and there were moments when he couldn't believe that this was real, for here he was, traveling on this quaint boat with all its local color, listening to rhythmic melodies and breathing the warm air of a clear night, in Almavivas, on the shores of a huge river, far, far from Golochov, from his mother and his loved ones.

During the following night, docked alongside another town, the same scenes were repeated, more or less: stories were told, songs were sung, and there was drinking. The songfest began dying out around two in the morning, as the high-spirited passengers, worn out by the previous night's revelry, began falling off to sleep. By early dawn, the only merrymakers left were two out-of-tune men who were completely drunk and just kept on singing.

"Shut up already, damn it!" somebody shouted.

"Come over here and make me, son-of-a bitch!" one of the drunks shot back.

141

But the man was so inebriated that the fight he was looking for didn't materialize, since he didn't have enough strength to stand up and had to limit himself to cursing in a hoarse and unintelligible voice until he finally wore himself out.

Two days later, around ten in the morning, the boat reached La Playada, its final destination. As soon as it docked, a stampede of passengers set off for the railway station, since the train was scheduled to leave at ten and missing it would mean having to stay in town overnight. Leon and the Lubinskys got a cab—a jalopy with a sign painted on the doors that read TAXI. The driver left them in front of the station, which was—they came to find out when they arrived—just two blocks from the dock.

They boarded the train and took their seats, surprised to see that the cars—unlike those in Europe—were not divided into compartments, but instead were fitted with wood benches on each side. From the station platform, peddlers hawked their merchandise, which they handed to the passengers through the train's open windows. "Hot *almojábanas!*" shouted women carrying large trays of flour and cheese pancakes on top of their heads. "*Buñuelos, buñuelos!*" others called out, selling deep-fried salty doughnuts. "*Bocadillos, quesillos, bocadillos!*" shouted three or four little boys, scurrying from side to side, holding their trays aloft to display small-size sweet fruit-jellies and cheese snacks. "*Piña, mamoncillos, guava, madroños, piña, piña!*" came the shouts of vendors carrying large baskets of pineapple slices and other tropical fruits. Leon and the Lubinskys saw people who had been with them on the journey up river hurrying towards the train. An hour later passengers were still boarding, and also among them were several from the mulatto's boat who had taken their time walking around the town before making their way to the train station.

It was 11:20 a.m. when "the ten o'clock train" pulled out. As soon as it started moving, the passengers felt immediate relief from the heat, with a bit of air coming through the open windows. It was a welcome breeze despite the fact that at times the air brought with it soot from the locomotive, causing irritation to the eyes of many passengers. Forty minutes later, having covered the distance between the river and the magnificent mountain range, the train began its ascent. The tunnels and bridges, and the sides of mountains that had been carved out provided a relatively level roadbed for the tracks, making the difference in gradations nearly imperceptible. Only the deliberate speed and the struggling engine betrayed the fact that the train was climbing, confirmed later by the gradual change in vegetation and temperature. The tall bamboo canes and the banana trees were the first to disappear from view, and as the exotic plants and trees were becoming more scarce, others, generally taller and of a darker green, were taking their place. After several hours of tortuous travel, the temperature had gone down considerably. They were still climbing when night began to fall. The leafy vegetation, now composed for the most part of pines and eucalyptus trees, would soon cease to be visible.

Leon noticed that Anna and her children had fallen asleep. He closed his eyes and felt sleep taking hold of him too. He realized that the train was gaining speed, which meant they were again traveling on a level grade or, more probable yet, that they were beginning to descend. It seemed to him that the train was lulling him and he felt himself entering a warm, dark space, until he fell into a deep sleep.

A few taps on his shoulder woke him. He wasn't sure at first where he was. Oh, yes, he was on the train. It was slowing down, almost ready to come to a stop. All the passengers stood up and were lining up to exit the car. Again someone tapped him on the shoulder, as if to make sure he was awake. He recognized the little man with the round, ruddy face who had offered him some fruit aboard the mulatto's boat.

"Get up, mister," the little man said, his hand still resting on Leon's shoulder, "and stay sharp, if you don't want someone to make off with your things."

"No comprende."

The round face became rounder as it beamed a big smile.

"We've reached Lárida."

Golochov

December 10, 1926

Dear Leon,

At last you've shown signs of life! Today the letters you sent your mother, your uncle Shmuel, Zvi, and me arrived—all at the same time. They were the hit of the year. We've been waiting over three months for news of you. Every day your mother waits for the coach to arrive with the hope that Mr. Marx will bring her a letter. At first, we all kept reassuring her, telling her that mail from America takes a long time, but after a while we no longer knew what to tell her; or what to think. The truth is that letters from the United States take four weeks to get here, five at the most (we know because of the Kleins who frequently get a letter from their son), and the last one you sent us from Le Havre was dated August 5. You told us you were leaving on the 7th for England, to sail from there to the United States. Imagine how worried we all were these last few months. We had started to fear the worst when your letters arrived from...Lárida! Lárida? How in the devil did you end up there? How crazy! I bet it isn't as important a city as you say. We were looking for it on the map and couldn't find it.

Write and give us some details about the place, what it's like, tell us more about the Lubinskys and tell me how you're getting on. And if you don't write to me, it's not important, just as long as you write your mother, because she's dying of anguish when she doesn't hear from you.

I'm happy to tell you that it is now my turn to leave Golochov, much sooner than I imagined. The fact is two weeks ago a delegate from Eretz Israel came to town. His name is Leibele, like yours. Leib Brenner, but he calls himself Arie. Lion, in Hebrew. Arie travels these lands, from community to community, organizing garinim, "nuclei" of young people to travel in groups to Palestine. I must tell you I signed up on the spot, along with seventeen other boys. More would have joined up if it weren't for their parents who opposed the idea. Itzik and Etl, for example, wanted to join the group, but their parents said absolutely not, since they're planning on going to the United States. The funny thing is the whole town is divided into three camps: those who intend to go to America (which is the majority); those who believe that the best thing is to stay in Golochov (the minority); and those who want to go to Eretz Israel. The opportunists, the fools, and the idealists, is how Itzik classifies them.

We are, in all, eighteen boys and girls in our group. We belong to an organization called Kadima, "Onward," in Hebrew. We meet three times a week, we chat, sing, and dance. At each meeting, we listen to a lecture by Arie on history, Judaism, philosophy, politics, and agriculture. Yes, you read it correctly, farming. We have to learn to cultivate the land because that is what we're going to do in Eretz Israel: redeem the land. Feter Yankl lent us the orchard that he has and we practice growing tomatoes, onions, and cucumbers there. I dream about the moment when I'll be able to touch the Holy Land with my own hands. You can't imagine how excited I am. The trip is scheduled for the spring, four months from now, and already the idea has me so excited I can hardly sleep. The plan is to travel to Trieste. We'll meet up with other garinim there to take the ship to Palestine. The matter of the boat still hasn't been decided and it's possible that instead of leaving from Trieste we'll leave from Venice. I hope it turns out that way so I'll have the chance to see a little bit of the world.

You ask me for news from Golochov. What a difficult task you've given me! Nothing happens here—nothing can ever happen here—at least, nothing of importance.

Nevertheless, I'll try to bring you up to date on the latest events. I'll begin by giving you a cordial Mazal Tov. You have a new cousin! Your Aunt Dora gave birth. Yes, sir, another boy. You can just imagine the disappointment that your Uncle Shmuel suffered, with this, his sixth male child. He didn't say anything, of course, but you

146

could see the disappointment all over his face. At the Brit Milah he didn't talk to anybody. He barely acknowledged the congratulations he received. I don't know why, but they gave the boy three names: Zalman Reuben Nachum. Poor kid, so little and with a name like that on his back!

The same day your cousin was born, Mrs. Riva Bronstein died in childbirth. The little fellow passed away the following day. It was a tragic episode that was felt throughout the whole shtetl. Who knows if the naming of your cousin had anything to do with what happened.

Do you remember I had written you that Ruchel Portnoy and her mother were leaving Golochov? Well, they already arrived in New York. Frimca The Dispenser of Advice must feel lucky to be in America, where she can meet so many new people who are ready to listen to her.

There have been two marriages in the town since you left. Pinchas Vinograd married Ida Kremerman who, as you will remember, was the love of his life. Her parents didn't want to let her get married because they say that Pinchas doesn't earn a living, but she threatened them (according to Mrs. Kremerman herself) that if they didn't let her marry Pinchas she'd never get married. Besides— and this is me talking—who earns a living in Golochov?

If the first marriage took place against the will of the parents, the second one took place against the will of the couple. The Rothcops arranged a sheedech for their daughter with the son of Rav Levinson. They probably paid the poor guy a nice dowry for him to agree to marry Zipora. Although, if not him, they would have had to pay it to someone else, because I don't believe there's a man to be found who would want to marry that girl. Neither do I believe that Zipora is thrilled about being married to an intellectual like Misha Levinson. She definitely would have preferred to marry somebody without too many smarts upstairs, at least to have the advantage over him in a few departments. They say that marriages are made in heaven, but this is one that surely wasn't.

I saved the worst news for last. It happened four months ago; so, it's not very fresh news, although it is for you. Rav Zuntz also left Golochov, not for America or Eretz Israel, but for heaven. He departed like a saint, at the end of prayers in the synagogue. He chose a mournful date to do it. It was the 9th of Av, at twelve noon, when he collapsed in the middle of the congregation. They all thought he had fainted from fasting, especially because on two recent occasions he had passed out; but Rav Zuntz hadn't fainted. His old heart had given out all of a sudden, just like that, and the old man departed this world from one minute to the next. The burial took place the next day and I tell you I never saw so many people at the cemetery. I didn't know the old man was so admired. I dare say that the fact of his having died in the synagogue, on the 9th of Av, had a lot to do with the big turnout for his funeral. As you know, the people from the shtetl are very superstitious. Even the pair of atheists from the town came to pay their respects. After all, the lerer had taught three generations of children. More than a teacher, Zuntz was a true erudite on questions of The Law, a humanist, and a philosopher. Right after his death, several of his writings were circulated through the shtetl and—according to what I've heard—the scholars here were very impressed. But I'll tell you what impressed me, and you're not going to believe this, but half way through the funeral— remember, it was July 21st, the middle of summer—a light rain began to fall, a luminous drizzle, as fine as the one that you and I saw only once in our lives—when they buried your father, last summer, in the same cemetery in Golochov. Do you remember the impression that detail made on us? I say "detail" because apparently no one remembers it. I believe that something similar happened this time too. The drizzle was almost invisible and not many people noticed it. If it hadn't been for our clothes getting damp, I think nobody would have realized it. I, on the other hand,

148

was very much aware of it. I had the feeling that it was heaven's response to what was happening, a participation in the grief, as if the angels were crying.

Affectionately,

Berl

12

On his first night in Lárida, Leon Edri slept under the open sky, stretched out on a bench in the city's main plaza. He had left the Lubinsky family in a small boarding house called Pensión Lárida, where only a single room was available. Doña Maruja, the landlady, a very pleasant woman, recommended other lodging nearby and told Leon how to get there, but without giving him an address. The boy walked around the neighborhood for more than an hour without finding the place (whose name, to top things off, he couldn't remember). Unable to communicate with anyone and feeling too ashamed to go back to the boarding house where his friends were, he began wandering the streets without any fixed destination, frequently stopping to rest his arms from the burdensome weight of his small suitcase.

Late in the day he came to a plaza where he found himself looking up at an immense building with a polished stone façade. It was only three stories high, but it occupied the entire block and had a row of windows that stretched the length of each floor. The magnitude of the structure and the presence of armed guards indicated that it was an important government building. A big black sedan, preceded by two motorcycles, had just stopped in front of the main entrance. Several policemen cleared the sidewalk of pedestrians to leave an open path from the car to the massive front entrance. Numerous onlookers, all of them men and, for the most part, young, crammed in against the police cordon to see what was happening. Leon drew closer. Truthfully, there wasn't anything special to look at. The black sedan remained parked next to the curb while the driver, in shirtsleeves, peered out impassively at the crowd gathered in front. In the rear seat, a handsome young man of about twenty or twenty-five, elegantly dressed, was examining the contents of a briefcase.

Who arrived?" a boy asked Leon.

Leon wasn't able to answer nor could he understand what had been said to him.

"Who arrived?" the boy asked again, addressing somebody else.

"No one."

"Well...?"

"Someone's leaving."

"Doctor Ulpiano Méndez de la Torre," said a third bystander.

"Isn't that him in the car?"

"No way, man! That's his son, Ulpianito Méndez."

Leon observed the young man looking over some papers he had taken from his briefcase but he got the impression he wasn't really reading, just making himself look busy; first of all, so he wouldn't have to look up at the intimidating crowd; and secondly, to give himself an air of importance. *One day I'll dress like that*, Leon fantasized. At a certain point, the elegant young man looked up and saw Leon. Of all those milling around outside the car, Leon was certain of one thing: the sophisticated passenger in the back seat was staring at him. *I must really look different*, Leon thought, aware that he probably called attention to himself with his coarse suit and old-fashioned haircut. He felt uncomfortable, but didn't lower his eyes. The immigrant Jew and the poised aristocrat continued staring at each other, as if locked in a confrontation, in a test of wills, each one having made up his mind not to be the first to give in and look away.

The door of the imposing building opened and a distinguished-looking gentleman came out, surrounded by an entourage. He was robust, with a dark complexion and a shock of wavy white hair; handsome for a man who was probably sixty. Someone opened the car door for him and he got in. Seated next to the young man, it was easy to see how much they resembled each other. *That must be his father*, Leon thought, not taking his eyes from his adversary. When the car started up, the confrontation of wills between Leon and the younger Méndez ended, without either one remaining the winner. Little did the young oligarch seated in the car and the bedraggled immigrant standing in the street imagine that their paths would cross again many years later. The two motorcycles started off in tandem, clearing the way for the black sedan to follow them at full speed. As soon as they left, Leon noticed that the rear license plate had no numbers, just letters: ***GOBERNACIÓN***.

The large building of the Provincial Government of Obondó faced the Plaza de la República, the city's main public square, which took up an entire block and was bordered on its other three sides by colonial mansions that housed many different kinds of businesses, the most bustling of all being the Café Real, through whose large, always open doors wafted the pleasant aroma of coffee that could be detected from quite a distance away. On one of the side streets, from the middle of the block to the corner, arose the imposing Cathedral of San Judas Tadeo.

The same physical layout that Leon had found in the country villages was repeated in the city, except that the dimensions were greater. A public square marked the center of town. Instead of a government house, there was a government palace; instead of a church, there was a cathedral.

The plaza itself struck him as charming, with its tropical ambiance, which differentiated it from the European plazas, even the most provincial ones. Four footpaths crossed it from side to side, two from the midway point of the streets at opposite ends and two from the corners diagonally opposite each other. Between the paths stood large trees and tall palms that gave the plaza the character of a park. Right in the center, on a large pedestal, and larger than life, was a bronze statue of a man in early nineteenth-century military attire, with his head held high, his left hand resting on the sword that hung from his belt, and his right hand over of his heart.

Since it was beginning to grow dark, Leon looked for a place to rest. Almost all the benches along the footpaths were occupied either by men sitting alone or small groups of men engaged in lively conversation. From a distance one bench that appeared to be free turned out to have a bundle on top, covered in newspaper. Leon walked past it and sat down on the next bench, alongside an old man dressed completely in white. Feeling fatigued from his journey, all he wanted to do was sit down; his suitcase was weighing him down and, even if he had the strength to keep walking, he didn't know where to go. Suddenly the bundle on the bench next to him moved. That was when Leon realized that under the newspapers were two little boys, about eight years of age, barefoot and in tattered clothes, sleeping with their heads in the middle of the bench and their feet pointed towards both ends. That's all Leon needed to make up his mind to follow their example and stay put for the night. As soon as the old man dressed in white stood up, Leon stretched out on the bench, laying his head against his suitcase, just as he had done in the train station in Budapest, six months and seven thousand miles earlier.

He slept soundly, oblivious to the hard bed and rigid pillow, undisturbed either by the street noise or the dampness of the night. When the cathedral bells woke him at six the next morning, it took him a few minutes to realize where he was, and when he figured that out and what time it was, a smile crossed his lips. He felt thankful; despite an aching neck and sore ribs, despite being cold and hungry, he was happy. He stretched. The boys on the bench next to him were already gone; the plaza looked deserted. Leon decided that it was too early to go back to the boarding house and that he would do well to wait before joining his friends. So, he stayed where he was for another hour, either standing or sitting next to his suitcase, delighting in feeling the warmth of the sun on his numbed bones and in watching the pedestrians and cars return to the empty streets. Something in his heart told him that he had reached his final destination.

The Lubinskys were eating breakfast when Leon arrived at the boarding house.

"Isn't there a bathtub where you're staying?" Anna asked.

"Do I look that dirty?" Leon said, evading the question.

"Yes, dear."

"Take a bath here," Chaim interjected. "There's no tub, but there's a great shower. And get into some clean clothes; we've got an interview."

"An interview?"

"Yes!" Chaim said enthusiastically, and then proceeded to tell him how, the night before, at the rooming house, he had met a certain Manes Finstein from Novoselitsa, who had arrived a year ago and was one of twenty Jews in Lárida. Finstein told him of another Jew, also from Besarabia, who had settled in Lárida thirteen years ago, a year before the outbreak of the First World War. He was the richest Jew in the city, which did not mean a great deal, since all the rest were poor. Still, it could be said that he was rich. Above all, more than money, he had a big heart. His name was Nathan Gottlieb. He lived with his wife and two daughters in a large, elegant house, which despite its fine touches, fell short of being luxurious. Nathan Gottlieb's home was always open to any Jew who showed up in this part of the world. Not only would Nathan receive him with open arms but—and this was the most important thing—he would help him find work. Gottlieb owned a textile store where he sold fabrics he imported from France, fine wools from England, and lesser quality textiles from Czechoslovakia. Whenever a *landsman* showed up (as Nathan called his Eastern European fellow Jews, although strictly speaking they were not "compatriots"), the good man would

155

hand him an assortment of fabrics to sell. The newly arrived immigrant, carting the bundle on his shoulder, would go from town to town, from house to house, selling his merchandise. Only when he finished selling all of it, would he return to Gottlieb's shop to turn in the money (keeping the difference in price for himself) and to pick up another batch. Manes Finstein earned his living that way, just the way several Jewish immigrants before him earned theirs. Now he, in turn, wanted to help the new arrivals, telling them who could be useful to them. He had no fear of competition, Manes assured Chaim Lubinsky, because, in his own words, "this country is so big there's enough for everybody and, besides, I intend to quit this line of work soon."

Around ten in the morning Edri and Lubinsky arrived at Nathan Gottlieb's store, located right in the center of the city. Above the door, the sign read: Ideal Fabrics. The store wasn't very wide but it extended far back. The walls on both sides were covered with rolls of fabric that reached to the ceiling and were supported on a wooden platform some eight inches above the floor. In front of the stacks of fabric was a row of long tables that the sales clerks used for laying out and measuring the cuttings. The two boys walked down the center of the store directly towards the back, where the bookkeeping was done. A bald, dark-complexioned, middle-aged man was writing in a large ledger that took up the entire desktop. He was working in shirtsleeves, but covering his right arm was a small piece of black cloth, an extra sleeve of sorts, to keep any ink from getting on his shirt. On his forehead he had a visor that shaded his eyes from the light bulb that hung just a few inches above him.

"Don Nathan," the man called out as soon as he saw the two boys coming his way. "Don Nathan, you are needed," he called out again when Chaim and Leon reached his desk, knowing beforehand what the boys were going to say.

"I'm coming, Don Pascual," a voice answered from behind a pile of fabric.

Pascual Barriga had been taking care of the books for Ideal Fabrics ever since Nathan Gottlieb opened for business some ten years ago. He had developed a talent for recognizing from a distance just what a person he had never seen before wanted: whether he was coming in to buy, to sell, to ask about the prices or to speak with one of the sales clerks, the owner, or himself. In the case of Leon and Chaim no special talent was required for identifying them as recently arrived immigrants, since that much was obvious by the look on their faces and the clothes they were wearing.

"Ah!" Nathan exclaimed on seeing the young boys and recognizing them as "landsmen." For the old, sentimental traditionalist that he was, seeing a pair of new faces obviously coming to swell the ranks of Lárida's Jewish community was reason enough for great satisfaction, and even more so when it involved young people who could contribute energy and enthusiasm. The old man rushed towards them.

"*Shalom aleichem*. Welcome, boys, welcome," Gottlieb said in Yiddish while embracing them.

Such an effusive and unexpected reception left Edri and Lubinsky completely baffled.

"Thank you, thank you," one of them said, nearly tripping over his words.

"Very nice to meet you. Thank you," repeated the other one.

Nathan Gottlieb had a special reason for his excitement. For several years he had been pressing those of his community to gather for Friday evening prayers, but his efforts in convening ten Jewish males, the minimum number required for conducting prayers, always fell short. Only during the days of Rosh Hashanah and Yom Kippur did they come to his house without him having to beg them. There were twenty Jews in Lárida—twenty-eight, counting the children—but he was never able to gather the required number of males. When

157

one wanted to, the other one couldn't; when one was not traveling, the other one was sick. What exasperated old Gottlieb the most was that there were almost always nine Jewish men available, not seven, or eight, but nine. The fact that he was one Jew short, just one, drove him crazy. Now, with the arrival of the two boys—and God's help— the *minyan* was assured.

"Come, boys. Sit down."

Gottlieb pulled up some chairs and arranged them around a small table. He sat down first.

"Tell me, where are you from?"

"Trilesy."

"I'm from Golochov."

"Ah, so you're not brothers?"

"No, sir."

"Tri… what?"

"Trilesy."

"Where is it?"

"In the Ukraine, near Fastov."

"Aha! …. The Ukraine."

Nathan Gottlieb was a man of medium height, somewhat heavy and a bit flabby. He was probably fifty years old, fifty shop-worn years; he looked closer to sixty. A native of Rumania, his skin had aged in the tropics. His eyes, of an indeterminate color, somewhere between gray and green, always had a fixed look to them, denoting curiosity, like those of a child watching a puppet. His abundant, white hair, always clean and a little disheveled, stood out above his broad forehead. His flabby cheeks, reddish like his neck and bulbous nose, drooped down over both sides of his thick lips. The most agreeable thing about that caricature of a face was the kindly smile that crossed it at every opportunity, exposing a pair of big upper front teeth gap between them.

Gottlieb spoke to the boys in a paternal tone, and as he asked them questions he told them about his own life. Chaim and Leon filled him in on details about where they were from, their families, and their aspirations.

"Fifteen and seventeen years old?"

"Almost eighteen," Leon said, stretching the truth a bit.

"But you're just kids! I was twenty-five when I left home. What's more, I didn't make the trip by myself; my brother came with me. The fact that your father died on the way, those are things that rest with God," the old man told Chaim. "But letting you travel on your own at your age," he added, addressing Leon, "that's pure madness. How did they ever let you?"

Edri shrugged his shoulders.

"And what about you, did you come straight to Lárida?" Leon asked, changing the subject.

"No, son, I didn't."

Leon felt moved. How good it sounded to be called son, even though it came from a stranger!

"I spent time in several countries before coming here," Nathan continued. "First, I stayed in Guayaquil, then I lived for a time in Quito; from there I went to Bogotá where I also attempted to put down roots. I tried other places until I finally stopped here. I liked it right away. The same day I arrived, I sold some watches I had brought with me and made good money off them. I had a feeling that things would go well for me in Lárida; and I wasn't wrong. That was 1914."

"You were the only Jew here, for sure," Chaim ventured a guess.

"No. There were two others here when I arrived, both Sephardic Jews: Salomon Ben Zion and Elias Shitrit. At first, they didn't want to know anything about me, perhaps because they had money and I didn't. They didn't say a word to me for years, not until I tried to organize a *minyan* for prayers at Yom Kippur." Gottlieb burst out laughing before continuing. "You don't know the trouble we had reaching an agreement! They say the prayers in a different order, not to mention the pronunciation or the melodies. But we managed to understand one another more or less. We were seven *Ashkenazis* and three Sephardic Jews. We ended up praying in a manner that was neither here nor there," he concluded, gesticulating with his hands.

The boys laughed, not so much because it seemed funny to them but because they felt that was what was expected of them.

"Where are you staying?" Gottlieb asked, sounding like someone bringing his interrogation to a close.

"At the Pensión Lárida."

"Doña Maruja's boarding house, yes, I know her. Boys, I want you to come and have dinner at my house on Friday evening. With your mother and your brother and sister, of course," he added, addressing Chaim. "Around seven, all right?"

"Thank you very much, Don Nathan," Chaim said on behalf of his family and his friend, and then paused before daring to continue. "The truth is that... we came to see you—"

"Ah, yes!" Gottlieb interrupted. "You two are looking for work."

"Yes, sir," the two boys answered in unison.

"Well, I think I can help you in that regard," the old man affirmed, and he went on to explain what they more or less already knew.

Nathan Gottlieb would provide each one with an assortment of twenty cuttings for them to go out and sell door to door. Each piece measured two yards, twenty inches in length, which was what was needed on average to make a dress or a suit. The merchant gave them an explanation of the different types of cloth and fabrics, their widths, quality, and prices. He also showed them styles and fashions, indicating which merchandise was more appropriate for men and which was more suitable for older women, middle-aged women, and young girls. Finally, he described for them the city and adjacent towns, specifying which districts they should cover in order not to conflict with the territory of other vendors. Leon and Chaim were able to begin working right then and there, if they wanted to, and they would earn ten percent on their sales.

"If you can sell about eight cuttings a day," Gottlieb told them, turning to look at Don Pascual Barriga, as if asking for confirmation of his calculations, "or let's say, some fifty pieces a week, you'll be able to earn a very decent living."

"Don Nathan," Leon Edri said in a firm voice, "if I sell five hundred pieces a week, will you pay me fifteen percent?"

Nathan Gottlieb smiled kindly.

"Five hundred, is that all?" said the old man, laughing with the candid laughter of those who have a sense of humor and know how to enjoy a joke.

Nathan Gottlieb had no idea how serious the boy was.

13

"Don Gaetano."

"Yes?"

"A young man wishes to see you."

"What does he want?"

"He didn't say. I think he's selling something."

"I'm busy. Tell him to come back tomorrow."

"It's the same young man who was here yesterday and you had me tell him to come back today."

"Well, tell him to come back tomorrow. Understand?"

"Yes, sir."

Gaetano Céspedes sighed heavily so that his assistant would hear him before leaving the room. It was his way of making sure he understood how much it annoyed him to be interrupted with trivial matters. In truth, Céspedes did nothing all day except cultivate his image as a busy company official. Whoever came into his office would find him with a fountain pen in hand and a stack of papers on top of his desk. Don Gaetano would lay the pen aside and shuffle his papers before speaking.

"Excuse me one second, please," he would say while putting things in order for the sole purpose of hiding under the pile of official documents the verses that kept him busy for hours on end. He considered it his right and well-deserved privilege to spend his time composing poetry rather than putting in an honest day's work. After all, those were some of the prerogatives of the important position he held and for which he was kept waiting for more than twenty-five years.

Gaetano Céspedes was not from a well-to-do family and consequently neither money nor influence could have gained him access to a high position in government. It came to him as a result of many years, not of hard work, but of flattery and perseverance. He was eighteen when he began working for the Autonomous Regional Corporation of Railroads, a government entity that was not known by its real name but by a much simpler one: National Railroads.

It is possible that when Céspedes went to work, weeks before the end of the nineteenth century, no one knew the Autonomous Regional Corporation of Railroads by that or any other name, owing to the fact that there were simply no railroads in any of the provinces. The Corporation was busy at that time planning routes and coordinating the work with the government of Great Britain, which would supply the rails, the technical assistance, and eventually the cars and locomotives. Gaetano was the assistant to the secretary of the assistant's assistant; he was, in practical terms, the office messenger. Two years went by before he made his first ascent (by means of smiles and a few fibs) on what was a long, slow series of promotions that culminated in being appointed head of the office in Lárida, the capital of the Province of Obondó, a job that he began barely a month ago.

"Come in!" Gaetano Céspedes shouted when he heard someone knocking.

The assistant opened the door part way and stuck his head in. He was an extremely thin man, pale and with bulging eyes.

"Excuse me, Don Gaetano. It's the boy again. He gave me this package for you."

Céspedes motioned with his head for him to come in. The assistant entered and placed the package on top of the desk. Gaetano patted it. It contained something soft. He tried to untie the cord, but gave up after a few seconds.

"Silvio, do you have a pair of scissors?"

"Allow me, Don Gaetano."

The assistant lifted the package to his mouth and began to take the cord apart with his teeth while his boss looked on impatiently.

"Well?"

"Almost done, Don Gaetano."

The man struggled a bit more until he managed to break the cord. He was going to place the package on the desk again when Céspedes grabbed it out of his hands and brusquely unwrapped it. On seeing the contents, he smiled approvingly. Before his eyes he had a first-rate, gray-striped English fabric, like that of the fine suits worn by the wealthy men of the city.

"Gee! What a beautiful fabric!" exclaimed the assistant.

Gaetano Céspedes shot him a glance as if to say: *What are you doing putting your nose in where it doesn't concern you?* Silvio lowered his eyes and made a gesture that clearly meant: *I'm sorry, Don Gaetano.*

"Is he still here?"

"Yes, sir. He insists on seeing you."

"All right…tell him to come in."

"Yes, sir."

The assistant left and returned seconds later, followed by a handsome young man.

"This way," he said, and when the visitor entered the office, Silvio left and closed the door after him.

"Excuse me a moment, please," Céspedes said while arranging the papers on his desk. "All right, that's that. They told me that you insisted very much on seeing me."

"Leon Edri," said the visitor, extending his hand and putting on his best smile. "Pleased to meet you, Doctor Céspedes."

"Nice to meet you," Céspedes answered, standing up to shake Leon's hand.

The astute Edri had been in the New World barely six months and was already learning the rules of the game. He had addressed Céspedes as "Doctor," just as he would address any high-ranking government official or any wealthy individual of modest education.

"Doctor Céspedes, I took the liberty of coming to see you after learning you were recently appointed to this important post and I assumed you, no doubt, are taking the necessary steps to turn National Railroads into an even greater enterprise than what it is today."

Gaetano Céspedes looked warily upon the young man who spoke to him in such a manner.

"I do my best."

"Of course, doctor, but I know how things are," Leon said with a little smile of complicity. "When there's a new boss everybody is waiting to see what he plans to do. Will he be a person without initiative? Or someone whose presence will make itself felt? Will he be a man capable of executing substantial improvements, a man who will leave his mark on the company?"

Céspedes felt uncomfortable and hardened his wary look.
"Be brief. What is it that you want?"

"I've got an idea that will greatly raise the standing of National Railroads and, while you're about it, put you in high regard with the board of directors."

The look of wariness gave way to curiosity.

"And may I know your idea?"

Leon approached Céspedes and quietly told him in a single word: "Uniforms."

Gaetano was perplexed for a few seconds before asking, also in a soft voice, as if it were a secret: "Uniforms?"

Edri nodded.

"Uniforms?" Céspedes repeated, this time aloud, stepping back.

"Yes, sir. Look…" Leon paused to gather his thoughts. "The last time I rode a train was a few months ago, when I traveled from La Playada to Lárida. During the whole trip there was something about National Railroads that troubled me, but I wasn't able to say exactly what. A few days later I was walking past the railroad station when, suddenly, I realized what it was that had bothered me. The employees of National Railroads don't wear uniforms!"

Leon waited for Gaetano Céspedes to say something, but all the man did was to stare back at him.

"As you've probably realized, I haven't been here long. Before coming to this country, I traveled all over Europe and got to see the most important railroad stations on the continent. It can be said that few people know the European railroads better than I do. I've traveled on many different trains: Russian, Austrian, German, French, you name it, and I can assure you, doctor, that nowhere in the world are there trains, or train stations, where the employees do not wear uniforms."

Gaetano Céspedes followed Leon's discourse with rapt attention.

"Just think what a bad impression a company without employees creates, especially for the cosmopolitan traveler. I say 'without employees' because, since your people don't wear a uniform, no one can identify them. What train station can function efficiently when the passengers don't know who to address? What respectable transportation company doesn't provide its workers with a distinctive uniform?"

"Does the uniform seem so important to you?"

"It's primary. It is the single, most important requirement if National Railroads is to acquire the prestige it deserves. And I am absolutely convinced that the man who succeeds in introducing that clear-sighted improvement will go down in the company's history as one of its principal driving forces."

Gaetano's eyes grew big. He was delighted with what he heard. He already saw himself being congratulated by the company's board of directors and promoted to a high post in the capital of the republic.

"Yes, yes, it's not a bad idea," he said, scratching his cheek. "To tell the truth, I had already thought of that but didn't plan to put it into practice just yet in light of the steep cost."

"That's where you're mistaken! Everybody thinks that uniforms must cost a bundle, but it's not so. If you were to purchase a thousand uniforms..."

"National Railroads has forty-five hundred employees," Gaetano interrupted.

"If you were to purchase that many uniforms," Leon continued, "it would easily cost an arm and a leg; but I have a different idea in mind. You go to a clothing manufacturer and contract for the type of uniform you want, except that you provide the material. As you know, doctor, factories earn a great deal on the raw material, but by supplying it yourself, you'll get a much lower price if you just pay for the labor."

"Yes, yes, of course... but it's not as simple as that. It would be a big headache getting authorization for such an undertaking. You can't imagine what it is to battle the company's board of directors! The problems with bureaucracy, with political conniving..."

Céspedes pursed his lips and shook his head from side to side, as if to say: *It's a lost cause.*

"Okay, but you don't have to outfit all the company's employees with uniforms right away. It can be done in stages," Leon reasoned, adopting a confidential tone. "What if we begin with your department? The Obondó Valley could set the example for all the provinces in the country."

"That would be... a fabulous thing."

"How many workers do you have under your direction?"

"About six hundred."

Leon and Gaetano Céspedes were now speaking confidentially, like partners in a business transaction. In a certain sense, they were.

"And is it within your authority to close a deal like this?"

"If it fits my budget, yes."

"Then we'll make it fit," Leon said with a smile.

14

When Leon Edri formalized the sale of some fifteen hundred yards of dark blue gabardine for National Railroads, Nathan Gottlieb almost fell over backwards. In the ten years since Ideal Fabrics opened, neither he nor any of his sales people had closed a deal of that magnitude. The biggest sale up to that time was not one tenth of what Leon had accomplished. Gottlieb didn't have enough blue gabardine in stock and had to put in an urgent request for ten hundred additional yards, and another ten hundred, and another and another, since on the heels of the contract carried out with National Railroads of the Obondó Province, orders came flooding in from the other provinces. Edri and Lubinsky perfectly complemented one another in their work. They traveled together, and while one was speaking with the head of the regional office, the other was busy convincing the accountant; while one handed out "free samples," the other was in closed-door meetings with the key people, getting their business. When they decided to coordinate their efforts and work as a team, neither of them imagined that they had become lifelong partners.

They traveled together for an entire year throughout the country's principal cities, closing deals with National Railroads in every province, just like they did with other public and private entities. It was a year of hard work in which they learned a great deal, got to know the country and, above all, the customs and mentality of the populace. That was the year in which, little by little, their lives were gradually becoming more normal. At least, they had settled somewhere.

The Lubinskys rented a modest little house in an upper middle-class neighborhood. They worked hard to fix it up, decorate and furnish it. Anna didn't rest until she saw her house impeccably clean, just the way she had maintained the home she had in Trilesy, which was older and smaller than the one in Lárida. The main difference, however, did not reside in the houses' age or size, but in their style. Everything was more modern in the New World: prettier, more comfortable, more pleasant. Chaim adopted the name Jaime, not so much because he liked being called "Don Jaime," but because that's how everybody addressed him, whether he liked it or not. And being addressed as "Don" really suited him, for he had developed into a very serious young man. He looked three or four years older than he was, barely seventeen, not only because of his physical aspect, but also because of his maturity and manner of speech. With dignity and no small success, he had assumed the role as head of the family. Anna, Mordechai, and Bertha only got to see him a couple of days a month, since his trips through the provinces kept him away from home. He never returned empty-handed; he always brought a gift for his sister and another for his brother. He generally gave his mother something needed for the house, which was, in fact, a gift for the whole family. Bertha helped her mother with the domestic chores. No one thought she should attend school, like other girls her age. In the eyes of the family, Bertha was no longer a little girl and her place was at home. Mordechai was, of course, enrolled in school, which would make him the only one in the family who would eventually be accomplished in reading and writing Spanish. It was a second-rate school, since Jaime was far from earning enough money for the tuition that the best school in the city charged and where he would have liked to send his brother. At that time, Jaime didn't know— although he would come to know, years later, when the day came to enroll his own son in the school—that having the money was not enough, that neither his brother nor any other Jew would be accepted into that institution. But Jaime couldn't be upset by what he didn't know. He was happy to see his little brother studying, to know his mother and sister were well, to have a comfortable home, to be earning a living and, above all, to have a future that looked promising. On the other hand, it pained Anna just thinking about what destiny had placed on her adolescent son's shoulders: the responsibility for maintaining a home. But down deep she felt proud to see him so confident and capable.

Leon had rented a room in a home and, like his friend Jaime, was happy to see that he was earning good money and that his future looked bright. Since he didn't have any major expenses, he bought dollars with the earnings he had left over, hiding them in his room and periodically sending some money to his mother, always fearful it would get lost in the mail, as in fact happened on two occasions; but what money he didn't send was also for her, since he had earmarked it for getting his family out of Golochov. He wanted to bring his mother and brothers to Lárida not so much because he missed them but because of his feeling of loyalty to them. From the moment Leibele Edri left home in search of a better world, he never felt the need of maternal warmth. True, he was just an adolescent when he left the *shtetl*, but he had the strength of character that would give him a sense of self-assurance in any situation. He had matured a great deal from that sun-drenched morning when he left the *Leicester Maiden* and stepped ashore on the soil of the Americas. He had turned into a tall, good-looking young man, successful with women and as passionate about them as he was about business.

After the first transaction with National Railroads, Nathan Gottlieb agreed to pay Leon and Jaime eighteen percent commission on their sales. It was an excellent commission and they knew it. But, despite that, a feeling that something wasn't right troubled them the whole time. They couldn't accept the idea of another person benefiting from their work more than they themselves. The arrangement with Gottlieb was to be short lived.

They liked dealing in textiles—in fact, it was the only thing they knew—and they decided to explore the possibility of establishing themselves in that field. Of the three textile factories in the country, two were in Lárida: Lanatex S.A., owned by the Méndez de la Torre

173

family and Lebanon Textile Manufacturers, run by Elias Jamal. Leon and Jaime went to them looking for merchandise to start their own business, but both factories turned them down for lack of satisfactory guarantees. On the other hand, the third factory, National Textiles, located in the capital, proved to be quite accommodating because— as the boys interpreted it—the company wanted to introduce its products into markets dominated by the competition. The new entrepreneurs enthusiastically embraced the opportunity and placed their first order. It was a relatively large purchase, especially for two young men seeking to go into business without any funds. They stocked the store they rented in downtown Lárida with merchandise from National Textiles, on the same street and practically in front of Ideal Fabrics. It isn't that Leon and Jaime planned it that way; on the contrary, they were troubled by the coincidence of a store being available in that precise location, but the central part of the city was small and it was necessary to take whatever was available. At Leon's insistence, they gave the store the presumptuous name of "A Touch of Royalty", even though Jaime would have preferred something less pretentious. Compared to what was available at Ideal Fabrics, merchandise at A Touch of Royalty was of inferior quality, the prices considerably lower, and consequently the profit margin was much smaller. But precisely because it was cheaper, the merchandise sold quickly. The volume of sales, good from the start, grew larger each time. The two young entrepreneurs decided to reinvest their earnings in the business, in equal shares, provided something remained after covering their personal expenses.

Since Leon's needs were less than Jaime's, his money began accumulating. The moment had arrived for him to bring his mother and brothers to America. There was no safe way of sending the money to Golochov, funds they needed for the trip, but neither was it indispensable for them to have it to leave the *shtetl*. His mother had sufficient means to travel as far as Paris, and he could get the money to her there. It was none other than Nathan Gottlieb who offered him the opportunity to do it through one of his suppliers in the French capital. Old Gottlieb loved the boys and, far from feeling bothered by their enterprising ways, he was happy to see that they had gone off on their own and that things were going well for them in their business. He came by frequently to visit them in their store, to chat with them and give them advice they didn't need. Envy was not a part of Gottlieb's character, and where "landsmen" were concerned, his good heart knew no limits.

Leon sent his mother a long letter in which he explained his plans and asked her to get ready for the trip. He wrote frequently, keeping her abreast of how his business was progressing. In his last letter, he informed her that he had sent immigration documents to Paris for her and his two brothers, as well as tickets with an open date for their passage from Le Havre. He gave exact instructions on how to claim the documents and even included a schedule of the company's sailing dates. He also told her that he would send her enough money to cover expenses while they waited for the ship's departure. Four months and a dozen letters later, he finally received the news that he was eagerly awaiting: his family was en route. Two more months would have to pass before he would see them approaching the dock in one of the boats that transported the passengers from the ship to the port of Bellavista. Leon had gone especially to receive them and had been waiting at the dock since early morning. The ship had dropped anchor at the break of dawn, but the passengers didn't begin disembarking until about nine that morning. Leon watched the boats slowly drawing closer to land, unable to distinguish anyone. But at the midway point, Leon spotted his mother. He knew it was she before he could make out her features; maybe by the pose she struck, maybe because of her clothes... Sara Edri. Who wouldn't recognize her from a distance? Leon began jumping up and down and shouting and waving his arms like a little kid. From the distant boat, the gray figure was waving back at him. He saw two more figures, almost her height, join her

175

and then, with her outstretched arm, she pointed to the spot where he was standing.

Leib Edri's reunion with his mother and his two siblings was a very emotional one. He marveled at seeing how much the boys had grown, especially Jonathan, who was chattering away the whole time, unlike Peretz who said nothing but just smiled. Sara wept with joy. Just as Leon saw changes in his brothers, Sara saw changes in her son. Oddly enough, she seemed to be the only person unaffected by time. They had so much to talk about, so much to tell each other, that they conversed well into the night. This continued for four more nights, on board the small motorboat—property of the Santa María River Transport Company—that they took the very same day they were reunited and that slowly carried them upriver, repeating the journey that Leon Edri had made two years earlier. Sara wanted to know every detail of her son's life in Lárida and Leon wanted to know about family and friends in Golochov. Uncle Shmuel and Aunt Dora, how were they? And Uncle Hoise and Aunt Lea? What about his cousins? Is it true that Gabriel is getting married? Had they seen Itzik? What news of Zvi and his brothers? Are they happy in the United States? Where do they live? Who else is leaving Golochov? So many questions, so thirsty to know the fate of a community that for him had become a nostalgic memory! Ruchel, the beautiful, golden-haired girl, was the only one he didn't ask about. Surely it wasn't because he had forgotten her.

The adaptation of the Edri family to its new surroundings was less painful than it had been for the Lubinskys, beginning with their disembarkation in Bellavista, where Leon had made all the necessary arrangements ahead of time so that the formalities would be expedited and ending with their getting settled into accommodations that awaited their arrival in Lárida: a clean, well-furnished house, equipped with all the basic necessities, from pots and soaps to sheets and toilet paper, besides a full-time indigenous domestic to look after things for the family. The ever-meticulous Leon had thought of everything; however, certain things didn't turn out as he had planned. His mother dismissed the servant, not so much because she couldn't communicate with her but because Sara, being a woman who had grown up in poverty and lived her entire life in a *shtetl*, where not even "the rich" had servants, felt uncomfortable having the girl around. Sara was of the opinion that she could fend for herself, that she did the housework much better than a domestic and, what's more, she didn't put much faith in the hygiene and honesty of a stranger in her house. That was her initial reaction, for in less than a year she would change her mind. Peretz and Jonathan didn't want to study. In fact, they were already too big to go to school. Leon had envisioned himself in the role of head of the house, checking the grades his brothers would get or going to the school to speak with one of their teachers, perhaps because he was influenced by the relationship between his partner Jaime and Jaime's brother, Mordechai, or perhaps because he visualized his brothers the way they were back in Golochov, in another period of their lives, without realizing that time plays tricks. For lack of any better occupation, the boys went to work as salaried employees of A Touch of Royalty, which didn't make them or the owners of the store very happy. They quit after a few months, first Peretz and then Jonathan, to try their hand at other endeavors, eventually becoming independent and forging their own destinies. In the meantime, the Edri family lived together under the same roof, in good health and well- being, always grateful to the Almighty.

A Touch of Royalty had barely been in business one year when the store became too small for the amount of business it had.

"The time has come to move to a larger location," Leon said.

"No," Jaime disagreed. "When a business is going well there's no need to move it. We'll open *another* location: the main headquarters. The store we have now will stay where it is and become a branch."

Four months later the main headquarters of A Touch of Royalty was inaugurated with a special promotion that lasted three days, a period in which more merchandise was sold than what the previous store achieved in a month. The ascendant careers of Leon Edri and Jaime Lubinsky had begun. Scarcely six months had passed from the opening of the main headquarters, when the third Touch of Royalty was opened, in Córdoba, a small but cozy city an hour from Lárida. Edri managed the branch stores and Lubinsky the main one, so that they only saw each other in the evenings, when they got together to discuss how things were going.

"Little by little we'll be able to open stores in different cities until we form a national chain," Lubinsky stated on one occasion.

"Yes? And how will we manage them? We barely cope with the three stores that we have now."

"It's all a matter of organization. We'll need to hire a manager for each store."

"No, Jaime, things don't work that way. The stores are doing well because we ourselves manage them. The moment you put a manager in charge and have less hands on, things will start going downhill. In no way should we branch out farther."

"Then what? Are we going to have three stores our entire lives?"

It was a rhetorical question, since both knew the answer was no. They were eager to expand into bigger things, and they stayed awake at night looking for a way to achieve their goal. They investigated the markets for food, clothing, and other goods, but didn't find anything that really grabbed their interest. From time to time, they ran across one business or another that they would have liked to take on, but they lacked the necessary funds to carry it out. One day Jaime came up with a new idea.

"We've done well for ourselves with fabrics, right?"

"Hm, hm," Leon assented.

"Have you ever thought that instead of marketing them, we could manufacture them?"

Leon gave his friend a serious look before laughing.

"Do you know what a textile factory costs?" he asked like someone reprimanding a child.

"I haven't the slightest idea. Millions."

"We don't have enough to buy even one piece of machinery out of all the ones we'll need."

"Possibly."

"So?"

"I was reading an article on the extraordinary advancement that's been made in textile technology. The machinery that was the most modern in the world five years ago is obsolete today. That means," and here he raised his index finger to emphasize his words, "that there are *obsolete factories*, factories that are certainly more modern than National Textiles, but which are obsolete *in England*. One of those factories, or rather, what in fact must be merely "the closed division" of one of the big textile manufacturers, can be bought for... I don't know, but for very little money. Don't you see? What is scrap metal in industrialized countries is gold dust here."

"You don't know what you're talking about. Even if the machinery were acquired at half the price, it would require an investment far beyond our means."

"Neither do you know what you're talking about. Where did you get that business of 'at half price'? Why not a tenth of the price?"

"My God, Chaim! Be serious! We can't even think about a tenth of the price. We don't have the money."

"We don't, but a bank does."

Leon raised his eyebrows.

"I was thinking that a bank could finance the entire deal," Jaime continued. "The credit would be backed by the machinery itself, whose value would be much greater here... The banks are loaded with cash and don't know what to do with it."

"Banks never finance a business at one hundred percent. You have to invest in the project."

"Of course, but that's not a problem. It's simply a matter of presentation. In requesting credit, we can present a study whereby the bank finances half and we the other half."

"Half?"

"Yes. That is...officially. The bank will cover the cost of materials for construction of the plant and provide the letter of credit for purchase of the equipment. We would have to finance the assembly, the raw material, the start-up, the marketing...That would only come to a small fraction of the total, but it involves a cost that's really hard to nail down; we could play with the figures a bit. And even that part we wouldn't have to finance in its entirety. For the initial raw material, for example, we could get credit from the supplier himself. Credit. That's the key. With credit we can run any business, buy whatever we need."

The idea that initially struck Leon as ludicrous gradually seemed more feasible to him as the days went by. To embark on a project like that, he thought it imperative to take three initial steps. In the first place, they had to find a bank, or more precisely, a banker who would be disposed to grant that kind of financing. Assuming the credit could be guaranteed with the machinery itself, that was the least of the problems. In Lárida there had to be a banker who would collaborate if they could strike some chord with him. The second step was to get the right textile plant, at the price and under conditions of payment that would allow the bank to justify the transaction. One of them would have to go to England and begin looking into matters there. Assuming they got the plant and the

180

money, the third step would be to map out the business, predicting every imaginable eventuality whose cost would have to be covered from start to finish. The financing at every stage would have to be worked out separately, leaving a margin of error for time as well as cost. It would be fatal to be left without funds or credit before the plant was up and running.

As they had assumed, they found a banker disposed to provide them financing. More than disposed, the man was eager to do business and pushed the young industrialists to move ahead with matters. Edri and Lubinsky secured an option to buy land in Lárida's industrial section, perhaps at a higher price than what it was worth, but with a five-year period to pay it off. The next step was to look for the factory and, if they found it, to negotiate a price equal to or below the base price set by the study. Neither of the two wanted to go to Europe and each insisted that the other one make the trip. Finally, Leon recognized he was the more suitable of the two to go. After all was said and done, he was older than his partner, had more experience and could get along better in English and French.

"Our problem is our age," Leon said. "No one takes us seriously."

"I don't see we've had any problems because of that."

"Maybe not, but things are different in Europe."

"You know something, Leib? If we formed a company, you could speak using its name instead of your own. I think that would create a better impression. Don't forget that the lawyer advised us to set up a corporation to formalize our partnership."

"We've done fine until now without any corporation."

"Yes, but why continue operating that way? If we're going to grow, let's do it the right way."

"All right, then, let's do it."

"I'll go see the lawyer tomorrow. That's a definite."

"The corporation must have a name that makes an impression. A name that shows strength, that inspires confidence... The name of a company is like a business card."

"That's exactly what I meant to say before."

"What do you think of *International Trading Company?*" he asked, saying the name in English. "Names in English make a stronger impression."

Jaime laughed. He knew his friend's weakness quite well: trying to impress.

"No," Leon continued. "*International Trading Corporation* is better. 'Corporation' sounds more important than 'Company'."

"Exactly what does the term '*Trading*' mean?" Jaime asked, pretending to take his friends words seriously.

"Mercantile. 'Trading' literally means 'exchanging.' "

"And what does that have to do with our business?"

" 'Exchanging.' That means 'commerce'."

"But that's a very general term. It doesn't say anything."

"Okay, we eliminate 'Trading.' The important thing is to keep 'International' in the title; it's a key word."

Jaime tried hard not to laugh. He always made fun of his friend's bombastic vanity.

"Why don't you try something that's more concrete?" he asked.

Leon thought for a few seconds.

"*Edri and Lubinsky International Corporation.*"

Jaime couldn't contain himself anymore and burst out laughing.

"What's the matter?" Leon protested. "What's so funny?"

Jaime was laughing so hard he couldn't answer.

"I put myself first," Leon explained, doubting if that was what was making his friend laugh, "because I wanted to keep the names alphabetical."

Jaime kept on laughing.

"Okay. You choose the name," Leon said, annoyed.

"Suppose we say something short, less complicated?"

"Tell me, then."

Jaime took a deep breath and looked up at the ceiling for a few moments.

"SILEJA Ltd."

"SILEJA? And what's that!"

"**SI**mply, **LE**on and **JA**ime."

Jerusalem

December 25, 1928

Dear Leon,

Here I am in the Holy Land. Jerusalem, finally! I arrived in Eretz Israel two months ago and up to this point I haven't been able to get used to seeing my dream turned into a reality.

You can't imagine what we went through to get here. The trip, which normally takes twenty days, lasted sixty. As you will remember, our departure from Golochov got postponed four times. In the end, we didn't leave from Trieste or Venice, but from Odessa. It seems that it's not my destiny to know even one little corner of the West. Ships left Trieste and Venice with groups that came from Poland, but they told us that there was no more room. Arie, our instructor, left with one of those groups. They sent us to Kishinev, where we joined up with another group led by a friend of Arie's. His name is Guiora; he stands six feet, five inches tall and has the same dynamism as Arie. From Kishinev we went to Odessa. There, a third group and a Turkish ship were waiting for us. All together there were thirty-six of us—boys and girls. The ship that had the Odessa-Sevastopol-Istanbul route was a filthy freighter, but our spirits were so high that we hardly noticed. We sang and joked nonstop for the four days of the trip. What none of us knew was that the ship was full of contraband. Evidently, the port authorities knew about it, because as soon as the ship docked, they arrested the captain and the whole crew. They didn't detain us, but they did confiscate our passports. According to the official in charge, it was a temporary measure until things were cleared up. I don't know what needed to be cleared up. We were foreigners in transit and had nothing to do with the contraband. Our explanations and protests did us no good. Maybe it would have been different had we been English or French citizens, but as Russian Jews we could expect very little. It goes without saying that "our" consul didn't lift a finger to help us. Would you

184

believe that they left us out on the street for a whole month, eating up the savings we had brought with us, without any possibility of continuing the trip, not until "things were cleared up"! And things only got cleared up when we pooled our money and gave it to the official in charge. We were so naïve that it took us all that time before we understood what we should have done from the beginning. I was left with the impression that everything in that old city of a glorious past works on the basis of bakshish, the traditional bribe. You can probably imagine how happy we were to leave.

Sailing aboard another Turkish freighter of dubious reputation, we reached Piraeus, where we had to wait three weeks until the ship that sailed ten days prior to our arrival returned, all because of the delay we had suffered. It was a Greek vessel that sailed the Athens-Rhodes-Limasol-Beirut-Jaffa-Alexandria-Athens route. I can't say we had a bad stay in Greece. We strolled around and learned a lot about the splendid Greek civilization. Still, during our last days there we nearly starved (believe me, I'm not exaggerating), since we didn't have a cent left to buy anything to eat. As you see, the road to the Holy Land is filled with hardship.

On the day that we were scheduled to reach port, I went out on the prow of the ship at dawn, scanning the horizon with the impatience of a lover waiting to see his sweetheart. I must have spent hours on end like that. My heart swelled with joy when I saw a tenuous yellow line in the distance, a blurred border that separated sea and sky. There it was, before my eyes, the Holy Land!

Sometime later the coast became more visible. It was completely flat except for where the city of Jaffa stood: a promontory right next to the sea. The sky was perfectly blue, without a single cloud, just as my mother told me it would be. The city seemed to have come out of the Thousand and One Nights. How pretty it was! Exactly what the name Jaffa means: pretty. I think that at that moment I found myself more or less in the same place where the whale swallowed Jonah. I don't know if Jonah's extraordinary adventure is true, but I can say

185

that I felt the way he must have felt when that enormous fish tossed him up on the coast of Jaffa: bewildered. I thought a miracle had happened.

When we disembarked, I knelt and kissed the ground. I'm afraid that I made myself look a little ridiculous, not for the sentiment I displayed but for the certainly melodramatic gesture itself. What's ironic—now that I think about it—is that, kneeling there on the dock, it wasn't the soil I love so much that I kissed, but the cement, which was probably imported from another country. I realized that some people laughed. It's not important. My gesture was symbolic rather than material. I was happy. And I wasn't the only one who kissed the ground either. Several people did, among them a devout Jew with an enormous black beard who traveled with us from Athens.

The port was alive with shouting and confusion. I was in a daze. I heard people speaking Yiddish, English, Arabic, and Hebrew. Hebrew! It was the first time I heard the language of the Bible as a living language. The vernacular that for centuries was reserved for the study of sacred texts was like music to my ears.

We didn't run into any hitches with the British authorities in completing the formalities for our immigration and an hour later we were on buses heading north. We passed through the city of Jaffa, which no longer seemed as pretty to me as it did from the sea. I would say that the Arab cities with their minarets are like ugly women with good figures: they look attractive from a distance, but under closer scrutiny their charm quickly crumbles when you see their bad teeth and pimply skin. The same can be said of the dilapidated houses that one sees when walking through the narrow, dirty, foul-smelling streets of Jaffa. As soon as one enters the Jewish section, the contrast is impressive. By comparison, everything looks new, clean, orderly. The town of Tel Aviv, which is like a neighborhood of Jaffa, sitting right next door to it, really caught my attention. Our guide told us that within a few years Jaffa would be a neighborhood of Tel Aviv. What optimism!

They divided us up among several kibutzim. I was assigned to one called Gan Shmuel: The Garden of Samuel. It consists of a series of little houses in the middle of orange groves and other crops. It has a population of around two hundred, so that our arrival—nine young people in all—was a big event. The people in the kibutz gave us a really warm welcome. They all called me Baruch, because Berl sounded too Yiddish to them and here they only want to speak Hebrew. Well, so now I'm Baruch. I'll keep the name, just the way you kept the name they gave you in your new adoptive land, my dear Leon.

At night there was a big party in our honor. It had been days since I had eaten so well. We sang and danced around a bonfire that night, under a starry sky. The whole evening was fabulous; I'll remember it the rest of my life.

But in the kibutz it's not all play. The next day we began working—each one with a different task—like we had never worked before. They had me dig a trench on the perimeter of the orange groves and I finished the day's work totally exhausted, with an aching back and my hands all blistered. The work was too hard for me and they had to give me something else to do. Now I'm laying irrigation pipes with a friend. We came to redeem the land and that gives us great satisfaction, but believe me, dear friend, it's hard work... very hard work.

This is the second time I've come to Jerusalem. Do you think I could stand two months in Eretz Israel without getting to know the Holy City? A few days after arriving at the kibutz, I went up to Jerusalem with a friend. I say "went up," not only because whoever goes to Jerusalem ascends spiritually, as they taught us in the cheder, but because the city sits physically on the heights, atop the mountains of Judea. You can't imagine the impact it has on you when you see it for the first time. From the distance it looks like a magical city atop Mount Zion, casting light towards the remotest corners of the world. In the early evening hours it has a pinkish hue, no doubt because of the setting sun that reflects off its stone houses. I imagine that's just how its conquerors saw it: the Babylonians, the Romans, the Arabs, the Crusaders, the Turks, and the English. Jerusalem, "City of Peace" that knew no peace, what destiny awaits you now?

Today I spent my time walking through the City of David, visiting its synagogues, churches and mosques, its walls and its streets. By chance my visit happened to fall on a Christian holy day, which was very interesting because the churches were packed with worshippers—pilgrims as well as Christian Arabs—and there was a lot of activity. To be honest, I never knew there were so many priests in the Holy City: Greek Orthodox, Russian, Catholic, Protestant, and Armenian. Clearly, the Christians are a small minority, compared to the Muslims and Jews. But, judging by the number of churches, one would think that the Christian community isn't so small. Their houses of worship compete with those of the Muslims in size and splendor, although the latter overshadow them with the Dome of the Rock, better known as the "Mosque of Omar" (except it isn't really a mosque but a monument); it has a beautiful golden cupola that stands out above the city. Barely a few steps away from the Mosque, which the Muslims built right over what is the most sacred place for us Jews, stands the Western Wall, the one Christians call "The Wailing Wall," one of those that encircled the Holy Temple in the glorious era when we were sovereigns in our land.

I stood in front of the Western Wall a long time watching the Hasidic Jews, dressed in their black robes and fur-trimmed hats, rhythmically rocking back and forth while they recited their prayers. They prayed at the foot of the Wall as if it were an altar. I think that in a certain sense it is an altar: imposing and solemn. I couldn't help

188

but feel moved before the austerity of the great white stones that have witnessed so much history in silence.

Now, in the home of my friend's relatives, in the tranquility of the night, I am writing you this letter that I have put off for too long. From the window of my room I have a wonderful view of Jerusalem. I have been thinking that I would like to live here. The city has something special, something that draws me in. Maybe it's not exactly the city itself, for there are others that are larger, cleaner, and more beautiful. It could be said that the emotional state of Jews makes them feel a magic that in reality does not exist. Still, non-Jews who visit the City of David also fall under its spell. There is no doubt the charm is real. There is a physical explanation for this effect and I believe myself to be among the few who have discovered what it is. It's the air. Yes, the air. It is light and perfectly translucent. It is the ideal air for meditation. Everything looks clearer: thoughts as well as objects. At this very moment that I am writing you, I have gone to the window and looked out at the sky. It is filled with stars, thousands of stars. I never believed there were so many. They shine like a shower of diamonds in the black firmament. Not nearly as many stars can be seen in the Russian nights, not even on the clearest ones. Looking at the sky on a night like this, any night in the Holy Land, one truly appreciates—not deduces but feels—how immense the universe is and how insignificant we are. Do you know something? It wasn't by chance that our ancestors decided to erect the temple to God here, in Jerusalem.

Affectionately,

Baruch

15

"Your attention, please...attention."

An immediate hush fell over the gathering. Everybody turned around to face the center of the room; all eyes were fixed on the person who had taken center stage.

"We're all here tonight," Jaime Lubinsky told his guests, "to discuss our future."

There were about forty people in the room: the Lubinskys, a dozen couples, and a dozen single men. Most had nowhere to sit, despite the fact that the hosts had set out all the available chairs. But the cramped quarters did not dampen the lively atmosphere or the pleasantness of the evening. Never before had so many Jews gathered in Lárida. Everyone who was invited showed up. Jaime had taken the initiative of speaking to each one in personally extending the invitation to his house. For her part, Anna Lubinsky prepared a delicious mango *strudel* (back then, apples were not available in Lárida) and a honey cake, which Bertha offered to the guests while her mother served coffee.

"When I arrived in Lárida, some five years ago, it was very difficult to organize a *minyan*," Jaime continued, pleased to see that he had everyone's attention. "With the passage of time I have seen many of our people settle here in Lárida. Every year three or four new families put down roots in our city. I calculate that today the number of Jews in Lárida, counting the children, is more than one hundred. In other words, we've reached the point where we no longer think of ourselves as isolated Jews. Whether we like it or not, we are now part of a colony, the Jewish Colony of Lárida."

"Excuse me, Jaime," Wolf Galitzki timidly interrupted. "We're not a 'colony' but a 'community.' A person can speak of 'the Dutch Colony of South Africa,' for example, but in our case the term 'colony' doesn't apply, since we didn't come here to *colonize* these lands."

"Thank you, Wolf," Jaime said, not seeing the importance of that semantic distinction. "Whether we like it or not," he continued, returning to the subject at hand, "we are part of a community."

"If Jaime and Wolf will indulge me for a moment," Julio Richter interrupted, "it seems to me the term that best defines us is not 'community' but 'collectivity,' since we don't live in a *communal* arrangement like, let's say, monks in a monastery. We're a group of individuals *with common interests* and together we form a 'collectivity.' "

What a difficult people we are! Jaime Lubinsky thought, little impressed by the intellectual inclination of his two guests. *We have to complicate everything!*

"Community or collectivity, what difference does it make!" Jaime proceeded, ignoring Galitzki's and Richter's comments, while the two men continued discussing the matter under their breath. "What really matters is that we're like wanderers, lost in the desert, each one going his own way, without direction or goal. I think the moment has come for us to organize ourselves."

"Yes, absolutely," Manes Finstein seconded. "We must organize so we can take the interests of the colony into our own hands."

"The collectivity," Richter corrected him.

From that moment on and for years to come, Richter and Galitzki didn't let a single opportunity pass without correcting whoever misspoke, insisting that the person use the term they considered to be the correct one. Despite that, "the colony" became a firmly implanted expression for designating the Jews of Lárida, and Jews and Gentiles alike used it routinely.

"The first thing we have to do is establish a fund, because without money nothing gets done," someone suggested.

"And who decides how much? And who's going to manage it?" another shot back.

"What do you mean who decides? All of us together decide! And we're going to manage it ourselves," asserted a third individual.

"Gentlemen, gentlemen…one at a time," Jaime Lubinsky interjected. "First, we have to form an entity that will be in charge of collecting and administering the funds. That entity must look after everything that's in our interest."

"What do you mean by 'an entity'?" Wolf Galitzki asked.

"I mean a corporation or a company, legally constituted, headed by a board of directors."

"What's that 'legally constituted' stuff?" came the shrill voice of Mrs. Tova Feigenboim. "Are we talking about a company, an honest-to-goodness business?"

"Of course, definitely," Jaime replied. "Just like any other commercial enterprise, constituted through a public filing, with name and statutes, properly registered."

"Oy!" Tova exclaimed. "How did you get such an idea! To become an organization? What will the *goyim* think?"

Everybody began talking at the same time. The arguments, sometimes expounded upon in Yiddish and sometimes in Spanish with a Yiddish accent, were brandished on all sides.

"If we had our community organization in Europe, why shouldn't we have it here?"

"In Warsaw, every time the authorities wanted to cause problems for us they already knew where to go: to the community institutions."

"Well, we never had any problems in Kolomyya."

"How can you compare Kolomyya to Lárida?"

"And how can you compare Warsaw to Lárida?"

"And who says we can't organize quietly, without anyone finding out?"

"We do this officially, the way it should be done, or not at all."

"The government would take a very dim view of any organization of Jews."

"My God! What's the matter with all of you? We're in America, for goodness sake. This is a free country."

"Why stir up problems with the *goyim*?"

"Silence! Silence, please!" Jaime shouted above the voices.

The noise abated sufficiently to allow him to have the floor again.

"We want to organize and we're not in agreement on how to do it. We have two possibilities. One is to have a closed organization, that is to say, almost secret, in which we would try to manage our affairs without moving beyond our own boundaries. I don't see any advantage in that. In the first place, it would limit our activities too much; in the second place, it could cause problems with management of the funds. What's more, I'm not sure, but I believe we would be violating the law. The other possibility is to have an open organization, in other words, an official community institution, tied to the laws of the nation and open to the scrutiny of the authorities. The way I see it, we must opt for the second choice, in view of the fact that we will be devoted exclusively to questions regarding our religion, charity, cultural activities, etc., in which case

194

we have nothing to hide. There can be no room for friction because we're not proselytes and we practice our religion without interfering in the lives of other people."

A murmur went up from those in attendance.

"If we're not in agreement," said Leon Edri, projecting his voice above the others, "we must solve our differences democratically. I propose that all who want to express their point of view do so, and then we'll submit it to a vote."

In the debate that followed, arguments surfaced that reflected the wariness, fear, and anguish of a persecuted people who still had not become accustomed to the freedom found in the Americas. Yet, a broad majority approved the formation of an official institution.

"The first thing the organization must do is build a synagogue," reasoned Enrique Shor.

"With what money?" Manes Finstein piped up. "Do you know what it costs to build a synagogue?"

"You don't need to build a synagogue to have one," Leon Edri said, speaking in a calm voice. "An acceptable place can be rented and set up to meet our needs."

Voices of approval were heard.

"Leon's right," Nathan Gottlieb said as he moved towards the center of the room. "We need a place to pray; we don't need to own it. We come to God wherever we are. Someday, when we have enough money, the first thing we must do is purchase land for a cemetery, not build a synagogue. We need a cemetery. It is incumbent upon us to do it," he said in a voice charged with emotion, "because... no one knows when... Here in Lárida there is a Jew buried in the Catholic cemetery. None of you knew him because he had already passed on when you arrived, but I know where he's buried. I know the exact spot. He was a poor soul who came to these lands alone... and that's how he lived and died: alone. The entity

195

that we are forming has the duty to get authorization to exhume his body and provide him a burial plot in a Jewish cemetery." Gottlieb took a deep breath before continuing. "And that is not the only duty... The community has to form a *Chevre Kadishe*, to assure its members of a burial in accordance with the Law; it has to provide the children a basic Jewish education; it has to procure a supply of *kosher* meat; it has to look out for the welfare of widows and old people, and in general any Jew in need of help." Gottlieb took another deep breath. "As you see, there is much to do before we build a synagogue."

"I propose we elect a board of directors of the organization," Wolf Galitzki said.

"The organization doesn't exist yet," Jaime Lubinsky pointed out, playing the role of moderator as usual, "but a provisional committee can be elected that will take charge of drawing up a plan for creating it. The plan will then be presented to the entire colony for its approval or modification."

"The *community*, Jaime, if you don't mind," asserted Galitzki, for whom the word "colony" was an obvious sticking point.

It was unanimously agreed upon that Nathan Gottlieb would be the president of the committee and that he, in turn, would name four others to serve. Gottlieb gladly accepted the nomination and immediately selected the other members of the committee. Jaime Lubinsky, of course, was one of them.

"Tell me, Nute," Tova Feigenboim said, addressing old Gottlieb in her familiar way, "what will you name the organization?"

"Well...I don't know. The committee will also decide that."

"We'll call it the Jewish Organization of Lárida," Al Pappu said decisively.

"That's all we needed!" Julio Richter protested. "Don't you know that the word 'Jew' has a pejorative connotation in the Christian world?"

"Huh?" grumbled Pappu.

"It sounds bad," Richter explained, putting it into simpler terms.

"The Hebrew Organization of Lárida would sound better," Wolf Galitzki asserted.

"No, not at all," Julio Richter said, taking pleasure in contradicting him. "Are we by chance Hebrews? Hebrews were those who belonged to that Semitic race of dark-skinned people who lived in Canaan and spoke Hebrew," he said in an authoritative tone before adding: "The proper term is 'Israelite.' The Israelite Organization of Lárida."

Damn it! Jaime said to himself. *Again with the semantics*!

"It seems all right to me if we call it Israelite," Leopold Reiss asserted, "but another word is needed. You can't say 'organization' and nothing else, without specifying what kind of organization. It's common to hear, for example, terms like 'sports organization' or 'gastronomical organization.' "

"What about 'The Israelite Philanthropic Organization of Lárida'?" someone asked.

"It's too long," replied one member of the gathering.

"Let's use 'Center' instead of 'Organization.' That shortens it enough," said a third individual.

Jaime grew impatient listening to so much discussion about a name, but he did not interfere in the debate. The important thing was to create the entity. That was why he had called the meeting and had the satisfaction of having achieved his goal. As for the others, let them call the entity what they wished. It made no difference to him.

197

"If we call it 'Cultural' instead of 'Philanthropic' we shorten it even more," proposed one who had already offered an opinion. "Besides, as a cultural center it will be less restrictive."

Each person had something to say. Words flew back and forth. "Association" replaced "Union," which took the place of "Federation," which changed to "League," which became "Alliance," which supplanted "Center." On the other hand, "Mutual Aid" replaced "Assistance," which gave way to "Biblical," which changed to "Community," which was switched to "Social," which replaced "Cultural." The discussion lasted almost an hour until the terms that were finally approved were those that had been dismissed at the outset. And so it was, very late at night—on November 16, 1931—at the home of Jaime Lubinsky that the "Israelite Cultural Center of Lárida" was born.

Jerusalem

May 12, 1935

Dear Leon,

I'm in love! Her name is Judith. She is slim-figured, not very tall, has chestnut hair, big, dark, expressive eyes, delicate features, and a precious mouth that smiles every minute. She's the most beautiful girl in the world. It's all right, go ahead and laugh. I'm madly in love. She loves me too. It had to happen someday.

I'm dying to get married, but my impatience isn't just because of my love for Judith. I want to have children and have my own home. I feel alone. In a certain sense, I've felt alone ever since I got here. As you know, I was the only one from my family to come to Eretz Israel. All my relatives and friends either stayed in the shtetl or went to America.

Judith's case is similar to mine, although more interesting. Her family is from Drogobych. She, like I, is an ardent Zionist. She hadn't turned seventeen when her parents took her with them to America. They settled in New York. Her father got work in a clothing factory where Judith was hired as a seamstress. Look at how small the world is. The other day, when she learned where I was from, Judith told me that a seamstress from Golochov worked in her division. Well it turned out to be—you won't believe it—Ruchel, the daughter of Frimca The Dispenser of Advice. Not only were they working in the same division, but they also lived in the same neighborhood. What do you have to say about that for a coincidence? Incredible, isn't it? Judith and Ruchel became best friends. They traveled back and forth to work together. Now that they're far away from each other they stay in touch by letter. Here's Ruchel's address if you feel like dropping her a few lines:

1291 Avenue L, Apt. 4B

Brooklyn, New York

199

Judith lived in the United States for three years until one day she made up her mind that it wasn't her place. And without hesitating, she packed her suitcase and came to Palestine with her older brother.

If you think my trip to the Holy Land was filled with adventure, theirs was a real odyssey. The British authorities denied them permission to enter Palestine. Judith and her brother stayed in London for two weeks doing everything possible to get their visas, but it was all in vain. Then they decided to travel to Lebanon in an effort to enter Eretz Israel by land, even if it meant breaking the law of the mandatory provisional government. In effect, they entered illegally, but in a very different way from the one they had envisioned. Just imagine what coincidences there are in life! Judith and Ephraim (that's her brother's name) had just reached Greece from Naples. They had to stay a few days in Athens to get the ship that was to take them to Beirut. One afternoon they found themselves in Piraeus, in a small café, when they heard a group of young people at one of the tables conversing in Yiddish. From the time they left home, six weeks earlier, they hadn't heard a word of Yiddish, and now, suddenly, in Piraeus—of all places! —the mother tongue appeared. The young people who were chatting in the café were part of a much larger group—350 in all—, members of the Jewish organization called "The Pioneer" that had come from Poland on their way to Eretz Israel. It wasn't just any journey they were undertaking. Organized in secret by the Jewish Agency, it didn't give away its real objective at all. The ship that officially was to sail to Italy with "tourists" from Poland, Czechoslovakia, and Austria was to veer towards the coasts of Palestine. This operation took months of advance preparation.

Judith and Ephraim joined the group, and that's how their lucky star put them aboard the "Vellos" when it left Piraeus in July of last year. The conditions on board were dreadful, since the ship was carrying two and a half times its maximum capacity of one hundred forty passengers. Fortunately, the crossing only lasted three days.

Captain Makros, the owner of the ship, reached the territorial waters of Palestine in late afternoon, but waited until nightfall before approaching the coast. He dropped anchor on an isolated beach, about twelve miles north of Tel Aviv. Several members of the Haganah (the clandestine Jewish militia) were waiting for them there. The passengers were taken ashore in lifeboats from the "Vellos" and aboard a few fishing boats that the Haganah had recruited. Some young people leapt into the water and swam ashore. As soon as they reached land, the immigrants were placed on trucks that set off in different directions to make the rounds of the collective farms, leaving twenty to thirty people at each one.

Despite the difficulties, those boys and girls saw their extraordinary enterprise end in success. Unfortunately, things did not go as well for a second group that tried to duplicate the feat two months later. The CID, or Criminal Investigation Department, (the English secret police in Palestine) discovered the plan before the "Vellos" weighed anchor. Upon the demands of the British government, Greece expelled the young pioneers who found themselves forced to return to Poland.

But getting back to Judith and her brother, after disembarkation, Judith was taken to a kibutz in the Valley of Yizrael, near Nazareth. Ephraim was left in Gan Shmuel, the same kibutz where they took me soon after I arrived in Palestine. I go to Gan Shmuel from time to time to visit friends. It was precisely during one of those visits that I met him. On another occasion, a few months ago, Judith was there and Ephraim introduced her to me. It was love at first sight. I can just see you there, smiling again. Don't you believe that love at first sight exists? Well, it does, and how!

I'm trying to find a suitable place for us to live, and as soon as I do, we'll set the date for the wedding. Judith is very excited. Of course, I'm excited too, but there are moments when I can't avoid thinking that despite all the happiness, there will be an element of sadness at our wedding: no one from our families will be there. Instead of parents, it will be Ephraim, Judith's brother, who will accompany her to the chuppah. Out of all the relatives she has, he'll be the only one there. From my side, there won't be anybody. My parents, who are so dear to me, are on another continent, far removed from my joys and sorrows. It's been seven years since I last saw them! I miss them very much. In general, I miss my whole family and, of course, my boyhood friends. If you were here at least, or Itzik or Zvi...

That, my dear Leon, is our destiny, the pioneers who came to redeem the Promised Land. We have the good fortune to be in Eretz Israel, but we pay the price of being far from our loved ones, isolated from the world and alone.

Affectionately,

Baruch

16

Nathan Gottlieb never came to know the Israelite Cemetery of Lárida for whose establishment he had pleaded so passionately. He was already dead and laid out in a casket when the gates of the cemetery opened to let him pass through. Irony apart, it could be said that he was making his triumphal entrance. From the time the Israelite Center was founded, four years earlier, and he was named president of the organization, he had tried to procure a cemetery for the community. "It isn't for the colony that I'm doing it," he would say half-jokingly and half-seriously, "it's for myself... After all, I'm the oldest Jew in Lárida."

"Don't worry, Nathan," Jaime Lubinsky would tell him, also half in jest and half in seriousness. "I won't let them bury you in a pasture. I'll get you a Jewish cemetery even if I have to go to another city to bring it here."

During his final months, old Gottlieb had been negotiating for the acquisition of a parcel of land that he considered the most suitable for the needs of the Jewish community, but a series of complications caused the matter to be drawn out and, at times, it seemed impossible to bring it to a conclusion. The owner of the adjoining section of land initiated a lawsuit alleging that the real boundary was a line of trees that ran six yards farther out, parallel to the barbed-wire fence that separated the two properties. Not only was the strip of land in litigation but the lot itself had been seized by a lender. As if this were not enough, the land belonged to heirs who were fighting over it among themselves.

"Couldn't you find a piece of property with more problems attached to it?" Jaime Lubinsky asked him jokingly every time they spoke about the situation.

The old man had convinced himself that it was the best piece of property available and persisted in his efforts to acquire it. Jaime, for his part, also tried to secure a suitable piece of land. They had asked such an exorbitant price for one that he liked that he didn't even present it to the board of directors of the Israelite Center for consideration.

The day that Nathan Gottlieb suffered a brain hemorrhage, Jaime was one of the first to reach the hospital. He stayed by Nathan's side until the old man finally succumbed, four hours after the onset of the stroke.

"Take him home," Jaime whispered to Karl Topol, the only member of the Israelite Center's board of directors who was present. "We have two days to organize the funeral."

Topol nodded without really understanding what Lubinsky meant.

Jaime rushed from The Samaritan Hospital of Lárida and, with his mind made up, went straight to the office of Apolinar Salcedo, the owner of the property that he liked. He was afraid he wouldn't find him in, since it was already well past five o'clock, but the businessman was still in his office, alone, going over some bills.

"Doctor Salcedo," Jaime said upon bursting into his office.

Apolinar Salcedo was startled, but as soon as he recognized his visitor he smiled from ear to ear.

"Señor Lubisi," he said at once, in the most amicable tone possible. "What a pleasant surprise!"

Lubinsky didn't bother to correct him. He took a seat before it was offered and without wasting time got right down to business.

"I've come to buy the property."

Apolinar Salcedo smiled again. This time he was truly pleasantly surprised. His visitor's eagerness was evident.

"Has something happened, Don Jaime?"

The tone was one of feigned concern. He stood up and came around from behind his desk until he was in front of the chair where Jaime was seated. Salcedo then leaned back against his desk and crossed his arms without taking his eyes off his visitor, who remained seated directly in front of him. An air of duplicity seemed to emanate from Apolinar Salcedo's tall, thin body, suggestive of those elongated figures in El Greco's paintings. He was dressed with consummate elegance, as was his custom: a three-piece suit tailored to his exact measurements, a white shirt with cuff links, and a silk tie. But his elegant clothes did little to counter the unpleasant impression created by his long, pasty-white face, scarred by smallpox when he was a young boy. He had curly, reddish coffee-colored hair, daubed with a fragrant, oily hair cream in an effort to straighten it, but without any great success. His straight and somewhat flat nose tapered off into very small nostrils. His pallid face was marked by three long, thin, horizontal lines: his mouth and his eyebrows, beneath which his small, dark but very alert eyes sized up his interlocutor.

"You seem very worried, Don Jaime. Is something wrong?" he asked again.

"No, nothing... I came to buy the property," Jaime repeated.

"Oh, yes... you're still interested in it."

"I came to buy it," he said a third time and in such an authoritative tone that Salcedo abandoned his leisurely pose and quickly retreated behind his desk, as if shielding himself from a possible act of aggression.

"Hmm... we had spoken..."

"What you quoted me," Lubinsky interrupted, "I'm prepared to meet your price."

"Well... you know, that was a preliminary talk and I merely tossed out a figure without giving it much thought... That is to say, what I asked may be a fair price, but I'd like to consider it further because... well... I'm not up to date on current real estate values."

Apolinar Salcedo wasn't born yesterday; he was a crafty businessman who wasn't going to miss out on an opportunity by keeping to his word. It was clear that his visitor was itching—out of urgent necessity, perhaps? —to buy the property, enabling him to convert a good business deal into an extraordinary one. But Lubinsky was smarter than Salcedo, even though the latter had the advantage in years, and wasn't going to let his arm be twisted.

"Well, the fact is that I am familiar with the real estate market and I know that your property is worth half of what you're asking for it; nevertheless, I'm prepared to buy it from you without haggling over the price and to pay you in cash."

"All right, but I told you I wanted to give it more thought."

"You have until noon tomorrow to decide," Jaime calmly replied while getting to his feet. "At twelve sharp you can find me in my office. If it's not to sell me the property at the price we discussed, don't bother to come. You will have missed a unique opportunity." He looked right into Salcedo's eyes and spoke more deliberately. "I give you my word of honor, Doctor Salcedo, that after that deadline, even were you to ask me on bended-knee to purchase it for less, I will not do it."

Jaime said nothing more. He wanted the warning, delivered in a dramatic tone, to be the last word that Apolinar would hear on the matter. He bid him farewell with a nod of his head and quickly exited, leaving Apolinar Salcedo frozen in his tracks. Salcedo didn't know what lay behind the Jew's motive for delivering such an ultimatum, but he didn't have the least doubt that it had been spoken in all seriousness. After twelve noon, even if it were only on a whim, Lubinsky would not purchase the property from him, not at any price.

Once he was outside, Jaime took a deep breath. He had to speak not only with his partner as soon as possible but also with the manager of the bank; certain financial arrangements had to be prepared, since—he was sure—the transaction was a fait accompli.

The burial of Nathan Gottlieb was a tragicomedy of sorts, without heroes or villains. An absolute disorder reigned. No one knew what to do. It was the first death in their community and the Jews of Lárida were not organized to deal with the situation. From one moment to the next, Doña Ida Gottlieb and her two daughters found themselves with a cadaver in the house. The three women cried disconsolately. The wailing would stop for a while, but when one began sobbing, it was contagious and all three started crying in unison. Karl Topol tried to calm them, telling them not to worry, that the Israelite Center would take care of everything. What a stupid thing to say. The Gottlieb women were not worried; they were hurting. So intense was their pain that they didn't even hear what was said to them, nor did it occur to them that something had to be done. Those to whom it did occur were the relatives and friends who went to the house, but no one knew where to begin. When they asked Topol, the poor man didn't know what to tell them. The corpse lay on the living room floor, covered with a white sheet.

"On the floor?" someone protested in a low voice. "Let's put him on the bed."

"No, no! It must be on the floor," another replied in an even lower voice. "Don't you see that afterwards someone will have to sleep in the bed?"

"In that case, a casket must be brought," said the first person.

"I can recommend a funeral home," said the woman who was their next-door neighbor, one of the few non-Jewish persons present. "Would you like me to call a priest?"

"No, thank you!" several voices answered at the same time.

"It's not our custom…" one of them explained.

Two hours later the casket that someone had requested arrived at the house. The polished wood coffin bore a crucifix on the lid and had to be returned. A couple who arrived in their car when the casket was being removed from the house followed the hearse to the funeral home believing that it was transporting the deceased.

The next day, around noon, Manes Finstein came running to the Gottlieb house with the news that at that very moment the acquisition of a plot of land designated to be the Jewish cemetery of Lárida was being formalized. Jaime Lubinsky had sent him with the news as soon as Apolinar Salcedo stepped into his office, some three hours before the documents—which still had not been drawn up—were signed.

That evening the board of directors of the Israelite Center met to discuss the matter of Nathan Gottlieb's burial, expected to take place the following day. A discussion immediately broke out about what must be done to convert the property into a cemetery. Each one was familiar with different rituals and no one was sure which were the prayers that had to be said. Well into the night an agreement was finally reached, in a process that left no one satisfied. If anything positive came out of the meeting it was the awareness that all of them were ignorant with regard to religious matters and that, therefore, it was imperative that they get a rabbi so that the community could manage its affairs in accordance with the Law. Jaime Lubinsky offered to go to New York to look for such a person and to contract for his services. Given his way of doing things, reticent when it came to his business dealings, he preferred not to mention that he was already planning a trip to the United States anyway for the purpose of acquiring machinery for the factory that he and Leon had started a few years before.

The burial was scheduled for twelve noon. At eight that morning the members of the board of directors were already at the site to officiate over the ceremony that was to consecrate it as a Jewish cemetery. Also present were some Jews who had been called upon for their greater knowledge of the religion.

"What foolishness do you intend to commit?" asked an indignant Emanuel Herzog, one of the most learned among them on matters of the Bible and the Talmud, when informed of the reason for which they had gotten him out of his house so early in the morning. "Nothing needs to be done for a cemetery to be a cemetery!" he continued angrily. "You only have to treat it for what it is. The important thing is to carry out the burial as prescribed by the Law. Who is in charge of preparing the body?"

There was a moment of silence. No one had given it any thought.

"You," Jaime Lubinsky asserted, taking on the role of de facto community president.

"All right. I'll do it at Gottlieb's home because there are no facilities here," Herzog said, visibly annoyed.

In view of the circumstances, he couldn't refuse accepting the responsibility. He was probably the only one who knew anything about that unpleasant task.

"I'll need two assistants," he added. "You, Lázaro, come," he said to one of those present while he looked over the rest, without finding anyone else to call upon.

"I can help," offered Mendel Fuchs, the feeble personage who had arrived from Poland a few months earlier and went around offering his coreligionists *kosher* chickens, which he decapitated in the patio of his house.

As soon as the trio of the improvised *chevrah kaddishah* withdrew from the cemetery, those who remained were divided into two groups: the ones who accepted Emanuel Herzog's judgment and those who wanted to sanctify the ground at all costs. They discussed the matter for a good while until someone realized that they were less than ten Jews in all and thus could not conduct prayers even if they wanted to. Then the second discussion ensued: where to dig the grave. One needed to plan the cemetery; it wasn't something that could be done willy-nilly. It was, therefore, imperative to establish a place for the first headstone and leave the planning for later. Each one insisted on digging the grave at a different spot and no one was ready to give in. They had to decide the matter by tossing a coin in the air several times to eliminate the various considerations one by one until just one prevailed, something that none of the nine Jews who were present, out of embarrassment, ever dared to tell about. And when they finally settled on a spot—and only among such complicated people could such a thing happen!—another discussion broke out: in which direction to set the longitudinal axis of the grave.

At twelve noon, while those who had come to the cemetery waited impatiently, standing under a scorching sun, neither the funeral cortege nor Menachem Barak, who two hours earlier had gone to get a couple of workers to dig the grave, had arrived. The cortege arrived ahead of Barak and immediately everybody began to despair. When they were about to go looking for him, Barak showed up, perspiring and out of breath, with two native workers equipped with pickaxes and shovels. They all stood around for an hour amidst the bushes until the grave was ready. The delay was helpful in that several people who had gotten lost were able to arrive in time for the service. Many had come not only to pay homage to Nathan Gottlieb, first president of Lárida's Jewish community, but also to get a look at the new cemetery. When they were about to lower the body into the grave—who would have believed it!—another discussion broke out: on which side should the head be placed and on which side the feet.

The lowering of the casket was somewhat problematic because no one had thought to bring a rope. They succeeded in lowering it a little bit at a time by sliding it down against the side of the grave with the help of tree limbs, while twenty people stood around giving instructions.

Nathan Gottlieb had no children, brothers or male relatives. It was Mendel Fuchs who, unsolicited, recited the Kaddish.

The grave was covered with dirt until an elongated mound was formed, marking the tomb among the weeds. The mourners began withdrawing without knowing exactly when the ceremony had ended, in the same way that no one had realized when it had begun. In a certain sense, there was no ceremony. Some felt troubled that they weren't able to wash their hands.

Many years later, Nathan Gottlieb's grave would be the only one not aligned with the other headstones laid out on the green, manicured meadow of the Israelite Cemetery of Lárida.

The day after the burial, Jaime Lubinsky signed the necessary papers for the legal transfer of the property, acquired in his name, as a donation to the Israelite Cultural Center. The action was widely commented upon in the heart of the community. Lubinsky was relatively rich, but he was far from possessing the immense fortune that he would amass over the years.

Shortly after the muddled burial of Nathan Gottlieb, the municipal government of Lárida imposed two fines on the Israelite Center: one for, in fact, creating a cemetery without previously having obtained the proper permit and the other for having carried out a burial without adhering to the legal formalities. The board of directors took up the matter of correcting the irregularities, but Jaime

Lubinsky, whose heart was bigger than his bank account, paid the fines out of his own pocket.

Lubinsky was named president of the community, which he served with affection and dedication. Years later, when he retired as president of the Israelite Center, he continued to stand out for his generosity, supporting the community institutions (which over time increased in number) and helping families in need, aiding Zionist and humanitarian causes and, outside the community sphere, undertaking benevolent works in general, such as orphanages and homes for the aged. It seemed that he had a pact with God: the more money he gave away, the richer he became. But his heart always continued to be bigger than his bank account.

17

Still panting, Leon lifted his sweat-soaked body off the woman and rolled over onto his back, face up, next to her. He turned his head to look at her. Her lithesome, bronze body glistened with perspiration, perhaps more so from his than her own. Her cheeks were flush with color.

"Ufff! It's so hot!" Graciela said as she traced her fingertips above her top lip, wiping away a few small droplets of perspiration.

Leon observed the delicate fingers, with well-manicured nails, neither very long nor very short, slide over her smooth, soft skin; that clear, dark skin whose perfection was as evident in her provocative features as it was in her sensual figure.

Graciela was somewhat taller than average, with long legs, narrow waist and firm, well-proportioned breasts. On her round and slightly high buttocks, two exquisite dimples provided the coup de grâce to her sculptured figure.

"Ufff!" she repeated, this time lifting her hair from the nape of her neck.

Her face was not of a remarkable beauty like her body, although indeed sufficiently winning for it to arouse interest all by itself. Her fleshy lips were a dark red, but with a tinge of pink coloring towards the interior, where they came together. Above the straight edge of her upper lip, marked by a V-shape in the middle, lay just a hint of down. When she laughed, she displayed a beautiful set of teeth whose whiteness contrasted exquisitely with her dark skin. She had a small, straight nose and high, clearly delineated eyebrows. The most commanding part of that lovely face, which was unacquainted with

213

make-up, were her big, dark eyes, shimmering and more loquacious than her mouth, outlined by her long, black eyelashes.

Graciela rolled over and contemplated Leon's face. They remained that way for a while, in silence, each absorbed in their thoughts. Leon reached out with his arm and took her hand, caressed it with his fingers, gave it a gentle squeeze and let go. It was an affectionate gesture more than a caress. With his flame of passion extinguished after a second orgasm, he was in no mood for caressing. She took his hand, which he had just withdrawn, and also squeezed it with her fingers and then continued caressing his forearm.

"I adore a man with hair on his arms."

Leon answered with a smile.

"Who has hair on his chest," she continued, "who knows many things and who talks nice, with a foreign accent, just like you; who dresses well... especially if he wears fine shoes. The shoes tell you what sort of person someone is; the shoes and the hands... I once had a sweetheart who was a mechanic. Not just a mechanic, but owner of his own garage. He was a real handsome guy. A foreigner, like you. A German. Suddenly, one day I got tired of him and left him. You know why? His hands. They were rough. I didn't like the feel of them."

After making love, she was the one who was always talkative. Leon listened and watched, impressed more by her beauty than by her monologue.

"The hands tell a lot about a person," Graciela said. "In the first place, they tell you if he works with them, which is like saying whether he has money. You can know by the appearance of the hands if a man is crude or sensitive, strong or weak, clean or dirty. You can tell by his hand movements if he is the nervous or restless type, if he has an artistic disposition, if he's effeminate... Leo, are you listening to me?"

"Yes sweetheart, I am."

"I thought you had fallen asleep."

"No, of course not."

"Last night I dreamed I was in a big house, a very elegant house, and was calling to you and you didn't come. Then I went outside to the street and realized there were no people around: as if the city were deserted. There were no cars or people, not even a dog. I began running, scared, and I was shouting, but no one answered me... Leo..."

Her beautiful dark eyes turned melancholy.

"You'll leave me one day, won't you?"

"Why do you say that?" Leon asked, figuring in a split second that it was better to reply with another question than to answer in the affirmative or lie.

"Because that's what every society man does."

"I'm not a society man."

"Yes, of course, you are."

"Where did you get that idea?"

"Every white person with money belongs to society."

Leon was not able to control himself and burst out laughing. She caught his laughter too, by contagion, but her expression of sadness quickly returned.

"No, sweetheart, I don't belong to society."

"But you hide me..."

Leon swallowed hard.

"You're ashamed of me," she said, sounding firmer in her tone.

"I..."

"Will you marry me?"

"No."

"You see?"

"What do I have to see?"

"That you're not sincere."

"I've never lied to you."

"Why won't you marry me?"

"Because... I can't."

"Because I'm poor? Because I don't talk nice? Because my family is trash? Because I'm not white?"

"You are white and very beautiful... and you do have a nice way of speaking."

"Then, why not?"

"Because I belong to another world."

"That's what I said."

"Another world, but not in the sense that you meant it... you wouldn't understand..."

Maybe she would, in fact, understand, but it was better not to explain. Anyway, she hadn't asked for an explanation.

Leon felt pity for that girl who loved him with all her heart even though it was an unrequited love. She was prepared to make any sacrifice for him, no matter how great the suffering, no matter how great the humiliation; he, on the other hand, was not prepared to even remain faithful to her. And he wasn't. He was unfaithful to her without any reason or, at least, without any physiological

216

justification, since the girl's heavenly body satisfied him with absolute plenitude. The winsome girl was always ready to offer him the charms of her sex, generously, to love him passionately, whenever and wherever he wanted. Leon felt ashamed of himself. Shame, not remorse. His conscience was clear, or he wanted to believe it to be so. Had he ever told her even once that he loved her? Had he promised her anything? No, not even by insinuation. And didn't he help her with the things she needed? He did it without her asking him. How was he to blame if she had fallen in love with him? How unfair one can be when one wants to rationalize! Of course, it was his fault she had fallen in love with him. From the moment he met her, he tried to seduce her with his charm, his pleasant smile, his wholesome face, his sparkling conversation, his worldly experience. And when he succeeded, he kept pouring on his charm with her to solidify his conquest. The vanity of a man who knows he's admired! It was true he helped her out from time to time with some money without her ever having asked him for anything. The first time he did it, it was an awkward moment for both of them, embarrassing in the extreme. He didn't want to offend her and she didn't want him to think it was that kind of relationship. Only Leon's intelligence and tactfulness got her to accept the money as the disinterested help from a wealthy friend to a friend in need, and not as payment for services rendered. It was also true that Leon was of noble spirit and took the initiative because he wanted to help her out of the dire straits she was in. But was his a truly disinterested assistance? Was it possible for him not to know that he was creating in her a bond of dependence? Would he have helped her all the same if he didn't have her unconditional love? So, in the end, how generous was his help? Compared to his income, what did the money he gave her represent? What proportion was there between what he gave and what he received? And finally, it was true he had never told her he loved her, but didn't he give her to understand it at every instance? He pampered her, treated her with tenderness, the way you treat someone you love. He had never promised her anything. Did he

217

perhaps need to promise her something? Didn't his behavior in and of itself make him beholden to her? Didn't his relationship with her create obligations?

"Yes, you'll leave me one day."

This time it wasn't a question but an affirmation. It troubled Leon that the conversation had taken that path. Why did she have to come out with such things? She was ruining what had been a perfect afternoon. Graciela's words irritated him, but at the same time he couldn't avoid a feeling of tenderness towards her. When all was said and done, she held a place in his heart.

He wasn't in love with the girl and never was. When he met her, her beauty was the only thing that drew him to her. It was the only thing that could have drawn him to her: the shapely, delicately molded body that she flaunted in the way she walked, in the way she had of sitting or standing, with the way she batted her eyelashes, the way she looked directly at a person or out of the corner of her eye, the manner in which she dressed—simple, neat, feminine, and yet slightly provocative. It was a purely sexual attraction—animal in nature—that she held over him. He had taken her for his carnal pleasure and continued taking her for his carnal pleasure. That was all. Nevertheless, he had become fond of her... the way an owner can become fond of a faithful dog. They had nothing to talk about, and yet they were always spirited in the things they said. They laughed together, found each other's company mutually entertaining, took pleasure in being together.

"What's troubling you, sweetheart? You look lugubrious."

"What's that?"

"Sad."

"Yes, because I know you're going to leave me."

"But I'm not leaving you."

"Not today, but one day…"

"Sweetheart, that day is so far off that it's silly to worry about it."

Graciela sighed.

"I don't know," she said.

"And this suddenly popped into your head today?"

"No. I've thought about it many times… I want that day never to come. I don't know what I would do without you. I'm scared of being left alone."

"Pretty girls are never left alone."

Leon said it to lift her spirits, but his words produced the opposite effect. Two tears ran down her copper cheeks.

"Sweetie, please don't cry."

He wiped her tears away with his thumb. The last thing he wanted was to make her suffer. She closed her eyes and two more tears appeared among her eyelashes. He felt his own eyes tearing up a bit.

"*Carajo*! Now you're going to make me cry."

Amidst her sobs, Graciela let loose a laugh on hearing him use that word. It was the first time she had ever heard him curse. It wasn't a really bad word, but for him it was completely out of character. Besides, carajo is a word that sounds funny with the slightest foreign accent.

Leon laughed too, not because it seemed amusing to him but to give her the push she needed to move past the middle ground where she found herself, between tears and laughter. That little push was enough. Leon took her in his arms, turned her towards him and embraced her. They kissed and Leon tasted the saltiness of her tears even before they began to flow. Surely many more were held in reserve, deferred until the inevitable day when he would leave her.

From a distance came the sound of a factory's long, strident whistle.

"What? Five o'clock already?"

Leon sat up and grabbed his wristwatch from the little night table.

"Hm, hm," he said in answer to his own question and jumped out of bed.

Keeping his naked body a safe distance from the window, he looked outside.

"All those dark clouds and it didn't rain; it's not going to rain either. It's already clearing up," he said, rubbing his head. "I'm going to take a shower."

There was no hot water, but what came out wasn't cold. It gushed out, at room temperature, and pelted his body with a pleasurable sensation. Leon took more delight showering at Graciela's than in the luxurious hot-water shower he had at home. Sometimes he felt like singing under the surge of water, but he constrained himself, not wanting to give the neighbors reason to talk.

Graciela went into the bathroom when he came out, and when she reappeared he was already dressed.

"Are you coming tomorrow?"

"Not tomorrow, but the day after, if I get away early."

Generally, Leon didn't visit her on two consecutive days nor did he make any commitment to return on any particular day, although there was no consistency in this. Thus, he could just as easily see her three days in a row as not see her for an entire week. The fact that he never missed her was proof to him that his fondness for Graciela was far from being love.

It was beginning to grow dark when he left. He took long strides walking to his car, which he normally kept at an auto repair shop, three blocks away. He strode past the little one-story houses, with whitewashed façades and red tile roofs, typical of the neighborhoods of the city's lower middle class, without paying attention to the women who were watching him from one window or another. For the first time, he was leaving Graciela's with a heavy heart. Something was bothering him, but he couldn't determine what. It wasn't what Graciela had said to him, but it had something to do with it. He tried to analyze his feelings. Was it possible he was becoming too fond of her? No, he wasn't any fonder of her than what he had been the year before. Might it then be the fear of her capturing his heart? Not that either. The experience he had with other lovers had taught him that the initial enthusiasm only wanes with the passage of time. Wasn't that probably what was bothering him? The loss of enthusiasm? Having only fleeting love interests, relationships with no future?

"Here it is, Don León, clean as a whistle."

He had reached the garage almost without realizing it.

"Thanks, Memo," Leon told the boy who had waited for him after having finished his day's work, and handed him some money.

The young man took it with one hand and opened the car door with the other.

"Thank you, Don León," he replied with a smile.

Leon Edri headed downtown. He drove slowly, not only because the streets of the surrounding neighborhoods weren't paved and he was being careful with his new car but because his mind was somewhere else. He had never given much thought to the matter, but the inevitable question suddenly surfaced. Had the time come for him to get married? How long was he to continue his life as a bachelor—a very pleasant life, to be sure—jumping from one

221

amorous adventure to another, without direction or future? He had enjoyed it and had more than his share of that life, and now he was beginning to tire of it. Coming home after work and finding a wife waiting for him must be a wonderful experience. And to have a son who would look like him? How exciting that would be! He laughed to himself. The car stopped bouncing. He was now driving on a paved and well-lit street, but all the same he didn't speed up. He was still absorbed in his thoughts. He could get married whenever he wanted since he was well established and financially set. He could and he couldn't, because the problem was something else: there was no one in Lárida for him to marry, or more precisely, there was no single Jewish girl his age or a couple of years younger that he liked. Neither did he have much to choose from. There were only three unmarried girls between the ages of eighteen and twenty-five: Bertha Lubinsky, Jaime's sister, terribly unpleasant; Erica Levinger, as ugly as sin; and Natasha Blumenfeld, unbelievably stupid. He suddenly realized that the problem was more serious than what it appeared. If there were no one for him to marry just then, neither would there be anyone in the coming years. In that case, his future wife was in another city, probably in another country. That thought had barely dawned upon him when the image of Ruchel came to mind. He remembered her as he had seen her for the last time, the day she came out to say goodbye when he left Golochov. Through the cloud of dust kicked up by the horse-drawn carriage, Ruchel was waving to him, holding her arm up high. The girl's features, in clear focus at first, faded into the distance and only her splendid mane of blonde hair, as shimmering as a star, remained visible until he lost sight of it.

Leon was driving along mindlessly. It seemed as if the car was driving him and not vice versa. He turned off the wide avenue and took one of the side streets that lead to the center of the city.

Ruchel had to be between twenty-one and twenty-two years of age now, assuming she was about twelve when he was sixteen. He was sure she was still single; otherwise Baruch would have mentioned it to him in one of his letters.

He didn't have the least doubt that Ruchel remembered him, even though ten years had passed, but would she remember him in a nostalgic way, as he remembered her? Or would she remember him as a vague image, one of so many without importance left over from her adolescent years? If only he knew... He thought he could write her a letter, but what would he say to her? He wouldn't even know how to begin. Dear Ruchel? Dearest Ruchel? Most cherished Ruchel? It would be laughable. When a boy is in love with a girl, he does not let ten years go by without writing. No, he would not write to her; he would not play the role of a fool. Then he got an idea, a diplomatic way of establishing contact without looking bad. He would send her a greeting through Jaime, taking advantage of his next trip to New York. A greeting, nothing more. Depending on the reply he got from Ruchel, he would know if he occupied some small corner of her heart.

Night had fallen when he reached the Plaza de la República. At that hour of the evening, many parking spaces were available and he found one right in front of his office building. The employees had left two hours ago, but Jaime, as usual, was still in the office.

"Hello," he said when he saw Leon come in.

"Hello."

"What were you up to this afternoon? Another of your amorous escapades?"

Leon smiled.

"Ready for the trip?"

"Almost. I want to sign the contract with Muñoz before I leave."

"Don't be silly. I'll take care of that if you're not able to wrap up the details."

The two partners shared an office where each one had his own desk. The other three rooms on the second floor of the old mansion served, respectively, as a sales office for the textile factory, an administration office for the chain of stores, and a general accounting office. They were beginning to feel cramped in their center of operations. They had acquired the house three years ago when they were looking for a suitable place to centralize their offices. The old, two-story mansion, where the popular Café Real was located, struck them as the ideal place for setting themselves up in the very heart of the city. They moved into the top floor and modified the lower level, dividing the enormous space once occupied by the Café Real into three separate areas, which allowed them to lease space to three different businesses and considerably multiply the income from the property.

"As soon as I reach New York, I'm going to take up the matter of the rabbi," Jaime said while putting away some papers. "I figure it'll take me a week to get somebody."

"You'll find one for sure," Leon replied, sitting down on his friend's desk. "The United States is full of religious Jews with time on their hands."

"Yes, but not just anybody will do. I have to find one who is suitable for the colony. You know, not too Orthodox, not very liberal…"

"Don't even think about trying to make everybody happy."

"Of course not, but I'd like to disappoint the least number of people possible."

"Do you think you'll manage to be back in a month?"

"Certainly. I intend to be in New York for a week, before going on to Philadelphia, Pittsburgh, and Detroit, and then return to New York for two more days. The trip shouldn't last more than three weeks total."

"Did you say Pittsburgh? But the equipment we want is only available in Philadelphia and Detroit!"

"Yes, I know, but a cousin of my mother's lives in Pittsburgh, her inseparable friend since youth, and I promised I'd go and visit her. Besides, it's on the way to Detroit."

An opportunity never slipped past Leon Edri. Jaime had just opened a door that would allow him to ask a favor without raising curiosity.

"By the way," he said in a perfectly casual manner, "my mother and I also have some very good friends in the United States. Their name is Portnoy and they live in New York. I'll give you their address. If you have time, stop by and give them our regards."

"It'll be my pleasure, Leib."

They got back to business. While they were talking, Leon was analyzing how well he had crafted his request. It was a veiled message of love, intelligible only to the person for whom it was intended, if she entertained similar feelings; to the unsuspecting party, it was nothing more than a simple greeting. He had prefaced it with "by the way." Could there be anything more casual? He didn't mention Ruchel at all. He only spoke of "friends," and not even his especially, but rather just "friends of his mother and his." He asked Jaime to visit them "if he had time." He felt calm about it. In no way would he play the role of the fool if his love went unrequited.

225

18

STILL NO RABBI--STOP--WILL REMAIN IN NEW YORK A
FEW MORE DAYS--JAIME

The cable was dated March 30, twelve days after Jaime Lubinsky
had reached New York. Edri crumpled the telegram until he made it
into a little ball and tossed it into the wastebasket a few feet away.

"Good shot."

He turned around to see who had spoken and saw the smiling
face of Alfonso Mendiola, the company's accountant.

"You always hit the mark, Don León," he added, while handing
him a paper.

"Not always, Alfonso. What's this?"

"The stock certificate for the one hundred fifteen shares we
bought yesterday."

"Why are you showing it to me?"

"Because with this purchase we now own more than five
thousand shares."

"You don't say!" Edri exclaimed with a smile of satisfaction.

"With five thousand shares, Don León, you and Don Jaime now
own ten percent of the bank."

Leon put his finger to his lips to signal their trusted accountant to
be more discreet.

Edri and Lubinsky had been working with the Mercantile
Guaranty Bank since 1928, when they first met the manager, Don
Ignacio Blanco Quijano, and proposed that he finance the purchase

of a textile plant. Blanco Quijano suggested they buy some shares in the bank so that, when the moment came to submit the deal to the board of directors for approval, he could cite, among other things, that the credit was consistent with the policy that the bank had for helping small investors. Not much to their liking, the young entrepreneurs purchased one hundred shares shortly before Leon traveled to England to acquire the machinery. For five weeks Edri searched in vain for the bargain of his dreams, a textile factory deemed obsolete for the sophisticated industrial standard in Manchester and Liverpool, but serviceable for the distant lands of South America. There was no bargain to be found in England or Belgium or France. Disappointed, Leon Edri returned to Lárida. The project had already been discarded when, scarcely a year later, in October 1929, the U.S. stock market crashed, precipitating that country's great economic depression and that of much of the world.

"This is our chance!" Jaime Lubinsky said emphatically, filled with enthusiasm.

"Don't you think we already wasted enough time and money on that idea?"

"No. This time I'll go."

And without a moment's hesitation, Jaime Lubinsky set sail for North America. He stayed in the United States for three months, three long months that seemed an eternity to Leon, since he was accustomed to managing the business in conjunction with his partner. Jaime sent telegrams periodically, announcing that "interesting things" lay ahead of him and that he would be delayed a little longer. The first cables were dispatched from New York; afterwards, from different cities in New England and the region of the Great Lakes. In the end, they were all coming from Philadelphia. None of the cables stated concretely what was happening, until one of the last ones heralded good news: COMPLETE SUCCESS -- DEAL CLOSED --EQUIPMENT PURCHASED --VERY

FAVORABLE TERMS --WILL EXPLAIN TO YOU PERSONALLY

Fifteen days later Lubinsky was on his way back to Lárida with the details he had not wanted to provide in his laconic telegrams. Financed by the Mercantile Guaranty Bank, SILEJA, S.A. had bought from the Midland Bank of Philadelphia at a ridiculous price, all the machinery the bank had seized from Pershing Cotton Mills, a textile enterprise that went belly up and left its creditors with a string of assets—land, buildings, machinery, raw material and a client list— —that could not be liquidated at practically any price, owing to the very serious economic crisis in which the country was submerged. It was a small factory by U.S. standards, but the equipment, far from being obsolete, was modern and well maintained. More than six years had passed since then when Jaime Lubinsky again set foot in North America, this time in search of a rabbi for the community, and additional machinery to expand the textile factory that had been operating for the past five years on the outskirts of Lárida. It was the first of four factories that, somewhere down the road, would form the great Sileja industrial complex.

When Jaime's first telegram arrived, announcing he had not acquired a rabbi and would remain in New York a couple more days, Leon didn't attach much importance to it; but when the second telegram arrived, saying more or less the same thing, he figured his partner was studying some business transaction that he intended to spring on him as a surprise. *I'll show him he doesn't have the monopoly on finding good deals*, he told himself. *I too will have a surprise ready for him when he arrives.*

With the purchase of the textile machinery completed, Edri and Lubinsky periodically went about acquiring shares of the Mercantile Guaranty Bank in small lots. They did it discreetly, every time the price went down, and since the shares were bearer shares almost no one knew they owned so many. The few who happened to know about it never imagined that the two partners held such a strong

229

hand. Leon and Jaime did not exercise their voting rights at stockholder meetings, thus keeping their position under wraps while they continued accumulating shares with their sights set on getting the required number that would permit them, at any given moment, to sit on the bank's board of directors. The acquisition of shares every four or five months, in small lots, was too slow a tactic for Leon Edri's dynamic personality. Perhaps that was an area in which he could have a surprise in store for his partner.

Jaime remained in New York twenty-one days, exactly three times longer than what he had planned to stay in that city. His third telegram arrived from Philadelphia and announced that he had been in contact with the manufacturers of textile machinery.

In the meantime, Leon had an appointment he had arranged with Don Claudio Barreneche Ossa, chairman of the Mercantile Guaranty Bank's board of directors.

"Come in, come in, my dear Leon," Don Claudio said, standing up and going to the door of his office to receive his visitor.

"A pleasure to see you, Claudio."

"The pleasure is mine, old chap."

The only old one there, was Claudio Barreneche, of course. The two were not as close as their familiar manner of addressing one another suggested, but they had known each other since the time the bank financed the purchase of the equipment from Pershing Cotton Mills. Barreneche Ossa had seen the extraordinary progress of the young immigrants and felt a great admiration for them.

"Jaime is in the United States, isn't he?"

"Yes. He went to see about purchasing machinery for the factory."

"Do you need any financing?'

"Thank you. This time, no."

"Hell! Before you know it, you two will be lending money to the bank, isn't that right?"

The banker laughed while again taking his seat. Not a single strand of his thick gray head of hair was out of place. Leon thought that Claudio Barreneche probably spent more time fussing over his meticulously groomed hair and neatly trimmed moustache than over matters of the bank. His flabby but smooth skin, his paunch belly, his elegant clothes, his heavy gold watch chain, the ruby ring: everything about him emitted an air of the good life. Only the dark circles under his eyes betrayed a possible penchant for excesses.

"How about a little drink, Leon?"

"No, thank you. Not at this hour of the day."

"A coffee?"

"No, thank you all the same."

"So far, your visit is costing me very little," the banker joked.

"Not only is it going to cost you very little, but you're going to come out with a profit."

"Oh! This is beginning to sound interesting."

Leon laughed.

"You bet it's interesting," he said. "Extremely interesting."

"Shoot, then."

"No doubt, those of you on the board of directors have probably commented on the bank's current premises not being adequate."

"Well... we..."

"Clearly, they're not suitable. They're old and unattractive, but worst of all, everything looks cheap. That's the really serious part. A bank's headquarters should give the appearance of prosperity and wealth; they should be a kind of temple to opulence. You know quite

231

well that money attracts money. A place like this, with no aesthetics, does not inspire confidence. Do you know how many deposits are lost because thousands of potential clients take their money elsewhere, drawn solely by appearances? Attractive premises are part of the modern banking strategy. Just look at what a beautiful building the Bank of the Sierra put up, a relatively new bank, small, and in my view the one that has progressed the most in recent years.

"And why are you telling me this?"

"Because I've got the exact premises that the bank needs."

"Which one?"

"The old Café Real, right in the Plaza de la República."

"Where the Monte Carlo is located?"

"And Metro Radio and Ideal Books. All the rental contracts were drawn up for three years and are about to expire. Jaime and I have our offices on the second floor, but we're a little cramped for space and decided it would be good to move to another location."

"So?"

"So we can hand over the vacant property to you within a couple of months (let's say, four or five) for you to raze it and put up the most luxurious building in the city, in the best location, befitting a prestigious banking institution."

"Hmm… it's an interesting proposition. It's a good location."

"Good? It's the best there is in Lárida!"

"And what do you estimate the value of the property to be?"

"A million and a half pesos."

Barreneche Ossa's eyes opened wide.

"You're crazy!"

"Not in the least. It's the only property on the plaza that's available. The only one. Until now we haven't offered it to anyone. I'm giving you a chance to get it *before* it goes on the market. It's possible that someone (one of the banks, maybe) is ready to pay more. Don't forget that it's more than thirty-two thousand square feet of space…"

"Yes, but… a million and a half!"

"Do you want me to give you an option?"

"I don't think my board will approve an acquisition of that size. The price is exorbitant. It comes out to about fifty pesos per square foot."

"It comes out to a little over fourty-five," Leon corrected him. "Because there are thirty two thousand eight hundred and fifty square feet total."

"It doesn't matter. It seems like a lot of money to pay for a piece of property, even if it is the best in the city."

"And suppose you purchased it without cash?"

Don Claudio raised his eyebrows as if to ask: *What do you mean?*

"What if, for example," Leon continued, adding a little bit of mystery to his voice, "you were to pay for it with bank shares…"

There was a moment of silence. Barreneche Ossa took a deep breath. He was the first to speak.

"The bank doesn't have any shares available. They're all in the hands of private investors."

"Yes, but the bank could announce an increase in capital… Let's say, thirteen thousand shares. You would pay me with three thousand shares at face value. That would leave ten thousand shares to place on the market… of which you could buy a sizable portion."

There was another moment of silence. The two men looked fixedly at each other. Both knew very well that the shares were worth fifty percent more on the market than their face value. A heavy silence reigned, one of those that prevails when two people understand perfectly how they can be useful to one another and prefer to act without exchanging words, so as to leave it understood that nothing had been agreed to. Finally, just as before, it was Claudio who spoke first. He cleared his throat.

"In accordance with the statute of the bank, investors would hold an option to purchase new shares, at pro rata to the old ones that they hold."

"Yes," replied Edri, who had an answer for everything, "but for a limited period of ten days. If the issuance of new shares catches them by surprise, you can be sure that many will not have the funds they need available. You, on the other hand, will be able to prepare yourself for the event."

For the third time a moment of silence ensued. Don Claudio Barreneche Ossa took another deep breath.

"Yes...," he said in a hushed tone. "It sounds very interesting."

Two days later Claudio informed Leon that he had called a meeting of the board of directors to take up his proposal.

A telegram arrived from Pittsburgh; it was from Jaime, saying that he had not bought any machinery in Philadelphia because he wanted to compare it with the equipment he would see in Detroit. Four days later, another cable reported he did not like what he saw in Detroit and was returning to Philadelphia.

Leon had just finished reading the cable when the telephone rang. It was Claudio Barreneche and he sounded very excited. The board of directors had approved an increase in the bank's capital by 6.5 million pesos, through an issuance of 13,000 shares at 500 pesos each, equal to the original shares, of which 3,000 were designated for acquisition of the lot.

"The deal almost didn't go through," Barreneche Ossa said, "but I managed to get them to come around to my point of view."

Edri smiled while he listened to the banker describe the details of the meeting. Claudio was talking as if the whole thing had been his idea and that he had launched a battle to get it approved. In fact, the members of the board had approved the plan without opposition because it also offered them the opportunity to purchase shares at face value. *They're all probably scurrying right now to line up their cash*, Leon told himself. In turn, he too would make sure he had maximum liquidity, since he intended to buy not just the one thousand shares on which he would receive option rights, (owing to the 5,000 already in his possession), but all the remaining unsold shares as soon as the option rights expired.

The telegram that Leon was waiting for from Philadelphia was not long in coming. Without going into details, as was his custom, Jaime reported he had bought the equipment the factory needed.

Knowing that Jaime had nothing left to do in the United States, Leon was hoping to receive a cable from New York the next day, informing him of his imminent arrival in Lárida. He was very eager to see his partner and hear the details not only of the negotiations but of his personal experiences, which were always amusing. For the next six days he didn't receive any news, but he was so busy that he wasn't able to give the matter any thought. He was running back and forth, trying to increase the company's liquidity and to get a suitable place for relocating their offices. On the seventh day, when he was beginning to wonder about his partner's silence, a telegram arrived from New York notifying him that he would be there a few more days and that he was staying at The Taft Hotel.

The cables constituted the only practical form of communication. Making an international call from Lárida meant staying by the phone several hours, sometimes a whole day, while waiting for the operator to make the connection, only then to hear a halting, barely audible voice amidst the whistling and crackling sounds on the line.

Leon was glad to know where Jaime was staying. Until then the communication between them had been a one-way affair, since Lubinsky reported on his doings without saying where he could be reached. Now that he had informed him, Leon was delighted that this time it was he who was sending the telegram.

CONGRATULATIONS ON PURCHASE OF EQUIPMENT-- EVERYTHING HERE IN ORDER--MOVING AHEAD WITH AN IMPORTANT DEAL--WILL EXPLAIN WHEN YOU ARRIVE

With that last line, he got back at his friend for the enigmatic messages he had sent him.

In the space of just twelve days, the Mercantile Guaranty Bank completed all the required formalities and undertook the issuance of 13,000 shares. The contract between the bank and Sileja was signed without any hitches. Leon had committed himself to vacating their offices within three months and searched feverishly for new quarters to rent.

Another cable arrived from New York informing him that Jaime would be delayed ten more days. Leon thought it strange, but he took the news in stride, since it gave him additional leeway to move ahead with his plans. First of all, he bought the one thousand shares at face value, exercising his stock options. That outlay of half a million pesos left him illiquid, but almost simultaneously he secured two loans from the other banks with which Sileja was working: 1.3 million pesos from the Securities & Exchange Bank and 700,000 from the Bank of the Sierra. The loans were guaranteed, respectively, with 3,300 and 1,700 shares of Mercantile Guaranty Bank stock. As was to be expected, the disclosure of those shares caused more than one eyebrow to be raised, especially among the directors of the Securities & Exchange Bank.

The new issuance and the exorbitant price that was paid for the lot resulted in the shares dropping by about thirty percent, which caused Claudio Barreneche and other investors to abstain from purchasing in the hope of an additional decline that never materialized. Ten days after the issuance, when the options expired, 3,480 shares remained available. Leon bought them all!

A third cable arrived from New York, stating that Jaime would be delayed for another week.

WHAT IN THE WORLD ARE YOU UP TO? Leon cabled.

THE BEST DEAL I'VE EVER PUT TOGETHER! came the reply.

Is this rascal capable of coming up with something better than I have? Edri wondered. The friendly competition would soon reach a climax and Leon was proud of what he had achieved. When his partner left on his trip, they owned ten percent of the shares of the bank; now, when he returned, he would find they owned twenty percent of the financial entity, whose nominal capital, in turn, had increased by twenty-six percent. Moreover, their seat on the board of directors was assured. The only thing missing to make it a complete surprise for Jaime were the new offices. Leon placed ads in the newspapers and queried all the real estate agents he knew, but nothing decent turned up. In the worst of cases, he told himself, if we haven't found anything in three months, we'll move the offices temporarily to the factory. Even though Jaime Lubinsky postponed his return two more times, Leon had not found suitable premises when the last cable arrived.

TUESDAY PANAMERICAN 101

Edri put the telegram in his pocket. As if he needed it to remember the day and the flight number! He was eager to see his partner and friend. He had missed him, more as a friend than as a partner. He figured out exactly how much time Jaime had spent in

237

the United States: two months, twenty-three days. And he said he'd be gone three weeks, the devil!

Leon arrived at Lárida's small airport half an hour before the flight was scheduled to land and was greeted with the news that it had been delayed by two hours. Jaime definitely had a magical talent for doing the inevitable.

In those days, a plane taking off or landing was an uncommon sight. Seeing a plane, period, was an uncommon sight. There were people who went to the airport simply for a day out, like someone going on a picnic, and they would sit down on the grass—or in the airport cafeteria when the weather turned chilly—to watch the arrivals and departures of the marvelous flying machines. On any given day no more than one or two flights landed in Lárida and the people waited hours on end to be on hand to witness those exciting moments.

Leon had been waiting for more than two hours when he saw Anna Lubinsky and her children, Bertha and Mordechai, arriving. He went up to them to say hello. He was upset with himself. Why hadn't it occurred to him, as it did to them, to call the airport to find out if the flight was on time? They had barely spoken when they heard the announcement over the loudspeakers. The plane from New York was about to land. Everybody rushed to the open area behind the building, in front of the airstrip. It was a cement platform, some 65x25 feet, closed off by a five-foot-high chain- link fence: a kind of corral for humans. Many children were there, but it was the adults who seemed the most excited. Half the people were awaiting the arrival of a friend or family member; half were only there to see the planes. Some young people pointed to the sky in a certain direction, but no one saw or heard anything. Minutes later someone called out: "Here it comes!" Only those who had good eyesight and knew where to look could distinguish the tiny dot in the distance, just above the horizon. It wasn't long before the modern Douglas DC-2 was landing to the cheers and applause of excited spectators. As soon as the engines were shut down, the plane door opened, and a stewardess with her arms pressed outwards against the doorframe waited while two workers in white overalls slowly pushed the steps up to the plane. Once they were fixed in place, the passengers began exiting, smiling, looking out towards the metal fence and waving their arms.

"Here comes Jaime!" Mordechai shouted.

"Where?" Anna asked.

"Over there, next to the fat man who's holding onto his hat, behind the lady in the green dress."

Anna didn't recognize her son from the distance because of how he was dressed, so different from how they were all accustomed to seeing him. Instead of dark trousers and a sport jacket, Jaime was wearing a white, three-piece suit, with brown and white oxford shoes, a red tie, and a white felt hat. His appearance was so striking that none of the four could stop staring. He even captured the attention of those who had come to the airport to meet other passengers. Anna was ecstatic. She thought she saw in her son a prince charming. Jaime passed in front of them, a short distance away, on the other side of the chain-link fence, smiling from ear to ear. The people began leaving the enclosed area to gather in the waiting area, in front of the door where the recent arrivals were to come out. At brief intervals, one or two passengers appeared and were immediately besieged by family and friends. When Jaime Lubinsky emerged smiling, Anna rushed towards him.

"Chaim!"

"Mom!"

They hugged and kissed each other.

"How handsome you look!" Bertha exclaimed.

"Hello, Bertha! Mordechai!"

"Hello, Chaim!"

He hugged everybody, and finally his best friend too.

"Leib!"

"Welcome home! Gee whiz!"

"It's so good to see you!"

"What can I say! I thought you weren't ever coming home."

"I want you all to know the reason for my delay," Jaime pompously declared, stepping aside and taking the hand of someone standing discreetly nearby.

All four turned around to look at the woman dressed in green and whom no one had noticed up until that moment.

"My wife," Jaime announced, brimming with happiness.

"Oh, Chaim!" Anna exclaimed, her voice charged with emotion. "What a surprise! She's beautiful!"

She was the only one who spoke, since the others were rendered mute with astonishment. Immediately, in a low voice so that no one would hear her, she added: "Is she Jewish?"

Jaime nodded.

"This is my mother," he said, addressing his wife and holding out his hand towards his mother, who had just breathed a sigh of relief.

The young woman, visibly nervous, forced a smile on her tense face and bowed ever so slightly. Jaime continued with the introductions.

"My sister Bertha and my brother Mordechai," he said, pointing to each one. "And this is my partner," he added, turning around to his friend. "Leib, you remember Ruchel, don't you?"

19

From the day she arrived in Lárida, Jaime Lubinsky's wife won over all who met her. With her gracious character, soft-spoken manner and warm smile, she quickly endeared herself not only to her new family but to the members of the small Jewish community, to her husband's employees and business associates, as well as to neighbors and servants who addressed her as "Doña Raquel," just as she had been introduced to them. Within a short time, the Spanish name replaced the one from the *shtetl*, as generally happened to immigrants, and Ruchel became Raquel, also to family and friends. Only those closest to her, as an expression of affection, sometimes addressed her with the Yiddish appellative in its diminutive form, and thus the name "Ruchele" surfaced from time to time, borrowed from the past.

Leon Edri never learned if Ruchel once had amorous feelings like the ones he once felt for her, and if she had, how intense were they and how long did they last after he left Golochov. Edri didn't even come to learn whether she, in fact, remembered him well. He never asked her; they never spoke of it. The surprise he received at the Lárida airport was more disconcerting than it was painful. In the end, he was pleased to see his best friend happy. Besides, what jealousy could he feel? That young woman—as desirable as she was—was a stranger to him. He did not recognize in the face of Jaime's wife the girl with the golden hair whom he continued seeing for so many years in his imagination. This woman had darker hair, a fuller face…It could be said she was another person. Yes, there was something in her features that reminded him of Ruchel's face, a distant likeness. The girl was probably twelve when the sixteen-year-old adolescent left home, his tender heart burning with the fire of his first love.

If the reunion ten years later served any purpose, it was to make Leon see that he was not in love with a woman but rather with an image from the past. In the face of the unexpected and harsh reality, that love—nostalgic memory more than love—dissipated like a cloud before the wind. In a certain sense, nothing had changed. Before, Jaime was his best friend; now it was Jaime and Raquel together who were his best friends.

A year after their arrival in Lárida, the young couple left Anna Lubinsky's house to set up their own place, a small but pretty two-story house, with a courtyard, a garage, and a huge patio that with time Raquel would transform into a lovely garden.

Jaime invited Leon to have lunch with them in their home every time they had to discuss important business matters, something that happened frequently, and Leon not only delighted in the new dishes that Raquel prepared but in the entire atmosphere of an ordered and happy home. If Leon had been thinking about marriage prior to his friend's trip, he was now thinking about it more than ever. He then decided that he too would go somewhere and find a Jewish wife. He was tempted by the idea of going to the United States, but he wanted to do something different from what his friend had done. It didn't take him long before he announced his intention to travel to Palestine for the ostensible purpose of knowing the Holy Land.

"Along the way I'd like to tour Europe, visit some of the more important cities there. I'd even like to go to Golochov, to remember and see what is new there," he told his mother.

"Tour all you want, son, but don't go to Golochov. There's nothing to do there, nothing to see, and not a single person from our people remains there."

When Jaime learned of his partner's plans, he was taken completely by surprise.

"Suddenly you want to travel?"

"Yes. I need to spread my wings a little."

"All right, but why so far?"

"I want to know Eretz Israel. Also, my best friend lives there and I want to visit him."

"I thought I was your best friend," Jaime protested in a mocking tone.

Leon smiled.

"You are," he said. "The other one was my best friend when I was growing up. It's been more than eleven years since I've seen him, but we write one another frequently."

"Do you know it takes a whole month to reach Eretz Israel?"

"Not that long. More like three weeks."

"Then, how long do you plan to be away?"

"Three months."

"Three months? You're crazy! How am I supposed to manage by myself for that long?"

"The way I did."

"You weren't alone that long and, besides, I wasn't touring."

"Oh, no?"

"No. I was looking for a rabbi for the colony and machinery for the factory. I worked hard and closed a good deal."

"You closed two good deals!" Leon joked, making an almost unintentional dig. "I worked too and I think I did all right. Let's see what kind of push you'll give the business while I'm away."

"Don't even think about staying away for three months."

"It's such a long trip that it makes no sense to do it for less. I have to stay there long enough to make it worthwhile."

"Yes, but three months?" Jaime protested.

"I'll try to do it in less."

Leon was away from Lárida for four months, and that without even stopping to tour Europe! He returned home the way his partner had twenty months earlier: smiling, elegant, happy, and with a radiant bride at his side. The day before he sailed, he sent a telegram from Tel Aviv, saying he had gotten married and that he would be returning with his wife. He sent the cable not so much because he wished to share his happiness but rather because, again, he did not want to copy what Jaime had done. The advance notice eliminated the element of surprise—his returning home as a married man—but it didn't eliminate the excitement. Waiting for him at the airport were his family, Jaime's family and numerous friends. Despite the fact that he had been greatly missed, it was really his wife they were all most eager to see. Their anticipation was well rewarded. Leon Edri had brought home a beautiful woman from the Holy Land. Of bronze complexion, with bright chestnut-colored hair, shapely lips, dazzling white teeth that were the epitome of perfection, high, dark eyebrows, her most striking feature were her green eyes that conferred on her face an exotic beauty. Her name was Esther and she was the oldest daughter of a distinguished family originally from Budapest. From the moment she arrived, she caused a sensation in Lárida, as much for the perfection of her face as for her elegance.

During those first weeks, Leon Edri and his wife received numerous invitations. The Jewish families invited the newlyweds to their homes for dinner, more with the intention of getting to meet the foreign beauty than of playing host to them. They all wanted to win their friendship, for Leon and Esther made a handsome couple: young, good-looking, intelligent, and prosperous. It wasn't long before Esther acquired the reputation as a distinguished and elegant woman. Maybe the clothes she wore were neither the finest nor of superior taste, but for the Jews of Lárida (each one a product of the shtetl) there wasn't anything more elegant. As the years passed, Esther Edri grew more sophisticated. Over time, her jewelry became lavish, her perfumes delicate, and her clothes supremely refined and of exquisite taste. Every new house they acquired was a showcase of subtle decor, the finest porcelain and crystal, the most extraordinary carpets, the most expensive paintings. Simply put, as the years passed, Esther was learning to be rich; but she had a lot to learn when she arrived in Lárida. Maybe the first thing she learned was to be selective. One need not accept an invitation from everybody; nor was there any need to invite just anybody. Esther, like her husband, was ambitious, but unlike him she displayed a haughtiness that frequently obscured her natural grace.

"Who has more money, you or Jaime Lubinsky?" she once asked her husband.

"We have exactly the same amount, because we're equal partners," Leon answered, surprised, and he added as if to show that the question had not been to his liking, "and we'll continue being partners in everything... equal partners," he emphasized.

Raquel Lubinsky and Esther Edri got pregnant more or less around the same time, in 1938, at the beginning of the year. The months of pregnancy dragged on. The bellies of both women grew; the Jewish community of Lárida grew, swelled by destitute immigrants who were fleeing European anti-Semitism; and Edri and Lubinsky's business grew.

The first to give birth was Raquel. The young Lubinskys were beside themselves with happiness. They had been blessed with the arrival of a healthy and beautiful baby boy. They quickly organized a big celebration for the eighth day after the birth, the day of the *Brit Milah*, when the ancient ritual of circumcision is held. Saul—the

245

name they chose for their son—would be the first male child of Lárida circumcised by Rabbi Abraham Singer, the very same one Jaime Lubinsky had hired in New York three years ago. Jaime wanted his son to be called Mahir, after his father, but Raquel insisted that they name him Saul, in memory of her father. What finally induced Jaime to concede was the argument, ably put forth by Raquel, that if for any reason they were not to have more children, she being an only child, her father's name would never be given in his memory; on the other hand, Jaime's father would never be denied that honor, since Jaime had brothers who would eventually marry and bring sons into the world.

Although there hadn't been much time for preparations, the celebration was a complete success. It was held in the big patio of the Lubinsky house, which had been decorated for the occasion with lanterns, palm leafs, and flowers. A group of musicians enlivened the evening. Thanks to Anna, who worked tirelessly in the kitchen all that week, the meal was a feast, brimming with delicious platters of food. The guests were thrilled with what was until then the biggest party ever held in the heart of the community. Almost the entire "colony" attended. The comment circulated among the guests that the Lubinskys wanted to celebrate not only their son's *Brit Milah* but their own marriage, since it had taken place without any great ceremony, when Jaime was in the United States, far from relatives and friends.

"What a nice party, wasn't it?" Leon Edri commented that night, when he was getting ready for bed.

"Yes, very nice," his wife concurred while removing her hairpins and taking down her elaborate coiffure.

"We must also give a party when our son... or daughter is born."

"Our son," Esther decided.

"Why are you so sure?"

"Because I am. It's going to be a boy; you'll see. And as for a party, of course we'll give one. And what a party it will be!"

Leon smiled. In the year they had been married he came to know his wife.

"I hope you're right. If we have a son, we'll call him Chaim, like my father."

"Like your partner. I don't like that name... there's nothing special about it."

"Well, I like it, and that's what we'll call him."

"Jaime didn't give his son his father's name, did he?"

"They named him after her father, Saul."

"Who was Saul?"

"I just told you: Raquel's father."

"No, I mean Saul in history."

"Saul? King of Israel. Didn't you study him? Saul was the first king of Israel. He was of the tribe of Benjamin. The people wanted to have a king, and Samuel, who was judge and prophet at the same time, anointed Saul so he could be king. Saul was also a great warrior who won important battles against the Philistines and against other nations that threatened us."

"Goodness! But you really know your history!"

"More or less... it's the only thing I studied."

The teachings of Rav Zuntz were still fresh in the mind of Leon. He had taken them with him from Golochov, along with his father's watch, the book of prayers, the two gold coins, and the faded photograph of his father and his uncle when they were boys. The old *lerer* had instructed him: the tradition of your people is their most important legacy, and it must be preserved above all else, to pass it on to your descendants as their heritage.

"How interesting!" Esther exclaimed, getting under the sheets. "Tell me more."

"At this late hour?"

"Yes. Why not?"

"What do you want to know?"

"More about Saul. What was he like?"

"The Bible says he was a very tall and handsome young man."

"And all the kings of Israel descend from him?"

"No, not at all! The second king was David, who came from a family in Bethlehem that had nothing to do with King Saul's family."

"David, the same one who cut off the head of Goliath?"

"The same one."

"Then, how did he become king?"

"Precisely because of that. The Philistines, seeing that the strongest of their warriors had been decapitated, fled in every direction. David's reputation spread throughout the kingdom. Saul, impressed by the young man's deed, gave him the rank of captain in his army and, later, his daughter in marriage."

"And when Saul died, David became king."

"But not in the way you think. It turns out that David was very popular and Saul began to be jealous of him, a jealousy that gradually transformed itself into mistrust and then into hatred. David—sensing that his life was in danger—fled the court and took refuge on the perimeter of Judea. There, hundreds of Jews unhappy with Saul joined him and mounted a kind of opposition against his rule. When Saul died, David was proclaimed king. Well… that's the story in a nutshell."

"Bible stories strike me as truly beautiful."

"If you knew the Talmud, you'd realize they're not only very beautiful," Leon said, sitting up in bed to turn off the lamp on the night table, "but they have a fascinating depth to them."

The bedroom was completely dark now.

Then Leon heard Esther say in a serene voice: "You know... we ought to name our son David."

Leon laughed.

"Sweetheart, what's gotten into you?"

"I believe it's a beautiful name; one worthy of a fine gentleman, a hero, a king."

"What do you think?" Leon asked in a comical tone. "Because you have the name of a queen that your son should bear the name of a king?"

"Why not? Besides, you also bear the name of a king."

"Me?"

"Of course! Leon is the king of the jungle," she said.

They both laughed.

"I'm serious," she insisted. "I'd like my son to be named David."

"In whose memory?"

"In King David's."

"We don't even know if we're going to have a son."

"I say we are. It'll be a boy."

Leon turned the light back on, sat up in bed, and looked his wife in the eye.

"If it's a boy, his name will be Chaim."

Esther had never heard him speak in such a severe tone, but despite that she was not ready to concede.

"Before the Torah we can name him Chaim David, in honor of your father," she suggested with delicate diplomacy. "Afterwards, let people call him as they wish."

Leon did not answer. On the one hand, he liked the display of character and intelligence in the woman with whom he was to share his life; on the other hand, her attempt to circumvent his wishes annoyed him. He turned off the light and lay back down, angry. Again he heard his wife's voice in the dark.

"Good night, sweetheart."

"Good night," he said, feeling obligated to answer.

Twelve days later, in the middle of lunch, Esther felt the first contractions. During the few hours that passed until she gave birth around seven that evening, one hundred ninety-one synagogues were burned and another seventy-six completely demolished; eight hundred fifteen Jewish stores were ransacked and wrecked; twenty-nine warehouses and one hundred seventy-one residences destroyed. It was the "Night of Broken Glass," the infamous *Kristallnacht*, a prelude to the most ignominious events in the history of mankind that were to take place during the next five years. But this was happening in civilized Germany, 6,200 miles from America, very far from Lárida. That November night was a warm and pleasant night in the Obondó Valley, and the anguished screams of the Chosen People—chosen for extermination—did not reach those fertile lands.

At the Santa Cecilia Hospital, Esther Edri gave birth to a handsome baby boy. On the eighth day following the blessed event, a *Brit Milah* was held in the home of the happy parents. Jaime Lubinsky was the *sandak*, or "godfather," just as Edri had been at the circumcision of Lubinsky's son. Esther got her way: their son received the name of Chaim David and—no one knows exactly why—from that moment on they all called him David. The celebration was bigger and more elegant than the one the Lubinskys had given. Esther made sure of it. That evening she was very beautiful, radiant: like a queen.

Jerusalem

February 26, 1942

Dear Leon,

The world has gone mad. The news coming out of Europe sends shivers through me, not of fear or desperation, but of fury and powerlessness in the face of the storm that is sweeping across the continent.

A report of a death that I heard on the radio made me think about you. I thought about you because the news was not from Europe, like almost everything we hear nowadays, but from South America, and it concerned a Jew who went to live there: Stefan Zweig, who three days ago ended his life. He committed suicide in Brazil, along with his wife, because his concern over the world situation had depressed him beyond what his noble spirit could bear. Not even in the comfort and security of your Latin America could he shut himself off from the terrible events of the old continent.

How far will the persecution and murdering go? We here, in Eretz Israel, despite the fact that we also have our relative comfort and security, feel the tragedy of European Jewry more intensely, not only because we are closer to the events, but because we receive the few fortunate ones who manage to escape the carnage. Some enter the country legally, supplied with immigration papers that the Jewish Agency obtains from the mandatory government. The English give those papers out like drops from an eyedropper, which is tantamount, really, to closing the doors of refuge for the Jews just when they need it most. Do you know how many Jews were indirectly condemned to death by the British government? If the English had kept the doors of Palestine open from the time of Hitler's rise to power until war broke out—precisely the period in which Jews could leave Europe but had nowhere to go—hundreds of thousands of our people would have been saved.

252

There aren't many that can escape now, but there are some. They try to slip into Eretz Israel illegally, risking their lives to cross the Mediterranean in ships that are not seaworthy and that reach desolate shores in the dead of night, with lights extinguished, to deposit on the sand their precious cargo: men, women, and children who risked their lives to enter the Promised Land.

A British fleet, whose mission is to intercept the refugee boats, constantly patrols the coasts. When it succeeds in frustrating the attempt at entry, the refugees are taken to Cyprus, where the English maintain detention camps. Other times the outcome is much crueler: the ships, which for the most part are in no condition to make the crossing, sink midway in the crossing. Everything: boat, passengers and illusions end up buried under the waters of the sea.

Just yesterday, also over the radio, we learned a terrible piece of news. The Struma, a ship that left the port of Constanza, crammed with Rumanian Jews who were fleeing the Nazis, sank off the coast of Turkey. Seven hundred sixty-nine people drowned! How horrible! The disaster happened three days ago, but it wasn't until yesterday that the Turkish authorities made the announcement. It occurs to me that that misfortune took place at the very moment in which Stefan Zweig was taking his own life, as if he perceived the anguish of his brothers and sisters transmitted from afar.

And in spite of everything, Jews do reach Eretz Israel. Judith is working as a volunteer at the Jewish Agency, providing help to the immigrants. She is really doing a wonderful job. After all, no one understands the needs of an immigrant better than another immigrant. She devotes a couple of hours every day to her efforts. Believe me, it's not easy for her, since home and children give her plenty to do. However, she arranges her hours to find the necessary time. Helping the new arrivals fills her with satisfaction. It's her way of serving the cause. As you see, I'm not the only idealist over here.

Only now is it dawning on me how diverse we Jews are, I, who thought I knew my people. It's impressive to see the number of races we have here: blonds from Poland, Caucasians from Russia, dark-skinned people from Yemen... They've come from all over the world and the strangest languages can be heard in the street. Every immigrant brings with him a particular culture from his country of origin. Each one has his own aesthetic concepts, his likes in food, his preferences in music. We are so different from one another, and to think that we are all Jews!

Love for Zion, even more than of religion, is what unites us. Zionists, the world over, feel a force of mystical attraction that pulls them towards the Promised Land. That's why they'll keep coming despite the British fleet and the detention camps. They'll come to join us, those of us who are already here, and to help us build our country. Let there be no doubt: We will have a Jewish State. The Third Reich will collapse like a house of cards, just like all the other empires that persecuted the Jewish people throughout history, and we will rise from the ashes to create our own State. Neither the English, nor the Arabs, nor anyone else will be able to stop it.

Affectionately,

Baruch

20

"Yes, señora, he seems to be a very lovable child," said Eustaquio Cardona, feigning a smile at the boy who was watching him with a frightened look in his eyes.

"He is, indeed. He's incredibly bright," Raquel said.

"What's your name?" Don Eustaquio asked, addressing the little boy.

"Saul," he answered timidly.

"Saul?"

The child nodded.

"And how old are you?"

"Five."

His voice was barely audible.

"Five?"

He nodded again.

"Aha! Very good, very good," Cardona murmured, again flashing his false smile.

"Dr. Cardona, I took the liberty of bothering you and asked for this interview," Raquel began apologetically, "to beg you to reconsider our request. I thought that knowing the boy personally you would be able to appreciate that he comes from a good home; I mean, that he has been properly raised and...well, that he's an orderly, well-mannered boy... intelligent..."

Raquel Lubinsky had swallowed her pride to ask for this interview with the director of Lárida's prestigious Upper School, which a week earlier, had sent home a laconic note stating that "the request had been denied." If she was prepared to bow her head to ask for the director's intervention, it was because she wanted to give her son the best education possible and, aside from the Lárida Upper School, there wasn't any other center of high academic standing in the city. The Lubinskys knew of several cases in which children from the Jewish community had been rejected, but they clung to the hope, given their superior economic position and their friendship with several persons of importance in the sociopolitical life of Lárida, that little Saul would be accepted into that select academy. Raquel was to lament the interview that she herself initiated.

"My dear lady," Dr. Eustaquio Cardona began in a tone of pompous arrogance, "the Lárida Upper School is not some run-of-the-mill institution. Look," he said, pointing with his index finger at a large plaque that hung on the wall, next to his desk. "That's our coat of arms, our emblem. You can read, can't you? 'Christ and Country.' For us that is not just a motto; it is a creed. Christ and Country! Those two words embody the essence of our entire philosophy... Since its founding in 1908, the school has dedicated itself, more than anything else, to elevating the spirit of our students and setting them on the path of rectitude and honor. Our goal is to make good citizens and good Christians of them. In no way can we make room in our classrooms for young boys who, in light of their social or religious background, will hinder us at the outset in achieving that goal... I believe that you understand me, don't you?"

"Do you mean to say that... you won't accept—"

"Precisely, señora. We won't accept—"

As if by agreement, both avoided the word "Jews."

"The policy of the school," Don Eustaquio continued, "is not to accept anyone who is not a Roman Catholic."

She wanted to reply, but the words stuck in her throat. She was
stunned.

Adding insult to injury, he continued: "If you will excuse my
frankness, señora, the truth is that those of the Hebrew faith
are not welcome in this institution."

They looked at each other. It was a brief look: hers, defiant; his,
cold.

Without saying a word, Raquel Lubinsky stood up, turned
around and hurriedly departed the office, pulling her son by the
hand. Saul did not comprehend what had happened, but he
understood that it was something bad and he was pale with fright.
Raquel, on the other hand, walked out with her face red, burning
with fury. And she cried with rage, but only after she reached home.
She had the small consolation that she did so without anyone seeing
her.

The doors of the Lárida Upper School were not to remain closed
forever. At some future date, they would be opened to receive a very
limited number of Jewish boys whose families had the right
connections and adequate funds. Indeed, sometime in the future, but
not while Dr. Eustaquio Cardona was the director and Professor
Nicholas Braun, a native of Bavaria, held the post of co-director.

The year was 1943. Europe was aflame under the furor of world
conflagration and even though Hitler had suffered some reversals,
many people in Lárida—and throughout Latin America in general—
thought that Germany could still win the war. Some vehemently
wished for such an outcome. It was a period when anti-Semitism was
in fashion. It was only when the war ended and the magnitude of the
holocaust was exposed, when the civilized world shuddered with
horror before the Dantesque spectacle of the crematoriums, the gas
chambers, the mutilated victims of macabre experiments, the
survivors of the concentration camps, in truth, walking skeletons,
and the immense piles of corpses covered with lime—only then—

that anti-Semitism ceased to be fashionable. But towards the end of 1943, when Saul Lubinsky and David Edri were five years old, the anti-Semites of the world still had not gone into hiding under the cloak of silence or a feigned tolerance.

Jaime Lubinsky was not in his office when his distraught wife phoned him.

"Do you know where I can find him?" Raquel asked the secretary.

"He didn't say, señora Raquel."

"As soon as he comes in, have him call me right away."

* * *

Jaime arrived at his office late that day. He and Leon Edri had spent the morning in the office of the Aldach brothers, Edmond and Clemente, distinguished members of the Lebanese community. Edri and Lubinsky were friends of the Aldachs, as were the oldest members of the Jewish community with those of the Lebanese community, generally speaking. They shared several things in common: their origins as immigrants from distant lands, their devotion to family, a dedication to commerce, and prosperity in business. They understood each other well. There were, of course, essential differences between the two communities. The Jewish "colony" was more closed, more united, better organized. The Lebanese did not need that type of social structure since, as a predominantly Christian community, they saw no threat to their religious patrimony. Unlike the Jews, they intermarried with the locals, and their integration into the social and political life of the country was much greater.

"On merchandise that's more than a year old and that you haven't been able to sell, we can take off your hands at fifty percent of cost," Clemente Aldach said. "That allows us to price it at a thirty percent markup, which is what we consider fair market. That's all we want. Our policy on prices is to make thirty percent profit on any product, nothing more."

"In that case," Leon replied, his mind leaping two steps ahead of the others, "you'll have to buy at cost plus fifty percent the merchandise that is sold at double the cost."

Days went by negotiating over the Touch of Royalty stores that the Aldach brothers wanted to buy as much as Edri and Lubinsky wanted to sell, without either side, of course, revealing its eagerness. The Aldachs were interested in the acquisition of the stores because they were a good complement to the chain of shops that they had in all the provinces and through which they distributed one fourth of the fabrics sold in the country, whereas Jaime and Leon were interested in selling because, simultaneously, they were moving ahead in secret negotiations with the heirs of the recently departed Claudio Barreneche, to buy all the shares in the Mercantile Guaranty Bank that he had bequeathed. Leon and Jaime thought their money would be better invested in shares of the bank where they would end up as main shareholders.

When Lubinsky reached his office around midday, his secretary hastened to inform him:

"Don Jaime, you've had about a thousand calls this morning. Your wife phoned twice, asking that you please get in touch with her. And also there's a gentleman who's been waiting since ten o'clock to see you."

"Fine. Get Doña Raquel on the phone for me, please."

A maid answered and informed him that his wife had gone out.

Jaime read the notes that his secretary had left for him on top of his desk. Attached to the list of messages with a paper clip was a business card. "Matías Kopel" it read in the center and just below it, in smaller letters: "Consulting Engineer."

"Who is he?"

"The gentleman who is waiting to see you. I don't know who he is."

"Have him come in."

The secretary left and a minute later a short, robust man entered and closed the door behind him.

Jaime Lubinsky and his visitor stood there looking at each other for a few seconds without uttering a word. The short, bald-headed man with glasses, began arching his mouth upwards little by little until there was a big smile. By the shape of the lips and the large and slightly protruding front teeth, Jaime recognized an image from the past, but he wasn't able to place it. The smile grew a little wider.

"Motty?" Jaime murmured.

The visitor broke into booming laughter at the same time that he was nodding his head.

"Motty!" Jaime shouted.

"Chaim!"

Jaime rushed over to the man and gave him a big hug. Holding each other tight, they rocked back and forth and emitted exclamations of joy. On hearing the noise, the secretary opened the door in a fright. When she saw the two men grasping each other's arms and looking so delighted, she changed her expression of alarm for one of perplexity and closed the door again.

"How great to see you!" Jaime exclaimed, barely recovering from the surprise.

"Chaim, you haven't changed a bit."

"Neither have you," Jaime fibbed.

"*Just* a little," Motty corrected him, patting his bald head.

"Well, we all change a little," Jaime conceded, patting his potbelly.

Both were laughing the whole time while looking each other over and talking.

"I see you haven't done too badly."

"Thank God. And what about you?"

"Eh. Not so great... thank God!"

The two burst into laughter.

"So now it's Matias, right?... What's with this Matías business?"

Motty shrugged his shoulders.

"Imagine if I had used the name Menashe," he said jokingly. "Menashe, in this part of the world! Matías, at least, is a Spanish name and it's the closest thing to Motty."

"And what did you do with Kopelovich?"

"I dropped the 'ovich' to simplify it."

They laughed again.

"And where did the 'Consulting Engineer' come from?"

"Oh, that's a long story..."

Motty, of course, had never set foot in any university in his entire life. Save for a few exceptions, none of the Jews who came from Eastern Europe had an education that went beyond elementary school. Poverty had obligated them to work from the time they were children and, for the majority, a couple of years in the *cheder* constituted their entire education. Motty belonged to that generation of unschooled, intelligent men who had come "to make America." He possessed an innate talent for mathematics and frequently amazed his acquaintances by performing calculations in his head that the most highly educated had difficulty working out with pencil and paper. No one beat him at chess. One day he decided that he was going to learn engineering and began studying on his own as many books on the subject as he could get hold of. He read books on physics, chemistry, and especially mathematics, abstract as well as applied in the branches related to resistances, mechanics of solids, mechanics of liquids, thermodynamics, methods and analysis. Engineering was more than a pastime for him; it was a passion. Having completed his self-education, at age twenty he knew more than anyone holding a university degree. When he arrived in South America, he decided to confer on himself the title of industrial engineer in order to earn a living. To the very few who insisted on seeing his credentials, instead of a diploma, he showed them some official documents written in Polish that no one understood. At the textile plant of his rich and generous friend he was to find the most important and most highly remunerated work that he had ever had.

"How did you find me?" Jaime asked.

"Through the Lubinskys of Lima. I've come from there. I remembered that your family was going to Peru, and when I arrived there, the first thing I did was to inquire about you."

"So?"

"When they told me an Alejandro Lubinsky lived there, I went straight to see him. I thought it was your father. Understand? I didn't remember his name."

"My father died while we were still in Europe. He didn't manage to reach America."

"Yes, I know. Alejandro told me. I'm sorry."

"And what about your parents?"

"They stayed in Poland."

"Are they all right?"

"I hope so. With all that's happening over there... I haven't been able to find out what's become of them."

"Are you married?"

"No. I'm afraid that the woman in my life doesn't exist."

"Nonsense. I met mine when I least expected it. Now I have three children: a boy and two girls."

"Yes, I know. Alejandro told me."

"And my sister Bertha also got married."

"Yes, I know."

"Good grief! I don't know a thing about you, and you come here knowing everything about me!"

"What fault is that of mine if your cousin told me everything?"

"Alejandro isn't my cousin; he's a second uncle. His father and my grandfather were brothers."

The telephone rang once.

"And do you have relatives over here?" Jaime asked, ignoring the phone.

"No. I know I have family in the United States, but I've got no idea where."

The door opened slightly and the secretary, without entering, called in:

"Don Jaime, your wife is on the phone."

The door closed again.

"Excuse me a moment."

263

Motty nodded while Jaime went over to the phone.

"Raquelita?... I was at the Aldachs. I think the deal is going to go through... Yes, they gave it to me. The girl didn't tell you I phoned?... I've just had a big surprise. Get this: I arrive at the office and meet up with a friend I haven't seen for seventeen years!... No, from Rovno, when we left Russia... I have him here, with me... Yes, very much. Listen, I'll bring him home tonight to have dinner with us... No, he's by himself... All right... Yes, I know. How did it go?... Hm!" Jaime exclaimed, sounding indignant while listening to his wife. "Hm!..." His face was growing tense. "Hm!... And what did you say to him?... Yes, well, of course!... Hm!... Don't take it to heart, dear. Calm down... Yes... All right, dear, see you later."

"Is everything all right?" Motty asked.

"Well... the same old thing."

That night, during dinner, anti-Semitism was the topic that occupied them the most. Raquel couldn't overcome her anger.

"We have our priorities backwards," Jaime Lubinsky offered. "We built a synagogue and then a social club, when the first thing that we ought to have built was a school for the children."

Jaime spoke those very same words to his partner the following day when he saw him, and he repeated them more vehemently at the meeting of the board of directors of the Israelite Center that he convened especially to deal with the subject.

"What is more important," he asked, launching the rhetorical question before the members of the board, "to have a place to play cards or one to educate our children?"

"You forget that the reason we didn't build the school before is because there were no children in the colony. There were no children and there was no money," Leopold Reiss pointed out.

"Well, now there are children and there's money!" Lubinsky exclaimed.

"I'm not so sure about that," Mike Spul intervened. "Has anyone taken a census of how many Jewish children we have in Lárida? Do it and you'll see that it's too small a number to maintain a school."

"That's not a problem," Arnold Liffshitz replied. "It can be supplemented with non-Jewish students."

"Who says we want *goyim* in the school?" Daniel Guttman interjected.

"Why not?" Liffshitz retorted, using the traditional Jewish technique of answering a question with another one. "And who said we want an exclusive school?"

"We want a Jewish school," Guttman insisted.

"Of course we want a Jewish school," Liffshitz argued, "but if the majority of the children belong to the colony, the school will maintain its Jewish character."

"What do you mean exactly by 'Jewish school'?" Isidoro Fischer asked.

"A school like any other," Arnoldo Liffshitz explained, "where, besides the subjects that are normally taught in schools, we'd offer courses in religion, Hebrew and Jewish history. Rabbi Singer, for example, could give classes in religion; someone like Emmanuel Herzog could give classes in Hebrew…"

"And Julio Richter could teach Jewish history," Daniel Guttman suggested. "It's incredible what that man knows!"

"If we have good teachers, our school could be one of the best in Lárida," Liffshitz said, enthused with the idea.

"One of the best, no. The best!" Jaime Lubinsky burst out.

Despite the general support for the idea in the community, the Jewish school was not established as quickly as Jaime had wanted. The community leaders, as usual, did more talking than doing. For hours and entire months, discussions continued regarding the name that the school should have, its size, location, how many non-Jewish students, the tuition, financing for the project, administration, the curriculum of Jewish studies, and an endless number of problems, real and imagined. Everybody had something to say.

"Why teach Hebrew? No one speaks that language. What should be taught is *mame loshen*: Yiddish."

"Yiddish? Us? You're going to teach us 'Turks' Yiddish? Rather we teach you Arabic."

"And why not Ladino? It's as Jewish as Yiddish."

"Hebrew is the vernacular of the Bible, the holy language. Thousands of Jews in Eretz Israel speak it. It's a living language. On the other hand, Yiddish is a language that's dying."

"Precisely because it's dying we have to teach it. To preserve its beauty, its special flavor."

"We need to teach both: Yiddish and Hebrew."

"There's no need to teach either of them."

In the end the institution was named the "Mount Sinai Hebrew School" and was inaugurated three years after Don Eustaquio Cardona, unwittingly, laid the first stone. It began operating in a rented house until years later it occupied the modern building that the community built at great expense. It wasn't "the best" school in the city, as Jaime Lubinsky had predicted, but it was one of the best. Saul Lubinsky and David Edri missed out on the opportunity though, because by the time the school began its operations it was too late for them. When they entered their fourth year of primary school, the Hebrew School was inaugurated with just three elementary grades: first, second, and third. There weren't enough students to start a fourth grade class. Every year, as the students passed from one grade to the next, the school expanded its services to include the next class, which was, unfortunately for the two boys, one grade below the one where they belonged.

Saul was enrolled in the New World Lycée, the only mixed school that existed in Lárida. It was also the only one headed by a woman, Doña Margarita Sinisterra de Longfellow, and most of its students came from foreign families. David was enrolled in the Sacred Heart Academy, considered the best in the city after the Lárida Upper School. The old institution for learning was run by Jesuit priests. Boarding students constituted approximately half the enrollment and the other half was composed of day students, like David, who attended classes from seven in the morning until four in the afternoon. In the school's old classrooms, in its long hallways, in the cobblestone patio, and in the austere dining hall, David spent an unhappy childhood. Rejected by his classmates, pushed around by bullies in the classes ahead of his, and humiliated by his teachers, not to mention Father Herrera's attempts to come on to him, David Edri only had unpleasant memories of his school years.

Jerusalem

June 12, 1948

Dear Leon,

The cannons stopped roaring as of yesterday, when the ceasefire went into effect. I'm taking advantage of this first day of relative calm to answer your letters before fighting breaks out again. If I don't write you now, who knows when I'll have the chance to do it.

First of all, it makes me happy to know that Esther and the children are well. Thank you very much for the photos. I must say that you all look wonderful. I was impressed by how pretty Suzy is and how Benny has grown. He is almost as tall as David.

In your letters you regret how vague the news is that appears in the press and you ask me a series of questions about what is happening here. You want to know my impressions and I am going to try to give them to you, although I don't even know where to begin.

The Jewish people are living the most glorious moments of the last two thousand years of their history. I think about what I am witnessing and I can't believe my eyes. I am seeing the rebirth of the Jewish State. Do you realize what that means? A country of our own, in the land of our ancestors! It seems extraordinary to me that we— you, I, all those of our generation—are passing through the world precisely at this stage. We enjoy a singular privilege, because what is a man's life in relation to History? It is a fleeting moment, a blink of an eye; but that blink of an eye fell to us exactly at the moment when the State of Israel was created. And the privilege is even greater for those of us who find ourselves in the Holy Land, because we lived the events up close, witnessed the State being born, and suffered the birth pangs.

On May 14, when the British mandate ended and independence was declared, I was beside myself with joy. I wanted to go out into the street and dance for joy, as I danced the evening of November 29

268

just past, when the people spilled out onto the streets in a spontaneous display of jubilation upon hearing over the radio the result of the vote in the United Nations on the creation of a Jewish state in Palestine. But this time there was no jubilation in the streets. There was no time for celebrating the birth of the state. The Arab attack had begun. It was an infamous aggression, aimed at annihilating the newborn baby on his first day of life. Egyptian planes bombarded Tel Aviv that very same night, May 14. On May 15 the armies of the Arab countries invaded the state that was not yet twenty-four hours old. From one day to the next, little Israel found itself in a war against no less than six countries: Egypt, Saudi Arabia, Transjordan, Iraq, Syria, and Lebanon. David facing Goliath. Rather, I should say, David facing half a dozen Goliaths, since the Arab armies are regular armies, well supplied, with tanks, planes and heavy artillery, and with soldiers properly equipped and trained by the Western powers. The Transjordanian Arab League, for example, is commanded by British military officers. Our army, on the other hand, is not what could be called in the modern world an army. It is, rather, a combatant force formed and trained in secret. While the Arab countries could freely assemble their war apparatus, we were impeded by the British, who did everything possible to leave us as cannon fodder when they pulled out. And, in effect, when the mandate ended and the last contingent of English soldiers abandoned the Holy Land, our "army," which had to face the combined armies of the Arab world the following day, did not have a single plane, not a single tank, not a single cannon. The Israeli soldiers did not even have uniforms; they went into battle dressed as civilians and each armed with a rifle of a different make. Under such circumstances, total Arab victory and the destruction of our national aspirations should have been inevitable. But what was supposed to happen didn't happen. Why? Frankly, I don't know. For me, it is completely incomprehensible. I could speak to you of the heroism of our men, of the motivation of our people, of the strength of an ideal; I could also speak to you of the fear, of what man is capable of doing when he has no alternative. Undoubtedly, all those are factors that affect the result of a war, but they are not decisive when such a disparity exists between the combatant forces. So, how does one explain the fact that we held back the onslaught? There is no rational explanation. The temptation is great—and many fell into it—to see divine intervention in the latest events. It isn't the first time this has happened, says the mystic: The Almighty watches over His people. Since I'm not a believer, I remain perplexed, unable to explain the impossible.

I'm not going to tell you in this letter how I performed in the war. It neither merits interest nor importance. Suffice it to say I fought and did my duty.

Yesterday the truce brokered by the United Nations went into effect. From the start of the war, the international organism tried to bring hostilities to an end, but the Arabs refused to accept a ceasefire because they thought that victory was theirs for the having. Now—being as perplexed as I am over the fact that instead of advancing, they began pulling back—they've decided to accept the United Nations' proposal. Fortunately for us, the Arabs committed a gross mistake. They intend to take advantage of the truce to get better organized and to attack with greater ferocity, but they haven't taken into account that when it comes to using time to one's advantage, we do it better than they. Our leaders are not sleeping. At this very moment, as I write these lines, a feverish effort is underway to improve our situation. Twenty-four hours a day, representatives of the provisional government of Israel in different countries are making extraordinary efforts to acquire arms and dispatch them here as soon as possible. A good supply of equipment has been reaching us in recent days. Also, Jewish volunteers from all parts of the world have come to participate in the fight. Today I am calm. If the Arab countries did not crush us in the first days of the war, they will never be able to do it.

When combat resumes—and it is going to resume, I have no doubt, because the Arabs announced their intention to not maintain the truce for more than four weeks—our enemies will suffer a tremendous defeat. In the meantime, we can't allow ourselves even a minute's rest. We have a colossal task ahead: to build the country. Much work remains. We must forge a nation like the one our parents dreamed of: a refuge for the persecuted people, a land to bring together all the Jews of the Diaspora; a country based on the principles of equality and social justice; a light unto the nations.

When I think that these ideals are about to become reality, I sometimes ask myself: Can it be true that we really witnessed a miracle?

Affectionately,

Baruch

Jerusalem

May 2, 1960

Dear Leon,

Fortunately we have holidays, like today, to catch up on correspondence. Today is the 5th of Iyar, Independence Day. How time flies! To think that twelve years have already passed since the creation of the State.

I would have liked to begin this letter telling you of the marriage of my son Ariel, but it seems I was mistaken in what I told you in my previous letter. Ariel had an argument with his fiancée a few days ago. I thought it was one of those altercations that all of us as couples have from time to time, but Ariel told me it is definitely over between Tamara and him. I don't know why I have the impression it isn't so and they'll soon make up, but if I'm wrong, a broken engagement is better than a failed marriage. There are so many divorces of late that one no longer knows what to think.

How times have changed! Do you remember when a father's greatest longing was to find his daughter a husband who was a "talmid chacham," a man wise in matters of the Law? Only the few wealthy families we had in the shtetl could give themselves that pleasure and have a son-in-law who, instead of working, devoted himself to study. Nowadays no one wants a son-in-law like that. It's true that the contempt for intellectualism, as displayed by the first pioneers, no longer exists; but our current crop of young people attends the universities more to acquire a profession than to be instructed. Rather than studying history or philosophy they study engineering and medicine. The learning that is valued is that which has a practical application. The world was never as materialistic as now. It amazes me to see how much today's kids want to be out ahead of everybody, to have a car of their own, fine clothes, an abundance of money... I see it in my children and to a greater

272

degree—it should serve as my consolation—I see it in the children of others. The spirit of sacrifice that characterized the young immigrants of my generation is something that belongs to the past. When we were growing up, we thought about the good of the country more than our own, we wanted to work for the future generations. How different things are today! Work is no longer in fashion; or at least, the physical work, the manual labor, in which those of us who came to redeem the land took so much pride. It isn't that idealism has disappeared. Kids today, like yesterday, are idealistic; and these young Israelis who, unlike us, have grown up free in their own country are not the exception. But their idealism is not a romantic one like ours was, we dreamers of the Diaspora. The young people have their feet firmly planted on the ground and understand life better, that is to say, better than we understood it at their age. Let's not kid ourselves, Leon, our children are not only better educated than we are but smarter and better equipped.

I'm enclosing the photographs I promised you. We took them at a picnic in Upper Galilee a week ago. We drove out from Jerusalem in three cars, along with my brother-in-law and some friends. We left the cars next to the road near Zefat and entered a small forest on foot. You know, one of those that the Keren Kayemet financed thirty years ago, when tens of thousands of trees were planted, each one in the small bit of soil that could be found between the rocks. If you could see how big and beautiful those trees have grown, providing a green mantle for the hills that for centuries—thousands of years, perhaps—remained barren. It was not in vain that our parents, one coin at a time, filled the little blue and white tin boxes that we used to see in the synagogue when we were children.

In that little forest we came across a spot with a splendid view overlooking Lake Kineret, which in the Christian world is known as the "Sea of Galilee" (although it isn't a sea). We found ourselves more or less in front of the site where the Kineret's waters run into the Jordan River and looked down from on high onto the city of Tiberias in all its magnificence, alongside the mother-of-pearl lake. What an intoxicating landscape! There wasn't even a single cloud in the blue sky. From that charming spot a person can view four countries at the same time: Lebanon, land of sleepy hamlets among hills that vanish next to the sea; Syria, on whose flank Mount Hermon majestically rises up with its crown of snow; Jordan, marking the horizon with its arid mountains on the other side of the lake; and Israel, sprinkled with settlements in the middle of cultivated fields with as much fruit and vegetables as the good land can yield.

Watching my grandson play with his friends, I was reminded of when we were boys and would go out to the country to swim in the river. It's a shame that destiny has separated us into two different worlds. Our children might have been friends; now, they don't even have a language in common.

In the photos where we are sitting on the grass, you'll recognize Ephraim, my brother-in-law, and Eva, his wife. Dalia and my son-in-law are the ones standing. Ariel isn't in any of the pictures because he was the photographer.

In the photo of just the children, my grandson is the second one on the left. He doesn't look like his father or his mother, or any of his grandparents, but—it never ceases to amaze me—he's the living image of my father. Do you remember him? He had a very distinctive face: eyes set wide apart, high cheekbones and a dimple in his chin. So, that's what Shai is like. Identical. Sometimes I think that it's him, my father reborn. Maybe all of us are reborn, reincarnated in some of our descendants. Deep down I know it's not so, which is a pity, since it would be very comforting to think that death only separates us from this world for a short time. Imagine, coming back to life and seeing your aspirations realized. That would be my father's case, finding himself reborn in the person of Shai: an

274

ardent Zionist, a dreamer who passed away, now a boy without fears or complexes, free in the land of his ancestors.

Affectionately,

Baruch

21

Leon Edri stepped out of the elevator before the door had finished opening.

"Good morning, don León."

"Good morning, Ligia."

"Don Jaime asked that you stop by his office."

"Jaime's already here?"

The question was superfluous. Jaime was always the first to arrive. Edri was in the habit of coming in later and generally leaving earlier. It isn't that he worked less but rather that he conducted a good part of his business outside the office, visiting the factories and maintaining several commercial contacts. Leon and Jaime worked in perfect accord. Demonstrating an extraordinary ability, together they had built a financial empire that, in that part of the world, was comparable only to the assets of the old oligarchic families, whose fortunes came through inheritance from generations back. It had been neither easy nor quick. With absolute dedication they struggled for more than thirty years to attain their current position. Unquestionably, luck had also played a part in helping them. Their factory, Sileja Mills, had become one of the principal industries in the province, with a sales volume close to that of Lanatex, the powerful firm of the Méndez family. Sileja Mills had two plants: one built at the beginning of the 1930s nicknamed La Vieja, and expanded on several occasions, and the other plant, nicknamed La Nueva, built twenty years later. Two subsidiary firms, Caribbean Fabrics and Siltex Industries, complemented what was known as the "Sileja Industrial Complex," which as a whole employed more than three thousand workers. But the assets of the "Sileja Group" were not limited to the industrial complex. They also included the Mercantile Guaranty Bank, in which it held a sixty-percent share; Liberty Insurance, entirely theirs; Farmers Corporation of Obondó Valley, with more than 10,000 acres of tropical fruit plantations; and Continental Construction Company, the largest in the province and the second largest in the whole country. Continental Construction had built up vast areas around Lárida and erected several buildings in the center of town, among them the luxurious Sileja Building, where the group's offices were located on the top floor.

"Yes, sir, don Jaime arrived early."

Leon went straight to his partner's office, located next to his. He entered without knocking. Jaime's rather large accommodations were furnished quite similarly to Leon's. A splendid wood bookcase, filled with several rows of books and some knickknacks, stood off to one side. Alongside the bookcase, next to a floor lamp, two comfortable armchairs faced each other on a diagonal. At the far end of the room, on a brightly colored carpet, and set up for meetings that never took place, was an oval conference table that accommodated eight people, with a pad of paper and a pencil in front of each chair. The big picture window provided a panoramic view of the city. The organdy curtain did not do much to mitigate the light that flooded the office and showed in silhouette the man seated behind the immense mahogany desk.

"Chaim…"

"Hello, Leib."

"With the cold you've got, I thought you weren't going to get up early today."

Jaime smiled.

"Have a seat," he said, motioning to the big armchairs.

Leon took a seat and Jaime got up from his desk to sit down in the other chair.

"Ligia told me you wanted to see me."

"Yes… I wanted to run a couple of matters by you."

Jaime had a very soft, high pitched voice, almost like a woman's. And just the way his voice was—gentle—so was his demeanor. His friends said of him that he was "a perfect lady."

Leon slid back in his chair and crossed one leg over the other.

"I'm listening."

"Let's begin with the most important one."

He remained pensive for a few moments, as if searching for the right words.

"In six months Saul will be finishing his studies," he began at last.

"Congratulations, Chaim."

"Thank you, Leib. God willing, we'll have an industrial engineer in the family."

"You mean, we'll have a good industrial engineer in the business."

"That's precisely what I wanted to talk to you about."

"There's no problem. We'll put him in charge of running La Vieja," Leon ventured, trying to anticipate his friend's thinking.

"Absolutely no! The boy is completely green."

"He's a bright young man, very capable."

"Yes, but as capable as he may be, he has no experience. What's more, we can't leapfrog him over Matías, just like that, from one day to the next. It wouldn't be fair. Matías has done a good job for us."

"So, what do you suggest?"

"That he begin working as an assistant engineer, responsible for one department. I think he could oversee the machinery in the maintenance shop. After a while, we'll be able to make him Matías's assistant, so that he'll gradually learn the business."

"All right… if that's what you want."

"I think it would be a good way for him to get his feet wet and familiarize himself with what's involved in running the factory."

"Hm, hm," Leon assented.

"The question of salary needs to be decided."

Edri smiled.

"What do you have in mind?" he asked.

"I don't know. It's a problem."

"There's no problem. Pay him five thousand a month and that's that."

This time it was Jaime who smiled.

"Do you want to spoil him for me?"

"I thought that—"

"Saul doesn't have a home to maintain. He lives with us and has everything he needs. It's better for him not to have too much money in his pocket; to learn that money doesn't grow on trees, to know he has to work hard to earn it."

"How much do you think he ought to make?"

"Twelve hundred."

"Twelve hundred?"

"That's the starting salary for an entry-level engineer and that's what he is: an entry-level engineer."

"He's your son."

"Of course. And he's not going to be stuck with that salary. He'll move up the ladder to a higher position and a better salary, but first he'll have to prove he deserves it."

"Well... if you think so."

"I believe it will be better for the factory and for him."

"And if you already had your mind made up about it, why consult me?"

Jaime looked directly at Leon.

"Because David will also be joining the firm shortly and I want him to come in under the same terms as my son's."

Leon didn't know what to say. The turn that the conversation had taken caught him off guard. It was true, less than six months remained before David would receive his degree in economics. From the time his son entered the university, Leon had dreamed of the day when he could work side by side with him. What could be better than having a son who was a recent graduate, totally versed in finance and economics, overseeing the firm's complex affairs? He had pictured David managing the company with more skill than he himself, but he had never given any thought to details such as exactly what position he was to occupy or what salary he ought to be paid.

"What do you mean?"

"That someday this business will belong to our sons. Not only David and Saul but the rest of the children, including sons-in-law whom we don't even know at this time. Everything will be theirs. We won't be around... but while we're here, we ought to plan things so they'll work together and get along with one another. We have to see to it that there's no cause for envy among them, and make sure their experience will be one of mutual trust and spirit of collaboration, the way it has been between the two of us. Do you understand?"

"Yes... Yes, of course."

"All right, so that's what I'm trying to do."

"I understand. And you want David to start at the bottom too."

"Yes."

"At twelve hundred a month?"

"Exactly. For him to climb the ladder little by little; for each one to go about finding his place within the organization, from where he can contribute to its smooth operation without interfering in the work of the others; for them to complement one another rather than compete."

"And what about their rights as shareholders in the companies?"

"Yes, eventually they'll be shareholders. But that's another story. For that we have the annual stockholders and board of directors meetings."

Jaime said it with a certain irony, since in none of the companies they owned was a stockholders meeting ever held as provided for by the statutes. These were not convened because the two partners, with equal voting rights and as owners of the totality of shares, did not consider them necessary. Neither was a single board of directors meeting ever held. Wherever and whenever the two partners met, that was the board of directors. During informal talks, like the one taking place at that moment, the clearest-cut decisions were made for the advancement of the company. Afterwards, the attorney for the firm would write up the minutes of the supposed stockholders and board of directors meetings, the sole purpose being to adhere to protocol and fulfill the legal requirements.

"There, in such meetings, they'll be able to air their opinions and make decisions," Jaime continued. "But in the meantime, let them get to know the business and learn to work together."

Leon Edri nodded in agreement. His partner was right.

"We'll do as you say, Chaim."

He thought for a few seconds before proceeding.

"A minute ago, when we spoke about salaries, you asked me jokingly if I wanted to spoil your son... Do you think I'm spoiling mine?"

Jaime also thought for a few seconds before answering.

"I'm afraid we've both spoiled our sons a little, but I think that under the circumstances it was inevitable. We wanted to give them what we didn't have, and at times it was possible we indulged them too much."

"If that was our only failing, I dare say we didn't go too wrong. We did the best we could, Chaim. We raised them to be healthy, physically and morally. They never saw a bad example at home. We instilled in them the spirit of decency and fairness. We sent them to the best schools and the best universities."

"And...?"

"And they haven't failed us. They studied hard, they're sensible, they respect us..."

"Then, why did you ask me?"

"I don't know... I have my doubts... Our children were born in the heart of two national identities, without belonging entirely to either of them; they grew up between two cultures, without fully identifying with either one."

"And why should they identify *fully* with one culture? Having assimilated both only makes them richer in spirit."

"But it bothers them. They don't know what they are."

"That's absurd. They know perfectly well that they're Jewish."

"Yes, they know they're Jewish; but they don't know how to be Jewish."

"I don't understand you. What do you want? For them to go around with their heads covered? For them to wear *peyot* and *tzitziot*?"

"No, but they could keep the tradition more."

"They keep it in their way. They respect the religion. They attend *shul* during the high holidays. They know they must marry within the Jewish faith. They understand they have received an important cultural heritage and that it is their duty to pass it on to their children.

"And you think they'll be able to do that?"

Jaime looked at his friend. He had asked himself that painful question countless times.

"At *Yom Kippur*," Leon continued, "when you go to temple, Saul is always at your side—"

"And he fasts," Jaime interjected.

"And he fasts," Leon repeated. "Do you know why he's at your side?"

"It's his place," Jaime replied, unintentionally skirting the answer,

"For the very same reason that David is at my side."

Jaime frowned and waited for his friend to give him the answer.

"Because he doesn't know how to pray. Because he needs you to tell him at every step what page you are on. Because he doesn't understand anything that is happening."

Jaime, with his brow still furrowed, kept looking at his friend. What he was saying was the absolute truth. Leon continued:

"He stays by your side because he feels unsure. But some day, when you are no longer here, he will sit where? At whose side? And all the other young men, the ones who sit down and stand up in imitation of the old men, who will they imitate when there's no one to show them the way?... No one. They'll stop going to synagogue because they won't have anything to do there."

Jaime nodded.

"The ranks of Jews without religion will grow," he said.

"Only for a generation, two at most, because just the way the religion is lost, everything else is lost: values, customs, tradition... How long can a Jew maintain his identity if he has no roots?

The question hung in the air. A generation, two at most, as Leon claimed? Neither of them would live long enough to find out. Like their coreligionists of "the old guard," all from Eastern Europe, they viewed the evolution of the community with mixed emotions. On the one hand, they were pleased with its prosperity; on the other, they were mortified by the assimilation that was gradually diluting its Jewish character more each time. With mistrust they observed the process of assimilation ("integration," as the young intellectuals called it) of that generation born in the New World, which didn't speak Yiddish or know the Talmud, or still worse, that of the generation of their children, which was ignorant of the most elementary foundations of Judaism and had neither patience nor interest in learning them.

They remained silent for a moment, pensive. It was a brief pause, since they hadn't met in the office, early in the morning on a workday, to talk about philosophy.

"You also wanted to discuss another matter with me," Leon said, breaking the silence.

"Ah, yes. Yesterday afternoon I received a strange telephone call from Rómulo Zambrano. Do you know who he is?"

"The owner of Southern Yarn?" Leon asked.

"The chairman of the board of directors. I don't know if he's the principal stockholder, but he represents the interests of the Zambrano family. In any event, he said he wanted to meet with me privately, if possible. I suggested my office at seven that evening, when I would be alone, and so we met here at that time."

"Mysterious," Leon joked.

"Not so much. He told me that Ulpiano Méndez made an offer to buy his company for twelve million pesos."

"He told you that?"

"Yes."

"And?"

"And… we spoke briefly, but basically that was it. He left me very worried. Do you realize how serious it would be if Méndez Carrizosa controlled Southern Yarn?"

"Very serious…"

"The man consumes practically half of Southern Yarn's production. If he were to get control of the entire production, he could leave us without raw material, or demand whatever price he wants."

"You really believe that the Zambranos are ready to sell?"

"Why not? They have very serious financial problems. They need an infusion of capital."

"We've got to stop the deal from going through. Any ideas?"

"For the time being nothing is going to happen because I told Rómulo that you and I would study the possibility of making him a better offer than the one Méndez proposed."

"Do you think we should make him an offer?"

"No. Absolutely not. I was playing for time while we ponder our options, but Southern Yarn is an ailing company."

"All the same, Méndez wants it."

"Yes, but cheap. It serves his purposes, to corner the market; not as a business per se."

"Maybe we could cut a deal with the Zambranos... Advance them a large sum of money in exchange for a long-term supply contract."

"It would be very risky. At any moment, they could find themselves forced to shut down production."

"Or buy a portion of their shares; I don't know, ten or fifteen percent."

"You would be investing in a poorly run company, without the ability to turn things around."

"Then what? It's bad if we buy, it's bad if we let Méndez buy."

Jaime nodded in agreement before speaking.

"The problem is we can't compete with Méndez Carrizosa because he's ready to pay more than it's worth."

Leon stood up, paced the room and stopped in front of his friend again.

"I've got an idea," he said. "I'll explain it to you now."

And leaving the explanation hanging, he approached Jaime's desk and pressed the intercom.

"Yes, don Jaime."

"It's me," Leon corrected.

"Yes, don León."

"Melba, get me Doctor Ulpiano Méndez Carrizosa on the phone."

22

David Edri parked the pickup two blocks from the mansion. He didn't want to be seen driving up to the party in a scratched-up truck with business lettering on it. That same day he had taken his car in for repairs and his father, upset over the accident the night before, refused to lend him the big family sedan. Using the rearview mirror David straightened his tie and ran a comb through his hair a couple of times. At twenty-one, he was supremely handsome, more handsome even than what his father had been. He got out of the truck, locked it, and strode towards the Castellanos's residence with a bit of apprehension.

For the first time in his life he would attend a party where he would be the only Jew. Lárida was a Catholic city inside a Christian universe, a place where David unavoidably had continual contact with people outside his religion. Still, he lived in a separate world: the world of the Jews. So closed was the sphere of "the colony," within which he was born and raised, that he had gone from childhood to adolescence and from adolescence to manhood without ever having formed any close link with a Gentile, without ever having attended any of their events, without ever understanding the Christian cosmos that surrounded him. It was only when he was a grown man that he received, almost by accident, the invitation to that party. And what a party! He was already picturing the expression on his friends' faces when he would tell them about it. In his mind he heard Cobi asking him about the girls and Ico making his pointed comments.

From the distance he admired the mansion, lit up as it was for the occasion. He thought that even if he had wanted to, he would not have been able to park closer, since the last block and a half was filled with luxury automobiles lining both sides of the street. A few cars had a chauffeur, either standing next to the vehicle or seated inside, prepared to wait until the late hours of the night to drive their young charges back home. The blaring trumpet of Pepe Chamaco, who enlivened the evening with his twelve-piece orchestra, could be heard from the street.

The parties given by Tulio Castellanos were famous among the young crowd of fashionable Lárida society. One would be hard pressed to find a better place for a party than the Castellanos's mansion. It had an immense ballroom that opened onto an equally immense terrace, which in turn faced a beautiful garden of illuminated grounds and palm trees. On moonlit evenings out there on the terrace, couples became enraptured dancing to the rhythm of the music that poured out through the arches of the room. In that luxurious setting, where only the most fashionable orchestras played and where the highest quality liquor was served, the evening gowns were more elegant, the young women more beautiful, the young men more handsome. That's why the parties that Tulio Castellanos threw were more successful than the ones held at the Bolívar Club, despite the fact that the rooms at the exclusive club were equally large, that it was the same orchestra that played, and that after all is said and done, it was the same young socialites who attended. Perhaps the fact that the parties were given at a private residence made the difference, especially since it was the residence of Doctor Belisario Castellanos Montejo, ex-minister of agriculture and the province's principal sugar cane grower.

Tulio was the eldest of Doctor Castellanos Montejo's children. The only male among four sisters, he was twenty-seven and the most eligible bachelor in the city. There was nothing strange about that. Belonging to one of the most distinguished families in Lárida, Tulio was good-looking, rich, a good conversationalist, and an excellent dancer. He had been working with his father for two years, helping to run the cotton, sugar cane, and soybean plantations that occupied

290

large expanses of land in different regions of the province. Doctor Belisario Castellanos had brought his son into the business almost by force, when he became convinced that the young man, more interested in reveling than in studying, would never complete his university studies. As soon as Tulio finished high school, Doctor Castellanos Montejo sent him to a North American university, following the custom of the wealthiest families in Lárida, who since the 1940's had been sending their sons to study in the United States. In those circles, to speak English was considered synonymous with having a good education. After seven years of "studying" abroad, the boy failed out of the university at the end of this third year. No one knew that, of course. Tulio Castellanos Bustamante, who returned to Lárida every year during school vacation, arrived home, this time to stay for good, and everyone called him "Doctor Castellanos," as they called his father, who didn't graduate with a degree in anything either.

David Edri met Tulio Castellanos by chance one Friday night when both were out on the town with their friends and Tulio, who had had too much to drink, ran into David's car. The young men got out ready to argue and trade punches if need be, but when Tulio saw that he had crashed into a luxury model sedan and that its occupants were apparently "well-to-do people," he addressed David in a gentlemanly manner, befitting a young man of his position.

"Hey, buddy, I'm really sorry. My brakes went out on me; but no need to worry; I'll take care of everything. I am Tulio Castellanos," he said as if he were announcing a title of nobility.

"I'm David Edri," David replied, feeling obligated to answer.

"Pleased to meet you. Look pal, here's my card. Call me tomorrow and we'll settle the matter," he added while taking out a card from his billfold, mystified over having run into a young person of means from Lárida whom he didn't know.

Though it was a city with a population that exceeded one million, it had less than a hundred well-to-do families.

David called Tulio Castellanos the next day and set up an appointment to meet at noon at his regular repair shop. Castellanos was very affable and not only reaffirmed his promise to pay the cost of the repair but extended an invitation to David to the party that he was giving at his house that very night.

"Don't mention this mishap to anyone, because if my father finds out, he'll kill me," Tulio said in a confidential tone. "Thank goodness the damage to my car is barely noticeable. There's no need to notify my insurance company; I'll pay the costs out of my own pocket. All right, then, now you know where I live. See you this evening."

And thus it came to be that David Edri attended Tulio Castellanos's party, a social event that was held once a year and practically defined, as far as the young set was concerned, who was considered to be among the elite in Lárida's high society.

Tulio wasn't at the door to receive his guests. Instead, a butler was stationed there, opening the door and directing the arrivals to the ballroom. David felt uncomfortable on entering and finding himself in a setting that was alien to him. His eyes roamed around the sumptuous room looking for Tulio or, at least, a familiar face. Edri, whose family was as rich as the Castellanos, had never seen such opulence in his life. Overwhelmed, he walked among the guests, not stopping in any one place so as not to appear to be alone and without having anybody to latch on to. He didn't know anyone. There were a hundred or more young people, all in formal attire. Those who weren't dancing were huddled together in small groups, conversing. David was impressed not only by the setting but by the guests. He never imagined there were so many attractive girls in Lárida, so pretty, so elegant. He got up the courage and approached a small group of these young socialites who were chatting beneath one of the arcades.

"Good evening," he said, not greeting anyone in particular.

"Good evening," someone answered.

A boy who had been holding court before David approached them then proceeded with his story.

David felt completely out of place, standing next to people he didn't know, listening to a story that was of no interest to him and about something to which he was not privy.

At one point, the group laughed and David was forced to feign a smile, in an attempt not to stand out from the rest. He could just as well not have made the effort, since no one even acknowledged his presence. The young man continued his narrative. David, seeing that the anecdote was going to drag on, decided to step away from the group. He did so and no one took any notice.

He moved slowly around the room, looking for someone to go up to. Another small group, smaller than the first one, caught his attention. In one corner of the room, two young men were chatting with three girls. He approached them.

"Good evening," he said.

They turned to look at him without saying anything.

"I'm David."

"Nice to meet you. Juan José Velasco."

"Totó," said the second boy, less formal than the first. "And this is Lidia."

The girl was quite pretty.

"Hello," she said, smiling.

"Amparito," Totó continued, introducing the others.

"Good evening."

"And Luz Helena, Juan José's sister."

"Pleased to meet you."

"The pleasure is mine," David replied, trying to appear affable.

"It seems to me that we met at Tulio's hacienda, didn't we?" said Luz Helena Velasco. "During a day of horseback riding."

"No, I don't think so. I wasn't there, although I love to ride."

"I thought I knew all of Tulio's friends," Amparo said, "but I've never seen you before."

"Well, the fact is I met Tulio only a short time ago."

"What did you say your last name was?" Juan José asked.

"I didn't say, but it's Edri."

"Edri?"

"Hm, hm."

"You're part of the Sileja people, right?" Totó inquired.

"Hm, hm."

"But that's a foreign surname, isn't that so?" Juan José asked.

"Hm, hm," David assented for the third time.

"It sounds Italian," Luz Helena interjected.

"But it's not," Velasco asserted, acting knowledgeable. "It's Tyrolian, right?"

"No. It's a Hebrew surname."

A few moments of silence ensued.

"So, you're Hebrew?" Totó asked, taken aback.

"Yes."

Another moment of silence followed, a bit longer than the first. They all felt uncomfortable; no one knew what to say.

"How interesting!" exclaimed one of the girls, more for want of something to say than out of admiration.

"Yes," said another girl, as if seconding the idea.

That's as far as the group's loquaciousness went. The silence that reigned this time was terrible, unbearably long. For a moment David considered excusing himself and walking away, but he didn't want it to appear as if he was fleeing an unpleasant situation. He remained defiant, waiting to see who would be the first one to break the silence. It was Totó who took the initiative.

"I have a great admiration for Hebrews," he declared in the spirit of improving the mood, but his discourse only managed to make it worse. "They're highly capable people. They run all the world's great businesses."

"I wish it were so!"

"But it is so," Totó insisted, convinced he was flattering his interlocutor. "Hebrews are the most able people in the world; that's why they practically control it."

"Not only don't we control the world, but we don't control any economic activity, here or anywhere else," David burst out with indignation.

"Not here, because you haven't had sufficient time," Juan José said, "but in countries where you've spent a hundred years, like those in Europe, or the United States, you're definitely in control. I mean families like the Kelloggs or the Rockefellers."

So refined and yet so ignorant! David said to himself while he considered whether it was worth the trouble to point out that neither of the two powerful families was Jewish. At any rate, he had no time to reply, since Velasco came at him with an extremely cynical comment.

"The problem with you Jews," he voiced in an authoritative tone, using the word "Jew" for the first time, "is that one can't count on your loyalty. No offense intended," he was quick to clarify, as if to contain David's reaction. "I understand there are reasons that explain it, or justify it perhaps, but the fact remains that you have more loyalty to Israel than to your own country."

It wasn't the first time that Edri had to defend himself against the accusation of dual loyalty, so frequently brandished against the Jews.

"I don't know if we have *more* loyalty to the State of Israel than to our own country. I, personally, do not; but I do, in fact, feel a certain loyalty to Israel," David calmly retorted, feeling sure of himself. "What's wrong with that? Is there a real conflict of interest? Why is it necessary to grab the child by the neck and ask him: 'Who do you like better, your mama or your papa?' Only a Jew gets asked that kind of question. Doesn't he have the right to love both his father *and* his mother? Yes, I have a dual loyalty... a triple loyalty and many more. The human is a complex being and has multiple loyalties."

"Multiple loyalties, yes," Juan José argued, "but only one for each individual attachment; in other words, loyalty to a single country, to a single political party, to a single soccer team..."

"To a single teacher," David added, extending the list. "To a single friend, to a single child..."

"It's not the same thing," Velasco protested.

"Why not?"

"Because..."

Juan Pablo didn't know how to answer.

"Take Spain for example," David firmly proceeded. "Don't you feel a certain loyalty to the country that gave you your language, your religion, your culture? Can you feel, let's say, for Bulgaria the same thing that you feel for Spain?"

"No, but... You're confusing love with loyalty."

"Love engenders loyalty."

"Not necessarily."

"Yes. Always."

"Let me ask you something," interrupted Luz Helena, who had been wanting to come to her brother's defense. "If a conflict arose between us and Israel, if a war broke out between the two countries, which one would you support?"

"The one that was in the right."

The quick, clear, simple answer disarmed them. It was a sincere reply that none of them was expecting. Now it was David's turn to ask a hypothetical question.

"If the government passed a law obligating you to do something that struck you as abusive or unjust, would you do it?"

"Of course I would," Juan Pablo asserted. "I couldn't contravene the laws of my country. It's my duty as a citizen. Of course, I'd try through all legal means to have that law abolished. In fact, that's what happens all the time in a democracy," Velasco concluded, satisfied that he had given a good answer. "Citizens fight to change what seems unfair to them, making use of freedom of expression, of the press, of public demonstrations, of elections and of everything that the political system allows them, but in the meantime they abide by the law."

"Excellent," David retorted. "Let's come back to that unjust and pernicious law and let's suppose that the Vatican calls upon all

Catholics not to comply with its requirements. Whose side would you take?"

Juan Pablo stood mute. He had fallen into the trap. Evidently, he too had a dual loyalty.

"What's gotten into you? All this talk about such serious subjects! This is a party!"

With those words and a smile Amparo put an end to the discussion.

"Listen!" Lidia exclaimed. "They're playing 'El Baile Mocho.'"

The music abruptly stopped, like when someone lifts the needle from a record halfway through the song. Voices and laughter filled the room and the music suddenly resumed. Out on the terrace, where most of the couples were dancing, the mood was buoyant, bubbling with energy. Several of the guests, catching the spirit of the vivacious music, split off from their groups and moved to the terrace.

"Would you like to dance?" David ventured to ask, addressing Lidia.

The young girl said yes with a nod of her head.

"Excuse us," Edri said to the others in the group, taking his partner by the hand and going out to the terrace.

As he walked off, he was certain that the four remaining members of the group were talking about him.

The music was carefree and had a distinct rhythm, like a combination of polka and the chotis. It was danced taking three little steps to one side, three to the other and endless twirls. When the music would suddenly stop, everybody would separate and rush to change partners. As soon as Lidia and David began to dance the music stopped.

"This doesn't count," she said with a mischievous smile.

"Of course not," he replied without letting go of her hand.

The music started up again and the two moved farther away from the arcades as they danced their way to the other side of the terrace. David was happy to begin relaxing.

"Hello! Glad you came."

Edri turned around to see who had greeted him. It was Tulio Castellanos, the only person he knew in the entire party. David greeted him with a wave of his hand, but his attention was immediately drawn to the girl who was dancing with Tulio.

What an engaging beauty! David was moved: her face, delicate in the extreme; her skin, a marble color; her lips, a soft crimson; the dainty nose; the eyebrows, dark, delineated to perfection; the lightly shadowed eyelids and long eyelashes that made the extraordinary beauty of her dark, expressive eyes stand out; and her dark brown hair, long and undulating, that fell on her shoulders and swayed coquettishly from side to side. She was wearing a white lace evening dress of an elegant, off-the-shoulder design.

She looked at David and for an instant their eyes met. It was one of those glances that immediately establish a communication, a sort of complicity. She was flustered and lowered her gaze; he, on the other hand, couldn't take his eyes off her. Even when she was twirling around the dance floor and was no longer in front of him, David could see in his mind the big, absolutely dark eyes that sparkled when they looked at him.

Lidia said something and David responded with a smile, without knowing what she had said, without even having heard her, so flustered was he over the captivating girl in the white dress. He looked around the room, having lost sight of her among the couples that filled the dance floor. When the music suddenly halted, he rushed to the side of the room where the girl had disappeared. He spotted her just as the music started up again. Someone was approaching her for the next dance. Hurrying towards her, David bumped into a girl who barely reached his chin and in turn was rushing in the opposite direction. Like two mechanical dolls, they began dancing, he with his eyes on the sleek beauty who was not more than an arm's length away and his partner with her eyes looking down at their feet. She was a freckled-face, blonde-haired girl, who laughed the whole time. Light as a feather, she easily followed David's lead, which allowed him to position himself next to the girl in white, who from time to time turned her face to look at him and flash him a smile. The music stopped and once more everybody hurried to pair off with another partner. David didn't have to go far. There she was, standing before him, radiant, waiting for him to approach. The music was starting. She held out her fingers to him and he took them in his left hand, placed his right hand against her slender waist and, filled with a sense of excitement, he began dancing to a slower rhythm than what the band was playing. He couldn't take his gaze from the girl's bewitching eyes.

"I'm happy to have this chance to dance with you... and meet you. I'm David Edri."

"Very glad to meet you. I'm María Cristina Méndez."

23

They met in the lobby of the Astor, the most elegant hotel in the city. It was really the only suitable place to meet. Leon Edri would not debase himself by going to the offices of Ulpiano Méndez Carrizosa, as if he were some insignificant citizen asking for an audience with one of Lárida's potentates. *It would be just like him—* Edri had thought—*to let me wait outside his office before seeing me.* He had not accumulated all his millions to humble himself before the city's economically powerful elite. And if Edri wasn't ready to go to Méndez Carrizosa's office, he could be sure that Méndez was even less disposed to go to his. Neither did either of the two men wish to invite the other to his home, since it was not prudent, at least at that stage of initial discussions, to elevate their relationship to the social plane. The meeting was strictly business. Doctor Ulpiano Méndez was a member of several social clubs in the city, while Edri was not and felt uncomfortable if invited to any of them. Holding talks over a meal in a restaurant meant turning the interview into an occasion, besides prolonging matters beyond what was necessary. In short, the Hotel Astor was the most suitable venue.

Leon Edri came alone, punctually at four. Five minutes later Ulpiano Méndez appeared, accompanied by a bodyguard who remained behind at the entrance while Ulpiano went inside to the lobby where Leon was waiting for him, standing next to the floor-length windows.

"Hello, don León, how are things?"

"Fine, thank you, doctor, and you?"

Nothing distorted the truth more than that cordial greeting. Mistrust and envy were the dominant factors in the conduct of both men towards each other. Nevertheless, one positive feeling could be pointed out in their relationship: admiration. Edri admired the way Méndez led his life, for despite his immense fortune he was not given to extravagance or ostentation; and Méndez admired Edri's ability in business and the tenacity that had made him one of the most important industrialists in the country. And as Méndez knew quite well, if Leon Edri continued progressing at his present pace, he would soon hold the top spot in the country's textile market. The Jew's wealth, made over three decades of hard work, was beginning to compete with Ulpiano's wealth, which had been passed down from generation to generation.

"Shall we sit in the bar? I think that we would be more comfortable there," Méndez suggested.

"Let's go."

In the short distance from the lobby to the bar, three people stopped Ulpiano Méndez to greet him. One of them, Congressman Roberto Núñez, took him by the arms and exclaimed:

"Hellooo, my dear doctor!"

"Hello, Rogelio. How are things?" Méndez answered amicably, repeating his favorite greeting.

Leon Edri waited impatiently for the two men to exchange pleasantries.

The cocktail lounge was full, but even so it was less noisy than the lobby. They sat down at a small table at the far end of the lounge.

"I've heard that you're being awarded the Industrial Medal of Honor, doctor Méndez," Edri said, trying to make small talk.

An expression of complacency appeared on the old aristocrat's face.

"False rumors, nothing more."

"Not at all," Leon proceeded, sticking to the subject that played to the man's ego. "I have it from a very good source. The president has three candidates for the Medal of Honor, and it seems that of the three he is most inclined in your favor."

"And what is your source of information?"

"Someone very close to the president," Leon answered, injecting a bit of mystery into his response.

They both smiled: Méndez out of satisfaction and Edri for having made it up. A waiter came up to them.

"What would you like, doctor?" Leon asked.

"A whiskey… with water," Ulpiano Méndez said, addressing the waiter.

"The same for me, with lots of ice, please."

Leon didn't generally drink. He had ordered something he didn't like and would force it down unblinkingly, since he knew that a person who drinks does not like to drink alone. Edri wasn't a man to overlook details. He had even thought to order his whiskey with lots of ice so that his glass would appear to be full.

They discussed matters regarding the economy for some ten or fifteen minutes, a minimum for small talk, since it was vital to establish an air of congeniality, but then the small talk ended, for neither man was given to flittering away time nor was either one comfortable in the company of the other.

"I understand you made an offer to buy Southern Yarn for twelve million," Leon Edri suddenly interjected.

"News really travels fast!"

"The Zambranos themselves informed me. They offered me a twenty-percent shareholder interest… for four million."

"And what did you say?"

303

"Nothing. I told them I'd think it over."

"And… have you reached a decision?"

"Yes… that the price isn't at all steep. The factory is easily worth twenty million."

Edri waited for a reaction, but Méndez kept looking at him, with an astonished expression.

"It was logical for them to approach me, since their game is to pit us against each other. Obviously, neither of us is going to sit with our arms folded while the competition acquires the principle source of the country's raw material."

"No, I suppose not," Méndez Carrizosa finally grunted.

"On the other hand, to get involved in the business of manufacturing yarn is to get involved in a bad venture; it means having to argue with the cotton dealers, fighting with the Ministry of Agriculture, and a thousand other headaches."

"I imagine you know why they offered you the twenty percent. They're in dire straits and need the money."

"Yes, they have financial difficulties, but they're not as desperate as you think."

"I don't *think*, señor Edri. I know what I'm saying. I had good reason to make them my offer."

"Undoubtedly, they informed me of your proposal so I'd know they had someone ready to bail them out; but at the same time they made light of the offer, saying it didn't merit consideration."

"It was merely an opening offer, for the purposes of negotiation."

"If you're waiting for a counteroffer, I'm afraid you're wasting your time. They're not going to make one."

Méndez Carrizosa swallowed hard.

"And what do you intend to do concerning their offer?" he asked.

"For a moment I thought I could make them an offer for everything. Then I told myself: Méndez won't pass up this opportunity. If I offer fifteen million, he'll offer sixteen. If I say eighteen, he'll come back with nineteen. In the end, one of us will end up paying through the nose, or we both come up empty. And it would be a shame to lose the deal."

"Elías Jamal might be interested."

"Nonsense. Everybody knows Jamal isn't in a position these days to make that type of investment. The Zambranos have no other buyer. It's just you and me, my dear doctor."

"Why are you telling me this?"

"Because I believe that we can work smart… You know?"

He leaned in closer to Ulpiano, so no one would overhear.

"I really believe Southern Yarn can be bought for twelve million."

Ulpiano in turn drew closer to Leon and made a gesture with his eyebrows as if to say: "How?"

"By no longer buying material from them. That goes for both of us. Then they'll really be in a bind."

They continued looking at one another in silence for a few seconds, until the old oligarch said under his breath:

"But we'd have to cut the production of fabrics considerably!"

"Not if we import the yarn."

"The Ministry of Commerce wouldn't grant us the import licenses."

"That's why we need your political influence, doctor."

"I don't think there's much I can do."

305

"Come now, doctor, don't be modest. You have a lot of pull."

Méndez remained pensive for a few moments, then, as if he were speaking to himself, he said softly: "I'd have to claim problems of quality with Southern Yarn's products."

"I'm sure you know how things are done, Ulpiano."

It was the first time that Edri had addressed Méndez Carrizosa on a first name basis. They flashed a smile of complicity.

"Leon," the old oligarch said, also addressing the other on familiar terms for the first time, "let's have a go at it. We'll put Southern Yarn in a position where their only alternative to selling is to go belly up."

"If the Zambranos make you a counteroffer, you've got to stand pat."

"Are you going to teach me how to negotiate at this stage in my life?"

"Excuse me. What I meant to say—"

"What you failed to say," Ulpiano interrupted, "is what kind of deal you're offering me."

"We invest one third subject to the same conditions as yours and we take one third of the profits or losses, but we share the decision-making power as equal partners."

"If you don't put up fifty percent, I don't see why you should get half the voting rights."

"Without Sileja's collaboration you wouldn't be able to close the deal. It's the premium that's owed us for making this happen."

"Leon, you're a sly beast when it comes to business!"

Edri didn't know if it was a compliment or a putdown. Neither did he know if the wordplay on his name was intentional or had slipped out by accident and, if that were the case, whether Méndez

Carrizosa had realized it; but when it came to matters of cleverness, he wasn't going to take a back seat to anybody.

"Doctor Méndez, I'm not as much of a fox as you may think."

24

"Tomasa!"

"Coming!"

The cook stopped what she was doing and hurried from the kitchen while drying her hands with a dishtowel. She was still wiping them when she reached the garden. She was a young woman of color, as black as coal, and enormously fat; her skin was smooth and shiny, one would say made taut by her corpulence; she had thick lips, a broad, flat nose, typical of her race, and a row of perfectly straight, beautifully white teeth that glowed with her every smile. She was wearing a short-sleeve, print blouse of blue, white, and yellow flowers that revealed the cleavage of her enormous breasts and huge, flabby arms that barely fit inside her sleeves. Underneath a pristine apron, she was wearing an impeccably clean white skirt that nearly touched the floor.

"Tomasa!"

"Coming, I'm coming!"

The servant scurried across the garden until she reached a small palm-leaf gazebo on the other side of the swimming pool, where María Cristina was chatting with a friend.

"Did you call, *señorita*?"

"Tomasa, set another place at the table. María Isabel is staying for dinner."

"Yes, *señorita*."

"Who called a little while ago?"

"I don't know. Your mother answered the phone."

"Has my father arrived?"

"Not yet."

"Look, Tomasita, do me a favor. If David calls—you know who he is, right?—and my father is around, don't say who is it. Okay?"

"Yes, *señorita*."

A pleasant smile of complicity accompanied the servant's reply.

"If you have to pass me the phone, say that Clemencia needs me... No, better yet, say that it's the Drama Club. Understand?"

"Yes, *señorita*," she assented, flashing a smile with her beautiful white teeth, "the Drama Club."

"Thank you, Tomasa."

"At your service, *señorita*."

Tomasa withdrew with the smile of complicity still on her lips.

"Do you really think he's going to call you?" María Isabel asked.

"I know he will."

"I think you're in love."

"Don't be silly, Isabel."

"He's really good-looking."

"I wouldn't say that. He makes a nice appearance, but nothing out of this world. More than anything, he is very nice. He has a way of talking that knocks me out. It knocks me out! I love talking to him."

"Me too. He's very intelligent. Do you remember the discussion that he had with Professor Martinguí after his lecture?"

"He made him look bad, didn't he?"

"Bad? He made him look like an idiot. He completely destroyed him."

"I adore boys like that, boys who have a brilliant mind. I find David mesmerizing."

"Sure you're not in love?"

"For goodness sake, Isabelita! Of course not!" María Cristina exclaimed. "But I'm almost there," she added saucily.

They both smiled.

"You're looking for trouble, sweetie."

"Why do you say that?"

"What do you mean why? You know that David is Jewish, don't you?"

"And am I by chance marrying him?"

"No, but you're falling in love and one thing leads to another."

"All right, let it lead," María Cristina said between giggles.

"You're crazy."

"They say that Jewish husbands are wonderful."

"Please, be serious!"

"Serious? I think that when one really loves somebody, one can't be selfish. If I fell passionately in love, I'd want to share my life with the person I love.

"In other words, you'd marry any man if you were seriously in love."

"If I were really in love, yes, but obviously I wouldn't fall in love with just anybody."

"Of course not, but if you fell in love with someone, would you be ready to marry without regard for the consequences?"

"I told you yes."

"Even if he was Jewish?"

"Even if he was Jewish."

María Isabel looked at her in shock.

"Your father would kill you," she said.

"And you wouldn't marry a Jew?"

"No."

"Even if you were very much in love?"

"I couldn't fall in love with a Jew."

"Why not?"

"Because… I don't know… They're so… different."

"You don't like them?"

"Well… Let's say, not very much."

"But why?"

"Because of what I just said. They're very different from us."

"In what sense?"

"They have their strange ways; their beliefs; their customs."

"Do you know many Jews?"

"I know enough of them."

"How many do you know well, but really well?"

"Well, the only one I know really well, is David… That is to say, I've spoken with him several times."

"Then how can you know what they're like?"

"Because a person knows. Those are things that people know."

"And didn't you say a minute ago that David is marvelous?"

"No. I said that David is a good-looking guy and I also like chatting with him. And so what? That doesn't have anything to do with anything. He can be very nice, intelligent and whatever you want, but that doesn't change the fact that as a Jew he has his strange ways."

"I don't see anything strange about him."

"Oh, darling!"

"Let's suppose you met a really handsome guy, super nice, loaded, well-educated and everything you can think of, and that you knew nothing about him or who he was. Let's say that you met him on a trip, or something like that, and that you fell madly in love with him and *afterwards* it turned out that he's Jewish. What would you do?"

"But that's exactly what I'm trying to explain to you: that something like that can't happen because one would realize right there that he's Jewish. One recognizes them immediately."

"I'm not so sure. I think a Jew can be like anyone else. Isn't it true all men were created in the image of God?"

"I don't know about that. Better you ask Father Izaza. All I'm telling you is that Jews are different."

"All right, but suppose you did fall in love with a Jew. Would you marry him?"

"No."

"Because of what people would say? Because of society? Because of fear of your parents?"

"Because of respect for my parents. Because of self-respect. Because of a thousand reasons."

"But what's wrong with marrying a Jew?"

"You're joking."

"No. I'm serious."

"Theoretically, nothing, but in the case of a girl of your position…"

"A Jew can convert and be a Catholic like any of us."

"So, if you had a Jewish boyfriend, you'd demand he become a Catholic for you to marry him?"

"It's not a question of demanding. Surely he himself would want to convert. Besides, how could we marry if he wasn't Catholic?"

"A person doesn't need to go through the Church to get married."

"For heavens' sake, Isabelita! Who do you take me for?"

"Since you seem to be so liberated…"

"You think me capable of forsaking my duty as a Catholic?"

"And what if he asked you to?"

"No one who loved me would ask such a thing of me."

A husky voice calling from inside the house interrupted the conversation.

"Cristina!"

"My dad is home," María Cristina said to her friend, and in a loud voice she answered: "I'm coming, Papa."

María Cristina stood up just as her father reached the garden carrying a bulky object in his hands. They walked towards each other.

"I brought you a surprise."

Ulpiano Méndez was carrying a large birdcage and was delighted to see the look of astonishment on his daughter's face. Directly behind him came María Cristina's siblings: Luis Eduardo, Jorge Horacio, and María del Pilar; and behind them were Tomasa and Dominga (the other servant); Alejandrina, the laundress who came

314

twice a week to wash clothes; Libio, the gardener, and Andrés, the chauffeur. They all trailed behind Doctor Méndez, admiring the beautiful macaw that he was carrying in the cage.

"Do you like him?" her father asked, holding out the cage.

"It's precious. What gave you the idea, Papa?"

"The garden needs a little bit of life."

"His name is Barajas!" Jorge Horacio exclaimed.

"Do you like him, young lady?" Doctor Méndez asked, addressing María Isabel.

"He's very pretty, Doctor Méndez."

"Papa, you remember Isabelita Palacios, don't you?"

"Of course. Club Bolívar's Beauty Queen last year, right? A richly deserved title, young lady."

"Thank you, doctor," María Isabel said, curtseying slightly.

"Isabelita is staying for dinner."

"I'm delighted," Méndez Carrizosa said, giving Cristina's friend an admiring look; then, addressing the servant: "Tomasa, take this," he said, handing her the cage with its colorful bird. "Put it where you think best, but not too close to the windows. Every once in a while he launches into some horrendous squawking."

"Does he talk?" Luis Eduardo asked.

"Indeed he does! And sometimes he says dreadful things," his father replied jestingly.

Tomasa took the cage and withdrew with the exotic bird and the retinue of curious admirers, who began talking all at once as soon as they felt free from the intimidating presence of Doctor Méndez.

An hour later, during dinner, "Barajas" was the main topic of conversation. Doña Lucila Campo de Méndez was the only person who was not delighted with the garden's new tenant, since it already had a dovecot, a monkey tied to a guayaba tree, and a spoiled dog, as scared of the monkey as the monkey was of him.

"What I really have here is more of a zoo than an garden," she joked. "Ulpiano was always bringing the children some small animal for their entertainment. I thought those days were over and it turns out now, with the children grown, he's started all over again."

"Darling, one doesn't have to be a child to enjoy nature. You're the only who's complaining."

"Once, when Cristina was six," señora Méndez continued, ignoring her husband's remark, "Ulpiano gave her a rabbit, and this dear child grew so fond of the animal that she never let it out of her sight for a minute. Well, one fine day the little animal goes and dies on us. You've never seen such drama! Who could bear to see this child reduced to tears! There was no way to console her. Ulpiano brought her another rabbit, but it was no help whatsoever because Cristina knew it wasn't the same one."

"It strikes me as a very touching story," María Isabel said.

"It is a very meaningful story," Doctor Méndez stated, "since it says a great deal about María Cristina's character. She forms attachments easily and is very obstinate in matters of the heart."

María Cristina smiled.

"She falls in love with rabbits," Luis Eduardo concluded, and they all laughed at his childish humor.

The table was set according to strict etiquette, even though the everyday dining room was being used. An additional place was set at the table which seated six and the formal dinnerware had been set out. The only bit of incongruity was the additional chair. Since that evening's guest was a young girl, really, the use of the main dining room—which seated up to twenty people and was reserved for banquets or special guests—was not necessary. The meal was simple

316

but abundant, in keeping with the custom of the region. Food in the home of that aristocratic family was not much different from that of humble homes, except for quantity, presentation and the way in which it was served. Doña Lucila never set foot in the kitchen, except to give orders when preparing a banquet and to coordinate the work among the household staff and chefs from the Club Bolívar who were hired especially for the event. The day Ulpiano brought home the macaw, Tomasa had prepared the same food for dinner that she fixed three or four times a week: papaya or pineapple for starters; chicken or beef consommé, with potato and yucca; for the entrée, veal sirloin with rice, beans, corn and fried plantain (there was always some kind of meat served, at lunch as well as at dinner and, sometimes, even at breakfast); for a beverage, a fruit drink made from *guanábana*, *lulo* or *maracuyá*; and for dessert, *dulce de guayaba* with half a glass of milk or a small cup of coffee. Despite the formal dinner service and cutlery, a relaxed and informal atmosphere was the order of the day when parents and children sat down to eat as a family. For brief periods, there was a single topic of conversation in which everyone participated, and brief moments when Doctor Méndez and his wife alone were engaged in some talk, María Cristina and her friend comprised their own coterie, and the younger children, in turn, formed their own little group.

"And what's the latest with you young ladies in the romance department?" Ulpiano Méndez suddenly asked, seeking to enliven the conversation.

"Not much to speak of, doctor," María Isabel answered with a smile.

"I can't believe it! If I were thirty years younger, I'd be chasing after both of you young ladies."

"You mean *forty* years younger."

"For heaven's sake, Lucila! If I were forty years younger, I'd be younger than Cristina."

317

"Papa, I'd take you at any age."

"And me too, Doctor Méndez," María Isabel added, playing along.

"We'd go dancing and leave this old woman at home," Ulpiano said, indicating his wife with a movement of his eyebrows.

Luis Eduardo laughed.

"Jorge Horacio would take me dancing. Isn't that right, sweetheart?"

"Of course I would, Mama!"

"And you'd take me too?" María Isabel asked in her most flirtatious tone.

The boy immediately blushed and was unable to hide his loss of composure. Spontaneous laughter broke out from everyone at the table.

"Jorge Horacio doesn't know how to dance," María del Pilar said.

"And you less," Luis Eduardo said in defense of his brother. "When you dance you look like a grasshopper with its feet turned backwards."

"Luis Eduardo, that's no way to talk," Doña Lucila intervened. "Apologize to your sister. Besides, you never saw her dance."

"I did so, at Germán's birthday party; and she's a terrible dancer."

"I saw him dancing at the party too," his little sister countered. "He looked ridiculous. Eduardo dances stiff like a lamppost. He takes one step forward, one back, then one step forward, then one back, without turning one way or the other; not even his head moves. He presses his lips together, tenses his neck and puts on the face of a sleepwalker that looks like a dead Jew."

Ulpiano Méndez broke into raucous laughter that vibrated around the room or more precisely, gave that impression because it coincided with the ringing of the phone. Doctor Méndez always enjoyed everything that came out of María del Pilar's mouth; to his way of thinking, she was the funniest little girl in the world. Isabel and Cristina exchanged looks.

"Tomasa, who is it?" Doña Lucila asked.

The servant had just entered the dining room.

"It's for *Señorita* María Cristina… from the Drama Club."

25

David had left the living room to make the call from the kitchen, far enough away so that his two friends couldn't overhear him. The delicious aroma of apple and walnut strudel filled the room, the kind his mother prepared with a bit of honey and some rose petals, according to the recipe that came from his grandmother.

A servant answered the call and told him to wait a minute, but several minutes went by until he heard the soft voice at the other end, which was like celestial music to his ears.

"Hello?"

David felt the blood rush to his head.

"María Cristina?" he whispered.

"How nice to hear from you! I had a feeling that you were going to call."

She was also whispering. David knew why, but he didn't understand why he himself was speaking so softly. It seemed to him that he was protecting her by speaking this way.

"I had to hear your voice," he said. "Since the last time we saw each other..."

He didn't know how long he spoke. Even though they were separated more by obstacles than distance, he felt her at his side; her exquisite mouth close to his face and his lips almost touching her ear. Maybe that's why he was whispering.

He had barely hung up when his friends came through the door. Jacobo, or Cobi, as his pals called him, was a tall, good-looking young man, with dark eyes and hair, a light complexion and very pleasant although somewhat hard features that made him appear older than he was, just having turned twenty-two. He bore a strong resemblance to David, which made many people take them for brothers. Isaac—Ico to his closest friends—was akin to the two friends in the way he thought and spoke, but in physical aspect he was very different. He had an aquiline nose and bright blues eyes that frequently smiled. Under his curly, blonde hair his mind was always looking for something to debate.

"So, did she say yes?"

Ico's voice made David turn brusquely around.

"Damn! Can't a person even have a conversation on the phone without the two of you snooping around?"

"Whoa!"

"Yes, it's the truth! I've run out of patience with you guys! You have to know everything!"

"So, tell us, what did she say?"

"Leave him alone," Jacobo intervened, pulling Ico by the arm.

"Don't you see he's playing dumb so he doesn't have to answer?" Isaac retorted. And again he asked: "Did she say yes?"

"No," David said dryly.

"Didn't I tell you?" Ico exclaimed victoriously, and added, accentuating each word: "I told you so. I told you so."

"Leave him alone, Ico," Cobi advised him for the second time.

"I told you so," Isaac said, continuing to hammer away. "Those girls never want to go out with a Jewish boy. Never."

"The truth is she did want to go out with me, but couldn't."

"And why couldn't she?"

"Don't be a blockhead, Ico!" Jacobo interjected. "Don't you know that they don't let those girls go anywhere alone? Not even to mass."

"It's different with them," David explained, as if his friends didn't know the situation perfectly well. "A guy can't invite them to the movies, or to go out for an ice cream, like ours. They can't go out with you, not because you're Jewish. If you were Catholic it would be the same thing. They simply can't go out alone with a man, unless it's someone they're engaged to. And even then, not at all hours or under all circumstances. But if it's just a friend, forget it! It's impossible."

"And if he's Jewish, all the more reason," Isaac added, as if he accepted David's explanation while stating precisely the contrary.

"The two of you have quite a complex!"

"It's not a complex," Cobi retorted. "They have their society and they don't accept us. We have ours and we don't accept them. And if you must know, that's all right with me."

"Well, I accept them in my society and I'm well received in theirs."

"That's what you think," Ico fired back. "In the first place, that business about you accepting them in your society is nonsense, because you don't own it. Every society has its norms and the individual can't control them. Your society doesn't accept the *goy*, and that's all there is to it. You can't do anything about that. It's neither a law nor a regulation. There's no agreement among the members of the community, not even a tacit one. It's simply a norm; it crops up naturally without it being up to anyone to implant it, and it functions because it's imbedded in our mentality. And as for them receiving you in their society, allow me to have my doubts. The fact that someone invites you to some gathering from time to time only shows a deference of that person towards you; it is in no way an

323

acceptance into the high society that will always remain closed to Jews. They don't 'accept' you; they 'tolerate' you, as an exception, because of your father's money."

"They accept me; and quite well. I have many friends and I feel comfortable with them."

"Friends? Rubbish!" Jacobo exclaimed. "I also have many Gentile friends, but not a single intimate one among them, not a really good one. There are a few I get along with really well; very good people, really nice, and... I don't know... I feel that it's not a deep friendship, that there is something that separates us. It's hard to pin it down, but you feel it when you talk with them... Maybe it's the way they think."

"The same thing happens to me," Ico said, picking up on what his friend was saying. "When I'm among *goyim* I don't feel at home. Maybe I'm even having a good time, but I always detect something artificial in the air that doesn't let me completely relax. Know what I mean? Something like there's 'us' and there's 'them.' "

"Damn. It's incredible, this complex the two of you have."

"To your mind we all have a complex," Cobi protested. "Come on. No fibs. The honest truth. Who are your best friends?"

"Well, you are, you jerks!"

"And among that entire heap of *goyim* friends that you have, is there really one intimate friend?"

David smiled, shaking his head no.

"You see?" Jacobo continued. "It's like Ico says. There's something that separates us from the *goy*. I maintain that it's a question of mentality."

"Mentality? What do you mean?"

"I don't know..." Cobi made a gesture with his hands to emphasize his words. "We have a more developed sense of family... we're more responsible... more sensible..."

"Hah!" David said, exploding with indignation. "Sense of family? Who has that? Carlos Levy, who left his wife and children out in the cold to run off with his secretary? What responsibility? Teddy Katz's, losing everything he had playing cards? What was the other thing you said?... Oh, yes. Sensible. Ask crazy Klachkin what sensible is, let's see if he has any idea; or Markowsky, the smuggler."

"Don't be naive," Jacobo retorted, adopting the same style of rhetoric as his friend. "How many Carlos Levys does our community have? He's the only one. And the swindlers and smugglers among us. How many are they? Among the *goyim* aren't there many more? Not to mention other evils of society. Did you ever hear of a Jew staging a hold up? Did you ever see a Jewish prostitute? Or a Jewish murderer? Even once? Just once?" he said, stressing the question so as to answer it himself. "Of course not. Because there aren't any."

"Of course there are! Idiot. Probably not in Lárida because the community is small, but where you have a large Jewish population, of course there are."

"Jewish criminals don't exist," Jacobo insisted.

"They exist, and how!" David asserted, looking straight at his friend, now that the discussion was evolving into a twosome. "They exist in Israel, in Russia, in the United States and anywhere in the world where there's a large Jewish population."

"It's not true."

"Believe what you want, Cobi. All I'm saying is that you have a lot to learn. All the evil that exists in other populations also exists in ours. Man is fundamentally the same wherever you find him."

"False. The human element that composes a society basically differs from one to another."

"No. That's a pure illusion of perspective. If you had a small, wealthy community of Gentiles, like ours, living in a city full of Jews, I guarantee you there wouldn't be a single Gentile among the thieves and murderers of the city."

"You're reasoning from a hypothetical basis to reach a conclusion that in reality can't be proved. The fact is that it is we and not they who live in a community. And it is the human element that determines the level of the community. Just as there are individuals better than others, there are also societies that are better than others."

David felt his blood beginning to boil.

"What do you mean? That we are better?"

"Yes."

"What fallacy!"

"It's as plain as day. Just look at the famous men we've given to humanity; in every period, in every field."

"Gentiles gave many, many more."

"Proportionally, no. And if you keep in mind that those famous Gentiles were products of *their* world, where the universities and opportunities were not open to Jews, our contribution becomes much more significant."

"For a hundred years we Jews have had the same opportunities as the rest."

"The same, no. But let's say almost the same; and look at what we've done with them. Look no farther than here, in Lárida. We're not even one tenth of one percent of the total population, and look at the percentage of Jewish students in the university. At least five percent, right? Look at the number of doctors and engineers that we contribute to the city, not to mention the successful industrialists and

326

businessmen that we have. If all this doesn't mean anything to you, you're in denial."

"Go to Israel and you'll see how many foul-mouthed workers, coarse peasants, ignorant hucksters, rude truck drivers, ill-mannered and stupid individuals we have, like any other normal country. The thing is that you keep making the same mistake in perspective that I mentioned. You take a Jewish community in Latin America, a microcosm that for historical reasons maintains a higher standard than that of the society in which it lives, you make comparisons and then apply your conclusions to the Jewish people in general."

"What nonsense! Pure intellectual garbage!"

"To an irrational person, every argument is garbage."

"Irrational?" Cobi shouted.

"What do you call the person who insists on comparing oranges to apples? Instead of comparing the Jewish elite with the Gentile working class, why don't you compare working class to working class?"

"If the Israeli people were like any other nation, the Arabs would have done away with them a long time ago. Or does it seems natural to you that fifteen Arab countries with over one hundred million people, backed by billions of petrodollars and armed to the teeth with the best that Russia and the West have to offer, can't do anything against a small country of three million Jews? There has to be some explanation."

"What?"

"That we're better."

"Only in the twisted mind of a racist."

"Wow! So, now I'm a racist?"

"Of course! How do you, a Jew, dare to think like that?"

"All Jews think the same way. Ask Ico."

"I don't think that way," Ico said, joining the conversation.

"Didn't you say before..."

"I said we're different; I didn't say we're better. All races are different, each with its own idiosyncrasies and talents. There are those that stand out in different things, let's say music for one, food for another, but there are no superior races. No one should understand that better than we Jews. That you can think like a Nazi is something that..."

"What kind of crap are you giving me! Who thinks like a Nazi? Do I believe that being better gives you some right over the rest? Am I persecuting anybody? Or do I think it ought to be done? ... Damn, how the hell did we get into this discussion?"

The three friends looked at each and smiled.

"The whole thing began because Her Ladyship, Señorita María Cristina Méndez, didn't deign to go out with our little David."

"She wasn't able to," David said, putting the record straight.

"Again?" Cobi protested.

"No. That's enough. But David's stubbornness really ticks me off. I warned him not to get involved with that crowd, that the only thing he was going to get out of it was a snub."

"What an exaggeration! No one snubbed me. Okay! You're right. She didn't say yes to going out with me. But you can be sure, she was as sorry about it as I was."

"Now you're going to tell us she's in love with you."

"No, but I'm sure she likes me."

"It's because you're so irresistible," Cobi joked, putting his hands together over his chest and making a high-pitched voice.

"She's the one who's irresistible."

David said it in such a serious tone that for a few seconds his friends looked at him in bewilderment.

"Yes, she's very pretty," Jacobo said finally.

"Hm, hm, very pretty," asserted the other.

"She's gorgeous," David affirmed with the same solemnity as before.

"Oy! This thing is more serious than we thought."

"Cobi, didn't I tell you?"

"Idiots! Am I getting married?"

"You couldn't even if you wanted to," Ico said.

"The world shouldn't be that way; I mean, just because of a whole string of dim-witted ideas two people who love each other can't get married."

"Two people who what?" Ico exploded at the same time that Cobi was choking.

"I'm not talking about María Cristina and me, you jerks. I'm talking in generalities."

"Well, the generalities sounded very specific."

"Don't go looking for problems," Ico warned him. "It's like Cobi said: stay with your own people; it's better that way. There's no need to get started with a love that can't be."

"Besides," Cobi added with a broad smile, "the world is full of beautiful women and without complications."

26

The luxury Lincoln Continental passed through the gate of Altamira and slowly advanced along the cobbled-stone driveway that led up to the elegant mansion on the slopes of the cordillera, a few minutes from the city. The imposing colonial manor blended perfectly with the surrounding landscape.

"Looks like we have visitors," Doctor Ulpiano Méndez Carrizosa said.

In fact, there were several cars parked on the other side of the expansive lawn.

"Yes, sir, seems so" the chauffeur agreed.

"Did Doña Lucila say she was expecting company?"

"No, sir. They must be friends of Señorita María Cristina."

He stopped in front of the house and honked a few times to announce their arrival. Méndez got out and took the briefcase that his driver handed him.

"Thank you, Andrés."

The limousine immediately drove away, trailed by another smaller, less elegant car that followed close behind. Méndez waved at the two occupants, his bodyguards, and turned to walk towards the house. The door opened before he reached the portico.

"Don Ulpiano," Tomasa said, flashing her big customary smile of gleaming white teeth.

"What's new, Tomasa?"

"Nothin' much, dotor."

"Who are the visitors?"

"Friends of Señorita María Cristina."

"And Doña Lucila?"

"She's upstairs in the bedroom."

Méndez crossed the foyer, walked through a second room and entered his study. He left his briefcase on the desk and looked out the window. There was a group of young people in the garden, next to the pool, engaged in some lively banter. He observed them for a few seconds, and then left the room. He climbed the wide wooden staircase with its polished steps and red carpet runner, and went into the master bedroom, a spacious area furnished with rococo style furniture. A crucifix hung on one side of the double bed. Doña Lucila Campo de Méndez was seated in front of the dressing table, painting her fingernails.

"Ulpiano, you're home early."

"Yes. I finished up sooner than I expected."

"Wonderful! You'll be able to rest a bit. Remember that tonight we're invited to the Peraltas."

"Oh, that's right. I'd forgotten. What a bore! Do we have to?"

"Absolutely, dear. We have to. Father Izaza called to make sure we'd be there. He probably wants to ask you for a donation for the benefit ball next month."

Ulpiano approached his wife, who had her back to him, and placed his hands firmly on her shoulders. It was a greeting, a kind of half-hearted embrace, as if he wanted to make a physical display of affection without having to bother to bend down. She lifted her free hand across her body and placed it on top of his, gently squeezing it against her shoulder. She did it without turning around, looking at him in the mirror over the dressing table. She patted him twice on the back of his hand, then continued fixing her nails. That concluded their mutual greeting.

Through the open window laughter could be heard coming from the garden where María Cristina's friends were gathered. Ulpiano went to the window and looked down at the immense garden behind their house. His daughter was chatting with a handsome young man whom he did not remember having seen before. They were standing next to the jacaranda tree, she with her back to the window and the boy facing it. How pretty his daughter looked! She was dressed in casual attire, all in white, with form-fitting slacks that accentuated her slender waist. Her chestnut-colored hair fell loose and wavy on her shoulders. For a moment, he had the impression he was seeing Lucila, his wife, twenty years earlier.

A little farther away, next to the swimming pool, there was another couple that was laughing the whole time; but the laughter he had heard before was coming from a group of eight or nine other young people, boys and girls, engaged in some animated talk, seated around one of the tables under the shade of a pool umbrella.

"Who are the young people?"

"Friends of María Cristina's."

"I know. But who?"

Ulpiano didn't like it when people gave him a vague answer.

"More or less the usual crowd: Tulio Castellanos, María Isabel Palacios, Amparito, 'Totó'..."

"I see some new faces," Ulpiano insisted, always interested in knowing who his daughter's friends were.

"One of the boys is Juan José Velasco," his wife continued, "and the others are Luz Helena, Camilo Pinto (Doctor Pinto's eldest son), and Ana María Bedoya... she was María Cristina's classmate..."

"Who's the one talking to María Cristina?"

Lucila stood up and looked out the window.

"His name is David. I don't remember the last name. He's a Jewish boy, the son of the people who own Sileja."

"Edri," Méndez grunted. "I met with his father a few days ago."

"What for?"

"A deal we were discussing."

"What deal?"

"A deal."

With that he closed the subject. Ulpiano did not like talking about business with those who had no understanding of such matters, and especially with his wife.

"Where in the world would María Cristina have met a Jewish boy?" he asked, querying himself more than his wife.

"Who knows? At some party, I imagine. Of late, one runs into all sorts of people at parties. Times have changed a lot."

She stepped away from the window.

"Yes, I suppose so," he said, also moving away from the window.

"Life is better nowadays; it's easier, more accommodating."

"Women say that, as if they were blind to the moral decay of our present times."

"People are no more immoral today than what they were years ago. What's different today is that things are said with greater candor and are done more openly; that's all."

"Come now! I didn't know you were such a... 'modern woman.' "

"I'm not a modern woman, Ulpiano, but one has to recognize that customs have changed."

"Well, I prefer things the way they were before. At least, one didn't see so much whoring around."

Lucila smiled.

"The moralist has spoken."

Ulpiano hesitated an instant, not knowing whether to get angry over the sardonic remark or to take it with a grain of salt. He opted for the second choice and returned his wife's smile. When all was said and done, hadn't he, after all, done his share in contributing to what he had just referred to as "whoring around"?

"I'll be right back," he said.

"Where are you going?"

"To meet the boys."

"Let them be. Don't be a busybody."

"I won't be long."

"Ulpiano, don't be ridiculous! It's just a group of young people. What are you going to do there?"

"I merely want to see what kind of people María Cristina has over to the house and I'll be right back."

"If you want to know who she invited, ask her later and she'll tell you."

"No. I want to know now."

"For heaven's sake, you're being ridiculous! You're going to upset her."

"Don't worry; I know what I'm doing."

"Ulpiano!" Doña Lucila exclaimed just as he was leaving the room.

Ulpiano went downstairs and out to the garden. A few feet farther ahead his daughter was still standing next to Leon Edri's son,

335

whose face was partially obscured by Cristina's head. He was doing all the talking. *How many sweet nothings is he feeding her?* Méndez wondered. *And does the bastard have to stand so close to her to talk?* He pricked up his ears but couldn't catch what the boy was saying, his words drowned out by the rustling noise of the breeze among the shrubs. At one point, the young man became aware of Ulpiano's presence. He stopped talking and stepped back, letting his arm fall to his side. Only then did the old man realize that the boy had been holding his daughter's hand. María Cristina turned around to see what it was that had disconcerted David. On seeing her father, she smiled and walked over to him.

"Hello, Papa! What are you doing there being so quiet?" She gave him a hug and kissed him on the cheek.

"Nothing, sweetheart. Merely taking in the scene..."

"Aha! Spying, right?" Cristina said.

She giggled and pulled her father by the hand.

"It seems that I'm interrupting a very interesting conversation."

Cristina led him to where her friend was standing.

"Papa, I want you to meet David."

"David Edri. Very pleased to meet you, doctor," the young man said, forcing a smile.

Ulpiano Méndez extended him his hand.

"Edri? I know your father quite well... I assume that Leon Edri is your father, right?"

"Yes, sir, he is indeed."

Ulpiano surveyed the face of the twenty-two-year old; it was a pleasant face, thin and clearly tanned from the sun. The wide forehead, the thick eyebrows and the straight but somewhat large nose, gave the face a certain look of seriousness hard to find in young men his age.

"Edri," Méndez repeated, his eyes fixed on those of the young man. "Interesting. I thought all Hebrews had last names like Goldstein, Greenberg or Rabinovich."

David thought he detected an anti-Semitic tenor in the observation, but chose to ignore it. Being unsure of the old man's attitude, it was better not to feel offended. The comment could simply be a question of harmless curiosity. The fact that Méndez had used the word "Hebrew" rather than "Jew" did not escape David's attention, given that the term "Jew" still held a pejorative connotation in that region of the world, and he did not know if the oligarch had avoided it on purpose or if the word of choice had come out spontaneously, without any special considerations.

"Surnames like the ones you mentioned are typically *Ashkenazi*."

Doctor Méndez held David's gaze with that look of intelligence that people muster when they hear a word with which they are not familiar, or something that they don't understand, but don't want to appear ignorant. He waited for David to continue, as people normally do, hoping to deduce the meaning of the word with the help of what was to follow.

"Edri is clearly a Hebrew surname," David continued, but the etymological explanation that he was about to give, contrary to Ulpiano's expectations, did not help to clarify the subject. " 'Eder,' which is also a surname, means 'flock,' and 'edri' means '*my* flock.' "

"Aha… Well, I hope you have a nice time," Ulpiano said, trying to change the subject to one he felt more comfortable with, finding foreign languages and everything connected with them to be intimidating.

"Thank you, Doctor Méndez."

"Cristina, do you want to introduce me to your other friends?"

"Of course, Papa. Excuse me, David," she said as she withdrew, being led away on her father's arm.

Edri watched them approach the group seated around the table. The bantering ceased while Cristina made the introductions. They were all good looking, well-dressed and displayed proper manners, befitting people of their class. Each one nodded and said a few words when it came his turn. Ulpiano was already taking his leave when David joined the group.

"All right, my young friends, enjoy yourselves!" the old man shouted as he walked away.

Upon approaching the house, he looked up. From the window of their bedroom on the second floor, Lucila was watching him.

27

Ever since its inception, ten years earlier, Father Izaza's benefit dance was one of Lárida's most important social events. Every year nearly five hundred people—the very upper crust of society—gathered at the Club Bolívar to eat, drink, and dance until dawn, for what was surely the most fun a person could have in supporting a charity. Couples paid fifteen hundred pesos each for the honor of attending. For the great majority, such an outlay—equivalent to twenty meals in the best restaurant—was inconsequential; for some, however, it was money taken from a family budget that barely covered monthly expenses.

Pepe Chamaco's orchestra filled the hall with music and high spirits. Seven blacks, five whites, and a female vocalist—a mulatto—comprised the group that had become famous in the region. Not only did they play and sing, but they put on an entire show with a choreographed routine that took them back and forth across the stage, sometimes together and sometimes in groups of three or four, swaying to the sound of their own music. They were dripping wet with perspiration, but they didn't stop moving or smiling. Their efforts produced the desired effect, their energy being transmitted to the dance floor where the couples gyrated wildly to the rhythm of the bongo and the maracas. The lively sounds of the music from the Caribbean coast, with its distinctive and contagious rhythm, capable of getting the most lethargic of mortals to get up and dance, blared through the loudspeakers. The volume was so loud that it drowned out the voices, making conversation practically impossible. The ones who were not dancing and didn't want to have to shout to have a conversation had to settle for watching the action on the dance floor, which was not bad entertainment at all, since several couples performed admirably, with a style to be envied. Yet, many of the men preferred watching the mulatto singer, who was pretty in a trashy sort of way but undoubtedly one of the best-looking women there. She was extremely well endowed, sheathed in a tight-fitting, ankle-length gold dress with a plunging neckline that came down almost to her nipples and an open slit on the left side that began at her hip. She moved masterfully, putting her physical charms on display. At times she swayed sensually, other times she danced in place, causing her shapely leg to peek out through the open slit and accentuating the roundness of her high buttocks, which created a shiny protuberance in the gold dress. The singer's name was Juanita Lozano, and there were those who believed that without her Pepe Chamaco's orchestra was worthless.

The orchestra did not come cheap, of course. It was charging twice as much as it usually did for private parties. Likewise, everybody else tacked on additional charges: those who saw to the decorations, the supplier for the liquor, the florist, and even the printer for the invitations; but no one knew this, not even Father Izaza, who was the one who paid the bills. Everybody ended up happy: those who made a nice profit off the event; those who enjoyed the party, who incidentally got double the enjoyment because, besides having a good time, they were convinced that they were doing a great work of charity; the organizers of the gala event who received much praise; and Father Izaza, along with the members of the committee for "Children's Aid Society of Santa Clara de Obondó," which despite being overcharged, succeeded in raising a good sum of money for their noble cause.

The food was abundant, but the amount of liquor that was gulped down greatly surpassed that of food that was consumed. The waiters paraded back and forth, bringing in bottle after bottle of whiskey, rum, and *aguardiente*, and taking away the ones that were empty. From time to time, a full bottle "found its way in" among the empty ones and would eventually end up at a party of the less well-

340

heeled, or—why not?—again in the company of the rich, offhandedly bolstering the meager wages of one waiter or another.

Between breaks, Pepe Chamaco looked after the members of his orchestra with a few rounds of *aguardiente*. The musicians took it as attentiveness on his part, but he did it to maintain them "in good working condition," like the driver who keeps an eye on the oil level in his car.

"Another round, Ulpiano? A short one?"

"No more for now," Doctor Méndez was quick to answer, placing his hand over his glass, which still had some whiskey in it.

"And what about you, Joaco?" Gonzalo Villalobos asked another of the guests.

"I'll pass too," Doctor Joaquín Pabón responded.

"Pablito, you're surely not going to let me drink alone, are you?"

Pablo Pinto smiled and held out his glass. Gonzalo Villalobos filled it and added a little more to his.

"All right, *salud*," he said, and took a quick swig.

"*Salud*," Pablo seconded and took a sip. "It's already going to my head."

"Don't go getting drunk on us, Pablito," Ulpiano Méndez said, "because we're too old now to carry you."

The biggest landowner in the country cracked a smile.

"It's true, we are getting old, Ulpiano. You've already got that father-in-law look written all over you."

"Not yet, Pablito, but with a grown-up daughter it wouldn't surprise me that one of these days, when I least expect it—"

"Well, you better be expecting it," Doctor Pinto interrupted at the same time that he discreetly pointed with his index finger.

The three men turned around to see what their table companion was pointing to. María Cristina Méndez stood out among all those who were dancing, perhaps for her beauty, but also perhaps because she was not dancing wildly like the rest, but rather was swaying slowly, as if dancing to the sound of some other music, in the arms of her partner. Ulpiano Méndez coughed.

"What are you pointing at, eh? María Cristina... is dancing."

"Yes... with the same boy, all night."

"Well, and what of it? Tonight she chose one boy in particular. Young girls have their whims. Or maybe he just won't let go of her. Who knows!"

"Come now, Ulpiano! Don't tell me you don't know."

Pablo Pinto was like an old gossip and was delighted to have found a way to tease his good friend.

"Know what!"

"Why, your daughter and David Edri. They're seen together everywhere."

Ulpiano Méndez was flabbergasted. He really didn't know anything about it.

"With who?" Doctor Pabón inquired, not certain of having heard clearly.

"David Edri," Pinto said. "Leon Edri's son, the Sileja people."

"Oh..."

All four turned around to look at the couple, at María Cristina and David dancing as if they had the whole world to themselves, in the middle of an island where the music reached them from far away and for their pleasure alone, transfixed in the pleasure of holding one another tight and gazing into each other's eyes with the look of two people in love.

Doctor Méndez was the first to speak; he did so without really saying anything.

"Well, yes."

With that he tried to close the subject. He turned around and sat up straight in his chair, as if trying to induce his friends to follow his example. But they remained immutable, their eyes fixed on the young couple.

"Well, yes," Ulpiano Méndez repeated, giving up, and turned around again to look at his daughter.

How beautiful she was! He frequently thought, whenever watching her from a distance, that it was Lucila whom he was seeing, the way she was twenty years before. It isn't that he noticed the resemblance between mother and daughter like so many others who had known Lucila in her youth surely did, but rather that he was suffering a real figment of the imagination: He saw his wife in the flower of her youth, when they were sweethearts and passionately in love. He had to restrain himself from rushing towards her because he knew that the reality was something quite different, that what his eyes were seeing was an illusion.

"They make a beautiful couple," Joaquín remarked.

"It seems like they've got their feet set in clay," Gonzalo Villalobos commented. "What kind of dancing do they call that!"

"It's just that the boy is a poor dancer," Doctor Pabón observed. "He's got no rhythm in his blood."

"Hm, hm," Gonzalo concurred.

"Since when have they been letting Jews into the club?"

Pablo Pinto's question was like a slap in the face to Doctor Méndez.

"Anybody is allowed in, so long as he's a guest of a member," Doctor Pabón explained, and he added with that tone that he

343

assumed every time the opportunity presented itself for him to show off his jurisprudent memory. "Article Seven, Chapter Three of the Club Statutes."

"Undoubtedly, your daughter invited him," Pablo said, addressing Doctor Méndez.

Ulpiano shrugged his shoulders and felt the blood rush to his head.

"Damn it, Joaco, with that memory of yours, you ought to have taken up some other line of work instead of going into business," Gonzalo Villalobos remarked.

The president of the National Industrial Union burst out laughing.

"As you can see, things didn't work out that bad for me, did they?"

"At least, better than they did for me, getting into the business of managing other people's money instead of my own," Gonzalo replied with a certain irony, since as president of the Securities & Exchange Bank he had contributed to the growth of his friends' assets, not to mention his own.

The conversation had taken another turn, but Ulpiano was no longer listening. He was red with anger.

"Excuse me," he said, standing up, and he withdrew from the table.

He went over to his wife who was chatting with several ladies at one of the tables off to the side.

"Lucila…"

"Are you feeling ill?" Lucila asked, immediately noticing her husband's flushed look.

"No, no…"

"Ulpiano, what do you think of the centerpieces?"

Méndez turned around to look at Doña Carmenza de Avila without understanding what she was talking about.

"The carnations are all from Carmenza's garden; she grows them herself," Doña Lucila interjected to help her husband understand.

"Ah, yes?" Ulpiano exclaimed, still not knowing what they were talking about. *Damned old bag with her stupidities*, he thought.

"Carmenza donates the flowers every year. The idea this year to put them in little tin foil boats was hers," explained Doña Edelmira de Peralta, president of the Children's Aid Society of Santa Clara de Obondó. "Carmenza always comes up with such good ideas that I must say, Doctor Méndez, that I don't know what we would do without her."

"Ulpiano, see what pretty flowers," Lucila said, pointing to the center of the table.

He had been seated in front of a centerpiece just like it for almost two hours without being aware of it, much less having noticed that every table was decorated the same way.

"Beautiful, really beautiful. As soon as I came in, the centerpieces caught my attention."

The ladies smiled, pleased, and Ulpiano added before they had time to say anything: "Lucila, may I have a word with you?"

"Of course, dear."

Méndez bowed to the ladies and took his wife by the arm. They walked a few steps to one side of the ballroom.

"What's the matter, Ulpiano?"

"María Cristina is with that Edri guy. Look at them over there. Do you see them? She invited him to the ball and has been dancing with him all night."

"Yes, I know."

"What are we going to do?"

"What do you mean, 'what are we going to do?' "

"People are beginning to talk."

"They can't say anything bad."

"For heaven's sake, Lucila!"

"Okay, so, what would you have us do?"

"To put a stop to this nonsense right now. I think that Cristina ought to go home immediately. I'm not in the mood to be the subject of everybody's conversation."

"How you exaggerate! Nobody's talking about you. When all is said and done, nothing has happened. You're giving the matter more importance than it deserves."

"I hope so. At any rate, if nothing has happened, better to nip it in the bud."

"All right. I'll speak to Cristina tomorrow."

"No. Right now. I want her home. The more they see her with that Jew the more they have to talk about."

"But what do I tell her?"

"You'll know what to say… Or do you prefer I speak to her?"

"No!"

The response leapt from her like a reflex reaction. She was afraid her husband was going to create a scene. She took a deep breath and added: "I'll speak to her. Can I tell her you are feeling ill and want us to accompany you home?"

"Tell her what you like. I'm leaving. I'll wait for the two of you outside."

Lucila walked over to the edge of the dance floor and stopped.

"Are you going to dance alone, Lucila?"

It was Irma Giraldo, the one who always felt inspired to bring every party to a close with a song. She was dancing with her husband. Lucila responded to the jest with one of her best smiles.

"Yes, dear." And she went onto the dance floor like someone jumping into a swimming pool of cold water.

"Cristina."

The girl immediately turned around.

"Hi, Mami!"

"Good evening, señora Méndez," David said.

Ill at ease, she replied, "Oh... Good evening," and then addressing her daughter, she added: "Cristina, your father is feeling ill and wants to go home."

"What's the matter? What's wrong with him?"

"Nothing serious," she hastened to say, wishing to ease Cristina's concern. "Nothing that a good night's sleep won't cure."

"No doubt, he had too much to drink," Cristina said, laughing.

"If you'll allow me, I'll be happy to take all of you home," David offered.

"Oh, that won't be necessary, thank you. We have our driver outside."

"Mami, wait," María Cristina said, "this is the perfect opportunity for us to get together. David and I have something important we want to discuss with you and Daddy."

Doña Lucila felt her heart drop to her feet. She must have turned pale, because David asked: "Are you feeling ill, señora?"

"No," was all she managed to answer.

347

She was trembling.

"Mama?"

"No, it's nothing."

She let go of David's hand as soon as he had grabbed hold of hers. She tried to control her faltering voice.

"I felt faint for a moment, but I'm all right now... Cristina, shall we go?"

"David, I think we'll have to leave the chat with my parents for another time."

"Of course," he answered, perceiving the reason for Mrs. Méndez's uneasiness.

"You'll call me tomorrow?"

David nodded.

"Good night, señora Méndez."

This time Lucila did not reply. She made a half turn and exited on her daughter's arm. She was still trembling.

28

Rage gripped Ulpiano Méndez. He was no longer in control of himself; the anger that dominated his corpulent body sent his blood pressure sky high, giving his face a reddish cast. He was having difficulty breathing and clenched his teeth. Every beat of his heart reverberated in his cheeks. Sparks of fury shot from his eyes and his hands trembled despite his closed fists. Never in all the twenty years that she had known him had Lucila seen her husband in such a state of anger. She took him by the arm, not so much to calm him but rather to be ready to control him by force if necessary, since she feared he might begin striking their daughter. In his current state of fury, he found it difficult to get hold of himself.

"Do you realize what you're saying?" he bellowed between clenched teeth.

"I love him, Papa."

"What romantic nonsense! Such stupidity! You're too young to know what you're saying. You don't understand life. Marry a Jew? Do you know what that means? Are you forgetting who you are?"

Ulpiano paused in an effort to calm down.

"You're a Méndez Campo," he continued, with a little more composure, "the offspring of the union between two of the most prestigious families in the country. Your grandfather, whose name I bear, was the governor of the province. Your great-grandfather, Absalón Campo Valencilla, was president of the republic... president of the republic," he repeated so that his words would sink in. "And you, from whom one expects the sense of honor and dignity befitting your lineage, resolved to marry a shitty Jew?"

"Ulpiano, please!"

"Mama…"

"You're so beside yourself you don't know what you're saying, Ulpiano."

"Let him speak, Mama."

"Yes, a shitty Jew, because all Jews are just that. You'll stain the family name; you'll dishonor all of us and bring great shame on this household. Is that what you want?"

"Shame is what you ought to feel speaking like this."

"Show respect, Cristina. Your father is expressing himself crudely because he's hurting, but down deep he is right. You don't know the Jews. They're a coarse and vulgar people. They're not of equal standing with you. It's possible that this David is a good sort, although I doubt it; I think you yourself don't really know him, but that's not the issue. The problem is that two families are joined through marriage: your entire family and his. Do you have any idea with what kind of people you would be linking us?

María Cristina didn't answer. With her big, dark eyes flooded with tears, she watched her mother nervously twisting a handkerchief, the same one she had given her after having spent several days embroidering it with little flowers.

"People who haven't the least bit of social grace," Doña Lucila continued, "who lack manners, delicacy; lower class people, contemptible. The thing that interests them most is money."

"And how!" Doctor Méndez interjected. "It's the only thing that interests them! I can attest to it, knowing them as I do. Thieves, cheats. When it comes to money, they're capable of anything. Filthy bloodsuckers!"

Cristina didn't know how to respond in the face of such a diatribe.

"David's not like that," she managed between sobs.

"They're all like that!" her father roared.

"My poor child!" Doña Lucila said softly, trying to influence Cristina and at the same time hinting to Ulpiano to change his tone. "You're in love, and when a girl is in love she can't see reality. Love is a beautiful thing, but to be happy one needs more than love. One needs to share ideals, principles... What can you have in common with a Jew?"

"But we have a lot in common," she protested. "We like the same music, literature, we enjoy all the—"

"Rubbish!" Doña Lucila interrupted. "Absolute rubbish! The musings of an adolescent in love! A woman of society can't feel comfortable with some poor so-and-so."

"Poor? Mama, you have no idea how well off the Edris are. David's father is a very rich man."

"You mean to say: *nouveau riche*. Jews are never rich in the true sense of the word; they don't know how to be. They're social climbers in the best of cases."

"They're greedy, miserly, despite all the money they have," Ulpiano Méndez blustered.

"Cristina, my dear, you're confused. You don't understand the gravity of what you're saying. I'm sure that in a couple of days, if you give it serious thought, you'll realize your mistake."

María Cristina plopped down on the sofa and burst into tears. Her parents watched in silence, then looked at one another. Lucila took a step towards her daughter, but stopped before the raised arm of her husband.

"Sweetheart..." her mother murmured, also on the edge of tears.

"Let her be," Ulpiano commanded. "She'll get over it."

"No! I won't get over it!"

Cristina stood up abruptly and angrily faced her father. She had stopped crying. She walked slowly but resolutely towards him. He watched her approach, poised, her eyes luminous, her chin held high. Her parents remained silent during those few tense moments before she would speak. In a calm voice, summoning courage from the deepest part of her being that not even she herself knew she had, she said: "I love David and I'm going to marry him. I'd like to marry him with your blessing, but if I don't have it, I'll marry him all the same."

Ulpiano Méndez stood aghast for a few seconds, but no more than a few seconds, the time that it took him to recover from the shock. His reaction was delayed but violent. He slapped Cristina so hard that she fell to the floor. Doña Lucila shrieked in horror, covering her mouth with her hands. She dreaded it when her husband turned violent. Her maternal instinct told her to throw herself against Ulpiano to protect her daughter, but she stood paralyzed. Such a heroic act, however, was not necessary, since Ulpiano turned on his heels and left the room cursing between his teeth.

Lucila bent down and took María Cristina in her arms. The girl was pallid and in tears, gasping to catch her breath.

"Sweetheart…" Lucila whispered, trying to help her get to her feet.

Cristina let go of her mother's arm and quickly got to her feet as if to say that she didn't need her mother's support, physical or moral. She turned half way around and walked towards the door.

"Cristina…" At the sound of her mother's voice, she stopped. "I'm sorry about all of this."

María Cristina turned around and the two looked at each other for a few seconds without saying a word.

"Now that your father isn't here, I think we can talk more calmly."

"Do you want to talk mother to daughter, or woman to woman?"

"In our case it makes no difference. You know I adore you, that I only want what is best for you."

If you love me so much, why do you make me suffer like this? she was about to answer, but held her tongue.

"Marriage isn't a game, sweetheart. It's much more serious than you can understand. When a girl chooses her life's companion, she can't allow herself the luxury of making a mistake. She needs to see all the drawbacks and ask herself: Is the man that I chose the ideal partner for me?"

"I only know that I love him."

"Yes, but you can't evade the question."

"And you, did you choose the ideal partner? Did Daddy really make you happy?"

"*Cristina*! What's gotten into you?"

"You prefer to evade the issue, right, Mama?"

"Don't talk nonsense. My story is already ancient history and isn't worth hashing over; but you have your whole life ahead of you. Do you want to ruin it for yourself? Do you know what you want, Cristina?"

"Yes," she answered resolutely.

"Do you know what you want?" Lucila asked again, as if her daughter hadn't heard her the first time.

"Yes," Cristina answered for a second time. "I want to marry David."

"You, from a family of believers, raised a Catholic, how can you think of joining your life to someone who belongs to an accursed people?"

After having resorted unsuccessfully to the mention of the family's prestige, to the parents' honor, to the damage to their social position and to the incompatibility of the cultures, Lucila's was trying now a new weapon.

"The Hebrew people of today have no reason to pay for the sins of their ancestors!" Cristina retorted.

"Sins? Such a nice little word for the horrific act they committed! They killed Christ! The Jews are a deicidal people and have no absolution. That's why God condemned them to roam the face of the earth."

Once more tears flowed from María Cristina's eyes.

"Do you want to lose your soul?" Doña Lucila continued, sensing that Cristina was beginning to weaken before the new line of attack. "Are you looking to damn yourself?"

"For heaven's sake! What do you want from me?"

"Leave him."

"No!... I can't."

"You have to leave him."

"No, mother. Don't you understand that I love him?"

This time it was Lucila who began to falter before Cristina's stubborn resistance. Reasoning with her was completely useless. There are no arguments that can stand up to the arguments of love, nor logic that can go against the heart.

"Sweetheart, would David convert?"

"I'm sure he would, if I ask him to," Cristina was quick to answer, heartened by the ray of light that managed to peek through.

"And would you be married by the Catholic Church?"

"I never contemplated otherwise."

Lucila took a deep breath.

"All right," she said, "we have to speak with Father Izaza to see what can be done."

María Cristina's face lit up. She took her mother's hands and kissed them, her beautiful eyes aglow with gratitude. But suddenly they turned sad again.

"And what about Daddy?"

"Your father?"

Doña Lucila lowered her eyes and sighed. She looked downcast. She loved her daughter and above all else longed for her happiness. María Cristina was still holding her mother's hands and had just given them an affectionate squeeze. Lucila looked up and made an effort to smile. Cristina, who knew her mother so well, sensed the uncertainty and fear that were hidden behind that smile.

"Your father? Don't worry, darling. Leave him to me."

29

Leon Edri had taken off his shoes, loosened his tie, and unbuttoned his shirt collar. Having made himself comfortable in the soft easy chair, he remained motionless, with his eyes fixed on the ceiling. David watched him. *It's just his body that's at rest*, he thought, since he knew that when his father assumed that posture his mind was working full steam ahead, analyzing matters regarding his complex business enterprises and planning his next moves. In a certain sense, David was doing the same thing: he was asking himself if this was the right moment to speak to him about what was eating at him without giving him a moment's peace. If he hadn't brought up the subject as yet, it was because he had lacked the courage to do so. Initially, he thought that it would be better to speak to his mother, but every time he was alone with her, his resolve weakened. Hurt her? She who adored him more than she adored anyone else? Besides, how would he face his father afterwards? No, he'd have to speak to him first. He knew that what he had to say would come as a mortal blow to him, but there was no way to avoid it. Sooner or later he'd have to do it. He came up behind him.

"What are you thinking about, Papi?"

"Oh, nothing in particular. Where were you all afternoon? I wanted to show you some papers."

"I was with some friends. What papers?"

"The contract with Mega Centers. It formalizes the orders for the next twelve months."

"Do you ever think about anything other than business?"

Leon smiled.

"Yes, of course."

"Such as?"

"About you, for one."

David returned the smile.

"What exactly?"

"Well, about your future…Who you'll marry, when, how many children you'll have…"

Here it is! His father had raised the subject himself. The time to speak had come. He cleared his throat…but nothing came out.

"And I also think about Benny, and Suzy, and your mother," Leon continued, "and about the whole family in general… those who are here and those who aren't. Do you know that I had an extensive family?"

Too late! He had let the opportunity slip away! He had it before him a second earlier, and now, without knowing how, it had slipped through his fingers.

"My Aunt Dora had ten children. The first one was a girl who died at birth, then came two boys and afterwards a girl who also died when she was barely a year old."

Leon enjoyed telling his children stories about the *alte heim*, "the old home," as he called the house where he spent his childhood, and his children, when they heard these stories, enjoyed it even more than he did. David especially delighted in hearing his father tell stories of a universe that no longer existed and seemed unreal to him. To think that in the *shtetl* where his father was raised there were no cars, no movies, no radio, no telephone, and that he was talking about Europe, no less, right smack in the twentieth century! The idea that the world had changed more in the last fifty years than in the previous one thousand fascinated him. The era of horse-drawn carriages, oil lamps, the long petticoat, and the corset had disappeared forever. Along with them went romanticism, modesty, and the fear of God. "It was another world," his father used to say and would add, not completely convinced, "but the present is better."

"My Uncle Shmuel wanted a daughter so much," Leon continued, "that my Aunt Dora gave birth every year until she had a girl, their tenth child, after having lost two girls and a boy when they were very little, and after having brought six boys into the world. I think that if the girl hadn't arrived," he noted with a smile, "my Aunt Dora would have continued having children until she was eighty."

David had already heard that story on more than one occasion, since the stories his father told about the olden days were always the same. In the presence of Benjamin and Suzy, his younger children, Leon narrated funny adventures from his youth, but when he was alone with David (who was more patient than the others, perhaps because he was the eldest), he seized the opportunity to talk about his family.

"They called the girl Braine. I never knew her because she was born after I left Golochov. From my Uncle Gabriel I also had three cousins whom I never met (he was a bachelor who got married when I was already in America); but with cousins my age, I had a marvelous time. If you could have seen, for example, how much fun the *Pesach seders* were. I never did see another *seder* like those again. There were about twenty of us around the table; I don't even know how we all fit. In spite of the fact that my Aunt Frida and Aunt Mina didn't come to Uncle Shmuel's house with their families but had their own separate *seder*. So that for all of us to be together—my aunts and uncles and cousins—we would have had to build a special room. After I left Golochov, not even in the biggest of rooms would we have all fit, since the family kept growing. Once I figured that there were seventy-eight of us when the war broke out …"

Leon stood up and paced the room a bit, as if lost in time.

"Yes, we were a very large family."

The expression on his face had changed and his voice sounded sad.

"Of the seventy-eight people, eighteen survived."

David was moved. Only once had he heard his father recite the doleful "statistic": eleven family members had previously traveled to America; of those who remained in Europe only two died of natural causes; six died as a direct consequence of the hardships caused by the war (one, literally of hunger); fifty-two were taken by the Nazis to extermination camps; seven managed to survive by fleeing to the East; in all, seventy-eight people.

"Yes," Leon repeated, "we were a very big family."

David would have liked to console his father, but he knew that there was no way he could. It wasn't a passing sadness that his father felt, but rather a profound ache, not intense, perhaps, but well ingrained in his mind, set in place, rooted in the most intimate part of his soul. *The Jews of his generation*, David thought while he watched his father's melancholy countenance, *will never be able to put the holocaust aside*. Not even those who, like his father, hadn't lived through it.

"That's how it is, son, we can't forget the holocaust. *We must not forget it.*"

He read my thought! David marveled, as he did whenever his father discerned what he was thinking, even though that happened with relative frequency.

"That was the biggest crime ever committed in all of human history. It's not that people haven't been murdered before, en masse and with equal cruelty," Leon explained, as if the explanation was necessary, "but it had never been carried out in a systematic way, building real 'extermination factories,' where with satanic efficiency science, industrial technology, and deception were combined to exterminate thousands of people day after day. Six million of our brothers and sisters were murdered! It is for their sake that we, those of us who survived, must remember."

Without these installments of regular indoctrination, my formation as a Jew with a complex wouldn't be complete, David thought. *Now, for sure, I can't touch the subject, not after a lecture like that. I'll have to wait for another opportunity.*

"What did you want to talk to me about?"

(*I'll be damned! He read my thought again!*)

"Me?"

"Yes. You were about to tell me something, weren't you?"

"Well, it's that…"

David couldn't get the words out.

"Tell me, son."

It was an invitation to speak, but it could be interpreted as an order. Now he had no choice. The time had come.

"Dad, I don't know how to tell you this, but the fact is that…"

David swallowed hard. Leon observed his son's nervousness and had a feeling he was in for some bad news.

"…I'm in love."

He had finished his sentence, but Leon kept waiting as if there should be more, forcing David to continue.

"…with a Catholic girl."

There! He had said it!

"And?" his father asked, trying to get more out of him.

"…and I love her very much."

"Aha!" Leon paused and added: "You'll get over it."

"No. I won't get over it. I want to marry her."

David saw his father turn ashen. The change was immediate and pronounced.

"David," the old man said, making an effort to make his voice sound natural, but it too had changed, "have you really thought about what you're saying?"

"Yes, Dad."

"That's what's been eating at you the last few months, isn't it?"

David bowed his head and lowered his eyes. He waited for his father to grab him by the shoulders and make him look him in the eye. But it didn't happen. Leon turned and walked over to the window, where he remained for a few seconds looking through the tulle curtain, slowly moving his head from side to side.

"You don't know what you're doing," he said dryly.

"Dad... I love her."

"You don't know, you don't know…," he repeated, not listening to his son.

He stood with his back to David, absorbed in his thoughts. Neither one said anything for a long while.

"In accordance with Jewish law, the *Halakhah*, a convert to our religion is a Jew in every sense of the word," Leon began reasoning in a very soft voice, as if instructing his son and talking to himself at the same time, "but the truth is that it's not the same thing."

David felt the blood rush to his head. His father had presumed that the girl he was in love with was going to convert. He bit his lip. He couldn't tell him that it wasn't going to be like that, not at that moment. It could cause him to have a violent reaction, perhaps make him sick.

Standing in front of the window, Leon continued mulling things over, looking off into the distance.

"In cases like this, converts generally aren't sincere. To facilitate the marriage, they embrace Judaism in the hope of allaying opposition and placating the Jewish fiancé's family. Sometimes a rabbi can't even be found who is willing to perform the conversion..."

Leon suddenly turned around and looked straight at David.

"How did you let yourself get dragged into this situation?"

"Can a person control his feelings?"

"Of course he can! A person knows who he is, with whom he ought to be joined, with whom he must *not* fall in love. He must place intelligence above feelings, cut the ties before becoming attached, not allow himself to become entangled. I thought that you had more common sense. Aren't there enough Jewish girls in Lárida?"

"No, Papa. None as beautiful or as refined as María Cristina."

Leon shuddered upon hearing the name. It was the name itself, not the person that made him shudder, for he hadn't the least idea about whom they were talking. Out of all the thousands of Spanish names in the world, it had to be that one: María! Precisely María! Could there be a more Catholic name? And on top of that: "Cristina." The *goyish* sound of the name drove the wound in deeper.

"What nonsense! Our community is filled with beautiful girls. Take the Feferbaum girl, for example. What a precious thing! You never found it in yourself to ask her out, despite all the times your mother begged you. Or the Frenkel daughters. He's got four, one better looking than the other. But no! No one was good enough for you. You're so foolish that you even turned your nose up at Monica Mayer. You can't find a prettier girl than her anywhere. And such

363

refinement! So polite, so well educated... and above all, son, from such a family! That's the kind of daughter-in-law I'd like to have."

David wouldn't debate the subject of beauty with his father. What did he know about beauty? He, who came from the *shtetl*, where the concept of aesthetics was practically medieval. For Eastern European Jews "whiteness" was synonymous with "beauty." A very fair-skinned girl was by definition beautiful, all the more so if she had rosy cheeks, like Monica Mayer. In the mentality of a people who for generations had suffered poverty, being of fair complexion and rosy-cheeked implied "good health," which in turn was associated with chubbiness. If a girl happened to be only moderately plump, well, that was also considered a form of beauty. Monica Mayer, white and quite stout, not only wasn't pretty but was, in fact, irremediably ugly. But what would his father know about that! And what did he know about refinement, when he himself, despite his keen mind, had never completely acquired it.

"Dad, none of the girls in the colony provide any attraction for me because I've known them since we were children; I played with them, I grew up with them and they hold no mystery for me," David stated diplomatically, showing the sagacity that he inherited from his father, and that under different circumstances would have made him so proud. "To fall in love with a girl from the community would be like falling in love with my own sister," he concluded.

"When I wanted to get married there wasn't a single Jewish girl in Lárida. Still, at no time did I contemplate the possibility of marrying a woman outside of my faith. I already told you how I traveled to Eretz Israel just to find a Jewish wife. And believe me, making a trip back then was not easy, but I did it because I knew that it was my duty. Thank God for giving me your mother for a wife. What kind of life would I have had married to a *goyah*? You wouldn't be in this world; that is to say, my children would have been different, without tradition, without light..."

"Why? Are you of the kind that believes we're better than the rest?"

"No, son. Not better, but *different*."

"And what's wrong with marrying someone who is different?"

"Do you ask this in all seriousness? Is it possible you don't realize that such marriages produce a culture shock? That inevitably you'll forfeit your heritage? That assimilation will be the end of the little bit of Judaism that you'll be able to bring to your home? Do you think that the influence of your wife's family on you and on your children, especially on your children, will not have any effect?"

"I'm glad you mention the family, since one would be hard pressed to find a family better than María Cristina's."

"Son, how little you know about life! Any Jewish family at all would have been better."

"How can you say that if you don't even know who we're talking about!"

"I neither know nor do I care!"

"Dad!"

"Yes, son. I don't care who they are. I don't want *goyim* in my family."

"You won't have anything to be ashamed of in that regard. On the contrary, you'll have reason to be proud."

David paused, as if to underscore the impact, before elatedly announcing: "María Cristina is the daughter of Doctor Ulpiano Méndez Carrizosa."

The impression that David intended to create did not happen. Leon Edri cast a cynical look at his son and asked: "Am I to understand that this is a great honor for us?"

"Yes, of course!"

365

"Well, it isn't," he calmly replied.

"The Méndezes are among the most important people in the country. What do you think?" David shot back. "That it's an honor for them to come into our family? Doctor Méndez's father was governor of the province. And yours, what was he? The watchmaker of Golochov?"

"Do you only go back one generation?" Leon's voice rose to a fever pitch. "Why don't you go back one hundred generations? Then you'll find my ancestors studying the Torah and those of Doctor Méndez's running half naked among the bushes."

David didn't know what to say. Father and son remained frozen in silence, each one furious with himself for having shouted at the other, and hurting over having caused any pain.

"I'm sorry, Dad."

"My son, you've dealt me a brutal blow tonight. I hope you'll think this over, that you'll see the harm you're going to cause yourself, not to mention us, your parents, who love you so much, or your brother and sister, whom you'll influence with your example. Have you spoken to your mother?"

"No."

"Good. Don't tell her anything. Don't make her suffer. Keep a clear head and don't act hastily. Let some time pass... Time has its way with things. It'll make you see your mistake."

David remained silent. He loved María Cristina passionately. He loved her with that fervor that becomes delirium, that doesn't allow for compromise, that blinds reason. He wanted to get married, to join his life forever with hers, but he couldn't tell his father more than what he had already said; not at that moment. He'd wait a little longer, holding his emotions in check.

"Stop seeing that girl for a while."

"No, Dad, I can't."

Leon looked fixedly at his son.

"Promise me, at least, that you'll give this some thought, that you'll reconsider the matter."

David did not reply.

"Do you promise?"

David nodded, but hesitantly.

"All right, son. Up to now nothing has happened... I'll pretend this conversation never took place."

There'll be another one, David promised himself.

Leon Edri closed his eyes. What moral commitments might David have undertaken? How far had he gone in making up his mind? He knew his son well and recognized that he had a will of iron, like his. If David had his mind made up, there was nothing that would make him change it.

The old man felt his legs go weak. He staggered towards his chair and plopped down. His face was pale and drawn. A tear rolled down his cheek; the first one in many, many years. David watched him in that pitiful state and he cried too.

"Dad... Haven't you ever been in love? ... Weren't you young once?"

The reply was slow in coming.

"Yes, son. I know what passion is... I too was young."

30

The receptionist at Sileja S.A. was taken aback at the look of the individual who had just gotten off the elevator. From behind the thick glasses, a pair of very blue eyes gazed out at her. The eyes looked exaggeratedly large because of the magnification caused by the lenses. The man had long sideburns and a thick mustache that framed both sides of his mouth and merged with a little goat-like beard. However, it wasn't the face so much that drew the young woman's attention but his clothes. On that hot morning, the visitor was wearing a black overcoat that came down below his knees. Resting over his sweaty forehead was a black felt fedora.

"I'd like to speak with Don Jaime Lubinsky."

By his accent the receptionist knew that he was a coreligionist of her employer.

"May I say who is asking for him?"

"Abraham Singer."

The name confirmed her assumption.

"Do you have an appointment?"

"No. It's a personal matter."

"One moment, please."

She lifted the receiver and pressed the button.

"Melba, a gentleman to see Don Jaime... No, he doesn't have an appointment... Yes, I know, but he says it's personal... Abraham Singer... Okay."

She hung up and said in a friendly tone:

"Don Jaime is in a meeting, but his secretary has gone to notify him. You'll have to wait a bit. If you'd like to sit down..."

"Thank you," the man answered and remained standing.

A minute later Jaime Lubinsky's secretary entered the reception area.

"Don Abraham? Would you like to follow me, please?"

Rabbi Singer followed the secretary to her boss's office. Jaime stood up as soon as the rabbi entered.

"Avrum," he said, walking to meet him, "What a pleasant surprise."

The conversation drifted into Yiddish, as generally happens when two Jews from the old country get together.

"Excuse me for coming to trouble you at work."

"I should say not! It's a pleasure to see you. What can I do for you?"

"A tragic case has come to our attention in the colony," the rabbi said, taking off his hat, under which he was wearing a little black cloth skullcap.

Singer sat down and Jaime pulled up a chair and sat down next to him.

"It has to do with Mrs. Lefkowitz, Dandush's widow. Do you know her?"

Lubinsky nodded. In Lárida all the Jews knew each other.

Elka Lefkowitz's husband, "Dandush the Shoemaker," had died five days earlier. Daniel Lefkowitz had been the shoemaker in Wieliczka, a little town barely six miles from Cracow. In Lárida he had a little grocery store, but his fellow Jews never stopped calling him by his old nickname: "Dandush the Shoemaker." There weren't many poor Jews in the city, but there were some, and Daniel was certainly one of them. He belonged to that class of people on whom luck never smiles, a real *shlemazel*, as Jews call those unfortunate individuals who drag through life. He never had children; of his relatives not a single living soul remained after the war, and as for friends, if in fact he had any, no one knew who they were. He remained on the fringes, perhaps more because he had no family than for being a *shlemazel*. When they buried him there were so few people at the cemetery that the members of the *chevrah kaddishah* had to phone their own friends to come immediately so they could complete the *minyan* and recite the Kaddish. Many members of the community didn't even know that "Dandush the Shoemaker" had died.

"As you know, one of the basic duties of every Jew is to help widows in need," Singer said while struggling to pull out a handkerchief from his pocket.

"Yes, of course."

"Mrs. Lefkowitz came to see me yesterday afternoon."

Jaime watched the rabbi wipe the perspiration from his face. Although Lubinsky hadn't been president of the community for years, from time to time, cases that were incumbent upon the Israelite Center came to him directly.

"Poor woman!" Abraham Singer continued. "She can barely walk and is in no condition to look after the store. And even if she weren't old and sick, that wouldn't matter either, because she knows nothing about running a business."

Singer paused, sighed, and then began again.

"But that's not the problem. The worst," he said leaning forward to be closer to Jaime, "is that Dandush owed money. Two days ago someone showed up at her house to collect on the debt. He had a note signed by her husband and threatened to seize the business if

371

the loan wasn't paid. The old woman is scared to death. She says she doesn't have a dime to her name."

"How much is owed?"

"Five thousand pesos," Singer said, drawing closer, and he added, almost in a whisper: "If you could help her out it would be a great *mitzvah*."

"There's no problem," Lubinsky said without hesitation. "I'll pay it."

Abraham Singer couldn't mask his surprise. He knew Jaime was a generous man and would surely be disposed to help, but the rabbi had figured that Lubinsky would only give part of what was owed and "to pull" that much out of him he'd have to haggle with him. For a second, it seemed he had misunderstood.

"Eh... You're going to lend her the five thousand?"

"No. I'll cover the note. Either we pay it off between Leon and me, or I'll pay it myself."

"Honestly... I'm at a loss for words to thank you."

"You don't have anything to thank me for. You're fulfilling your duty and I'm fulfilling mine."

"God bless you, Chaim."

"Bah," he replied, shrugging his shoulders.

"Doña Elka is about to have a nervous breakdown. She'll be happy when she hears that you're going to give her the money."

"Absolutely not! She is not to know where you got the money: not her, not anybody. Agreed?"

"Definitely. That's how it should be when lending help. Do you know something? There are different levels of morality, or rather, degrees of nobleness, within which one can make a donation. Do you have a few minutes?" he suddenly asked, realizing he might be taking up time in an important businessman's day.

"It's all right," Jaime replied, looking at his watch, "I have a few minutes."

Truthfully, he hadn't any time to spare. He had some letters to dictate and several phone calls to make before leaving for a board of directors meeting of the bank, but he sensed that the rabbi was getting ready to teach him something about the Talmud and nothing could please him more. To be seated in front of a learned man and listen to the ancient doctrine of the scholars of Israel transported him back to his childhood, to the room with its whitewashed walls whose cracks he clearly remembered, to the *cheder* where the teacher gave his young students their first knowledge of the Bible.

"Every good deed is worthy of praise," Rabbi Singer began. "To give money to a needy person, no matter how it is done, is a good deed, a *mitzvah*. Still, the same act of charity can have greater or lesser merit before God, depending on how it is done. The lowest stage is when everybody learns about the gift, that is to say, when the donor makes his generosity public."

"Like when Moisés Birenbaum publicly announces that he is going to donate fifty thousand pesos to the Hebrew School," Jaime interjected with a smile.

"Exactly. It's the donation that is announced in speeches, that is printed in the newspapers or, simply, that runs from mouth to mouth. It's the donation that remains on public record in the minutes of a meeting, on the inscription next to a door, on the commemorative plaque... The second level is when no one knows about the donation, except the donor and the recipient. It is the case of someone who tells a needy person: 'Take this money, but don't tell anyone; this is just between you and me.' "

"How interesting!"

"The third level is that of the anonymous donation. It is when the donor arranges it so that no one knows who gave it, not even the recipient."

"Is that the highest level?"

"No. There's one more. It's when not only nobody knows about it, but when the donor himself doesn't know who the person is who benefited from his generosity."

Lubinsky wondered if in practice such a situation could arise.

Abraham Singer stood up.

"All right, Chaim," he said, putting the handkerchief that he had held in his hand the entire time back in his pocket, "I won't take up more of your time. You have shown, once more, that you have a big heart."

"It was a pleasure," Jaime replied, firmly shaking his hand. "I'll be at your house tomorrow with the money... in cash."

"Tomorrow's Saturday."

"Oh, yes! It slipped my mind. Monday, then."

"Perfect."

"Give my best to your wife."

"Thank you. Likewise. *A gut shobes.*"

"*A guit shabes*," Lubinsky repeated, giving the traditional Yiddish greeting the pronunciation characteristic of Russian Jews: "Have a good Sabbath."

Jaime remained alone in the room. He went back to his chair, behind the big mahogany desk. While pondering, he picked up a pencil and twirled it on his fingertips. He contemplated the possibility of the Jewish community of Lárida acquiring a house; a kind of shelter, where people like Mrs. Lefkowitz could spend the final years of their lives comfortably and without worry. Then he thought it wasn't such a good idea. What old or infirm people there were in the community had relatives who were ready to look after them at home. The case of Elka Lefkowitz, a widow without children or family, was an exception. It would be better to create a fund that the Israelite Center could manage at its discretion, to help the poor of their community in the event of grave necessity. Yes, that indeed was a good idea. How much money would the fund need to have? Five million? No, that much wasn't needed. Three million? Maybe. The total amount could only be determined on the basis of the income that the fund would produce, and the pertinent question was: How to invest the money? Jaime remembered he was going to meet someone that very same evening who could give him some advice on the matter.

The telephone rang and interrupted his deliberations. Of the two telephones on his desk, it was the one with the private line.

"Hello?"

"Hi!" It was Leon Edri's voice at the other end.

"Where are you?"

"I'm stuck at the R.O. I'm going to be delayed a little longer," he said, speaking from the Registry Office of Industrial Property.

"I can't wait for you. I've got a board of directors' meeting at the bank."

"Okay, it doesn't matter. Let's leave it for Monday morning."

"All right, see you then."

"Please tell my secretary I'll be in the office within an hour."

"Right away. Listen, when we see each other, remind me to speak to you about another matter."

"About what?"

"A donation."

On Friday evenings someone always was invited to dine at the home of Jaime Lubinsky. He established the custom, following the tradition of Eastern European Jews, whereby on Friday nights each family tried to host some of the poorest people in the *shtetl*. In Mahir Lubinsky's modest home—Jaime clearly remembered, even though he was a child— students from the *yeshivah*, assistants to the dairyman, tanner apprentices, and workers from the neighboring stables of the regional commissar came to dinner. The guest he remembered most vividly, perhaps because he found him so appalling, was a beggar his father picked up one night coming out of the synagogue. He was revoltingly filthy, a ragged and foul-smelling man, who claimed to be a Jew from Kiev passing through Trilesy on his way to Kazatin. Despite his repulsive appearance, he received the same cordial treatment that Mahir extended to every guest, even though Anna grumbled the entire night.

There were no indigent Jews in Lárida, thank God, and the custom was modified so that anyone could be invited: an individual, a couple or group of people, who weren't necessarily poor. What mattered was that there should be always a guest for dinner, generally a relative or friend.

When it began to grow dark, Raquel would light candles and recite the corresponding prayer, thus ushering in *Shabbat*, the day of rest. None of the children missed dinner, not even Saul, who frequently went out to eat with friends. They all stood around the table, in respectful silence, while Jaime Lubinsky recited the *Shabbat* blessing and the benediction of the bread and the wine.

That last Friday of the month, August 1961, the dinner guest was Professor Erich Halberstam, an eminent economist from Stuttgart University. In 1934 the government had hired Professor Halberstam to submit a plan for restructuring the tax code. When he finished his work, after a year in the capital, he decided to make that city his permanent residence and not return to Germany, where the situation for the Jews was growing worse by the day. Since he wasn't married it was easy for him to decide to stay; the government gave him citizenship, the National University offered him a professorship, and several companies asked him to serve as a business consultant. Twice a year Professor Halberstam traveled to Lárida to review the financial state of Sileja S.A. and to offer his wise counsel to the firm's owners. Jaime Lubinsky always invited him to his home during those visits, which were professional in nature.

"I don't even know why you pay me to come here," the professor joked. "You know more than I do."

"We know how to run a business, Erich; what we don't know is how to avoid paying taxes without breaking the law," Jaime said laughingly.

"And you think I do?" Halberstam replied, laughing even harder.

"A little more roast, professor?" Raquel asked, moving the serving dish closer.

"No, please, thank you," he protested too late. "Everything is delicious, but I don't have any more room," he said out of breath while Raquel served him another portion.

"What's for dessert, Mama?" asked Vivian, the youngest of the Lubinsky children.

"Compote."

"I don't want any."

"Who's asking you? When it comes time to be served, you can say: 'No, thank you.' "

"It didn't do the professor much good."

They all burst out laughing.

"Well, young man, and what about you? How is your work going for you?" Halberstam asked, addressing Saul Lubinsky. "Very hard?"

"No, sir."

"What do you do?"

"I'm in charge of the old textile plant and I'm managing more or less all right."

"More or less all right?" Jaime interrupted. "Don't be modest, son. You're doing a really great job. Do you know, Erich, that he was able to increase production by nine percent and at the same time reduce variable costs by three percent? I still don't understand how he did it."

Saul smiled. His father was proud of him.

"He would do even better," Raquel interjected, "if he spent more time on work and less on girls."

Vivian and Sandra, Saul's sisters, started giggling.

"Let him be, Raquel. What do you want? The boy is twenty-two."

Erich Halberstam was a man of vast culture and an excellent conversationalist. Jaime, although quieter and less learned than the professor, did not fall short of him in the ability to express himself and to delve deep into a subject. They spoke about the most suitable type of investment for a public fund, where safety and valuation are more important than income. They also discussed politics, history, and other subjects. When they did say goodbye, it was midnight.

Leon Edri arrived at the office on Monday morning later than usual. He walked past his office and went straight to Jaime's, where the secretary greeted him.

"Good morning, Don León."

"Good morning, Melba. Is Jaime in?"

The question was superfluous. His partner always arrived before he did. He opened the door without knocking.

"Hello!" Jaime said when he saw him come in.

"Hello!"

"You got up early today."

Leon ignored the jest.

"Any news about the price quotes?" he asked, sitting down in front of his friend.

"They haven't arrived yet, but I ought to get them any minute. Four in all: two from Germany and two from the United States. The best brewery equipment is German, but for bottling there's nothing like American machinery. The ideal thing would be to build the factory with equipment from both countries."

"Possibly. We'll see when the offers arrive."

"What did you find out at the Registry Office?"

"The name that we liked, 'Imperial Corona,' isn't registered, but the brand names 'Corona' and 'Imperial' are. I think that to avoid problems it will be better for us to come up with another name."

"Like what? 'Sileja Beer'?"

The two erupted into a big laugh.

"We'll think of something soon," Leon assured him.

"Leib, I want us to come to a decision as soon as possible on the land for the factory. Do we buy the Martínez parcel? Or do we look for something in the new industrial area?"

"I knew I had something to tell you! I found out they're going to expand the industrial area by building a street that will run straight to the Southern Freeway."

"Interesting… Some good opportunities can turn up there."

"I have a draft of the project in my office. That Indian fellow from the mayor's office, Vélez, got it for me. Hold on a minute; I'll bring it to you," and saying this, he headed for the door.

Before leaving, he stopped abruptly and turned around.

"Chaim, you told me to remind you to tell me something about a donation…"

"Oh, yes! A sad case in our community came to my attention. It's a person in dire straits. Five thousand pesos would solve it, and I want to help out. I'd like for the money to come from the two of us."

"Who is it?"

"Someone."

"Someone? You can't say who?"

"No."

"At least tell me what kind of problem."

"I'd rather not."

Leon smiled.

"You're very mysterious, Chaim."

"You'll be doing a *mitzvah*."

"If you say so, I'm sure that it is. Okay, count me in. I imagine that you want it in cash."

This time it was Jaime Lubinsky who smiled.

"You've set yourself on the fourth level."

Edri returned the smile and left the room, without understanding what his friend had meant.

Leon went to his office. Waiting for him on the desk was the day's correspondence. He went to the window first, as he always did as soon as he entered his office, and drew the curtains back. The splendid view of the city appeared before his eyes, the Obondó Valley in the distance, and off to the side, the imposing hills of the cordillera. Light flooded the room. He sat down at his desk and quickly perused the names on the correspondence, without opening any of the envelopes.

This Chaim is a case! he told himself. *Always going around worried about the other guy.*

He removed a folder from the file drawer, placed it on his desk and began leafing through it. He found the paper he was looking for and was ready to pull it out when he heard a blood-curdling scream that caused him to drop the folder. He heard a second scream. It was a woman's scream and came from the corridor. He hurried outside. A few others had gone out into the hall. Before the open door of Jaime's office, which was next to his, he saw Melba, with her back to him. She turned around slowly and looked at Leon with her eyes grown large, her face tense. She had her hands over her mouth, a look of anguish about her. Edri entered the room. On the floor, next to the big mahogany desk, lay Jaime Lubinsky, face down and his feet drawn up. Leon rushed to his side, turned him over, unbuttoned his shirt collar, and filled with angst slapped his face a few times. There was no response.

"Chaim!" he shouted.

As if enshrouded in a mist, he heard voices around him. Even though Melba was speaking softly, her voice was the one he heard above the others.

"I was bending over, arranging the bottom drawer of my desk," she said, "when I seemed to hear a thud, like something that had fallen. Then I called Don Jaime over the intercom, and when he didn't answer I went to see what had happened..."

Leon felt his heart beating wildly. He was trembling.

"A doctor! A doctor!" he shouted.

Before him was the pallid, completely lifeless, face of his friend and partner, with his eyes shut and his mouth half open. He placed his mouth over Jaime's and began blowing desperately. At regular intervals he pressed down on the inert torso with his hands, without knowing exactly how to give artificial respiration. And if he had known, it would have been in vain.

Jerusalem

September 25, 1961

Dear Leon,

It was really a strange coincidence for you to get my last letter, with my commentary on death, precisely when you returned from the cemetery; but what strikes me as being even more bizarre is that also there in Lárida—at the very moment of Chaim's burial—there should begin to fall that luminous, nearly imperceptible drizzle, which we have come to associate with death. What a curious phenomenon! What do you think it means? If I were a believer, I would surely see some divine manifestation in it. Maybe you interpret it that way, but I don't know what to think. The truth is that it is hard for me to accept as a mere coincidence the fact that you as well as I, on opposite sides of the world, have seen the same mysterious mist that we saw at your father's funeral that August afternoon, thirty-six years ago, and which, once again, has appeared under tragic circumstances.

I am deeply sorry for the loss of your friend and partner. With all my heart, I am with you in your grief.

Fifty years old! What a pity! He truly departed at a young age. He departed when he reached the age at which a man should step back a little from the world of business and devote himself to enjoying his money, his free time, wife and children... the grandchildren that he did not live long enough to have.

They say that you love your grandchildren more than your own children. Maybe; but I don't believe it. I think people just don't remember how much they loved their children when they were little. Grandchildren arrive so many years later, that a parent doesn't really remember how much he adored his children. What happens is that children become adults, and the love that we held for them necessarily changes as they change and turn into "other" people. It is natural. The adult always has a bit of cunning in him, a bit of dishonesty, and can't inspire as much love as the tender, innocent child. Be that as it may, a man's greatest happiness is to be surrounded by his descendants and to watch them grow.

Your children must be grown-up by now. If I remember correctly, David must be twenty-three, Benjamin twenty-one, and Suzy eighteen. Right? Don't be surprised if at any moment one of them announces to you the desire to get married. Ariel already informed me, and he's even a couple of months younger than David. He's going to marry Tamara, the same girl we thought he was going to marry a little more than a year ago. Do you remember I told you at the time in one of my letters that I didn't think their breakup was final? See, I was right.

Judith and I are very happy that things have turned out this way, since we like the girl and her family. We get along wonderfully with her parents and, believe me, that's important too.

We'd like to have grandchildren and enjoy them during the years we have left. You'll say that it's ridiculous to talk this way at our age; however, what happened to Chaim Lubinsky gives one a lot to think about. His death is a forewarning: for those of our generation, our time has come.

I imagine you'll laugh if I tell you that I bought two cemetery plots last week, for Judith and me. When the time comes, one day, we'll rest more peacefully lying next to each other, together for eternity. You see, even those of us who are nonbelievers have our mystic slant.

My purchase also has a practical side: I'll simplify matters for my children on two occasions and afford them the prospect of paying their respects before the graves of their father and mother in a single visit. As you see, without being rich, I also have investments in land. Nothing compared to your holdings; nevertheless, it could be said that forty square feet of Holy Land are worth more than forty

384

thousand acres of tropical plantation. They are worth more, but obviously they cost less. That's how things are in this materialistic world.

I won't ask you to extend my condolences to Ruchel because I prefer to do it directly. I'm going to write her a letter right now.

Two weeks ago was Rosh Hashanah, the first day of the year 5722. What irony! On the same date I sent you my last letter, I mailed a card to the Lubinsky family wishing them a "Happy New Year." I don't even want to think about how untimely it was. Poor Ruchel and the children. It had to be a terrible blow for them, but they'll recover. The passage of days will ease their sorrow, since it is true what they say about time: it heals all.

Affectionately,

Baruch

31

Barely ten minutes from the city, along the road that winds towards the cordillera to then descend tortuously towards the sea, on a grassy plateau beside the road, sits Altamira, the stately mansion of the Méndez Carrizosa family. The gate was wide open, but Leon Edri stopped his car before taking the cobblestone driveway that led up to the house. In previous years, when his children were little, he used to go for a holiday drive on the same road, looking for a high, breezy spot to spread a blanket and sit down with his family for a picnic. He had passed by the gate at Altamira many times without stopping and had admired the placid green plateau with the house in the distance. Not even in his wildest dreams had it ever occurred to him that one day he would be entering the mansion to speak with its owner on a subject as delicate as the one that brought him there that afternoon. His wife had urged him to meet with Ulpiano Méndez, and so the meeting was hurriedly set up, only two hours beforehand. To keep the appointment, he had to cancel several previous commitments. Surely, Méndez had to do the same.

"You have to speak with him as soon as possible," his wife had told him flatly. "You've got to do something."

For two weeks, after David again spoke to his father about his feelings for María Cristina, an atmosphere of gloom and anguish hung over the Edri house. Leon had made up his mind not to tell his wife right away, but it wasn't easy to hide something from Esther Edri. The day following the confrontation between father and son, at lunchtime, Esther began hounding her husband.

"What's troubling you, Leon?"

"Nothing."

"Don't give me that 'nothing.' Do you think I'm blind? Ever since yesterday you've been on edge."

"On edge?"

"Come now, Leon, don't go playing stupid. Something's troubling you. Tell me what's wrong."

The issue that was troubling Leon was one that he had thought was over and done with, because following the first conversation with his son he had gotten the feeling—choosing to believe what was expedient—that David's feelings for Doctor Méndez's daughter were a thing of the past.

"Something... has come up, but I'd rather not discuss it for the time being."

"Stop this foolishness! If you're going to tell me, you're going to tell me right now. What's going on?"

Leon wasn't about to fight the pressure. Nor did he have any reason to; the problem belonged to both of them.

"It's David," he said in a faint tone. "He's in love with a Catholic girl."

Esther stared at her husband, first surprised, then amused; finally, she broke into laughter.

"Is that all?" she asked, somewhat confused. "Is that what has you like this? What do you expect? It's completely natural. He's twenty-three."

"It's more serious than you imagine, Esther. The boy is madly in love and... he wants to get married."

Esther's smiling expression quickly turned serious, as if the weight of the matter had suddenly sunk in. She repeated her husband's last words, very slowly, incredulous.

"He wants to get married?"

"He's going to get married," Leon said, enunciating each syllable with a mixture of fury and hurt.

"How do you know?"

"Because he told me. Because I know him."

A heavy silence filled the room. Leon stood up and walked over to the window. He remained there for a while looking through the tulle curtain, as he had done the first time that David had spoken to him.

"We were right here when he told me."

"How long has that relationship been going on?"

"One or two years."

"And in all that time he wasn't able to speak to you not even once?"

"Yes, he spoke to me a few months ago, but I thought it was something that with time he'd get over."

"Obviously, time made it worse."

"They fell in love the first time they saw each other."

Esther couldn't repress a tenuous smile on her lips and a twinkling in her eyes. At forty-five she was still a beautiful woman.

"He told you that?"

"Yes."

"Who's the girl?"

"A daughter of Ulpiano Méndez."

"Doctor Ulpiano Méndez Carrizosa?"

"Hm, hm."

"Well, at least he didn't get involved with just anybody."

389

Leon Edri cast a fierce glance at his wife.

"I mean," she added in a manner of clarification, "that it could have been worse."

"It's already bad enough."

"Do the girl's parents know what is happening?"

"That's my understanding."

"And what do they say?"

"I don't know."

"I assume they're opposed."

"Without a doubt, yes, but unfortunately I don't think that changes things much. When young people lose their heads..."

"I'll speak to David as soon as he comes in."

"He won't listen to you. He's completely lost his head."

"We'll see..."

The conversation that Esther had with her son that same day was as painful for him as it was for her. David understood perfectly what it meant for his parents—perhaps for himself too—to marry outside the faith. From his home he had received a rich cultural storehouse of knowledge, and with a heavy heart he was prepared to sacrifice it for the woman he loved. With his mother he did have the courage to state clearly what he only dared to insinuate to his father: He would be married in the Catholic Church, because that was the condition that María Cristina had made. It pained Esther to have to ask her son to renounce what his heart most desired, what he perceived to be his own happiness. David, in turn, suffered doubly: for feeling he was voluntarily distancing himself from his people, and above all for causing heartache for his parents. But love is a powerful emotion, stronger than fear or compassion, more tenacious than reason;

especially the passionate love between a young man of twenty-three and a girl of nineteen.

That wasn't the only discussion David had with his mother. Over the course of the ensuing days, the conversation was repeated, sometimes alone with his mother, sometimes just with his father, sometimes the three of them together. The tone of the conversation varied on each occasion, from calm discussion to heated confrontation, with accusations, reproaches, and threats. Neither his father's mature reasoning nor his mother's emotional exhortations had any effect whatsoever. David Edri was unyielding. He would never forsake María Cristina. He couldn't ask her to convert to Judaism and he was prepared to renounce everything for her. His decision was final: he was going to marry her, and that was that.

The problem hung permanently over the house and even when no one mentioned it, the atmosphere remained charged.

One day David coldly announced to his parents that the date for the wedding had been set for December 17. It would be on a Sunday, perfect for a society wedding. María Cristina and he had intended to be married sooner, he told them, but Doña Lucila had asked her daughter to give her at least two months to properly plan the event.

"What do you intend to do?" Esther asked Leon when they were alone.

The feeling of sorrow that had burdened them had turned to anguish now that a date had been set and everything that was falling in on them seemed inevitable.

"What can I do?"

"The marriage is a fact, Leon. Nothing is going to stop it. We have to accept it. David is going to marry that girl and we haven't even spoken with the parents. They are high society people. I don't know what kind of wedding they intend to give, but we can't fold our arms. We are Jews. We enjoy standing and a good name in our community. We have to do something to save face. We can't abandon David; we must help him in some way."

Leon shrugged his shoulders and took a deep breath.

"*Goyim* in my family!" That was the only thing he could say.

"Leon, what's wrong with you?"

Edri sighed again, more deeply than before.

"All right," Esther said, her voice charged with emotion, "you're not going to sit *shivah* and cry over your dead son."

Leon turned around and looked directly at his wife.

"No... Of course not."

"Then, for heaven's sake, do something!"

"What would you have me do?"

"Call Méndez right now and go speak to him. Stand up for your son. Try at least to have them put on a wedding where David doesn't lose all his dignity as a Jew."

"Right now?"

"Yes, yes," she said, pulling him by the arm towards the telephone. "Tell him you want to speak to him as soon as possible."

Leon took the receiver in his hand and stared at it for a few seconds. The dial tone seemed to haunt him.

"You have no idea how unpleasant it is to speak with him. The last time we were together his breath smelled of booze."

"Go on, now, call him."

He took a deep breath, dialed the number, and lifted the receiver to his ear.

It was a little more than a hundred yards from the gate to the house. Leon Edri began approaching, driving slowly up the

392

cobblestone driveway. From the second-floor window of the old mansion, Ulpiano Méndez and his wife watched the car drawing closer.

"Here he comes," Doña Lucila said.

"Yes, here he comes… Just what I needed: Jews in the family!"

"Don't let that sly fox fluster you."

"What do you think!"

"Speak to him in plain words."

"You have no idea how unpleasant it is to speak to him. The last time we were together his breath smelled of onion."

"Go on, now, he's almost here."

A female servant opened the door and led Leon Edri into the living room.

"Please wait here. The doctor will be down momentarily," she said and disappeared.

Leon remained standing. Ulpiano Méndez delayed his entrance for a few minutes.

"Leon." This was all the aristocrat said when he entered the room.

"Ulpiano," Edri reciprocated, as a manner of salutation.

Méndez Carrizosa met Leon's eyes with an austere look, and Leon in turn did likewise, without blinking. The two men stood face to face without exchanging even a single word; they merely observed one another, each trying to deduce what the other was thinking. It was the second time this happened, but neither one remembered the first occasion when, seated in the back of a big black sedan, thirty-five years earlier, the son of the governor had fixed his eyes on those of the young immigrant who was observing him from the sidewalk.

"Such a great urgency to see me," Méndez said, breaking the silence. "I suppose this time it's not about Southern Yarn."

"You know why I'm here."

Ulpiano made a face and sighed.

"Yes. It seems we're going to be in-laws, right?"

"Yes, so it seems, whether we like it or not."

"Yes, sir, whether we like it or not," the old oligarch repeated, as if to leave no doubt that if there were those who were opposed to the joining of the two families, he was among them.

"Frankly, I must confess I'm surprised you've consented to this marriage."

"Consented?" Méndez replied, indignant. "I did everything possible to stop it, but María Cristina would have none of it. I had to accede; if not I would have risked having her elope with your son one day, and that would have been disastrous."

"You're not the only one who is unhappy over this situation. I also did all that I could to prevent it. Destiny put us in the same boat, Ulpiano, and we have to accept it."

"So it seems."

"The problem is that we Jews only marry among ourselves."

"Well, that's your problem. My daughter is going to marry a Catholic, since David converted a few days ago."

Leon Edri felt a shiver run through his body. Méndez had to have noticed it, since he asked:

"What, he didn't tell you?"

"No…"

"Father Izaza performed the ceremony. He baptized him in the Chapel of Saint Filomena, with the boy's own name: David."

Leon Edri was stunned for a few moments, but his agile mind was quick to rationalize. He knew his son well; he knew what he believed in and what he didn't believe in. The conversion had been a tactical step aimed at facilitating his marriage to María Cristina and no conviction whatsoever lay behind his submission to the ritual. What sometimes happens with Christian girls who convert to Judaism—because the fiancé's family demanded it—had worked in reverse this time.

"Well, you see," he said finally, "basically that doesn't have much importance for me. They could have bathed him with holy water and he'd still be a Jew all the same."

Ulpiano laughed at the thought. It wasn't a time for laughter, but the image of a Jew soaked in holy water struck him as quite amusing.

"An individual possesses the quality of Jewry by the simple fact that he's a Jew," Leon explained, trying to impose on the conversation its initial tone of gravity, "and there's nothing that can be done to take that away from him."

"All right, if you're not troubled by it, so much the better. This way we're both satisfied. For you David is a Jew and for me he's a Catholic."

"Tell me, what kind of wedding are you planning?"

"What do you mean: what kind of wedding?"

"I mean from a formal point of view. They could be married in a civil ceremony. The law considers it..."

"Absolutely not! My daughter is going to be married in a Catholic Church. On this point there is nothing to be discussed. David agreed to it, and so, I gave my consent."

Leon remained pensive for a few seconds. He had lost the first round.

"And as for the reception, what do you have in mind?"

"Well, I'm glad you came to see me. Lucila and I were going to phone you in the coming days. When all is said and done, our families are being joined and there are certain decisions that we must make together... Will you have many guests?"

"No. Very few."

Doctor Méndez felt relieved. The last thing that he wanted was to have a bunch of Jews at the wedding. They would detract from the elegance of the occasion, not to mention anything of the embarrassment they would create.

"How many, more or less?"

"I don't know. Very few. Why?"

"To plan the reception. We want to host it at the Club Bolívar. It will be a quite elegant affair."

"Since you told me that there are certain decisions that we must make together, allow me to express my opinion."

"By all means. Tell me."

"Why not hold the reception at the Hotel Astor?"

"And why at the Astor? The Club is more fashionable."

"Because it seems to me that if we will be inviting very few people, you ought to do the same. And if it's not going to be a really big reception, why not the banquet room at the hotel? I think it's more suitable than the one at the club."

Edri was careful not to state the real motive for his preference. The Club Bolívar did not accept Jews, and Leon thought that such an invitation would be an affront to his coreligionists, even though there would be some who would be happy to attend.

"But the Astor is so... so mundane," Méndez Carrizosa objected.

It was the only criticism he could think of since the Hotel Astor was the best hotel in the city, much newer than the Club Bolívar, and with a banquet room just as appealing and luxurious as the club's.

"Believe me, the hotel would be so much more appropriate," Leon insisted.

"You know what? If we're not going to host a big event, let's keep everything small. Let's say, about one hundred guests; a select group. Then we'll be able to hold the reception at my house, something really elegant, as it should be."

"Excellent idea!" Leon Edri exclaimed.

He had won the second round.

"All right then. They'll be married in church in the morning and then, depending on what Lucila decides, we'll have lunch in the garden or a reception in the evening."

"And do they have to be married in the church?"

"Then where, if it is a religious ceremony?"

"What I mean to say, can't the ceremony be held here at your home, just before the lunch or the reception?"

"Well, it's not customary."

"But it can be done. I imagine there's nothing standing in the way of the priest performing in your home what he would in church."

Méndez understood that Leon didn't want the Catholic aspect of the wedding to be emphasized.

"Frankly, I don't know," he replied, thinking that it could even be in good taste to do something different from the conventional. "I'd need to look into it."

"If it's possible, I'd greatly appreciate it being done that way."

"We'll see."

The third round had been left undecided.

"At any rate, Ulpiano, tell me what everything will cost, since I think we should share the expenses."

"Nonsense! This is my party and it's on my tab."

"All right, at least let us help. My wife, for example, could take care of the invitations."

Edri was trying to arrange matters to minimize as much as possible the impact that his son's wedding would have on the community. He thought about every detail; even about the wording on the invitations. Sometimes he won a few points, sometimes he lost, but they were non-decisive rounds in a match that he had lost before it got started.

32

Even with the wedding growing closer, Leon and Esther didn't speak about it again with their son, but the absence of discussion didn't help much to clear the air. November followed October, and December followed immediately thereafter. In vain, Leon tried to make time standstill. It didn't, not for an instant. December 17, 1961 arrived as anticipated, immediately after December 16.

Everything in life has its appointed day. There's no escape, Leon reflected while buttoning his shirt in front of the mirror. *The day on which a son is to be born; the day on which he is to marry; the day on which he is to die... At least, usually, a father is no longer around for that one...*

"Leon, are you ready?"

"Almost."

"Hurry up. I'll wait for you downstairs."

"I'm coming! I'm coming!"

He adjusted his bow tie, put on his jacket, and went downstairs.

"What took you so long?" Esther fussed at him.

"Buttoning twenty thousand buttons. Where's David?"

"He's been waiting in the car."

"And Suzy and Benny?"

"In the car too."

"Let's go, then."

They sat in back next to David. Benjamin and Suzy were upfront, next to the chauffeur.

"I thought you'd never get here. We're going to be late," David said impatiently.

"We have time," Leon replied. "The invitation is for nine and it's not even eight o'clock."

"Yes, Dad, but we have to be there at least an hour before."

"Take it easy. No guest arrives on time."

Twenty minutes later they passed through the gate at Altamira and drove up the cobblestone driveway. The mansion, with all its windows lit up, stood at the end of the drive. Ulpiano Méndez was waiting for them at the door.

"Good evening," he said.

One by one they replied in kind.

"Excuse our tardiness, Don Ulpiano."

"No need to worry, my boy; you arrived in plenty of time. Come in, please."

"No one else has arrived?" Leon asked, merely to make the point to David that his father was always right.

"No one. We're the only ones here. Sit down, make yourselves comfortable. Lucila will be right down. So, how are you feeling, young fella?" he asked, putting his arm around David's shoulder. "Nervous?"

"No, sir."

"If you prefer, you don't have to stay with us the whole time. You can join your friends and come in a few minutes before the ceremony begins."

"Yes, sir."

"And what do we have to do?" Leon Edri asked, not without a certain irony.

"Nothing. Watch the ceremony from the first row. Can I offer you a little drink, Leon?"

"No, thank you, Ulpiano. Later."

"Señora?"

"No, thank you."

"What about you, young man? You won't turn me down, will you? Have a short one. It'll do you good. Paco! Three whiskies!"

The bartender brought three whiskies.

"Come, Leon. You can't turn me down on drinking to our children's happiness," he said, taking a glass in each hand and holding out his arms, one towards Leon and the other towards David. "To health, wealth, and happiness!" he exclaimed, raising his glass and forcing his guests into a toast.

"To health!" Leon and David exclaimed in turn.

"Good evening."

The voice came from upstairs. All turned around to see Doña Lucila Campo de Méndez who had just appeared at the top of the stairs. She looked like an empress, and not because of her long sumptuous black and red taffeta dress, nor because of her jewels, which sparkled in the distance, but rather because of her lofty gaze and regal bearing.

Very elegant, Esther thought. *But I look better.*

Very pretty, Leon thought. *It's easy to see where María Cristina got her looks.*

Lucila descended the stairway and greeted all the Edris with a kiss.

During the two months leading up to the wedding, the Méndez family had been to the Edri home, and the Edris to theirs. Even though they were no longer strangers, they continued observing each

401

other with a keen interest. The family of the old aristocrat and that of the wealthy Jew had a certain apprehension regarding one another and while getting better acquainted, each side observed, studied, and analyzed the other.

"This young man must be your youngest, right, Lucila?"

Esther was referring to the eight-year-old boy whose suit looked like seventeenth-century formal attire.

"This is Jorge Horacio. We had a special suit made for him for the wedding."

"I think he is the only one of your children I hadn't met," Esther said while turning to the boy and adopting an expression of admiration. "How elegant you look! Are you happy that your sister is getting married?"

"Yes."

"Yes what?" Doña Lucila interjected.

"Yes, ma'am."

Esther smiled.

"Would you like to see how we fixed up the garden?"

"Thank you, Lucila, I'd be delighted."

Señora Méndez left the room with her younger daughter, María del Pilar, and Esther and her daughter followed them. The men remained in the living room, chatting, but when they finished their drinks they too went out to the garden.

They had arranged for the reception to be held in the garden because on summer evenings it was more pleasant to be outside than indoors, especially at Altamira, which was about seven hundred feet above the city and caught the refreshing air that came down from the mountains. The garden was very pretty, illuminated with reflecting lights hidden in the tropical vegetation and on top of the palm trees.

The artificial lighting made the big green leaves look larger and greener, giving the garden a surreal atmosphere and infusing it with the charm of places people dream of. On the flat, open area of the garden, on the well-tended lawn that looked like an immense green carpet, there were some fifteen round tables with seating for eight, set according to strict etiquette, with white tablecloths, fine white porcelain china, silverware, and three crystal goblets at each seat. Every table had a floral centerpiece and was lit by a little candle lamp.

From behind some shrubs came the sharp warbling of a bird. María del Pilar laughed, imitated the sound, and the warbling repeated itself.

"It's Barajas," she explained.

"It's our pet macaw," her mother added to be more exact. "Pili, go and tell Tomasa to lock Barajas in the garage until the party is over."

The little girl went running back to the house.

From the other side of the garden, Ulpiano signaled to his wife.

"It seems the guests have started to arrive," Lucila said, motioning for Esther and Suzy to follow her.

The individual who had just arrived wasn't exactly a guest, but rather someone who was indispensable to the wedding ceremony. Ulpiano Méndez hurried to receive him.

"Virgilio, I was beginning to wonder where you were," he said as a form of greeting.

Father Izaza came in smiling.

"Hello, Ulpiano. How are you? Lucila, good evening."

Ulpiano took the priest by the arm and accompanied him to the garden.

"Come, Virgilio, I want to introduce you to the bridegroom's parents... Don Leon Edri."

"Very pleased to meet you," Leon said, with a nod of his head.

"And Doña Ester..."

Not knowing Esther's maiden name, which Ulpiano wanted to mention ahead of her family name on introducing her, he hesitated for a moment, "...de Edri."

"Very pleased to meet you, father."

"Father Izaza is an old and dear friend of the family. He baptized all my children. We've known each other for at least thirty years. Isn't that right, Virgilio?"

"I think it's a little more, Ulpiano. Thirty-five years more or less; from the time I was a seminary student... And these are David's siblings, I suppose."

"Yes. Benjamín Edri—"

"Benny," Esther interrupted with a smile, trying to break the formal tone of the conversation.

"And Suzy."

"Very good, very good," Izaza muttered, nodding affirmatively. "You don't know how happy I am to see all of you tonight."

Virgilio Izaza was as mixed-blood as they come, but he affected a slight Castilian accent because he was convinced that it made him more engaging. His mannerisms reflected the profound influence exercised on him by the teachers at the San Bartolomé Theological Seminary, who were all Spanish priests during his time.

"My son," he continued, addressing David, "today you are taking one of the most important steps in your life."

Leon couldn't suppress a cheerless smile. *So, now David has another father!* he told himself.

"I've heard a lot about you," the priest said, this time directing his remarks to Leon.

"Good or bad?" Esther Edri interrupted, showing off her congeniality.

"Oh, very good things, señora, very good things. I had the pleasure of meeting your associate, Señor Jaime Lubisi. What a gentleman! He had a very good way with people! I met him as a result of a donation he made to the Children's Aid Society of Santa Clara, but what impressed me most is that afterwards he gave me a donation for the chapel and, well, not being Catholic... Quite definitely, a gentleman. A gentleman through and through. I am so sad over his passing... Will Señora Lubisi be here this evening?"

"Regrettably not, father," Leon explained. "Until a year of mourning has passed, neither she nor her children will attend any social event."

"Yes, of course. I understand, I understand."

Leon Edri felt himself beginning to perspire. Someone rang the doorbell.

"Oh, people are arriving now," Doña Lucila said. "Ulpiano, stay here in the garden. I'm going to ask Andrés to have the guests come this way and I'll be right back. Excuse me," and having said this, she quickly went inside.

Seconds later Doctor Benedicto Méndez Carrizosa, Ulpiano's brother, and his wife, Doña Eulogia Peña de Méndez, appeared. They were the first of one hundred and eight guests who for the next fifty minutes would be ushered into the garden of the elegant mansion.

Esther nearly fell over backwards when she saw Manes Finstein and his big-nosed wife, Rosa *mit a nus*, as the matrons of the Jewish community liked to call her. Basically, Esther didn't have anything to be ashamed of, since neither of the two was ignorant or coarse, but she was shocked to see them in everyday clothes. It couldn't even be said that they were poorly dressed. Finstein had put on his best suit, with a white shirt and tie, and Rosa was wearing what she considered to be a cocktail dress; but in that well-lit garden, where all the men had on tuxedos and the women long gowns, the couple constituted a blot on the perfect harmony and elegance of the occasion. Esther didn't want to invite them to the wedding, but Leon had insisted.

"He's one of the first persons I met when I came to Lárida; he helped me get started, he was my friend and I have no reason to exclude him from the wedding."

The Finsteins hadn't dressed according to strict etiquette simply because they didn't own any formal attire. Other Jews whom Leon considered friends and who weren't rich either came dressed in ordinary clothes. Esther Edri was about to explode—she didn't know whether from rage or embarrassment—and she only managed to calm down when a couple invited by the Méndezes showed up also dressed in everyday outfits. That wasn't the only couple to serve as Esther's consolation; there was another—related to Doña Lucila, no less—who came in ordinary attire. From that moment on, Esther relaxed. *Now we don't look so bad*, she thought, without it mattering to her that among those who were not properly attired there were four guests of the Méndezes and sixteen of hers.

Ulpiano, his wife, Leon and Esther remained standing at the entrance to the garden. Leon was perspiring. It wasn't hot, but he was sweating. The sensation of his damp shirt against his neck and around his wrists annoyed him.

Every time a guest of the Méndezes arrived, Ulpiano made the introductions to the Edris; and when the guests of the Edris arrived, Esther introduced them to the Méndezes. Because of his prominent position in the financial circles of Lárida, Leon knew a few of the guests of the Méndez family personally, and almost all by name.

Presumably, Ulpiano Méndez and Doña Lucila didn't know any of the Edris' guests.

"Doña Ester de Edri. Doctor and Mrs. Pablo Pinto Zamora," Méndez announced pompously. "Pablito, you know Leon, don't you?"

"Of course! Good evening, Don León. Very pleased to meet you, señora."

"Very pleased to meet you."

"Our sincerest congratulations. I told Ulpiano some time ago that your son and María Cristina made a handsome couple."

Méndez shot his friend a murderous glance.

"Inés, Pablo, go on out to the garden, please. Find a table and make yourselves comfortable," Doña Lucila said in a tone of extreme affability.

Thus, one by one, the guests continued filing in and passing through the ritual of introductions. After the *de rigueur* greetings, a few words of polite social chat were exchanged. The phrase "Very pleased to meet you" was said a million times.

"Hello, Hans, Sonia! I'm delighted to see you," Esther exclaimed. "May I present Doctor Méndez Carrizosa…"

"Very pleased to meet you."

"And Doña Lucila de Méndez."

"Very pleased to meet you."

"Doctor Hans Guggenheim is our physician."

"We invited him tonight in case I pass out," Leon said in all seriousness.

They all broke into laughter.

Very funny, Leon thought. *I pray it doesn't happen*! He was distressed, but not nervous. That wasn't a reason to perspire; however, he was perspiring the whole time. Could he have a fever? No… he didn't feel ill. Why in the devil was he perspiring so much?

"Leon, allow me to introduce you to my sister Claudia and my brother-in-law, Néstor Ibarra Salazar. Leon Edri and Doña Ester de Edri."

"Very pleased to meet you, señora."

"Delighted."

"It's so exciting to see how the family is growing, isn't it?" Esther said, dryly.

"I should say so," Néstor Ibarra affirmed without much conviction.

"Might you have another son for our daughter?" Doña Claudia asked in a cheerful mood. "I was telling Lucila recently how lucky she was that her daughter was marrying a boy from your community. They say that Jewish husbands are the best."

Ulpiano Méndez Carrizosa and Néstor Ibarra Salazar exchanged glances.

At this point, almost everybody had arrived. Señora Méndez scanned the tables filled with guests and looked pleased. Dinner would be served later, but the waiters had been busy for some time serving drinks. Leon Edri also turned to look out across the garden. He saw that the guests had chosen to drift off into groups to form what could be termed "Christian tables" and "Jewish tables," and that the latter were all located in the same area.

"Miriam, good evening."

"Good evening, Ester. Hello, León."

"Lucila, Doctor Méndez, I want to introduce you to some good friends: Miriam and Julio Richter."

"Very pleased to meet you," Ulpiano said.

"Very pleased to meet you, doctor, señora."

"The pleasure is mine. I'm very happy to meet Ester and León's friends."

"I'm pleased to meet you too. Ester mentioned you often. Even my husband has spoken to me of you and your wife."

"Your husband?" Doctor Méndez asked, intrigued.

"Well, not exactly about you, but about your family name."

"How so?" Ulpiano asked again, even more intrigued.

"My wife meant that on one occasion I spoke to her about the name Méndez. Did you know, doctor, that your ancestors may be Jewish?"

Ulpiano turned red. All except Julio Richter noticed it.

"I don't understand. Could you explain?"

"Méndez is an illustrious Jewish-Spanish surname. In sixteenth-century Morocco and Algeria the Mendezes constituted a very important family of rabbis and wealthy merchants. Some came to occupy very prominent positions in Amsterdam and London."

Richter, whose interest was Jewish history, spoke with authority.

"And in London we have a Fernando Mendes, one of the most outstanding physicians of his period; physician to the kings and queens of England, no less. His grandson, the playwright Moisés Mendes, and his descendants, Sir Francis Bond and Solomon Mendes, were very prominent. But one shouldn't confuse Fernando Mendes with Antonio Mendes, who was also a physician at the English court. All those Mendeses were *marranos*. Of course, it reached a point in time when their lineage ceased to be Jewish."

Ulpiano was about to explode, but restrained himself. He didn't want to create a scene on the very night that his daughter was getting

409

married, in his own home. That business of "all the Mendeses being *marranos*" sounded like an insult to him, but if he held back from reacting it was because he wasn't sure. He didn't want to appear ignorant. He was sufficiently astute to understand that he was missing something. He could deduce it by the fact that this Julio fellow who was talking wasn't the least bit hostile. *That little expression of his must have some other meaning*, he told himself, *because this asshole is convinced that he's most congenial.* In effect, Julio Richter spoke enthusiastically, happy to have fallen headlong into a subject that was his forte, without realizing the anger that he was creating in Doctor Méndez or the discomfort he was causing the rest.

"There were also two rabbis who left their marks on the North American Jewish community: Frederic de Sola Mendes, promoter of the reform movement in the United States, and Dr. Henry Pereira Mendes, M.D., who was one of the principal leaders of North American Orthodox Judaism."

"Very interesting," Méndez Carrizosa mumbled.

"The subject of Jewish surnames is extremely interesting," Leon agreed, diplomatically steering the conversation away from the particular to the general.

But Julio Richter had locked himself into a single topic and refused to let himself be derailed.

"There were many very wealthy Mendezes, like Francisco Mendes, who founded in Lisbon one of the most important banks in Europe, with branches in Flanders and France. But the most affluent of all, I believe, was Francisco's brother, Diogo Mendes. As a young man, he settled in Antwerp, where he became so powerful, that he lent money to the governments of Holland, England, and Portugal."

"Incredible how you know so much," Doña Lucila stated in a tone as if to say: *Bravo*! *I congratulate you; now shut up and go away*.

"Julio is a professor of history," Señora Richter proudly pointed out.

Ulpiano was still red with fury and forcefully clenched his jaws. The revelation that his surname was Jewish was killing him. It didn't displease him to hear that there was a Méndez so supremely wealthy that he came to finance several countries in Europe, but that business of the *marranos* continued to disturb him.

"The nineteenth-century French poet, Catulle Mendés, was the son of a Jewish banker, and the previous—"

"Sweetheart," Miriam interrupted him, "I think you've already enlightened us enough."

"Oh…" Julio Richter said, realizing that he had gotten carried away. "I was only trying to say that the previous prime minister of France, Pierre Mendés-France—"

"Is he also of Jewish origin?" Lucila asked.

"No, señora, he *is* Jewish."

"All right," Edri said with the authoritarian intonation that he used when he wanted to settle a negotiation, "but not all the Méndezes who were in Spain prior to the Inquisition were Jews."

"No, of course, not," Richter conceded.

"In that case," Leon concluded, "the present-day Méndezes can be descendants of either Jews or Catholics."

"That's right," Richter again conceded.

Doctor Ulpiano Méndez Carrizosa recovered his color a bit. The arrival of David Edri at that moment put an end to the conversation.

"I think we're almost about to begin," he said.

411

"Ulpiano, go get Cristina," Lucila told her husband, and addressing David and his parents, she added: "Come with me, please. We must take our places up front."

Doña Lucila and the Edris walked towards the edge of the lawn where a long, narrow table had been prepared in the form of an altar. It was covered with a white tablecloth of rich texture. A silver cross was displayed in the center, anchored vertically on its own base, and bordering it on each side was a candle in a silver candelabrum. Virgilio Izaza had taken his place in front of the altar, looking out across the tables in the garden. When the guests saw that the priest was ready to begin, they left their tables and gathered in front of the altar, leaving room down the middle for an aisle cordoned off by stanchion posts with a pair of taut rose-colored velvet ropes. From one side of the garden came the clear, majestic music of the wedding march. A chamber ensemble consisting of five teachers from the Lárida Conservatory had been hired especially for the occasion.

"Lohengrin," Esther whispered to her husband.

Leon gave her a look of incomprehension.

"Wagner," she said, placing her mouth close to his ear. "An anti-Semite like that! Why him?"

"Oh?"

"There being better ones… and our own."

"What are you saying?"

"Mendelssohn," she said abruptly. "The 'Wedding March' from 'A Midsummer Night's Dream.' Just what the occasion calls for this evening."

"I don't understand a thing you're saying."

Esther reprimanded him with a stare. *If no one knows or understands*, she told herself, *I suppose it doesn't matter.*

Leon's face was soaked with perspiration. He pulled out a handkerchief and wiped it.

From the door of the ballroom that faces the garden, an attractive young couple made its appearance. Tulio Castellanos, dressed in tails and high hat, and sporting a yellow carnation in his lapel, was smiling broadly and casting his eyes right and left in greeting. The beautiful young woman at his side was María Isabel Palacios, María Cristina's best friend. She was wearing a bright yellow, floor-length evening gown with décolletage and carried a bouquet of flowers in her hands. Arm in arm, they took two steps and stopped. Another couple appeared behind them, also young and attractive; and behind that couple came another; and another and another. Five couples in all, all around twenty years of age, the men in tails and high hat, and the young ladies in bright yellow evening gowns and a bouquet in their hands, comprised the court of honor. They advanced slowly to the sound of the wedding march, pausing briefly every two steps.

The couples stopped in front of the altar, the bridesmaids on one side of the aisle and the groomsmen on the other. Immediately afterwards, little Jorge Horacio came through the same door in his seventeenth-century style suit. With both hands he held a silver tray bearing two rings. Like the entourage of bridesmaids and groomsmen, the boy advanced slowly, pausing every two steps.

Trailing behind him came a file of adorable couples ranging in age between five and seven. The girls wore bright yellow dresses and the boys black pants and white shirt—without a jacket. Instead of the bouquet, the girls carried little baskets filled with rose petals that they sprinkled on the ground as they moved forward. This second entourage, composed of children and grandchildren of the relatives and friends of the Méndezes, added a touch of special grace to the ceremony.

Jorge Horacio stopped in front of the altar and the other children stood aside.

413

The music was suspended for a few seconds to resume with greater vigor, increasing the ostentatious effect of the wedding march. At that moment, Doctor Ulpiano Méndez and his daughter made their entrance. A murmur of admiration sprang up from the guests. María Cristina's beauty was dazzling. On her father's arm, she walked gracefully towards the altar. The train of her beautiful white gown followed her like a trail of light.

Upon reaching the head of the Honor Court, Ulpiano Méndez stood aside for David to take his place. Slowly, side-by-side, the bride and groom took the few steps that separated them from the altar. They looked magnificent: he, so gallant, she, so beautiful. They gazed straight ahead, like sovereigns on their way to their own coronation.

The wedding march concluded, leaving an impression of absolute silence. Leon and Esther were off to one side of David, slightly behind. On the other side, in the same position with respect to the bride, stood Ulpiano and Lucila Méndez.

"May the grace of Our Lord Jesus Christ, the love of the Father and the communion of the Holy Spirit be with you always," resonated the voice of Virgilio Izaza.

The mass had begun. First they prayed "I, A Sinner." The priest officiated the mass in Latin and the faithful said their prayers in Spanish. There was some bewilderment when the Jews in attendance remained standing while the Catholics knelt. Both contingents looked at each other and no one was sure what to do. Some of the men spread their handkerchiefs on the lawn so that the women could kneel. María Cristina's parents, not wanting to make their guests feel uncomfortable, remained standing. Several of the Catholic guests also remained standing, but it wasn't clear if they were doing it for the same reason or because they didn't want their evening attire getting soiled on the grass.

"We have come together this evening to join in holy matrimony two of the Lord's children."

With these words Father Virgilio Izaza began his homily. He started by explaining that marriage is one of the seven sacraments, an outward symbol instituted by Jesus Christ that produces a state of inner grace. He elaborated somewhat on the theme, spoke about the indissolubility of marriage and read some verses from the Gospels.

"If anyone knows of any reason why this marriage should not be carried out, may he speak now," he said, looking up from the breviary that he was holding.

There were a few seconds of silence. Esther looked at her husband out of the corner of her eye. Leon Edri remained still, a lost gaze in his eyes.

As if giving a warning to the congregation, Father Izaza proclaimed: "You are all witnesses…" He waited a few seconds before continuing. "David," this time addressing the bridegroom, "do you give yourself as lawful husband and take María Cristina, here present, as your lawful wife, and promise to be faithful in sickness and in health, in poverty and wealth, in sadness and joy, to love and respect all the days of your life, until death do you part?"

"I do" came his clear reply for all to hear.

Doña Lucila Campo de Méndez was crying, filled with emotion. Esther too; and even Leon Edri got teary-eyed. Many of the guests interpreted the tears as a manifestation of happiness; others knew exactly what they were.

The priest addressed María Cristina and posed the same question to her that he had to the bridegroom. Her reply was identical.

"I do."

Virgilio Izaza motioned to Jorge Horacio and the boy approached, held out his arms and raised the tray slightly. The priest leaned over and took the rings.

"I bless these rings, symbol of love and happiness," he said, and he handed them to the bride and groom.

David put one ring on María Cristina's finger and she put the other one on his.

"David and María Cristina, you are now husband and wife forever," Father Izaza solemnly declared. "I bless this union in the name of the Father, the Son, and the Holy Spirit."

Leon Edri thought the ceremony was over and turned half way around to step away from the gathering. He felt the need to be alone. When he saw that everybody remained in place, he discreetly turned to face front again. The recitation of the Creed was beginning. His son was married now, but the mass was just starting. Still to come were the Offertory, the Consecration, the Adoration, the Communion, and the Giving of Thanks. He waited impatiently for the mass to be over, absent-mindedly observing the sacramental rites, as if he were viewing them from afar, with his vision clouded and his mind overwhelmed by an endless number of thoughts he was unable to put in order.

"May the blessing of God Almighty, the Father, the Son and the Holy Spirit, be upon you both and abide with you forever," Virgilio Izaza proclaimed in an affecting tone.

The mass had ended. Father Izaza wiped the chalices and arranged the items used in the ritual.

Following behind the children (who no longer had the patience for filing out in an orderly manner), the bride and groom withdrew from the altar, beaming with smiles and escorted on both sides by the honor court until it dispersed.

All the guests gathered around the newlyweds and parents to offer their congratulations. Leon Edri felt overwhelmed by the avalanche of congratulations, handshakes, embraces and kisses. He bore the outpouring decorously, returning embraces with embraces, blessings with expressions of gratitude, congratulations with smiles; but when the noise died down he made the most of it to leave the crush of people, moving to the center of the garden where he began walking among the empty tables that were just beginning to fill up, wandering bewildered, aimlessly, like a child lost in the forest. While avoiding the guests who were returning to their tables, he heard bits of distant conversation.

"The ceremony was very beautiful," one lady said.

"And original," another woman added.

"Carlitos, old man, I thought you were away," one elderly gentleman greeted another.

Edri ambled over to an empty table and sat down. A lady smiled at him and he thought it was because he looked ridiculous, sitting alone at his son's wedding. He stood up and went to sit down at a table of fellow Jews who were engaged in lively conversation. When they saw him, they changed the subject. Leon greeted them mechanically; he got up and continued his stroll. Suddenly, he heard trumpets and maracas. The rhythmic music of the Caribbean filled the air with happiness. Leon raised his eyes to where the quintet had been and saw that in its place was an orchestra of some twelve musicians, all black, dressed in multicolor shirts opened at the chest and white pants that reached no farther than their shins. He hadn't even realized when the change had taken place. "Opa!" one of the musicians shouted from time to time. Some couples strode over to the tiled area to dance. Leon walked towards the opposite side, more bewildered than ever, and stepped off the lawn to meander behind some bushes. He tried to move farther back but the shrubs made walking difficult. Unconcerned about getting his suit dirty, he sat

417

down on the ground. Pulling out a handkerchief, he mopped his brow. It was soaked. He felt some relief in being off by himself, away from the gathering. He could hear the music in the distance. The darkness made him feel better. He remained like this for a few minutes until he felt calmer. When he was about to return to the reception he heard someone talking. Two men who had also withdrawn from the noise were chatting leisurely on the edge of the lawn, directly in front of him. He decided to wait for them to move off so they wouldn't see him coming out from among the bushes.

"The house is immense," one of them remarked.

"They say there's more than half a million square feet of garden here," the other said.

"Why does one person need a garden this size?"

"Beats me."

From their manner of speech, Leon realized that both men were fellow Jews. He looked between the branches and saw Emilio Gluck and Asher Rosenthal.

"The nobility in Russia had houses like this."

"Today, some ten families live in every one of those mansions," Gluck commented.

"But there are people who continue living like the old nobility. Don't think for a minute that the big shot party officials in the Soviet Union enjoy less opulence than the rich do here."

"Oh no! Of course not! The Communist paradise is like anywhere else: a few rich people and all the rest living in poverty.

"Okay, let's not exaggerate either. Things have changed in Russia."

"What about here? Do you think all this is going to blow up one day too?"

418

"I don't know… There's so much misery… On the other hand, everything seems calm on the surface; inertia rules everything."

"Well," Gluck concluded, "at any rate, as long as this lasts I wouldn't mind living in a little shack like this."

He chuckled to himself, looked in the direction of the mansion and sighed.

Damn it! Leon said to himself. *How long are they going to keep talking?*

He was growing impatient. He remembered once, when he was a little kid, a thousand years before, in a world that ceased to exist, he had hidden behind a pile of wood in his Aunt Dora's kitchen. He was cutting himself a slice of honey cake when he heard her come in. He thought that he ought to have asked permission first, got befuddled, and in a single bound hid behind the stack of wood. While remaining out of sight, he thought his "crime" hadn't been so terrible, but he felt ashamed should his aunt see him come out from where he was hiding. So he stayed where he was for an hour, huddled and motionless, hoping his aunt would finish her tasks and leave. It was the similarity of the two situations that brought that day to mind, one which he had forgotten about many, many years ago. Shielded among the shrubs in the garden, he saw his Aunt Dora, heard her voice quarreling with Uncle Shmuel in Yiddish over something that surely was not worth the trouble, and even smelled the aroma of her kitchen. No kitchen in the New World smelled like those of the *shtetl*. Could it be because in those kitchens the women baked bread and made things that are no longer prepared at home? They cooked *kasha*, *guefilte fish*, *kuguel*, and *kholodetz*. On Friday afternoon they made *chulnt* to eat the following day. Many foodstuffs were stored: pickled cucumbers, long strings of garlic, walnuts and goose fat. They made *povidl* and all kinds of preserves. Even wine and butter were made at home. Homemade remedies also came from the kitchen, like herbal teas and *goguel-moguel*. a potion made of hot

419

milk, egg and honey, used as an expectorant. What times they were! He saw himself running with Itzik through the streets of the town. "Hey, you kids!" Fishel yelled at them when they nearly knocked over the pails of milk he was carrying. Frimca "The Dispenser of Advice" began explaining to Fishel that if he walked in the middle of the road there would be less chance of someone bumping into him. One half of the hair on Frimca's head was curly while the other half was straight; as for her eyebrows, they were thick like a man's, and her cheeks were big and rosy. She looked more like a caricature than a real person. In a certain sense, all the people in the *shtetl*, seen in retrospect, seemed like caricatures: Hersh the Carrot Top's teeth were almost all gold, while Ghitl the Matchmaker's were nearly all silver, and Shloime the Tailor's were marked by gaps in the upper front. Then there was Big-Nosed Simcha with his unusually large ones, and Pinky the Half-Pint who had only two teeth that stuck out from his lower gum like two tombs in a barren field. In the Old World people were more animated, had more "flare," more personality; in the new one they were all alike, insipid... Or might he be making a mistake in perspective? To which of the two worlds did he belong? His Uncle Gabriel, the bachelor, laughed in his face. No, it was somebody else now. It was *féter* Yankl who was smiling. The old man extended his hand to him, as if asking him for something. Leib removed the *talit* from his shoulders and handed it to him. He felt cold. He saw himself with Berl, Itzik and Zvi splashing around in the water in the river. "If we stayed in the sun all day, every day, we'd turn black," Itzik said. They all laughed. Suddenly they grew serious. The presence of *Rav* Zuntz intimidated them. They were in the *cheder* with its whitewashed walls and the old *lerer* was stroking his beard. "Get thee out of thy country, and from thy kindred, and from thy father's house unto a land I will show thee," he told them, quoting the Holy Scriptures. "I will make of you a great nation."

Asher Rosenthal's laughter brought Leon back to reality. The two men continued chatting.

"And even to this day people refuse to believe it," Emilio Gluck said.

"Blind and foolish people, so blind and foolish!"

"Well, that's life. Be that as it may, you can't deny it was a lavish wedding."

"You call that a wedding?" asked Rosenthal with the cynicism that was so typical of him. "That was a burial."

"Oy, Asher, stop with your silly jokes!"

"It's no joke. I'm telling you what we witnessed today was a burial."

"And who, may I ask, is the deceased?"

"The Judaism of Lárida. The Judaism of Latin America," Asher solemnly replied.

"Well, I see Judaism very much alive here."

"Yours and mine, perhaps. But the Judaism that died is that of our descendants."

It was at that moment that Leon Edri realized what had happened. He wasn't sweating nor had he perspired earlier. It was the air that made his face and neck feel clammy, the air that on that evening was imbued with a kind of luminous, nearly imperceptible dew. It had descended from the sky in the form of a very fine drizzle, silent, invisible... as on that distant August afternoon in the Golochov cemetery.

Glossary

aguardiente: liquor made from fermented sugar cane

Ashkenazi: Hebrew for "German." A term applied to European Jews, or Jews of European origin, except those whose ancestors were expelled from or fled Spain ("Sephardic Jews") during the Spanish Inquisition

Av: The 11th month of the 12-month Jewish calendar

9th of Av: the date of the destruction of the Holy Temple of Jerusalem, according to the Hebrew calendar

Bar Mitzvah: a boy who turns thirteen, the age at which he is no longer a minor and assumes the duties of Jewish life; literally "son of a good deed." The words are often used to mean the ceremony performed when the boy becomes a *Bar Mitzvah*

Brit Milah: God's *Covenant* with His people, sealed by the act of circumcision performed on the eighth day following birth

carajo: in Spanish, a common curse word, more or less the equivalent of "damn" or "damn it"

casher: Hebrew for suitable, fit, proper, legitimate; *kosher* in Yiddish. Kosher food: food which is in accordance with Jewish dietary laws

charoset: apple, nut, spice, and wine mixture

cheder: in Hebrew and in Yiddish, "room"; primary school in the now disappeared Jewish communities of Eastern Europe

chevrah kaddishah: Hebrew for Holy Society. A group of persons that assumes the obligation of providing a burial in accordance with Jewish ritual

423

chevre kadishe: Yiddish for "Chevrah Kaddishah"

chotis: a dance popular in Spain in the nineteenth century

chuppah: a marriage canopy erected on four long poles, under which the Jewish wedding ceremony is held

dulce de guayaba: a sweet dessert made from the guayava fruit and sugar

Eretz Israel: Israel is the name given to Jacob by the angel sent from God, which by extension is applied to his descendants, "the Israelites as a people." For greater clarity, it is customary to use three expressions:

1) "Bnei Israel," meaning the people of Israel: the Jews

2) "Eretz Israel," the territory of the ancient kingdoms of Judea and Israel: the Holy Land

3) "Medinat Israel," the modern state: the republic of Israel. Since 1948, this last meaning is understood when the word "Israel" is used alone

Far vos bist du avec gueganguen? Yiddish for *Why did you leave?*

feiguele: Yiddish for "little bird"

Goldene Medine: in Yiddish, "Golden Land." A nickname given to the United States by immigrant Jews at the beginning of the twentieth century

goy: in Hebrew and Yiddish, a non-Jew

goyim: plural of "goy"

guanábana: strong acidic tropical fruit used mainly in liquefied form in fruit drinks, mixed with milk or water and sugar

Keren Kayemet: National Jewish Fund, founded in 1901

kibutz: a collective agricultural settlement (from the Hebrew word *kvutzah,* "group."

kibutzim: plural of "kibutz,"

kosher: Yiddish pronunciation of the Hebrew word "casher"

lerer: Yiddish for "teacher"

lulo: strong acidic tropical fruit used only in liquefied form in fruit drinks

Iyar: 8th month of the Jewish calendar

mame loshen: in Yiddish, "mother tongue"

maracuyá: "passion fruit"

marrano: "pig"; a derogatory term applied at the time of the Inquisition to Spanish and Portuguese Jews who converted to Christianity either by force or for self-preservation

matzah: flat, toasted unleavened bread, baked with unleavened flour

mazal tov: in Hebrew, "good luck." It is used in the sense of "congratulations"

minyan: a quorum of ten Jewish males, thirteen years or more in age, required for the recitation of certain prayers

mitzvah: in Hebrew: "a good deed"

muzhiks: in Russian, "peasants"

Nueva, La: in Spanish, literally "The New One"

parashah: episode or "chapter" in the Bible

Pesach: in English, Passover; a Jewish Festival or Holiday celebrating the Exodus from Egypt

peyot: curls or locks of hair that Orthodox Jewish men allow to grow in place of sideburns

Rav: title given to scholars concerning matters of (Biblical) Law, below a "Rabbi" in rank

Rosh Hashanah: "New Year" in Hebrew

Salud! "health": in the Spanish-speaking world, this is a common form of toasting, much like saying "Cheers" in English

seder: in Hebrew, "order": Name of the ceremonial meal for the Jewish Passover

shalom aleichem: in Hebrew and in Yiddish, a traditional greeting: "Peace be with you"

sheedech: Yiddish pronunciation of the Hebrew word "shiduch"

shiduch: An arranged marriage (generally, by the parents of the couple)

shtetl: village, small town, especially in Eastern Europe

shul: Yiddish term for synagogue

sidur: Jewish book of prayers

talit: shawl worn over the shoulders and back by Jewish men while praying

tzitziot: the fringes that adorn the edges of a prayer shawl. Orthodox Jewish men wear a small *talit* with *tzitziot* all the time

Valle Rico: Rich Valley

Vieja, La: Literally, "The Old One" in Spanish

yarmulka: "in Yiddish," a skullcap worn by Jewish men during prayer or any Jewish ceremony. In Hebrew, it's "kipah"

yeshivah: Rabbinical seminary

Yom Kippur: "Day of Atonement." It is the most sacred day in the Jewish religion. Rosh Hashanah, which is celebrated ten days before, follows it in importance.

Made in the USA
Middletown, DE
25 June 2018